Restless Rake

SCARLETT SCOTT

Restless Rake
Heart's Temptation Book 5

This book is a work of fiction and any resemblance to persons, living or dead, or places, events, or locales, is purely coincidental. The characters are productions of the author's imagination and used fictitiously.

All rights reserved.
Copyright © 2018 Scarlett Scott
ISBN: 978-1983683893
www.scarsco.com
Cover Design: Wicked Smart Designs
Interior Design: Dallas Hodge, Everything But The Book

All rights reserved. This book or any portion thereof may not be reproduced or used in any manner whatsoever without the express written permission of the publisher except for the use of brief quotations in a book review.

The unauthorized reproduction or distribution of this copyrighted work is illegal. No part of this book may be scanned, uploaded, or distributed via the Internet or any other means, electronic or print, without the publisher's permission. Criminal copyright infringement, including infringement without monetary gain, is punishable by law.

Printed in the U.S.A.

Dedication

For Steve. Thank you for making me laugh every day with your quick wit, for knowing how to fix anything (just ask the girls), for being brave for me when I'm not, for making the best of each bad situation we've faced, and for always being my champion. I love you.

Contents

Chapter One

London, 1884

He was pockets to let and he was bloody well tired of whoring himself for the well-to-do ladies of the Marlborough House set. Drinking seemed an excellent course of action for the moment.

"Lord Ravenscroft, you've a visitor."

Julian finished pouring his brandy before flicking a glance to his grim-faced butler. Osgood's expression was one of distaste, as though a fly had flown into his mouth and his august bearing wouldn't allow him to spit it out. Osgood was a relic of the previous earl's days. A gargoyle made of stone, guarding against evil spirits and indiscreet late-night apparitions with unsavory intentions.

Oh, this wasn't the first time an unexpected visitor had made her way to Julian's front door. Nor, he suspected, would it be the last. It was a certainty that the visitor was female. They always were.

Osgood was far too loyal a retainer to make his thoughts about such callers known. He was a third generation butler who had served the Earls of Ravenscroft for the entirety of his life, and he was above reproach. But Julian could read him like a bad gambler.

No face for *vingt-et-un* on that one. Indeed, Julian thought as he sipped his brandy with great care, eying the old fellow, no face for much of anything save being a wilted stickler for propriety. Even if his employer was living on credit and bad debts, every sign indicating that he ought to flee the proverbial sinking ship like a rat.

But Osgood wasn't a rat. And Julian wasn't in the mood for visitors, especially not the unexpected variety.

He frowned at his butler. "I'm not at home. I believe I made that known."

The butler cleared his throat. His expression remained suitably dour and pinched. "Yes, my lord, of course. Forgive me, but the visitor in question refuses to leave. Would you care for me to have a footman brought round, my lord, to extricate her?"

Some devil in Julian rather enjoyed watching Osgood squirm. After all, with ruin so certain a future, this may well prove his final opportunity to needle the man. He took another sip of brandy, enjoying the burn down his throat. Damn it, he wished it was enough to numb him. It never was.

"Such persistence ought to be rewarded." His tone was careful and mild. "Do you not think so, Osgood?"

Osgood remained immovable, however. "I do not presume to think, my lord."

"No?" Julian was feeling perverse tonight, dredged in the freeing wickedness of a man about to lose everything. "Terrible shame, that. Not to think. Or perhaps it's a lie, Osgood? Surely it cannot be said that a man does not think. You must have an opinion. Tell me, should I be at home to this creature who dares to call so late at night?"

His butler paled, clearly not relishing the untenable position of being forced to comment on his disreputable master's social niceties. "My lord, I'm certain I will be pleased to follow your instructions, whatever they may be."

Ah, perhaps it had been a whimsical notion on his part to believe he could wrangle a concession from the block of ice before him. "Bring her in, then, Osgood. The night grows late and I'm in need of diversion."

His butler's expression didn't alter, but Julian could sense the disapproval like a clap on his back. No matter. Disapproval had haunted him his entire life. He wore it like a mantle rather than a shroud.

Osgood bowed and disappeared. Julian took another long sip of brandy and contemplated the visitor who wouldn't leave. He wondered, for a brief, fanciful moment if it was Lottie.

Not Lottie, his instincts told him, for Osgood would have recognized her. It hadn't been that long ago. What, a year? Not a great deal of time when one considered the span of a lifetime.

The door to his study opened. His butler did the pretty. A feminine figure entered, clad in a luxurious pelisse overtop a promenade gown that was, unless he missed his guess, a Worth. His visitor was petite but curved in all the right places. Her nipped waist, visible even beneath her layers of fabric, emphasized her generous bosom. An ostentatious hat adorned with a stuffed bird and veil hid the woman's identity from his view, but he scarcely cared. He'd find out who she was soon enough.

He stood. "Thank you, Osgood. That will be all." The door had only just snicked closed before he bowed to her. He wondered what lay beneath that veil. The little he could discern of her features appeared even, unremarkable. "Madam, if I may be so bold, please be seated and make the reason for your unexpected visit known."

Her steps did not denote confidence. Rather, they were mincing. Hesitant. As though she feared him. She stopped a notable length from his desk. "My lord, I'm here to make you an offer."

Her voice was soft and sweet, her enunciation rounded like pebbles worn smooth by a stream. There was beauty in that honeyed voice, and it rolled over his senses like a touch. She was an American, he'd venture to say. Perhaps one of the many heiresses who had exchanged her immense dowry for a title and now found herself ensnared by ennui. Or disillusioned, her girlish dreams of snagging a coronet and living a fairytale dashed by the reality of a balding duke with a paunch and a penchant for bedding servant girls.

Julian supposed he shouldn't be surprised. He frowned. "I fear I'm no longer interested in offers of any sort." He'd long ago grown tired of playing this role. Of whoring himself to wealthy ladies for enough money to keep from utter penury. A man could only swallow his pride for so many years before it choked him.

She clasped her hands at her waist, the sole indication of apparent indecision. "Perhaps you would care to hear my offer before you so summarily dismiss it, my lord."

Bold of her. Now he could place her accent, the leisurely drawl. A Virginian. Julian closed the distance between them, not stopping until her pelisse brushed his trousers. "I daresay it couldn't be an offer I haven't already heard before."

"You may be surprised." She held her ground, tipping up her chin.

Feisty as well as bold, he thought, studying her with new interest. The veil was an unwanted deterrent that kept him from seeing if her face matched the lilting beauty of her voice.

He stepped closer, her skirts crushing against him, and hooked an arm around her waist. She stiffened. "What is it, love? You want me to join you and your husband in bed? You want him to watch as I fuck you? No? Perhaps you want to feel pleasure for the first time. Is that it? You've settled for a title but he doesn't make you come."

Her quick intake of breath told him he'd shocked her. She sounded young. Perhaps she was a novice to this sort of game. He should be merciful and send her on her way, but his mood was dark. A man on the edge had little to lose, and he needed distraction badly. Here was a plaything, a well-dressed naïf who had landed in his study like a benediction.

He reached beneath her veil, cupped her cheek. The contact jolted him. Her skin was smooth and warm, soft. His thumb found her lower lip, lush and full, stroking. Her lips parted. He'd consumed too much brandy tonight, it was certain. Otherwise, why would he feel such heat, such unadulterated attraction for a faceless woman with a Virginia drawl and an atrocity of a hat?

She didn't say a word, just held still, allowing his touch but not reacting. Her breath fanned over his skin, quick and shallow, the only sign she was affected. Was her lack of response borne of shock? He couldn't be sure.

"You've heard I'll do anything for a price, yes?" His thumb dipped ever so slightly inside her mouth before retreating. "That is why you're here, is it not?"

She swallowed, and he absorbed the ripple in his fingertips that rested lightly beneath her jaw. Then, her drawl, steady and calm, cut into the silence. "Do you think to frighten me into fleeing, my lord?"

The lady was even more audacious than he'd supposed. Fine. How far would she take their gamble before she broke? The hand that held her waist slid with unerring precision to the buttons lining the front of her gown. He could undo buttons faster than the most skilled lady's maid. With one hand, with his teeth, with a knife—whatever the moment and the woman required.

He watched his handiwork. Her pelisse hung open. Her bodice gaped. He could see the elegant embroidery of her corset cover, the white ribbon at the top of her chemise. Her breasts were full and high, straining against the constriction of her tight lacing. She still hadn't moved. "Are you not frightened yet, love?"

Perhaps he would consider her offer after all, if only for the night.

"Would it please you if I were?"

Her cool question stayed him in the act of removing the final button from its moorings. Damn it, what was he about, practically ravaging some poor sod's wife merely because she'd appeared in his study? And for what gain? To prove a point to himself? To the enigmatic lady whose face he'd yet to behold?

Part of him wanted her to run away into the night and take with her all reminders of the man he'd become. Shouldn't she be terrified of him, of what he could do to her? Or was she not as innocent as she seemed? Did a depraved heart beat beneath her ivory breast? He had to know. "Does fear excite you?"

"No, and neither does your posturing."

He could so easily make a lie of her words. Julian knew when a woman was attracted to him, and this one was no different than a hundred others before her. She wanted him. He trailed his hand down her throat, feeling tension in the corded muscles. Tenderly, he caressed her as if she were already his lover. Some part of him understood that she would be, that this pull between them was inevitable. If not tonight, another.

The time for playing games was at an end. "What is your offer then, love? The night grows late and I'm tired of entertaining my whims."

Her hands remained clasped at her waist, just below the last button he'd yet to undo. The knuckles rose in stark relief from her fine-boned fingers, belying the ease with which she spoke. "I thought you were no longer interested in offers."

She possessed a considerable amount of mettle. He smiled, for he thoroughly enjoyed himself now in a way he had not done in quite some time. "Can a man not change his mind?"

"Of course. Man is rarely constant, I've discovered."

There was a reproach in her words, though whether it was aimed at him or another, he couldn't be certain. "Your offer, madam. What is it?"

"My offer is simple." She unclasped her hands and

reached up to remove the hideous hat and veil.

Good God, the face didn't match the voice at all.

No indeed, it surpassed the mellifluous lure by leaps and bounds. She was beautiful, more exquisite than any goddess splashed across a canvas. Her golden hair was plaited into basket weaves. Her eyes were wide, blue, unblinking. Her mouth full and lush, her cheeks pink, her cheekbones high. She was the most gorgeous creature he'd ever seen. Who was she, and how had he never set eyes upon her before? For he couldn't have crossed her path. He would have remembered a splendor so rare.

"Marry me," she said.

The silence almost undid Clara. She hadn't intended to blurt her offer so artlessly. She had rehearsed this moment at least a dozen times in the privacy of her chamber, and never had she faltered. She'd planned a lengthy soliloquy cataloging the virtues of the barter she presented him—his time and name in exchange for a share of her tremendous dowry.

But when she had practiced the bloodless listing of facts and reason, she had been alone. No one had stood before her with the looks to rival a fallen angel. No one had touched her, undone her dress, or uttered the most wicked, debauched words she'd ever heard aloud.

Dear God, perhaps she had made a mistake in choosing him. This man, tall and muscled as most English lords weren't, more handsome even than she'd recalled from the handful of times she'd seen him from across a ballroom… This man was not at all what she had imagined, what she had prepared for.

And then, he laughed. Threw back his head and laughed as though she'd just delivered the cleverest joke he'd heard in ages. Clara reached for her buttons, beginning to set them to rights. Humiliation threatened to devour her from the inside out. She was the joke. He thought her offer of marriage so ludicrous, it seemed, that he couldn't stem the flow of laughter pouring from him.

Maybe the earl was mad. He was certainly odd. She hadn't been able to shake the impression that he was a great cat and she a little mouse, his to toy with, to lure and then strike when she least expected it.

If only she could repair the damage he'd done as quickly as he'd accomplished it. She had four buttons back in place and he was still laughing, damn him. That irked her into saying something else when she knew she likely should keep her peace and go back from whence she came, finding a different way to return home to Virginia.

"One hundred thousand pounds is humorous to a man in your dire financial straits?" she asked.

That finally tempered his good humor. He sobered, fixing her with that penetrating stare of his. "Who are you?"

So he didn't recognize her, then. They had never been formally introduced, of course. She ought not to be disappointed, but some small, vain sliver of her was. "I am not a woman who should be laughed at, my lord."

"Oh, I wasn't laughing at you, love." He grinned, and it did wicked things to her senses, that grin. "It was the absurdity of the moment. Surely you don't think to entrap me into marriage by arranging this tableau?"

"I didn't invite you to molest my person," she reminded him, flushing. Of course, she had—she was ashamed to admit—been enthralled by him. It was as if he'd cast a spell over her with his beauty and his knowing touch.

"Of course not, but I must be excused for imagining that my reputation precedes me, and that only a certain sort of woman seeks out my company at this time of night." His voice was low, suggestive. "That sort of woman seeks pleasure, not wedding vows."

Pleasure. The mere words on his lips sent a frisson of something wanton and altogether alarming settling over her. The things he had said. Lord almighty, but she'd never heard the like in her entire life. The man was everything she'd heard and, quite probably, worse.

"I sought you out for simple reasons, my lord." She decided to strive for bald honesty in the hopes that she could avoid any further references to matters of the flesh.

"Pray forgive me if marriage seems the inherent opposite of simple," he purred.

He was a dangerous man, impossible to read. So beautiful at this proximity that she ached just looking upon him. Hardly any wonder he had bedded half the women in the aristocracy if rumors were to be believed. No woman could look upon him and not melt on the inside.

"I'm not looking for a true marriage, my lord," she explained.

He caught her chin in his thumb and forefinger, holding her still for his unsettling inspection. "What are you looking for then, dear girl? Cease talking in riddles and place all your cards on the table."

"A marriage in name only." She met his gaze, unflinching.

"Ah," he said softly, stroking her jaw as he spoke the single syllable, drawing it out as though the next moment held great import. "What makes you think I'd sell myself for one hundred thousand pounds? You cannot believe you're the first to attempt such an arrangement?"

She'd been certain she would've been the first. His words gave her pause. Clara had thought out this plan with meticulous care. She had researched, planned, chosen the man before her because he'd seemed an indolent voluptuary and was rather infamously pockets to let. An easy sell, she'd been certain.

But the earl she'd watched these last few weeks, the man who flirted with other men's wives and drank too much at balls, who courted scandal at every turn, that earl was nowhere to be seen on this dark night in the privacy of his study. For the real Earl of Ravenscroft had a wit as sharp as a Bowie knife and the personality of a coiled rattlesnake. She'd ventured where she didn't belong. Had imagined him to be a different person entirely.

But she'd come this far, hadn't she? Her father and stepmother and their legion of servants were not easily fooled. Sneaking out with the aid of a bribable driver her father had recently hired had taken an endless amount of daring and tenacity. She'd made it here, into his study, past his sour-faced butler. She couldn't simply turn tail and go home.

"I may not be the first to present you with such an offer, my lord, but I believe my offer to be the best." There. She could brazen it out. She could make him see reason. She hadn't a choice. Ravenscroft was her only hope of escape now, for if word of her failed attempt at freedom reached her father, he'd change the terms of her marriage settlement as he'd threatened, leaving her with nothing and no recourse. No way of ever returning home. "I understand that you're in need of funds. You have sisters in desperate want of a season. I neither want nor need anything from you. A great deal of wealth shall be settled upon me after I marry, and I'm willing to give you a hundred thousand pounds of that wealth unencumbered so long as you allow me to return to Virginia."

"I thank you for the offer, my dear, but the answer is a resounding no." His fingertips skimmed down her throat. Such a light caress, barely even there, and yet the effect was maddening. "It's a damn shame you aren't someone else's wife. I could have shown you so much."

He had refused her, yet he hadn't released her. He touched her with a familiarity she hadn't ever known, not even with Henry. Now she understood the whispers. Understood why ladies spoke about him behind their fans and sent him longing glances. He could make a woman feel as if she were the most desirable woman in the world, even as he was telling her no.

"Will you not even consider it?" she asked him. "I believe that one hundred thousand pounds could solve a great many of your problems."

He smiled without mirth, watching his fingers as they settled in the hollow of her throat and then swept lower still, across the bare expanse of her breast that he had revealed with such skilled ease. "Not the biggest problem, I'm afraid. But that is neither here nor there. How much longer will you stay, love? I cannot in good conscience encourage you to linger. If I ruin you tonight, I won't go to your father in the morning begging for your hand. It really is in your best interest to go. Now."

But his fingers skated a path of fire near her nipple even as he warned her, and he lowered his head so that she could smell his cologne and feel his hot brandy-scented breath upon her lips. Would he kiss her? It didn't matter. She forced her mind back to the task at hand, convincing him of the wisdom of his capitulation.

"Wouldn't you like to see your sisters have the seasons they deserve? You must love them very much. You could see them settled forever. You could return your estates to their former glory, and I would barely require anything from you for your cooperation."

"There is only one way in which I'd like to offer my cooperation at the moment, and it is this." He cupped her face with his other hand and that quickly, his mouth was upon hers. The kiss was not anything like Henry's had been. It was masterful, a revelation. His lips angled on hers, his tongue sweeping the seam of her lips before coaxing her to open. He tasted of brandy and sin. His fingers slipped from her cheek to her hair, loosening the heavy plaits, holding her in place. His other hand slid beneath her chemise and corset, finding her hardened nipple without err.

She gasped at the sensation, arched into his hand. His kisses slowed. He nipped at her lower lip then sucked on it gently. He pressed a kiss to the corner of her mouth, to her ear, his tongue darting out to trace the shell and lick the sensitive area she hadn't known existed just behind her earlobe.

"Why did you come here, little dove?" he whispered into

her ear. "Tell me what you want."

He had turned her mind upside down. She couldn't think. His shoulders were broad beneath his waistcoat and shirt. She hadn't even realized she was touching him, but she opened her eyes now and stared. This had not been her plan. Not at all. He was never meant to touch her, and yet he was sucking the tender flesh of her throat, kissing a path to the curve of her shoulder, nipping her with just enough pressure to send an unwanted flood of something primitive and wholly foreign straight through her veins. Her pelisse was somehow on the floor, her bodice partially shucked. Lord God in heaven. What manner of scrape had she gotten herself into now?

"My lord, will you not see reason?"

"Is it reason that brought you here to me tonight?" he whispered and then continued his path of fire down the curve of her breast. He dragged her corset down with both his hands, nearly exposing her.

"Yes." And no. But largely yes. She forced herself to think, to recall all the things she'd meant to say. "I want my freedom. Do you not also want yours, my lord?"

Another tug, and her corset was beneath her breasts. He shocked her by sucking on her nipple through her chemise. He captured it between his teeth and tugged, sending an answering pull of want low in her belly. When he released her, he glanced up, meeting her gaze, and she couldn't help but notice how lucid and direct he was. He'd been toying with her again, she realized, and she had fallen so neatly into his trap. Had he even been affected?

"Freedom is an illusion," he said coolly. "Perhaps you're too young to have realized that yet, but the truth will inevitably come to you. We are all trapped here in one way or another, and the only escape is death."

Such a harsh, cold view of the world. Clara shivered. "One hundred thousand pounds, my lord, and all you need do is wed me and let me go."

Chapter Two

JULIAN STARED AT THE DELECTABLE WOMAN IN HIS ARMS. She was half dressed. Completely lovely, her sensitive skin marred by the nips and licks he had given her. She was responsive after all. It had merely taken some coaxing on his part. But no matter. Of course he could make a woman—any woman—want him. It was simultaneously his gift and his curse.

But it wasn't her surprisingly sensual reaction that gave him pause or her undeniable allure. It was her words. One hundred thousand pounds was no trifling matter. A man could pay off his debts with that kind of coin and still live more than comfortably enough, provided he had a care with what remained.

Naturally, it could be a ruse, a hyperbolic lure to lead him to the altar. Sacrificial lamb, etcetera. She didn't seem the cozening sort, however, and he fancied himself a superior judge of character. She blushed prettily now beneath his frank regard, though whether her embarrassment stemmed from the liberties she'd allowed him or her daring proposal, he couldn't be sure. Perhaps a healthy smattering of both.

"You want to pay me to marry you, little dove?" The

mere suggestion sounded so absurd that he almost laughed again. He decided to discomfit her instead, caressing her jaw and touching his thumb to her lower lip once more, precisely where he'd nipped it. "Was this meant to be my taste of the wedding night, then?"

Her lips compressed into a tight line, blue eyes snapping fire at him as she shrugged from his loose grasp and stepped back. "As I've already explained, there will be no wedding night, sir."

"On that we are agreed." His gaze flicked to her breasts straining against her chemise, her nipples stiff little temptations beneath the white fabric. They begged to be sucked, those nipples, without the barrier of cloth. "For there will be no wedding."

He set her away from him. Pity she was either a bit touched or green enough to believe the plots and schemes she read in Gothic novels could be applied to her life. He would have dearly liked to finish what they'd begun. True desire had become a rarity for him but he felt it now, pulsing through him like a starved beast. She was lovely and innocent, and he longed to awaken her to pleasure. To take the artlessness of her and consume it for himself.

Pity too that his days of selling himself were at an end. She'd almost be worth it.

"Not even for a hundred thousand pounds?"

That rather caught him off guard, for it was almost as if she'd read his bloody mind. Something else stirred in him then, warring with the lust. Anger. He stalked back to her, crowding her with his body. He should have some mercy, at least allow her to finish buttoning herself back up, but she'd scratched him deep enough with her question and her offer to make him bleed.

"Who told you I would sell myself so cheaply?" He settled his hands on her waist, drawing her flush against him. "Even whores must set their price, my love. One hundred thousand pounds is a pittance to spend the rest of my life shackled to someone, regardless of how pretty her bubbies are." And the bubbies in question were, undeniably, flawless, crushed to his chest in the most tantalizing manner.

Her lush mouth dropped into a perfectly shaped O before she gathered her wits enough to plant her palms on his shoulders and push. "If you find insult in my offer, the fault is mine. Only allow me to go and I shall never again trouble you."

In her ire, her drawl deepened. He could listen to her speak all day in that accent.

But the wrath within him still burned a steady, vital flame, and so he wouldn't think about her soft, lilting patterns of speech. "Why should I let you go when I have you precisely where I want you, little dove? I don't suppose this was part of the madcap plans you hatched in your bedchamber, was it? No, I daresay not. I was meant to only be pleased by the honor you pay me in offering to sell the rest of my life for a hundred thousand pounds."

A new, telling shade of red tinged her high cheekbones. "I hardly asked for the rest of your life. I wish to return to my home in Virginia. One hundred thousand pounds for a marriage that can be over the moment I step aboard a ship bound for America hardly seems a devil's bargain to me."

Perhaps it wouldn't to someone like her, but Julian had been selling himself for over half his life. It had begun with Lady Esterly and it had ended with the Marchioness of Lyndhurst. The intervening years had held too many names and faces to recall.

He didn't release her as she wanted, held her still. She would not escape so effortlessly. No, she had been the one who had decided to come to him. She'd had an entire carriage ride to question the wisdom of her decision and had still proceeded. "Selling one's self is a devil's bargain, regardless of the price and circumstance."

This slip of a girl, quite beautiful, was no different than the rest. She wanted something from him. Wanted to use him in exchange for financial compensation, but this time it was his name instead of his body. Jesus, how had he gotten here, to this place in his life where at thirty-one years old he faced a golden angel in siren's form who was scarcely twenty if she was a day, who thought she could damn well buy him and then toss him away like rubbish?

"It is an even exchange, my lord."

She was brave, this lovely American girl. She faced him without flinching. Even now, she held her head high, her bodice gaping, her throat marked with what he had done to her, and she did not cower. He could admire bravery. Foolishness was another matter.

"Who sent you to me?" he asked quietly, for he wanted to know. Very much. They'd never crossed paths. He still didn't know her name. And while he was aware he possessed a reputation, he couldn't think she'd dreamt up this farce on her own.

"If you think I've been sent here by one of your former…friends, you're wrong."

"Friends," he repeated. "Come now. None of the ladies you're so delicately referencing were ever my friends."

"Your paramours, then. No, it was not any such person. Proposing this agreement to a gentleman was my idea, but a good friend of mine suggested you as an ideal candidate. Of course, I must now wonder at the wisdom of her recommendation!" Her eyes went wide, and she seemed almost as startled as he by her outburst. "Does that please you, my lord? Why do you toy with me now? Have I not entertained you enough for one evening? Can you not be merciful and allow me to go if you've no interest in my offer?"

Could he not be merciful? Well yes, he supposed he could, but some small part of him was actually enjoying this game. He stared at her, considering her words with care, and as he did, muted hollering reached his ears from somewhere else in the house. The front door, perhaps.

It was the sound, he was sure, of a madman. The sounds grew louder. Closer. Julian could discern words from the guttural caterwauling now.

"Where the hell is he?"

What the devil? His little dove stiffened in his arms, and he knew instantly that she recognized that booming voice. That drawl, so similar to hers. And he recognized it as well just as suddenly. Jesse Whitney, the American businessman. They'd had occasion to cross social paths before more than once.

But the woman in his arms was not Whitney's wife. She couldn't be…

"I demand to see my daughter!"

The voice was near to Julian's study now. Positively murderous. Osgood's affronted, proper tones could be heard next. The sounds of a scuffle ensued.

"Jesus." Julian stared at the woman in his arms, wondering if she had planned this. The stricken expression on her face suggested otherwise. "Never say you're Whitney's get?"

"What can he be doing here?" She shook her head, trying to make sense of the unwanted interruption. "How can he have known?"

The sound of a boot heel hitting his study door crashed into the silence between them. The door flew open, banging into the wall and sending plaster shards raining to the tired, old carpets. With a grim feeling settling in his chest, he set the girl behind him and faced his second unwanted visitor of the night.

Her furious papa.

This was a conundrum he found thoroughly distasteful. The Earl of Ravenscroft had committed a great many sins, but ruining an innocent—much less being discovered in the process by her irate sire—had never been one of them.

"Goddamn it, Ravenscroft! Unhand my daughter at once!" Jesse Whitney pulled a revolver from his jacket and took aim at Julian's heart. "Step away from her, you son of a bitch."

The sound of the hammer cocking echoed through the chamber, punctuating his demand with visceral effect.

Clara was almost afraid to peer from behind the Earl of Ravenscroft's broad shoulder. He was a tall man, blotting out the sight of her furious father and the gun she'd heard him cock, shielding her state of *dishabille* with his large body. Lord have mercy, her father didn't touch arms of any sort. Not since the war. She hadn't even known he'd possessed a gun. Never mind making sense of the notion of her good-natured father whisking into the earl's home prepared to commit murder.

"My lord!" The imperious butler she'd faced earlier now sounded rather breathless and concerned. "What would you have me do?"

"That will be all, Osgood." The earl sounded remarkably unflappable for a man who had a gun pointed in his direction.

Her father wouldn't harm Ravenscroft, would he? Clara stole a peek from behind the earl's right arm. Her father's expression revealed he was in a fine rage. She didn't recall ever seeing him so angry, and she had certainly provided ample cause for that emotion in the past. Admittedly, she had not adapted well to life in London or to a father she'd spent most of her life without knowing.

"Clara." Her father spotted her. "Has this miscreant done you any harm?"

"Of course not, Father." Her unsteady fingers found her corset and struggled to tug it back into its proper place. She'd never button her tight-fitting bodice back up without her undergarments in order. The thought of her father witnessing the evidence of her wanton behavior with the earl was enough to make her feel ill. "Please, do calm down."

"I object to your use of the term miscreant, Whitney," the earl said in an indolent tone, as though he didn't have a revolver pointed at him, a man's finger on the trigger. "I'm a peer of the realm, you must realize."

"We both know what you are, Ravenscroft." Her father's voice was dark, void of the irrational amusement the earl seemed to derive from the situation. "Now kindly get the hell away from my daughter so that I can take her home where she belongs."

Clara longed for home, but home was not and never could be the Belgravia mansion where she lived with her father, stepmother, and their growing brood of children. It had been years since she'd last seen Virginia, her beloved homeland. After tonight, her chances to ever see it again were almost certainly dashed. Her father would lock her in her chamber until she agreed to marry the next florid duke in need of her marriage settlement.

"Afraid I'll ruin her?" The earl's voice was cocky. Goading. "Perhaps that's already been done, old boy. I suppose you didn't think of that in your haste, did you? My hands are quite quick, and I know my way around a lady's skirts."

She stilled in the unattainable feat of righting her corset and decided to simply do her buttons instead, just as quickly as her fingers could fly over the small fabric-covered discs. An almost feral sound emanated from her father, so great was his rage. Mercy, why would the earl say such a thing? Did he intend to ruin her thoroughly before rejecting her? He was unpredictable enough, perhaps even cruel enough, to enact such a misguided sense of retribution.

"If you touched her, I'll put a bullet in your miserable hide. Don't doubt that I will," her father warned.

Clara settled the final button into place and stepped out from behind Ravenscroft, praying she didn't look as thoroughly kissed and debauched as she felt. "Father, please do calm down."

"I touched her." Ravenscroft issued the statement conversationally, as though he were imparting a fascinating *on dit*. "More than touched her, if you must know. Will you shoot me now, or wait to take a better aim? Will you shoot to maim, Whitney, or will you shoot to kill? The mind reels with the possibilities."

Mad, Clara decided. The earl was, without question, utterly mad. She gawped at him. He was handsome and elegant, as cool and charming as he'd be in any ballroom. And yet, he had just admitted the unthinkable to her father, a man with the barrel of a firearm trained on his heart.

"You miserable cur." Her father's expression was filled with more rage than she'd imagined possible. He spared her a quick glance as if to ascertain that she had not been unduly physically harmed before pinning Ravenscroft with his glare once more. "Where I will shoot you depends a great deal on what you say and do next, Ravenscroft."

Clara stepped in front of the earl, shielding him. If there was one thing she had come to know about her father, it was that he meant what he said. If he threatened the earl with bodily harm, he was deadly serious. And it was her fault that the earl faced the end of a Colt now, wasn't it?

"Father, this is a dreadful misunderstanding. I'll go with you. Please, do put the gun away. His lordship has done nothing wrong." Not precisely true, that. But what could she expect from a man of his reputation when she had barged into his home alone? And she had been a more than willing participant.

"Step away from him, Clara." Her father's jaw clenched. He lowered the revolver to his side but didn't seem inclined to holster it.

"Come, darling." The earl sidestepped her and slid his arm around her waist, drawing her against him. "You needn't defend me. The fault is all mine, is it not? It was I who asked you here. I who couldn't wait another moment to have you in my arms."

What in heaven's name? Clara stared at his chiseled profile. He didn't appear mad, rather the opposite in fact. He exuded an ease, a calm charm that was at odds with the situation. Did he think somehow to protect her by feigning culpability for her disastrous plan? If that was his aim, she had to put an end to it.

"My lord, this isn't necessary." She was responsible for her own unwise actions. She'd face her father's wrath. She'd answer for her sins, since it seemed she couldn't atone for them.

"But it is, it would seem, my sweet little dove, for your sire has rendered it so with the honor of his presence and the commotion he's made with his…" The earl allowed his words to trail away in indolence for a moment, as though he were the one in control of the state in which they now found themselves uncomfortably mired. He made a fluid gesture toward the Colt. "With his armament."

"It's a decision maker, you rotten scoundrel." Her father's eyes narrowed. "You can decide to remove your hands from my daughter, or I'll maim you. I'm a former soldier, sir. Don't think my aim isn't exceptional."

Clara's mouth felt painfully dry. Dear Lord, there was no way her father would dare to shoot the earl, was there? He raised the revolver once more, training it on Ravenscroft's left foot. Clara attempted to slip from the earl's grasp so that she could shield him again, but he held her fast. What was he about? He had dismissed her offer with arrogant disdain. Had told her he would never marry her, not even for a handsome portion of her marriage settlement. And then, he had kissed her, touched her, placed his mouth upon her most sensitive and forbidden places. Now, he seemed almost to be her champion.

"Would you maim your future son-in-law, Mr. Whitney?" Ravenscroft's question cut through her whirling thoughts. "It seems unwise, as it would not only possibly make your daughter the object of all manner of scurrilous gossip but also invite the law to come down upon you. Just think of what would happen, sir, if you should kill me while my babe is in your daughter's womb and she hasn't even yet enjoyed the benefit of marriage to me."

Her father's expression, Clara was sure, mirrored her own. Stunned shock warring with disbelief. She may be an unwed lady, untutored in much of the pleasures of the flesh, but even she was not ignorant enough to believe that anything which had transpired between them would have gotten her with child.

"My lord," she protested, attempting another escape from his grasp.

His fingers tightened on her waist, telling her with actions what he hadn't told her with words. This man was not letting her go. Had he decided that her offer was worthwhile after all? Could it be?

"Hush, darling Clara." He looked down at her now, and she didn't like what she saw at all. He appeared hard, his blue eyes dark and cold, his beautiful mouth pulled taut in a grim frown, all harsh angles and a sense of foreboding. His words suggested that of a lovelorn suitor. His gorgeous face, however, showed nothing of the kind. "I am sorry that I've compromised you so completely. Sorrier still that your father has had to learn the news in such an undesirable manner. But the damage is done, and it cannot be mended. We'll need to wed as soon as I can acquire a license."

"You've compromised her?" Her father lowered the revolver again. His expression was even more grim than the earl's. "We can keep the details of this night a secret. No one ever need be the wiser, Ravenscroft. How much for your silence?"

Clara couldn't shake the feeling that she'd been outwitted by the sinfully handsome earl. He was quick and complex, a rattlesnake, yes. It would seem he had chosen to strike. "But you didn't compromise me, Lord Ravenscroft."

"Darling." He drew her to him and pressed a kiss between her brows, as though he were besotted. He didn't fool her for an instant. "You are far too innocent to understand that I have." He looked back to her father once more. "I have no price, Mr. Whitney, that will buy my silence. I'm afraid it will be marriage to your daughter or nothing else. I'm in love with her, you see, and she is in love with me as well. Is that not right, my darling?"

Misgiving filled her. Not one bit of her plan had unfolded as she'd so meticulously strategized. Yet now, the earl was giving her precisely what she wanted. The opportunity to marry so that she could leave England forever after she received her marriage settlement. The lush magnolias and verdant fields of her youth called to her now. Home was suddenly within reach.

"Yes." She trained her gaze on her father, not without a pang of sympathy for him. She had grown to love him over the past few years, but he was inflexible on the one thing that meant the most to her—returning to Virginia. "Father, I am in love with Lord Ravenscroft. I wish to wed him as expediently as possible."

"What makes you think I'll give you even a shilling, you misbegotten bastard?" Jesse Whitney demanded.

Julian sipped his brandy, still wishing for the easy obliteration of liquor that never seemed to find him. Miss Clara Whitney had been trundled home in her papa's carriage, the better to protect his future wife from further scandal. Now he faced the angry father bear, who still looked inclined to take up his Colt revolver and send a bullet straight into Julian's black heart. Perhaps it was well-deserved, especially given what he'd decided to do.

The tattered remnants of his conscience could bloody well go to hell and wait until his soul inevitably joined it there one day. He turned his mind to the task at hand.

"I merely expect the terms of the marriage settlement to be fair, Mr. Whitney. It stands to reason that a man doesn't wish the daughter he loves to live in penury, without a roof over her head or bread in her mouth." Julian shrugged. "I'm afraid I cannot provide her with the life she's accustomed to living."

Julian had no experience in angry fathers or dowries or the finer art of arranging marriage settlements. Angry husbands, he could ward off with his fists quite nattily. An unsavory business, this. But if he wanted to save himself and his sisters from ruin, he knew what needed to be done. He thought of Alexandra and Josephine, who certainly deserved to be spared the legacy of their father's profligacy. The little Virginia termagant had been right.

"You seem to have forgotten something, Ravenscroft," drawled Whitney, "I don't have to allow her to wed you."

By law, an heiress needed to reach one-and-twenty before she could marry without her parent or guardian's permission. Apparently, his bride had not yet reached her majority. A bit young for his tastes, but he would make do with her, and the prospect wasn't at all unappealing.

But there was also the possibility of her father refusing to provide a dowry or providing a marriage portion that was hers alone to control. He would need to proceed with caution, deftly maneuver Whitney into seeing things his way.

"Of course not, and yet there is, one must note, the matter of her possibly carrying my child." He kept his tone mild. "If you wish her to give birth to a bastard and be forever ruined, I cannot change your mind. However, I can obtain a license and we can be married with such haste that no one will ever be the wiser should a child arise from our…indiscretion this evening."

Julian wasn't a man who was prone to prevarication. Nevertheless, he was currently and unabashedly engaged in an outright, utter lie to Clara Whitney's father. Something had shifted inside him as he'd stared down the barrel of that revolver. It had all seemed rather serendipitous suddenly. He'd been on the brink of ruin, and into his study sailed a beautiful American heiress, ready to pluck him from the maws if he just played his cards properly.

He still had a price after all, it seemed.

But he wasn't selling himself for one hundred thousand pounds. He was selling himself for a far greater amount, for Jesse Whitney's wealth—even greater now that he had joined forces with Levi Storm of the North Atlantic Electric Company—was quite well known, even to Julian. After all, if Clara had been willing to part with one hundred thousand pounds, it stood to reason that there was a great deal more to be had. His little dove thought she'd bought him and was about to set sail for her homeland with the bulk of her marriage portion. Poor, sweet dove. She hadn't realized he'd never agreed to her terms.

Whitney clenched both fists, his countenance rigid with his anger. The Colt stayed mercifully in its place for the moment. "You do realize the…possibility to which you allude is the sole reason I haven't either already beaten you into oblivion or shot you dead where you sit, don't you? I suppose you do. You don't seem stupid, Ravenscroft. Merely lazy and greedy, which is why you decided to make poor Clara your unsuspecting prey. My daughter deserves far better than a lowly parasite who would ruin her to line his own pockets, goddamn it."

Yes, she did. Julian couldn't argue that point with Whitney, for no one deserved him, a man who had whored his body and pretty face since the age of fourteen. A man who had never done anything more important than bring misguided duchesses and countesses to shattering orgasm with his tongue. Ah, well. It was a skill, he supposed, making a woman come. Not every man could claim to do so, and certainly not as proficiently as he.

He considered the man who would be his father-in-law, who didn't appear to be terribly advanced in years. Indeed, he'd wager they were somewhat of an age, which was deuced awkward. He'd guess old Whitney had about nine years on him. The man must've been little more than a stripling when he'd become a father.

"Mr. Whitney, I do so hate to dispel your assumption that I'm a fortune hunter who importuned your daughter, but I must correct you on that score." Ha, what utter tripe. But he had to make his soliloquy convincing or he'd never get this boulder-headed American to give up his daughter or his coin. "We've fallen in love, you see, and tonight when I begged her to visit me, I had no intention of compromising her. I would never dream of causing her harm in any way. It was merely my love for her that—"

"Cease talking," Whitney interrupted, his ire evident in his heavy drawl and the booming thunder of his voice. "Do you think me a bumbling fool, Lord Ravenscroft? Do you think your protestations of love will ever be believed by me? Oh, I have no doubt that your silver tongue charmed my sweet Clara. But it has no such effect upon me. I can see a hog's turd for what it is."

The man was as pugnacious as a prize fighter. Damn it.

"A hog's turd, am I?" He made a great show of looking down at his person. "And here I thought myself a peer of the realm. An earl."

"Titles mean nothing to me," Whitney growled. "They aren't the measure of a man."

Well. This certainly would not be the first or the last time that someone had found him morally lacking. Hardly shocking. "I'm a man of reason, Mr. Whitney. I shall count your remarks as those of an overset father. Regardless of your opinion of me, I am the man who will marry your daughter. Do let us try to remain civil."

"Civil is me refraining from shooting you."

"But we are here to discuss the marriage settlement, are we not, and the marriage itself?" His head had begun thumping, and no amount of brandy could cure what ailed him. Best to tie up this matter neatly. "I can secure a license as quickly as possible. We will marry quietly. I propose a dowry of two hundred thousand pounds to refurbish the estates and provide your daughter with a standard of living to which she is accustomed and another hundred thousand pounds in stocks of North Atlantic Electric. Whatever else you decide to settle on her will be hers, free and unencumbered as the law states."

"Son-of-a-bitch. You've been planning this, haven't you?" Whitney's hand was creeping back toward his revolver, which he'd holstered at his waist like a common outlaw.

Actually, his sweet little dove had planned it. Julian had merely turned the tables on her. She was a clever thing, he'd give her that, but no match for a man of his ilk. "Of course not, sir. But I do know what the estates require and what your daughter will require as my wife. Should you think it judicious to bless her with more, that is your choice."

"You're a cunning bastard, I'll say that for you." Whitney stood abruptly. "Before I agree to anything, I'll need to speak with my daughter directly. I'll send word to you in the morning. In the meantime, sleep well knowing I'm a merciful man who spared you a painful death tonight because I love my daughter. And never forget, Ravenscroft, just how much I love her. For if anything should ever happen to make her unhappy, retribution will be mine."

Perhaps it would be best to allow the man to retreat, lick his wounds. Julian was fairly confident that Clara would maintain his ruse. She wanted her freedom. So too did he.

He stood and bowed to Jesse Whitney. "I will expect to hear from you tomorrow."

"Four years in the hell of war, Ravenscroft. I know how to kill a man." Whitney tapped the revolver-shaped lump beneath his jacket. "Never forget."

Julian didn't suppose he would any time soon. Fortunately for him, murder remained a punishable offense. But he knew a worthy foe when he'd met one, and Jesse Whitney was certainly that.

Chapter Three

CLARA RECEIVED THE SUMMONS SHE'D BEEN DREADING just after breakfast. Her stepmother gently knocked at her chamber door, apparently the messenger.

"Clara dear? May I enter?" Lady Bella's voice was tentative, worried, muffled by the wood separating them.

No, Clara wanted to deny. *You may not.* She eyed the window with dedicated purpose. It wasn't the first time she'd contemplated an escape via the deep ledge and accommodating architectural effects adorning the front of her father's stately home. But perhaps it would be the last. She'd cast her fate in Ravenscroft's study, and she'd be lying to herself if she didn't admit that decision had brought with it enough trepidation to shake an entire phalanx of soldiers.

She clasped her hands before her and took a staying breath. All night she had waited for someone to address what had occurred. Her father's wife had said little as she'd escorted Clara from the carriage upon her return from the earl's home. *What have you done this time, Clara?* A footman had promptly been stationed at her door as if she were a prisoner.

She'd waited, still dressed, until her father had returned home, having realized far too late that her buttons were one off and her bodice tellingly skewed. And still, nothing had happened. No one had come. No caterwauling, no hollering, no wildly waving revolvers. There had been instead a deep, troubling quiet.

The silence told Clara quite a lot, for she'd indulged in more than her fair share of scrapes and troubles over the years following her mother's death back home in Virginia. There had always been remonstration, reprimands. There had never been such deafening, dread-inducing tranquility.

"Clara? I'm afraid I'm going to enter whether you'd like me to or not."

Yes, she had supposed as much. No more procrastination then, though the sleepless night had rendered her a bundle of ragged nerves, bloodshot eyes and all. "Enter as you will."

Bella breezed over the threshold, effortlessly beautiful and elegant as always with her raven hair styled *au courant*, high on her head with a fringe of bangs. She wore a silk morning gown of cheerful yellow trimmed with flounces. But her expression was that of a funeral mourner.

"Clara." Her stepmother's tone carried a visceral sense of disappointment, her mouth tightening into a pinched line of dread.

"My lady." Clara performed a perfect curtsy. The occasion seemed to merit it.

"Your father wishes to speak with you." Bella crossed the chamber and took up Clara's clasped hands in a show of tender concern. "He has allowed me the favor of this tête-à-tête with you first."

How wretched.

Clara didn't want to talk to anyone. Not about what had happened. Not about her supposed ruining. Not about anything. She still wasn't entirely sure herself what had happened, truth be told. As traces of dawn had stolen across the sky, she'd begun to wonder if she hadn't been outmaneuvered at her own chess game. All she wanted was to leave for her homeland with enough money to pursue her cause of women gaining the right to vote. But she mistrusted the earl's sudden capitulation. She mistrusted it very much indeed.

She struggled to tamp down her disquiet as she met her stepmother's frank gaze. "Must we talk, Lady Bella? You are well-intentioned, I know, but I would prefer not to delay the inevitable."

Her father waited, the agonizing hours of quiet at an end. He was a kind man, a fair man in most ways. But in the earl's study, he'd been unhinged. Her fault. Guilt crept over her, mingling with the foreboding. Perhaps she had finally managed to produce her own stunning, inglorious downfall. And she'd thought herself so sharp. Alas.

"Indeed, we must." She guided Clara to the sitting area, an uncomfortable set of gilt settees she found rather loathsome. "Do let us sit down."

Clara sat on the edge of the cushion, folding her hands in her lap. "I suppose my father is angry."

Her stepmother settled herself daintily. "He's quite overset, as would any father in his position be. You can consider yourself most fortunate that your driver had a conscience and returned at once to unburden himself. Who knows what would have transpired if Jesse had not reached you when he did."

So it was the new coachman she'd bribed with a hundred pound note who had been her undoing. The rascal. But now was not the time for ruminating. She had a feeling Lady Bella was being rather magnanimous in her description of what—if her father's reaction last evening had been any indication—was his utter fury. "He nearly shot Lord Ravenscroft dead in his study, my lady. Did you know that?"

"I'm sure you're being melodramatic, my dear. Your father would not murder a peer of the realm, regardless of the man's crimes." Bella paused, her expression growing strained. "Speaking of crimes, the reason for my visit this morning is to…ascertain the extent of the earl's actions."

Ah. Perhaps they feared Ravenscroft had forced himself upon her. He had not, of course, but he'd been no gentleman. She thought of the depraved things he'd said, the likes of which she'd never heard. The way he'd undone her buttons and kissed her until she'd felt as if she'd drunk too much wine. The way he'd sucked on her nipple straight through her chemise, fabric no barrier to his prurient ways. A sharp pang of yearning shot through her, startling her, making a new ache settle between her thighs.

Her cheeks went hot. She shifted and focused on settling her skirts into place. "I would prefer not to speak of it, my lady."

"But you must." Her stepmother's tone was soft, almost pitying. "Did Lord Ravenscroft hurt you, Clara?"

Shocked her? Yes. Done wicked things to her body? Yes. Hurt her, however, he had not. "Why, no. Of course he didn't."

"He didn't force you?"

"No."

"You understand that there's no shame if he did, do you not? Be honest with me, dear heart. The law does not allow the misuse of innocents, and we shan't hesitate to prosecute the earl should it be necessary."

Lord in heaven, did everyone think the earl so evil that he'd force a woman? He must possess some redeeming quality, something to which she could cling for the short time she'd be his wife.

"The earl didn't force me," she repeated. There would be no hauling Ravenscroft off to some dank prison cell, even if she did have a deeply troubled conscience over the wisdom of her decision.

"Did you lie with him?"

Clara's cheeks went hotter still. Lord have mercy, she hadn't anticipated such direct questioning. "I do believe his lordship has compromised me."

She didn't want to fib to her stepmother. When Clara

first met Lady Bella, they had clashed horridly. Clara had been young, newly motherless, and fresh on the shore of a strange land where she'd been brought to live by a father she scarcely knew. But Bella had been firm and kind and caring. She'd earned Clara's respect.

Her stepmother pressed a hand to her heart now as if it pained her. "Oh, dearest girl. I know you love your scrapes but this time you've gone much too far. You cannot recover from this without marrying Ravenscroft."

"I wish to marry him, my lady." If only she could speak the words with more conviction. Marrying him would get her what she wanted, after all. She thought of the rolling hills of Virginia, the beauty of her home. How she missed it. She didn't belong here in this stilted, aristocratic society laden with titles and rigid custom. She was a Virginian by birth and by nature.

"You don't even know him." Bella appeared to consider her next words with care. "Are you aware that he has a…certain reputation?"

"I too have a past, my lady. I'll not judge him."

"Others do, however. You may not be welcomed at certain homes as his wife, Clara. He is an earl, but his reputation is quite black."

Irredeemable, or so her good friend Bo had claimed. It was part of her reasoning in choosing him. A man with such a dark past had nothing left to lose. But his past and his repute didn't matter to Clara other than that they made him an ideal candidate for her plan. After all, she hardly intended to be his wife for long.

Bella's gaze was earnest upon her. Clara tamped down her guilt. She was doing what she must. Her father had told her he refused to allow her to return home on her own, and that he would withhold all monies he intended to settle on her so that she could not leave England upon reaching her majority. He'd forced her into it, really, with his stubbornness.

She forced a sunny smile to her lips. "Never fear.

Virginia ladies are made of stern stuff. I'm sure I shall manage life as Lady Ravenscroft with aplomb."

Her stepmother frowned, her expression akin to that of a woman watching her loved one board a canoe with a hole in it for a voyage across the Atlantic. "I certainly hope you are made of the sternest stuff, my dear. For you shall need to be if you marry the Earl of Ravenscroft."

There had to be worse fates. She thought of his sinful mouth, his beautiful face, his lean and hard body. And then she thought about the real him, the Bowie knife and rattler. An unwanted shiver stole down her spine.

Julian's sisters sat before him in the same study where he'd so recently defiled his bride-to-be. They'd been summoned from their impeccably proper aunt's home, where they'd been staying lest his reputation taint them, for the purpose of his grand announcement.

He loved his sisters, and the latest mark upon his soul was partially down to that fine emotion. He wanted to see them happy, wed to decent men, gaggles of children about their skirts one day. They deserved everything good, sweetness and light, this lovely pair of innocents.

Alexandra and Josephine. Just three years apart in birth, they were marked opposites in all ways aside from their age. Alexandra had fiery red curls and stood almost as tall as Julian. Handsome rather than beautiful, she was without doubt the issue of their mother's affair with a hulking, redheaded Scottish groomsman on their country estate. Josephine was petite and dark-haired, fine-boned and exquisite in appearance, almost certainly not their father's daughter either but her lineage was rather more muddled, given their mother's dozen flings in the last year of her life. She'd died shortly after giving birth to little Jo. Julian still recalled looking down at the red-faced, mewling infant and hating her for taking their mother away. Seventeen years had not faded the memory.

Edward, though, the perfect son—the son who should have been the firstborn, according to their father—had instantly been taken with Jo. Julian had always put it down to how much Edward had reviled both Julian and their mother. And Julian had, in turn, reviled Edward with equal vehemence. Edward, a faultless sycophant to their father, had never once experienced the old bastard's fists.

But that was all a lifetime ago now, Edward long gone to the Continent, and his sisters awaited the reason for their summoning with ill-disguised curiosity. "You will be moving here with me," he told them.

Alexandra, ever an imp, was first to respond. "*Tante* Lydia won't allow it, you know. She says your reputation rivals only the devil himself."

Julian kept his expression carefully blank. The ancient bit of baggage had certainly never spared him any love, so he supposed he shouldn't be surprised to hear her opinion of him. She did, after all, share blood with the former Earl of Ravenscroft, who was currently rotting in the family plot just as he deserved. "Great Aunt Lydia is not your guardian. I am. She can bloody well carry on with attending temperance meetings and sewing for charities like the wizened old bird that she is."

"Wizened old bird." Josephine grinned. "One must admit it's an apt description."

"She is rather a dragon," Alexandra conceded. "But why now, Julian? *Tante* Lydia says you're in debt up to your nose. She says Edward ought to have been the earl rather than you."

"Not even enough coin to keep proper servants," Josephine added. "No housekeeper to speak of. Quite a shame, she says, that you've squandered every last shilling on harlots and drink. Edward never would have done, according to her."

He grimaced before he could think better of it, tamping down the old rage that surged inside him at the mentioning of his brother's name. "*Tante* Lydia damn well ought to keep her misinformation to herself. I strongly doubt Edward would have fared any better than myself at managing the mountain of debt the previous earl saddled me with. As it is, the paragon is too busy gallivanting across the Continent at present to grace us with his illustrious presence. Moreover, the task of outfitting this house with a proper staff will belong to my wife."

His sisters gaped.

"Are you soused?" Alexandra asked. "*Tante* Lydia said our father was a drunkard and a wastrel and that you've chosen the same sad path."

A chill went down his spine at being compared to that particular rotter. He was nothing like his father. Not one goddamn part of him. But that was neither here nor there, for the dead earl and the misery he'd inflicted upon Julian was best left buried in the past along with any thoughts of his brother. Edward was just as dead to him as the bastard who'd fathered them both.

"Of course I'm not soused." But he was fast losing patience with the overly opinionated ladies before him. "Has our paragon Aunt Lydia forgotten to remind you two of the necessity of possessing manners? I'll thank you not to repeat anything else the crone has said."

For the first time in as long as he could recall, Julian was sober as a teetotaler. He hadn't a drop of drink since three days prior when he'd suddenly acquired his future countess. He'd nearly completed negotiations with Miss Whitney's still-irate papa. He'd made his bargains and his peace with the tattered remnants of his conscience. He was in possession of a marriage license and soon, he'd be in possession of a great sum of coin and stocks and one beautiful little dove.

His to do with as he chose.

Surreal, all of it. Too facile by far. He felt like Hades securing himself a Persephone. Fitting, that comparison. He'd lured the girl into his underworld without even trying.

She'd set foot in his dark world first, God help her.

Alexandra had the grace to look a bit sheepish. "In truth, I think she's growing addle pated in her dotage. Quite hard of hearing."

"None of that explains your alarming lack of civility." He would hire a proper chaperone for them immediately. Or send them far away to a Swiss finishing school. Yes, perhaps that would be just the thing. How had he thought them a lovely pair of innocents mere moments ago?

"Your wife?" Josephine repeated. "Have you one, then?"

Damnation, he hadn't recalled that his sisters were this trying. Admittedly, it had been some time since he'd abandoned them to the disapproving protection of *Tante* Lydia. He resisted the urge to roll his eyes heavenward. At least someone was moving the conversation forward at last. "I will have a wife within the week."

"Not you." Alexandra's tone dripped with disbelief.

Josephine stared at him as if he'd suddenly manifested magical powers and had transformed himself into a mythical creature. "Damn it all, did you say within the week?"

He glowered at both of his troublesome siblings. These girls were a handful, by damn. "Precisely what has our esteemed, ossified great aunt been teaching you about comportment? I begin to think I did you an injustice in leaving you in her care."

Alexandra grinned. "But near-sighted, almost deaf aunts make perfect chaperones."

"Wonderfully easy to elude." Jo's smile was serene.

Hellfire. He didn't dare imagine the sort of scrapes the girls had gotten themselves into while *Tante* Lydia snoozed into her needlework. Their familial reprieve, it seemed, was coming at a crucial moment. "Do try to at least pretend to be civilized ladies, you lot. If I'm ever to find you suitable husbands, you'll need to stop cursing and exhibiting such cheek."

"No one will wed us anyway." Alexandra waved a hand

as if to dash away his concern. "We haven't any dowries and our brother is the Earl of Ravenscroft."

His mood grew more dire by the moment. "While I'm afraid I cannot change the fact that I'm your brother, a dowry you both shall have. Upon my marriage, I'll be a very wealthy man, and I intend to use a generous portion of that wealth to see that the two of you are happy for the rest of your lives."

Josephine and Alexandra exchanged a prolonged glance of incredulity.

Julian tapped his fingers on his desk, irritation needling him. Was it truly that difficult to believe he was marrying? "Dear sisters," he drawled, "never say my reputation is so black that you don't believe me."

"You're not…you wouldn't force a girl to marry you, would you, Julian?"

"Good Christ." The tenuous thread of Julian's remaining patience snapped. He bestowed his most rebuking glare upon Alexandra, who had asked the question. "Do the two of you take me for a monster? Precisely what is it you've heard about me?"

Josephine wrinkled her nose. "I daresay you may not want to know."

One of the benefits of being regularly inebriated was that he hadn't a clue just how irredeemable the world apparently believed him. Even his own flesh and blood, Chrissakes. Meanwhile, here he was, about to sacrifice himself at the matrimonial altar for their futures. "I'm falling upon the sword for you two incorrigible minxes. I expect, at the very least, a modicum of gratitude in return. From this moment forward, I'll thank you to hold your tongues if you haven't anything civil to say."

Alexandra's brows shot up practically to her hairline. "But—"

"Silence," he bellowed. "I'll not hear another word about my reputation. Ever again. Are we understood?"

If he expected his sisters to meekly comply, it would

appear he'd forgotten they shared at least half of a family tree. Josephine blinked. "A bit of a sensitive subject, is it?"

He gritted his teeth so hard his jaw ached. What the hell had he been thinking, to saddle himself with the vexing scraps of petticoats before him? He should have allowed them to continue moldering with Great Aunt Lydia and retained his sanity.

Julian took a breath, calmly studied the threadbare patches in his carpet, and counted to five before responding. "Each future instance of insolence will cost you dearly. One less dress. One hundred less pounds for your dowry. That goes for each of you. Am I understood now, you ill-mannered imps?"

His sisters stared in unison. Apparently his generosity had robbed them of speech. A rarity, that. His generosity and their lack of verbosity both.

And then Josephine ruined it utterly. "Do you mean to suggest we shall truly have a trousseau and dowry?"

"Yes of course." Damn it, his benevolence was fast being depleted by the trying nature of his madcap sisters. "You were always meant to have the both. It was merely a pittance before, but now it shall be handsome. Very handsome indeed."

"What paragon of riches are you marrying to allow such a generous amount to be settled upon us both?" Alexandra demanded, apparently having heard none of his stern admonitions of the past half hour.

"One Miss Clara Whitney." Damn if the name didn't feel odd on the tongue. Foreign. But it was a name she wouldn't possess for much longer, for soon she would be the Countess of Ravenscroft. His lady. And damn if that title didn't feel equally odd. A slip of a girl, an American at that, would be his bride.

She was a beauty, his little dove. Clara of the golden hair, winsome smile, lilting drawl, and intoxicating innocence. It was a damn shame to spoil that innocence, but spoil it he would. The sisters before him, the servants belowstairs, the roof over his head—all depended upon that very spoiling now. The darkness in him would thoroughly enjoy every second of it.

Clara faced her father not without some wilt in her posture, which, she reckoned, was only understandable. For she loved her father, despite the fact that she hadn't known him in her formative years. She didn't want to hurt or disappoint him. But it seemed she was forever doomed to do both. He was as immovable as a boulder, stubborn as the cornerstone in the foundation of a grand old manor house.

His expression was as eerie as a death mask. No hint of smile. No hint of the laughing, teasing father she had come to know. "You've finally managed to mire yourself in a situation from which I cannot save you, Clara," he said in somber tones reminiscent of the reverend who had presided over her mother's funeral several years before. Her father had been at her side then, and he sat opposite her now, on the other end of an imposing and ornate desk.

It was, she thought for a silly moment, as though they were two nations at war. Much like their country had been not so long ago. She felt like a stranger, almost, brokering a treaty. An armistice? Or was it her terms of surrender? She didn't rightly know. "I neither want nor need saving, Father."

He made a moue of supreme displeasure. "You mean to suggest you wish to marry this…waste of flesh lord who has never earned a cent in his life without taking some bored society wife to bed?"

She shifted subtly on her uncomfortable chair, attempting to ease the pressure of her corset and her nerves. Her cheeks were hot and red, she was sure. This was not the sort of conversation one wanted or expected to engage in with one's stern and protective father. It didn't matter that she'd had days to prepare. "I'm sure I don't know what you speak of, nor would I wish to. Lord Ravenscroft is a good man."

Ha! Even to her own ears, her words rang horribly false. In truth, she didn't know the earl. Not at all. But Father didn't need to become aware of that pathetic fact, did he? Of course not.

"Good is not a word to be spoken in the same sentence with that son-of-a-bitch."

When Father was angry, his drawl was a great deal more pronounced. And the thickness of his drawl suggested he was very, very angry indeed. "I love him."

Another lie. Guilt struck her heart. She was a bad daughter, a rotten daughter, to prevaricate. He left her with no choice, however. He thought he knew better than she what she wanted, what she ought to do with her life. But she knew. She had a heart and a mind of her own, and that heart and that mind longed for Virginia.

Virginia was where she belonged, fighting for her cause. She'd had her taste of the gilded world of English aristocracy. It was flimsy as her silk stockings. No limbs of its own, if you asked her. Not that anyone ever did.

"Perhaps you foolishly think yourself in love," her father scoffed at such a notion, as though it were as ridiculous as an apple woman being presented to Queen Victoria at court. "But I can assure you that your lovesick swain has a different perspective entirely. He already had a settlement in mind, Clara. It is not you he is in love with, regardless of whatever nonsense he may fill your ears and innocent heart with. It is your wealth."

Of course it was. Gold was one of the oldest and surest lures in the world. And it had gotten her what she wanted, hadn't it? She held her head high. "Am I to be shocked to learn his coffers have nearly run dry? I'm given to understand that many noblemen find themselves in similarly unfortunate predicaments. Surely that makes him no different than most of his peers?"

"What makes him different is his reputation, Clara." Her

father's eyes bored into hers.

She dropped her gaze lest he read her too well, examining his clenched hands upon the desk. There were papers scattered about, some crumpled, some with entire sentences redacted by a bold strike of his pen. Marriage settlement documents, perhaps? She'd been told by her lady's maid that her father's redoubtable lawyer had made a long and solemn call upon him already that day.

What had Father said? Oh yes, Ravenscroft's reputation. It would seem she must forever answer for his wicked ways. "I'm not as ignorant as you believe me to be. Indeed, I am a woman grown, completely possessed of excellent reasoning and logic."

"You are aware that he has whored himself to half the ladies of the peerage?"

Clara flinched. Such an ugly insinuation. Ravenscroft himself had used the same word to describe himself. *Even whores must set their price, my love.* How low the earl's self-worth must be. For some reason she didn't care to examine, the thought disturbed her.

"Were every man or woman to be judged by his past misdeeds, no one would be welcome in any drawing room or ballroom," she countered.

"Clara." Her father turned his eyes heavenward for a moment, as though beseeching the Lord himself to intervene and strike some sense into her. "Clara, my darling daughter, I want so much more for you in a marriage than a hasty farce forced upon you by a rattler masquerading as an earl."

He was aggrieved, his pain palpable. Her conscience prodded her to make one last attempt at winning her freedom. "Perhaps there is another way to salvage my reputation without marriage to the earl. You could send me back to Virginia, Father. My mother's kinfolk would welcome me there."

Her father cocked his head at her, studying her in that way of his that saw far more than she would have preferred.

"Never tell me that this was all another one of your larks, Clara, that you somehow devised this madcap scheme in the hopes that I would send you back to Virginia rather than marry you off to a scoundrel."

Well, not precisely. But he was too close to the mark for her liking. She didn't wish for him to unravel all her careful plans, not when she was so near to achieving her goal. "Of course not. As I said, Lord Ravenscroft is the man I wish to wed. I'm sorry for the manner in which it need occur. I was foolish to go to him as I did, and for any shame or distress I've brought upon you and Lady Bella both, I apologize."

Unfortunately, her mentioning of her indiscretion with Ravenscroft hardly blunted her father's ire. Rage fairly emanated from him, overtaking him with a force so strong he could no longer remain seated and shot to his feet to pace the length of his study.

"What he did to you…ruining you…your stepmother has spared me the excruciating specifics of the nature of your encounter. But Clara, I need to be certain that he didn't force you or otherwise ill use you. Tell me the truth."

"He did not force or hurt me," she answered, one of the few honest statements she'd made since their interview had begun, much to her shame.

All the fight seemed to drain out of her father then. He stopped, appearing far less omnipotent than he always had to her. Far more human. Far more weary. "Then I will accept his offer for your hand. You'll wed him as expediently as possible. I'll grant him the two hundred thousand pounds he's asked for, but he's only getting fifty thousand in North Atlantic Electric stock. As for you, I will give you ten thousand a year and the other fifty thousand of North Atlantic Electric stock your husband requested for himself. You'll be a wealthy woman in your own right, and that is the best I can hope to do for you now. Under the law, you'll maintain control over anything you bring to the marriage aside from what is directly settled upon your husband."

Two hundred thousand pounds.

Clara had only offered Ravenscroft one hundred thousand to marry her and then annul the marriage. Dread settled over her. She had to know for certain. "He asked for the two hundred thousand directly?"

"You're damn right he did," her father gritted, his voice grim as ever. "Don't fool yourself into believing this is a love match, Clara. The son-of-a-bitch wants your dowry."

The same sense of foreboding she'd been feeling ever since returning home crept over her now, stronger than ever. If only asking her father to settle all the funds on her would not arouse his suspicion. No, she couldn't afford to chance he would change his mind. The web she'd spun about herself grew more tangled by the moment. Perhaps she'd been outmaneuvered in her own game.

Checkmate.

"You needn't worry over me. I know how to look after myself," she told her father. She'd been raised in the shadowy aftermath of America's deadliest war, and her upbringing had hardened her in a way none of her fellow society misses would ever understand. She could hold her own in a battle of wits and wills with an English earl whose only recommendation was his face. If he thought to best her, he'd never met a girl from Virginia.

Chapter Four

Ravenscroft stared at Jesse Whitney with disbelief. The man had gumption, he'd give him that. "You wish for me to court your daughter," he repeated slowly, doing a poor job of masking his irritation. Now that he'd settled on his course, he wanted his prize: his little dove and her tremendous American dowry. In truth, he wanted her almost as much as he wanted the vast amounts of coin that would accompany her. Certainly more than he cared to examine.

"Those are the terms I'm willing to offer you," Whitney affirmed. "Either you court her for a fortnight, well-chaperoned and without further ruining her, or you can't wed her."

To the devil with it. Now the man wanted him to bow and scrape and come sniffing about his future wife's skirts like some lovelorn swain when he'd all but secured her hand. To dance at balls. To attend dinner parties and the theater. To seriously pretend to be smitten by her, in public, and most certainly to manage all this while maintaining a façade of respectability and abstaining from drink. Why, he hadn't been sober long and he already found it deadly dull.

"I ruined her, you daft man," Ravenscroft grumbled, not feeling even a pinch of guilt at the lie. Well truly, he'd done some damage, put his hands and mouth where they didn't belong, but he hadn't bloody well swived her as he'd implied. No, that would come later. If she still truly believed there wouldn't be a wedding night, he would thoroughly enjoy changing her mind. With his tongue.

"Few are aware of what transpired." Whitney's rebuttal was smooth, calculated.

Well played. But no one could do brazen better than he. No one. "There is the matter of possible issue from what transpired," he reminded his father-in-law-to-be, also without a hint of guilt. "If I refuse to court her and you won't allow her to wed me, what shall happen when her belly grows? For then, it will be too late for doing the pretty at balls and dinners."

Whitney went ruddy, presumably from pent-up rage. The poor fellow didn't appear to enjoy reminders that his precious daughter could perhaps sire a bastard. "Do you want me to kill you after all, Ravenscroft?"

Julian made an elaborate show of scrutinizing his future father-in-law's person as though looking for the telltale silhouette of a pistol beneath his trappings of finery. "I don't see a weapon today, Mr. Whitney. Or shall I call you Papa? No? A bit too soon, perhaps."

His opponent apparently wasn't given to being blithe. He slammed his hands down on the admittedly battered study desk. "Listen to me, you son-of-a-bitch, this—my daughter's future—is not a laughing matter."

No, it wasn't. Poor girl, about to be shackled to him forever. Little levity in that, unfortunately for her. But Julian couldn't help himself. He rather enjoyed goading people. It was a trait he'd always possessed. Most damning in the eyes of others, no doubt. "Dear me, old fellow. I don't recall laughing, but if I did I'm sure I ought to offer you an apology."

Whitney's hands snapped closed into tight fists, the

knuckles showing white. Those knuckles bore the signs of his past. Mayhap he'd engaged in hand-to-hand combat during the war. Very likely Julian ought to tone down his bombast, but the man irked him.

"The next time you call me 'old fellow,' I'll knock out your teeth. You owe me at least a dozen apologies by now, none of which you seem willing to give." Whitney pounded the desk for emphasis. "Most importantly, you owe an apology to my daughter. Clara is an impulsive girl but a good girl nonetheless. You aren't fit to tidy up after her horse, let alone wed her. Give her a proper courting for a fortnight. The wedding will still be rushed, and tongues will still flay us alive, but at least we can build a case for love rather than necessity."

Julian took exception to all threats against his teeth. As it happened, they were even and straight, quite white, and one of his vanities. "I fail to see how a fortnight of courting will cause any less damage to her in the eyes of society than a simple, immediate marriage will."

Moreover, it had occurred to him that perhaps Whitney was attempting to use this fortnight to prove that Clara was not, in fact, *enceinte*, and that their nuptials would no longer be necessary. After all, depending upon where she was in her monthly courses, she could make a liar of him tomorrow. Or this very afternoon. Of course, it wouldn't be in her interest to do so, but Julian couldn't be sure just how far the wild-looking former soldier before him would go to protect his daughter. Examination by physician? He doubted it, but then again, if he'd learned anything in his life it was that the actions of most people couldn't be either trusted or predicted.

"I don't give a damn what you do or don't see, Ravenscroft," growled Whitney. "These are my terms. Court her for a fortnight. Act the part of lovesick swain. It must all be quite proper. And in return, I will give my reluctant blessing upon the marriage, along with the dowry you requested with one exception. Half the North Atlantic

Electric stocks will go to you and the other half to Clara, hers by law, along with whatever settlement I choose to bestow upon her, also entirely hers."

Strange that Julian didn't care to quibble over the division of the stocks but he did want to argue about a fortnight of waiting to make his little dove into his countess. Fifty thousand here or fifty thousand there, what was it when one had the expectation of nothing? He'd be a far wealthier man than he'd ever fancied possible either way. But he wanted the wedding, damn it, and he wanted it now.

Because he wanted her. Somehow, inexplicably, the plucky Virginia girl who'd shown up in his study unannounced had woken up a part of him he'd thought he no longer had. Desire. He hadn't truly longed for a woman since Lottie.

To the devil. Perhaps he ought to rein himself in a tad. It wouldn't do to become so enamored of her before he even *knew* her, for Chrissakes. "Mr. Whitney, allow me to be blunt for a moment. You don't want your daughter to marry me, and I perceive this courting nonsense as an attempt on your part to stop the nuptials from taking place. However, I am, you'll find as you grow to know me better, an amenable bloke at heart. I propose, therefore, a *détente* of sorts. I will do as you wish in return for your written oath that the wedding will carry on two weeks hence. Our lawyers will discuss the specifics of the agreement, I trust."

Whitney nodded, regaining a modicum of his civility. "Clara claims to love you, and if there's anything I know about my daughter it's that no one, not even the Lord, can stop her from accomplishing something she's set her mind to. I'll not stand in the way, but as a father I must protect her reputation as best as I may."

An odd sensation overcame Julian then, reminiscent of the way he'd felt when his mother had instructed one of the footmen to drown poor Alexandra's favorite puppy as a punishment for being cross with her nurse. He still recalled the sound of his sister's mournful howls. Three years old, poor lass. Pity. He supposed that was what he was experiencing just now. Pity for the father coming to terms with letting his daughter go to a notorious reprobate who he feared had only ruined her to gain a fortune.

But he hadn't ruined her, not truly. Nor was he marrying her with the sole aim of securing her dowry, though that had certainly been the factor that had influenced him to sell himself one last time. He wouldn't lie to himself about that. Part of his motive was mercenary. Part pure lust.

Wouldn't do to think about that now, for he'd just allowed himself to be roped into a fortnight-long betrothal. Courting. Observing the proprieties. Fuck. When was the last time he, Julian Danvers, the seventh Earl of Ravenscroft, had been respectable?

"Draw up the papers," he said, standing, uncomfortable with himself suddenly. Uncomfortable with the lies he'd perpetuated and the way he had so effortlessly and carelessly manipulated not only the man before him but also his beautiful, innocent daughter. "Draw up the papers, and it shall be done."

Perhaps it was time to find his whisky.

Clara had drunk far too much wine at dinner the night before. Had it been three glasses or four? Five or six? It little mattered now, for the end result was the same either way. Her father had made his announcement. Her fate was sealed. She'd almost heard the clang of the prison doors thundering shut on her right there in the dining room. Her glass had been waiting at her hand, filled with a deliciously mind-numbing claret, refilled by an efficient footman whenever she drained it. Which, as it had turned out, had been often.

Unaccustomed as she was to indulging too heavily in spirits, she felt as though an entire regiment of soldiers had marched across her head while she'd slept. Pity that she felt so wretched, up before dawn with a mouth as dry as Virginia dirt in August after a month without rain. She pressed her forehead to the glass pane of her bedchamber window, absorbing its coolness. She was heated, flushed, and she didn't know if it was down to the aftereffects of the wine or the terrifying fate she'd so stupidly chosen for herself.

Both, more than likely.

She wasn't getting the hasty wedding she'd expected after all. No, not precisely. Instead, her father had somehow brazened it out with the earl, the results of which meant she was to be courted for a fortnight to make a case for their love match. Paraded before the society her father had embraced—the society she herself found so affected and silly—as though she were an ornament from the hunt.

The street below was beginning to wake. The grim, seemingly inescapable London fog was fiercely thick this morning, overtaking everything beyond her window so that all she could discern were some splotches of light and the dash here and there of a liveried carriage. Perhaps it was the hour when gentlemen returned from their clubs or from their mistress's beds. All Clara knew was that it wasn't an hour she would ordinarily be awake.

Courted. Her stomach roiled at the thought. She'd suffered enough pomp and pageantry the last few years. Finishing school, etiquette lessons, dancing instructions, her comeout, introduction to the queen… It had been endless, strict, laden with rules and tricks, wolves in sheep's clothing. And now, just when her escape had seemed within reach, she was to be delayed by a *courting,* of all things. It may as well have been a hanging for all she looked forward to it.

What madness. She couldn't shake the feeling that she'd become mired in something far larger than she'd ever planned. She'd imagined a quick marriage, her coffers filled, the freedom to do whatever she wanted. It would have been a tearful farewell with her father and Lady Bella, for she truly did care for them. But then it would have been off to the place where she belonged, the place that called to her heart in ways she had never been able to convince her dear father of. *Your home is in England now*, he'd counter to her every complaint. *You will find this country's appeal in time.*

But she hadn't. Time had passed—years had gone by—and she still disliked almost everything about the country in which she'd found herself unceremoniously mired. She'd committed nearly every act of rebellion she could dream up, short of simply running away, in an effort to dislodge her father from his stubborn determination to keep her in a place that was cold and rigid and dreary.

She turned from the window as her maid arrived, fresh-faced and irritatingly chipper. She brought Clara's correspondence on a tray along with some tea. Clara seated herself at her desk as was her morning ritual and riffled through the letters while Anderson attended to her coiffure. A slashing scrawl caught her attention, and somehow she knew the owner of that bold penmanship. It seemed he too had risen early. As if it were him touching her and not a mere scrap of paper, warmth unfurled within her belly, and her fingers tingled.

Little dove,

Your father has convinced me—N.B. said convincing transpired sans the use of any firearms—that we must do our best to appear honorable and respectable for the next fortnight. I'll call this afternoon. Dare I trust you'll be at home?

Yours,
R.

Clara stared at the scrap of paper in her hand and realized she was smiling. Oh, he was a charmer, the rake she'd chosen for her mad plan. She'd do well to guard her heart against him. Catching her lip between her teeth to quell her unwanted reaction, she took up pen and paper to fashion her response.

Lord Ravenscroft,

While I'm gratified to hear my father didn't threaten your person upon this occasion, I'm afraid I won't be receiving callers.

Sincerely,
Miss Clara Elizabeth Whitney

She received a response just after breakfast, under the watchful eyes of her stepmother and the Duchess of Devonshire, who had paid a call on her social rounds. Feigning disinterest, she slipped the note into the pocket of her morning dress as though she weren't enjoying their game of cat and mouse. She longed to read the contents of the note but dared not seem too eager. Nor did she wish to arouse the suspicions of Lady Bella any further.

The duchess and Lady Bella continued chattering about the duchess's ball, which was to be held the next night. What music was to be played, what refreshments—certainly not any aspics, which the duchess deplored—but plenty of champagne, who was to be in attendance, etcetera, etcetera, and all rather boring stuff to Clara. A footman interrupted their lighthearted banter shortly, bringing with him a large arrangement of stunning white lilies.

"For Miss Clara," the young fellow intoned.

Lady Bella directed him where to place the flowers before inspecting them. "Quite lovely, Clara." She turned to the footman. "Was there not a note accompanying them?"

"I'm afraid not, my lady." He bowed and exited the room.

Clara didn't require a note to know who had sent them. The earl.

"Perhaps the answer is in your pocket, my dear," the duchess observed shrewdly, never one to mince words.

Clara fished the note from her pocket with reluctance, opened the envelope, and found once again a missive marked with his bold scrawl.

Dearest C.E.W.,

I never said he didn't threaten my person. Merely that he didn't use a firearm. Something very much like 'Do you want me to kill you after all?' I'll call at 3.

R.

Lord in heaven. She was smiling again. Realizing she had an audience, she folded the note, marshalled her lips into a rational line, and cleared her throat. "No, I'm afraid this note is from Lady Bo. Perhaps the lilies were sent here in err." She stuffed the note back into her pocket for good measure.

"Pish," the duchess dismissed, waving her hand in the air as if combatting an irritating fly. She was animated, bold, beautiful as a butterfly, and older sister to Clara's dear friend Bo. Once, Her Grace had acted as Clara's chaperone at a country house party where Clara had unabashedly run her quite ragged. They'd forged a camaraderie of sorts, with the duchess taking Clara under her wing. Of course she could see straight through Clara like a window pane that had just been washed. "If you wish to keep your secrets, you may. But the smile upon your face is quite telling, dear girl."

"Our Clara fancies herself in love," Lady Bella revealed with a grim air as she searched Clara's face, perhaps for a sign of repentance. Or madness, perhaps? One shouldn't presume to guess.

Some part of Clara—the wicked part—still sometimes found the blindingly beautiful English rose her father had married a rather irritating interloper. In truth, Clara was the interloper, and perhaps that was the real issue. She'd never, from the moment she'd first stepped ashore in England, felt as though she belonged. Their world had already existed without her, and hers without them.

"I don't fancy myself in love," she lied, not without compunction. But she'd told the tale so many times that it came more naturally now. "I *am* in love. I sincerely hope to make a love match with the earl."

Knowing her stepmother and the duchess as she did—the two could not have been closer had they been sisters born and raised—Clara was certain that the duchess was privy to what had transpired. Ah, well. It seemed there were never any well-kept secrets in London anyway, and soon she would be far, far away from this nonsense.

"A love match with Ravenscroft?" Tia inspected her with keen interest. "I've known him for years, and I've never known him to be the sort who charms young ladies or entertains them in his study at midnight. If you were a widow or a wealthy married woman with a husband who turns a blind eye to peccadilloes, I would believe your story. But you're too young for him, too sweet, too…innocent."

Innocent she was not. She recalled all too well what the earl had done to her. What he'd said to her. Part of her wanted it again. Wanted more. No innocent lady would have such a response to his depravity. But here was a rather salient piece of information. The duchess and her husband-to-be were acquaintances.

"You know Lord Ravenscroft?" Why hadn't she realized that? "What precisely do you know of him?"

"He is a charmer and a flirt, but I do believe he has a genuine heart. He was quite good to my sister Cleo, and they remain friends." Tia paused, appearing to choose her next words with judicious precision. "You are aware of his reputation, I trust?"

There it was again, the ever-present reminder that the earl was a wicked man. And he was, for she had experienced his skill firsthand. "His past is not my concern, Your Grace."

"Ah," was all Tia said, and Clara couldn't shake the feeling that her abbreviated response said far more than anything else could.

"It is not too late to turn away from all this, Clara," her stepmother entreated. "You can change your mind. The damage has not yet been done. Don't be at home if he calls today."

"I will be at home." Clara was firm, unrelenting. If anything, Lady Bella's heartfelt persistence swayed her in the opposite direction of her intent. "Her Grace says that he has a generous heart. Does that not mollify you?"

Lady Bella pursed her lips as though she'd tasted something sour. "Not in the slightest. A generous heart does not excuse a blackened reputation. The earl is a scoundrel of the first order. How I wish you would see he's not the man for you."

"I can see why you'd be drawn into his web. He's deadly handsome, I'll own," the duchess continued. "But dear Clara, don't forget that surfaces can be deceiving. Bitter scars can hide beneath the most beautiful of facades."

Clara didn't care to hear any more of their well-intentioned guidance. She had a singular pursuit now, and that was marrying the earl so she could gain her freedom. It would seem that if she had any hope of either of those two things occurring, she needed to play the game her father had devised for her. She needed to be courted.

Julian arrived at the Whitney residence precisely at three, buttoned up, jaw freshly shaved, smart waistcoat, rakish hat, looking for all the world like a gentleman intent upon wooing his lady. In short, he'd been ready for a proper courting. Or rather, as proper a courting as a man who'd fucked half the ladies of the Upper Ten Thousand for his supper could manage.

But he'd been met by a harried Lady Bella who'd informed him there was a family matter—urgent, her mother suddenly ill and in need of attendance—that would prevent her from acting as chaperone. A lady's maid would not be sufficient. The bloodthirsty Mr. Whitney was not at home, leaving no way for Julian to see Miss Whitney. She was so very sorry, but could he possibly call another day when the dowager marchioness was not ailing?

So he'd done the gentlemanly thing, bowed and apologized, offered his sincere hopes that the fierce old curmudgeon that was Lady Thornton would prevail. He'd gone back to his carriage, but as he drove along, he'd seen the strangest thing. A lone woman hurried along the street, head down, dressed in the first stare of fashion though she clearly sought to be unnoticed, a large hat tilted to conceal her face. He recognized that form, even though he'd held those lush curves in his arms but once. She turned and he saw her face.

Damn it all to hell, she was a troublesome one.

He instructed his driver to stop and alighted, closing the distance between them with easy strides. "Miss C.E.W., can it be you?" He kept his voice carefully low and intimate as he drew alongside her, touching her elbow lightly.

"Lord in heaven," she exclaimed in her airy drawl. Surprise mingled with alarm on her beautiful, expressive face. "You gave me a fright, sir."

What the devil was she thinking, sneaking away from her home with no chaperone, in the midst of the day? Did she truly believe no one would see and recognize her, that she wouldn't ruin herself? That there wouldn't be hell to pay? The girl's temerity knew no bounds. She was either slow-witted or possessed of tremendous audacity. Though, to be fair, she *had* stolen her way into his study at midnight and proposed to him—that alone suggested audacity of a most unbecoming and tremendous sort. The sort he quite admired, in fact.

But none of that meant that he was going to allow her to ruin his plans to wallow in her dowry and thoroughly debauch her after she'd become his countess.

"Come," he said in his most authoritative tone. Clearly, she needed his aid before she committed any more egregious sins. And wasn't that a laugh, the Earl of Ravenscroft looking after a lady's reputation? "Into the carriage with you."

"I can't go anywhere with you." Her eyes were wide and

bluer than the clearest country sky.

"You can and you will." He cast a glance around the busy street. It was only a matter of time before they were both recognized. "For your sake, little dove, get into the carriage. I'll take you safely back home."

"I'm safe enough." She cast a pointed look toward her reticule, which bulged in most peculiar fashion. "I carry a pistol with me always. I've done this many times before."

Damnation. He had no doubt that she had. Perhaps she was as much of a cutthroat at heart as her dear papa. "Into the carriage. You cannot run about the streets of London unchaperoned. Mr. Whitney was most firm in his stipulations."

She frowned at him, her eyes sparkling with mulish heat and her chin tilting in the air. "What business is it of yours whether I run about the streets? I'm my own person, my lord."

"Of course you are, little dove, but you are also to be my wife. You're under my protection now." As he said the words, he couldn't resist touching the tip of her stubborn chin.

He felt her warmth through his gloves, and the scent of her, orange and musky and dazzling as sunshine, slammed over him. It was delightful, intoxicating. *She* was intoxicating. The notion that he was now her protector oddly aroused him—the juxtaposition of his life of sin with her purity made him harder than a randy youth with his first woman. Right there on the street.

To hell with it. If he didn't gather his wits and her both, he'd be doing something rash. Like taking her maidenhead in his carriage. It had its appeal, of course, but there was something delicious about waiting, about making her his in good time. No woman he'd bedded had ever been his, whether in heart or in status, and he rather liked the notion of her being the first.

"Lord Ravenscroft, I'd like to be on my way," she prattled now, oblivious to the mayhem her beauty and bold naïveté wreaked upon him.

"No," he said thoughtfully. "I don't think so, my dear." Without relinquishing his grasp upon her elbow, he hauled her toward his waiting carriage and the relative safety of the privacy waiting therein.

She balked, tugging back and attempting with all her might to resist. But he was stronger than she, and trundling her into his carriage was a small matter indeed. He quietly instructed his driver to take several laps around the neighborhood before returning her to her father's home. After all, he reasoned, who was he to turn away such a gift from the fates?

He settled himself on the squab opposite her and studied her just long enough to make the blush rise to her cheeks. Seducing her would be most enjoyable. His gaze dipped to her bosom, full and high, and he recalled how the sweet bud of her nipple had felt in his mouth through the fabric of her chemise. Ah, yes. Seducing her would be his manna.

"I fail to see why you insist upon abducting me, my lord." She was in high dudgeon. "I cannot imagine this is what my father had in mind when he requested a proper courtship."

He ignored her jibe. "Tell me, love. How often have you snuck away from your father's keep to prowl the streets of London with a pistol in your reticule?"

Her brows snapped together into a frown. "That's none of your concern."

But it was. She was. And he quite liked it. He quite liked *her*, much to his bemusement. "Perhaps I ought to try a different course, Miss C.E.W. You seem to have no dearth of courage and—one might even venture to say—foolishness. Why not simply steal away from your father's house in the night and take passage back to America on your own? Your gift for sneaking out of your home is surely unparalleled by any other young lady of an age with you. Why seek me out?"

Her full lips curved into a rueful grin, somehow making

her all the more entrancing. "I would beg to differ, sir, that I am anything but a fool. My father is a stubborn man, and in a misplaced effort to keep me close to him, he's sworn to deny me all funds unless I marry here in England. Think me as feather-headed as you like, but I know the fate that would befall me should I try to return on my own without a cent to my name."

Jesus, an innocent lovely like her on her own wouldn't last long in the rough underbelly of the world, even if she actually knew how to fire the pistol hidden in her reticule. At least she wasn't naïve enough to think to brazen it out on her own. But still, she had sought out him, the blackest soul in all London, to be her savior. And he too was leading her astray. Taking advantage of her just as any other faceless man along her journey would have.

He didn't like that realization, so he tamped it down, past the place where his conscience once lived. Good and buried, that brief sense of guilt. "I think many things of you, but feather-headed, rest assured, is not one of them."

She nodded, looking more flustered than ever. "This carriage ride seems to be taking longer than necessary."

A shrewd little thing, too. Good. He'd never enjoyed the company of vapid women, though he'd suffered it for the sake of survival. "Belgravia is an absolute crush at this time of day."

"Hmm."

"Where were you off to, my dear?" He decided to change the subject, distract her quick wit. "As I recall, you were meant to be properly courted by me this afternoon."

"Of course I was, until Lady Bella's mother took ill. I dislike being cooped up in a city, if you must know. It makes me feel itchy. So I take walks."

Itchy. She was the oddest female he'd ever encountered. He found her utterly captivating. He'd wager she was a fair shot with the pistol she kept in her reticule, too.

"You take unchaperoned walks," he observed drily.

"Don't pretend to be honorable now." She waved a

dismissive hand. "Everyone has been delighting in reminding me how thoroughly jaded and wicked you are."

"I'm all the bad things you've heard about me and then some." And damn if that didn't rankle, far more than it should. After all, the truth ought not to hurt. "But as we've already established, we each have a mutual need for the funds your father will bestow upon you. I'm now subject to his whims the same as you."

"You, subject to anyone's whims? Somehow I find that difficult to imagine."

Ah, but the sad reality of it was that he'd been subject to the whims of others for more than half his life. Lady Esterly had been old enough to be his mother when she'd plied him with attention, gifts, and drink. He'd been fourteen, orphaned by a father who reasoned with his fists and a flighty mother. The interest of an older, worldly, beautiful woman like the Countess of Esterly had been a siren's lure. And just that easily, he'd been trapped. His time and his body had never again been his own.

Until now. Although even now, he had still trapped himself. But this time, he was old enough, wise enough, to know what he was about. This time he saw a beautiful woman, smart and prickly and bold and odd, and he was fascinated. Fascinated in a way that had nothing to do with the fortune she brought with her. No, if he were brutally honest with himself, he'd admit that his actions weren't entirely mercenary. A sobering thought if there ever was one, that.

"We're all subject to the whims of others in one fashion or another," he told her as he muddled his way through the painful remnants of his past. Remnants he hadn't realized still required muddling, after all this time. "Some of us are merely better at fooling ourselves into thinking we aren't than others."

"I suppose you're correct in that assessment, my lord. We are all at the mercy of someone else at times, are we not?" Her drawl was soft and under-pronounced. A delicious trill.

There was her exotic, citrus scent again, teasing him. Luring him. He leaned forward, closing the distance between them in the confines of the carriage, and traced the silken curve of her cheek.

"And now you've placed yourself at my mercy, little dove." He withdrew, bit the tip of his glove, and shucked it. Bare skin, the better to touch her. To tempt them both. He cupped her cheek, then traced a delicate path to the supple curve of her rose-pink mouth. His thumb ran over her lush lower lip once, twice, thrice. The seam of her Cupid's bow parted and he sank his thumb inside, feeling her wet heat. God, how he wanted that. How he wanted her. To hell with his promise of a proper courtship. This woman was his, damn it. "Why would you choose me, of all men?"

She nipped his thumb, startling and intriguing him all at once. Of course she would bite. He pulled back.

"I'm at no one's mercy," she denied. "Not any longer. That is precisely why I chose you."

"Do you think me so easily controlled, then? Do you think you can wave your papa's money in my face and make me come to heel like your pet?" Anger rose within him, swift and strong. He recognized that this fury was old, pouring from a deep wound, that it was not necessarily hers to bear. But he wanted her to understand that he was not weak. He was not—would not ever again be—a plaything, a man to be toyed with by a woman whose needs he fulfilled. He had played that role for far too long.

"Of course not. Ours is an even exchange. You get your portion of my dowry and I get mine and—most importantly—my freedom."

Her reasoning was calm, unperturbed. As if she weren't sharing an enclosed space with one of the lowliest rakes in London, sans chaperone. Some beast within him rose up then, wanting to shake her from her tranquility.

"What if I've decided that I want more than you bargained, little dove?" he asked, touching the smart trimmings on her bottle-green street suit directly above her madly thumping heart. Bless fashion. Bless her, all stubbornness and beauty and sunshine. "What if I want you?"

Her supple lips pursed into a moue that he found equal parts fetching and irritating. "Our agreement is not negotiable."

So she thought. Ah, silly chit, believing he possessed a shred of honor. He slid a casual but firm touch around her neck, his fingers catching in the silken web of her carefully coifed hair. His grip tightened, pulling her head back with just enough strength to show her who was truly in control. "I could take you here. Now. I could slide my hands under your skirts, over your calves, straight to your soft thighs and the slit in your drawers. We both know you would welcome me."

She stared at him, her bosom rising and falling with the violence of her breaths. She wasn't alarmed. Rather, she was…intrigued, he'd wager. Aroused. His little dove possessed a wicked streak, it would seem. Her lips parted ever so slightly.

"You wouldn't dare." Her words were a low, throaty whisper. Her pupils were large and round in her brilliant blue eyes. She looked for all the world like the lushest, sweetest peach hanging before him on a branch, all ripe and ready to be plucked. Or, as it were, fucked.

He grinned. "Oh, I'd more than dare." With his free hand, he demonstrated, reaching beneath her voluminous skirts to find the hollow of her knee. Her heat singed him through her silk stockings, and of its own volition, his hand traveled higher still, coursing over her frilled drawers to cup the delicious curve of her outer thigh. "Part your legs for me, darling."

Her eyes went wide, her body tensing beneath his touch. She wasn't accustomed to such familiarity, of that much he was certain. But her untried innocence appealed to him in ways he hadn't anticipated, and despite his best intentions for a proper courtship, the urge to show her pleasure was strong. He longed to bring her body to life, to give her the first, forbidden taste of passion.

"We're meant to have a proper courtship, my lord, and then a marriage in name only," she reminded him breathlessly.

"Mmm, but that is all deadly boring. Let me make you spend, love. Just once." He was like an opium addict now, drawn to what he craved—Clara, her passion, her innocence, the illicit —and he couldn't stop until he sampled at least a bit of it.

Her thighs fell open to his questing touch. He found the slit of her drawers, damp with her dew. Lust surged over him. His fingers traced her soft mound in slow, gentle strokes, circling her pearl. She jerked and tensed beneath him. He stroked her, toyed with her. Back and forth. She caught her lip in her teeth, head tipping back against the carriage squab. Ah, she was sweet. Slick and hot. He wanted to taste her, to put his mouth where his hand was and lick and suck her until she came undone.

Her eyes closed.

No, he was having none of that. He increased his pressure ever so slightly. "Look at me, Clara."

She refused, turning her head to the side, remaining otherwise open to him. Her cunny was as responsive as ever, her wetness bathing his finger. But he wanted her completely, wanted her gaze to meet his as he gave her the first taste of pleasure.

"Look at me," he demanded again. He'd played many games with many lovers over the years. But this was different. This wasn't about control or domination or titillation. It was about her, and it was about him and things he had never even imagined he'd desire.

She gave in at last, turned back to him, her eyes clashing with his. A pant stole from her. "What do you want from me?"

Her question surprised him. *Everything,* he wanted to say.

Every part of you. All your innocence, all your passion, every bit of your delectable body. Instead, "I want you to lose yourself. Give in. Watch me as I bring you pleasure."

He was well aware of his depravity, leading a maiden down the garden path of the dissolute. She'd kissed with a charming inexperience that suggested she'd kissed a scant few men, if any, before him. She was a virgin, a naïf he'd sworn to chastely court. And yet here he was, hand up her skirts, inside her drawers, playing with her, craving not only her climax but also her complete abandon. He was already teaching her how to be wicked.

It was as if she'd heard his words herself, for a change came over her. Her hands flew to his chest, pushing him back to the squab opposite her. He went, allowing her to overpower him with ease. Perhaps she wasn't quite ready to be as wicked as he wanted her to be. Perhaps she lied to herself. She straightened her posture into a stiff, ladylike pose, fidgeting her skirts into place.

"A marriage in name only, my lord," she reminded him with the cool, august bearing of a queen. She could be proper when she wished, the spitfire before him. "As I said, the terms are not negotiable, and I'll thank you not to place your hands upon my person again." She blushed furiously as she said the last.

But he wasn't about to accept her dismissal so easily. He raised his fingers, still glistening with the evidence of her desire, to his mouth, and tasted them. Sweet and musky. His cock went painfully rigid against his trousers. "Never again?" he asked with a wicked grin.

She stared at him. He'd shocked her. But he'd also intrigued her, and he could see it quite plainly. "Never again," she repeated, her tone rather faint. She swallowed. "Our agreement won't change. Now if you'd be so kind as to return me to where I belong? I don't suppose it truly takes this length of time to get a carriage back to my father's home from where you found me, regardless of the *absolute Belgravia crush.*"

She was turning his own words against him. Yes, she was a clever minx. But even the most clever of minxes could be outfoxed. He'd win her yet, even if he did dread the day he'd have to face her wrath when she realized he had no intention of allowing her to go traipsing back to Virginia like the lamb bound for slaughter.

"Very well," he agreed with a relaxed air he was far from feeling. He rapped on the carriage, signaling to his driver that their circling was, alas, at an end. Not all wars could be won in a single battle, but he was prepared to lay siege of the very best sort.

Chapter Five

THE EARL HAD PUT HIS HAND UP HER SKIRTS.

And she'd let him.

Clara could not force the thought from her mind. Not as she went about her preparation for dinner that night. Not as she dressed for breakfast the next day. Not as her father addressed her with the frigidity of a stranger. Not as she politely inquired as to the wellbeing of Lady Bella's mother. (Still as much of a harridan as ever and merely the victim of a bad fish course conflated with a tendency toward melodrama). Not at all.

Worse, she'd enjoyed it. Her mind relived that heart-stopping moment in the carriage again and again. He'd been handsome, dressed to perfection, no plum half-moons beneath his intense eyes as he'd had that night in his study. And he'd been intent upon her, looking at her as though he longed to devour her, catching her in his seduction as easily as if she were a butterfly trapped in a net. One swift journey up her skirts, and she'd been done.

And Lord, the way he'd made her feel. It had been sinful for certain, but she'd never experienced anything like the molten heat and honey, the dizzying pleasure of his long fingers touching her very core as he watched, as he made her watch. He'd touched the part of her even she'd dared not touch. Now she wondered why, for it was clearly a most receptive and delightful place for such a thing.

Heaven have mercy on her, she'd only been alone in his presence twice, and the man had already made her as much a sybarite as he. A most disquieting realization. Perhaps something was wrong with her. She certainly felt out of sorts, as though her body were too heavy or her skin too tight, her thoughts all wound up inside like a ball of twine.

"Clara, dearest? Where is your mind?"

Clara jolted from her sinful musings, cheeks going hot before she could collect herself as she met her stepmother's gaze. Ravenscroft was to call upon them today for tea. More flowers had arrived that morning, so sumptuous and lovely and dear that she was certain he couldn't afford them. They'd been accompanied by a note with a single word.

Again.

Yes, that was precisely what ailed her—the portent of a lone, menacing, thrilling word. "Forgive me, Lady Bella. I was merely gathering wool." She attempted a smile she didn't feel. In truth, she simply wished to have done with this ridiculous courting nonsense Papa had devised. The sooner she could wed the earl, the sooner she could leave him and his troublesome hands, wicked mouth, and beautiful face behind.

"You were granted a reprieve yesterday," her stepmother observed. "Have you not wondered if perhaps it was providential? You could still refuse him, deny him access to you, forget all about this madcap sense of romance you've allowed to rot your brain."

Providential indeed, she thought weakly. "Not in the slightest, my lady. I'm committed to staying the course. Do you not love my father?"

Lady Bella's expression softened, and somehow the effect rendered her even lovelier than she already was. "I love your father very much."

"And what if someone had told you not to wed him? Would you have listened?" Clara knew another twinge of guilt for asking the question and using her stepmother's weakness for her father against her. However, her cause needed all the help it could manage to swindle, borrow, or steal.

Lady Bella's lashes swept down over her gaze. "Your father would not have allowed anyone to come between us. But what we share is rare, Clara. It's a special bond, the sort that cannot be nurtured in a hasty courtship or a longing glance cast across a ballroom."

Truly, did Lady Bella suppose Ravenscroft the sort of man who made eyes at a lady over the quadrille? She was about to answer when the earl himself was announced. Here was the man she couldn't shake from her mind, and he was just a mortal after all, with hair that was a bit too pomaded this afternoon for her liking and a shade of stubble upon his jaw. While his wardrobe was perfection—tailored trousers and a gray waistcoat, all the mode—the darkness beneath his eyes had returned.

He bowed, and she had to admit that he cut a lean figure. Not at all the build one would have expected of a man given to indolence, womanizing, and drink. His hips were narrow, shoulders broad, and she spied not a hint of a paunch beneath his layers of fashionable clothing. He was an enigma, at turns precisely what she'd expected and then at other times quite the opposite.

"Lady Bella," he greeted, the epitome of polite sophistication. His gaze lingered on Clara for a beat longer than necessary, and an unwanted surge of heat swept over her. "Miss Whitney."

The tea was weaker than Clara preferred, though she didn't particularly care for the English custom of teatime. The conversation was stilted in the extreme, steeped in Lady Bella's obvious disapproval and displeasure. For his part, Ravenscroft either didn't notice or didn't care. He carried the conversation with his easy brand of charm. He knew how to banter, and he knew how to win over virtually any opponent.

"How are your sisters, Lord Ravenscroft?" Lady Bella asked, still cool though the earl had undeniably begun to thaw some of her ice. "You have two, yes? Lady Alexandra and Lady Josephine?"

He inclined his head. "You are, of course, correct as ever, my lady. Both are well, thank you, but perhaps a trifle in need of some sisterly guidance from a female. It's my fervent hope that Miss Whitney might become dear friends with them."

"I'm sure Miss Clara would enjoy such an arrangement, in the event of your marriage." Lady Bella said the last as if it tasted bitter upon her tongue. As though their marriage were still a questionable matter.

Clara stared at the earl's hands upon the fine china of his saucer. So large, those hands, holding such a delicate porcelain. He could easily crush it in his fist, but he was gentle, his long fingers curved over the handle as though it were a lover's body. Pity that she'd never again be capable of looking upon his hands without recalling what they'd done to her.

"Clara, dearest?"

She blinked and forced her attention to her stepmother, who had apparently asked her a question. A question she hadn't heard, mired in wicked thoughts about Ravenscroft's hands, of all things. Not even his mouth, though another stolen peek confirmed it was equally as fine as she'd recalled, well-molded and sensual.

"I would dearly love a turn about the garden, Lady Bella," she blurted, suddenly in need of air. Lots of air. "Forgive me, my lord. If you'll excuse me?"

"I'll escort you," the earl offered, playing the role of the gallant knight all too well as he shot to his feet.

"My lord," Lady Bella argued.

"We shall stay in view of the windows at all times, Lady Bella," he countered. "I'll not do Miss Whitney any harm, I swear. Not a hint of scandal."

Her stepmother's gaze was as sharp as a guillotine. "Ravenscroft, my husband will have your hide if you so much as touch her elbow inappropriately."

The earl nodded, unperturbed. "I wouldn't dream of molesting Miss Whitney's elbow, I assure you."

Such a droll wit, his lordship possessed. Clara repressed her smile. Lady Bella did not appear equally amused.

"I'll be watching from the window, my lord." Lady Bella's tone was frigid. "Five minutes. No more."

"Thank you, my lady, but fifteen would really be much more the thing."

"Seven and a half, not a second past."

"Ten," he countered, "and a disappearance behind a tall, accommodating hedge."

Clara couldn't stifle her shocked laughter at his daring.

Her stepmother pinned her with a remonstrating glare before turning the full force of her disapproval upon the earl. "You think everything a lark, do you not, my lord? Eight minutes and absolutely no accommodating hedges to speak of. You're fortunate indeed that I haven't called for my husband to beat you to a pulp for your insouciance."

"Ah, I suppose being a peer of the realm possesses its merits," he said drily.

"Being a peer of the realm has nothing to do with it," Lady Bella corrected. "Clara professes to care for you. And that, my lord, is your only saving grace."

He smiled, but the effect did not reach his eyes. On the whole, it was a rather grim smile, harsh and unforgiving. "On that, my lady, we are agreed."

A turn about the gardens for eight minutes with an overbearing stepmama watching from a window for the slightest misstep. Damnation, he supposed this was his punishment for toying with innocents. Or perhaps it was his very own form of Purgatory? One of Dante's circles? Jesus, who knew.

The only fact Julian did know as he stood in the garden with Clara, her hand on his elbow—the better to avoid an improper touch, and all that—was that if he didn't soon take her to bed, he'd go mad. How had he thought that touching her in his carriage was a good idea? How had he believed he could slide his hand beneath her skirts, experience the welcoming, wet heat of her, her newly awakened desire, and then ride home to his impudent sisters, threadbare home, dwindling cast of servants, and empty bed? How had he ever fancied he could carry out polite conversation before Lady Bella and not recall what Clara tasted like? Sunshine and honey and the earthy musk that was deliciously, innately hers.

Fuck.

Someone needed to brain him. Plant him a facer. Trounce him. Take up the cudgels and beat him senseless. For that was the only way he could shake the deliriousness this innocent slip of a girl had visited upon him.

"I wanted to come out here alone, you know," Clara said then as they stopped before a perfectly trimmed hedge. Not tall enough to serve his purpose, but a green slash of boxwood nonetheless. The sun was blotted out by fog, and the air was far from fresh. But the garden was, somehow, rebelliously green and alive in their city of filth.

A casual glance over his shoulder confirmed the wraithlike face of his chaperone on the other side of the pane. Blast. She was true to her word, Lady Bella. He turned his attention back to his betrothed's profile. A perfect, petite slash of nose. A high cheekbone. A smattering of freckles. How *de trop*. How refreshingly real. He hadn't noticed before. Nor had he noticed the way her left brow winged out in imperfection. "You sought to avoid me, little dove? Why, I wonder? Do you not trust yourself with me?"

She made an impatient sound, almost a harrumph, keeping her gaze trained on the hedge. "You flatter yourself,

Lord Ravenscroft."

"Did you not enjoy my touch yesterday?" He couldn't resist goading her with the question. Some devil within him wanted to see her cheeks filled with roses once more, to shake her from her nearly flawless equanimity. "Tell me, love, when you lay alone in your chamber last night, did your thoughts not stray to our carriage ride at all?"

Her lips compressed into a firm line, hammered out by irritation, he had no doubt. "No, my lord, to both impertinent questions."

He grinned. Perhaps there was something to be said for being watched in a garden while he conducted a proper courtship. He'd never aroused a woman with mere words before.

"You didn't even think of me once, darling?" he pressed, stepping nearer to her with a subtlety he hoped would spare him notice from the hawk-like chaperone at his back. His trousers curved into the voluminous fall of her gown, their sides almost touching. Yes, there was something to be said for the wait. Somehow, their lack of intimate contact only heightened his desire. That gilded scent of citrus wafted to his nose, and his cock went as hard as a marble bust.

She turned her head toward him at last, rewarding him with the full effect of her beauty, the high forehead, delicate tawny brows, luminous eyes, the lush mouth, slightly retroussé nose. Even her ears were lovely, goddamn it, the plump little lobes calling for him to bite and lick.

"I didn't think of you at all, Lord Ravenscroft. I thought of my home, the place where I belong. I thought of freedom, of the scent of the earth in Virginia after a summer rain, of the sun rising over Richmond. I thought of the call of whip-poor-wills and a sky that isn't blanketed in noxious fog and endless drizzle."

Her impassioned reply had him knowing a sharp pang of jealousy. What would it be like, he wondered for a fleeting moment, to be thought of with as much unadulterated passion as the woman before him directed upon a place on a map? The urge to usurp her homeland in her affections rose within him, as ridiculous as it was unrelenting. Tea was not a panacea, it seemed. Nor was an eight-minute turn in the gardens with a grim, window audience.

He leaned nearer to her, just near enough to maintain propriety but capture the full attention of the woman before him. The woman who expected him to believe she carried a mere place in the same regard as a man's touch. Virginia couldn't damn well make her come, now could it?

"Perhaps I was remiss in my efforts." He allowed his gaze to dip to her lips. "Next time I shall use my tongue."

Her eyes flew open wide. He'd shocked her again. Such an innocent, his future countess. But just as quickly, she schooled her features into unaffected elegance once more. "For what purpose, Lord Ravenscroft? I'm sure you've already wielded your tongue upon me with your verbal prowess on each occasion of our meeting. Sometimes with manners, but usually without."

Ah, she wanted to play the game? He hoped to hell that Lady Bella wasn't about to swoop down upon them and put an end to their invigorating tête-à-tête, for he was enjoying himself immensely. "Sweet, innocent darling, you cannot think I meant to use my tongue for something as boring as speaking."

She swallowed. "My lord, this conversation is quickly becoming improper."

"If you wanted proper, you sought out the wrong earl, little dove," he reminded her with a touch more bitterness than he intended. "Proper is for clergymen and maiden aunts. Proper is dull as hell. Improper, however, is infinitely more rewarding. Do you want to know what I'd do to you with my tongue?"

She did. Her expression, her sparkling, intelligent gaze, all clamored with curiosity. "Perhaps you ought to bite your tongue, my lord," she suggested airily, refusing to give in to that inquisitiveness. "That seems to be the wisest course of action for all concerned."

"Wisdom and desire so rarely go hand in hand," he returned, smiling at her rejoinder before bemusement overtook him.

He enjoyed her wit, her determination, and even her dedicated love for her homeland, her wrongheaded pursuit of liberation from her father's perceived tyranny. He liked bantering with her as much as he liked kissing her and touching her. Now there was a rarity indeed. Few women had ever called to him on a deeper level than mere animal lust. That this innocent firebrand from Virginia, this slip of a girl with golden hair who smelled like sunshine, who'd shown up in his study and proposed marriage to him did—somehow, this seemed like God's greatest joke of all upon one of His most sinful servants.

"On that notion, my lord, we are in agreement," she said, interrupting his musings with such abruptness that for a moment he wasn't certain what she referred to. "You'll not sway me. A marriage in name only. I don't care how handsome you are or how fine a kisser."

As she said the last, she raised her fingers over her mouth as though doing so could recall the words. Color still tinged her cheeks. With his free hand, he covered her fingers where they rested in the crook of his elbow. Just a slight touch, but she was teaching him that there could be power in the smallest of gestures.

"You think me a fine kisser, Clara?"

She glared at him. "You must already know that you are, sir."

"Perhaps." He considered her with great care. "But hearing it from you is the greatest of compliments. I do believe your delightful stepmother is about to swoop down upon us any moment. But do think tonight when you're alone, darling, where you'd like to have my tongue. You'll find I'm a most obliging sort."

Think about where you'd like to have my tongue. Indeed! The man was a rake, a cad, a voluptuary, a… Why, Clara had run out of insults already, but there it was. Plain and stark and true. The Earl of Ravenscroft was every bit as wicked as she'd been led to believe. She didn't know which was worse, his obvious dearth of morals or the way he'd managed to intrude upon her thoughts far too often when he was nowhere in sight. His sinful suggestion had stayed with her, and she was ashamed to admit that her fanciful imagination had envisioned more than one place upon her person where she'd like to have the bounder's tongue.

It was wicked, wanton, and altogether at odds with her plans for a hasty marriage, even hastier dissolution, and her happy return to American shores. She took a calming sip of the champagne she'd forgotten she held. Then another. And another. She'd tucked herself into a corner of the Duke of Devonshire's ballroom, where she hoped she could remain undetected by her fellow revelers, her stepmother and father chief among them, for as long as possible. Invisibility wasn't a virtue, but in the maelstrom of her life, it had suddenly become a condition she craved.

"Clara, dear heart." The familiar, feminine voice in her ear had Clara whirling to find her closest friend, Lady Boadicea Harrington. Bo was auburn-haired and tall to Clara's petite fairness. The two of them had become fast friends in finishing school, bonding over their mutual hatred of such an insufferable institution. They'd both been seen as too spirited by their families, too rebellious in nature, desperately in need of some ladylike polishing. *As though we're candlesticks*, Bo had once lamented, rolling her eyes.

Bo grinned at her now in that vibrant, carefree way she had that made anyone who looked upon her feel as if they were sharing in a great secret. "I feel it's been ages since we've seen each other. I've missed you so."

"And I've missed you." Clara was relieved to see her friend and confidante at last. "There's so much I must tell you."

She hadn't dared to write Bo with news about her plan for fear her father was reading her letters after all the trouble she'd brought raining down upon him. Lord knew he'd done it before when he suspected her of becoming too familiar with the Earl of Dalmain's third son. In truth, Henry had kissed her but twice, though his long and ardent love letters—intercepted by her irate father—would have suggested otherwise.

Henry's kisses had been nothing at all like the earl's. They had been pleasant but hasty, a quick press of his wet mouth upon hers. Not entirely unpleasant, but neither had it left her longing for more in the way Ravenscroft's masterful mouth had. Lord have mercy, there her wicked mind went again, at full gallop into enemy territory. She had to grab hold of the reins.

"Has your plan commenced?" Bo asked quietly, her eyes sparkling with mischief. Bo enjoyed larks. In finishing school, she'd once switched out the headmistress's cheese plate with a rather convincing array of sliced soap. Madame Desjardins had not been impressed to be the butt of such a joke. "Do tell."

Clara nodded. "My plan has more than commenced. I'm marrying the earl in a week and a half's time."

"Truly?" Bo's eyes went wide. "How can it be when I haven't heard a word?"

"My father is doing his best to blunt the scandal. Unfortunately, I'm being forced to endure two weeks of proper courtship before we can wed."

"Shrewd of Mr. Whitney," Bo agreed before a frown creased the otherwise flawless cream of her high forehead. "But does this mean you're really going to leave me here in this unforgiving wilderness on my own?"

"You have sisters," Clara reminded her.

"Of course, and I love them all dearly, but none of them have ever crept into the darkness of a Swiss night with me to rig a saucer of honey to fall on Lady Louisa Wormley's head after she left her chamber in the morning."

Clara laughed at the reminder of one of their more memorable adventures. "Lady Louisa deserved a saucer of pig excrement. The honey was too kind."

"You see? Where will I find anyone else with such a delightful sense of justice?" Bo clapped her hands to her wasp waist and gave her a severe look. "Don't answer me. I despair."

Her friend's feigned melodrama had Clara relaxing slightly, and momentarily distracted her mind. "You may visit me in Virginia whenever you like. My doors will always be open to you."

"Is Ravenscroft in accord with your intentions?" Bo asked.

"Yes. He's pockets to let as you said, and he needs the funds. He keeps his portion, and I return to my home. It will all be easy." She flushed as she said the last, for her thoughts again strayed to his wicked suggestion, and to thoughts of his touch. Of how much she'd enjoyed it, and of how difficult she found it to resist him.

"He's the devil's own sort of handsome, is he not?" Bo seemed to sense the sinful course her thoughts had taken. "Is he as good a kisser as they say?"

Her pride wanted her to lie, but this was her friend. Her compatriot. The very lady with whom she'd released frogs into the knickers drawer of one Miss Caroline Stanley. "I'm afraid so," she admitted weakly, embarrassed. "Bo, he's every bit the rake they say he is too. Perhaps worse."

"Never say it." Bo looked impressed.

She likely was. Bo was unique and bold, and she aired her mind without caring who she offended or what rule of society she bent. She was a true original, the last of her sisters on the marriage market. As such, her parents were quite eager for her to make a good match before she created a horrible scandal. Bo herself was in no such hurry.

"I wouldn't say it if it weren't true," Clara grumbled. "Though it grieves me to admit it. I'd certainly never tell a soul other than you. Well, and perhaps the earl himself. I do believe I foolishly told him just such a thing yesterday in the gardens."

And he'd been pleased, the rapscallion.

Her friend's gaze searched Clara's, seeing far too much. "You like him, don't you?"

Like him? Of course she didn't like the Earl of Ravenscroft. He was odd, a contradiction, too handsome for his own good. He was a reprobate who'd used his looks to cuckold husbands all across London. He drank too much. He didn't seem to hold anything sacred. He'd never done anything worthwhile in his life, aside from taking on the title of earl and walking about as though the world was his theater. Why, the greatest suffering in his life was likely nothing more dire than a leaky roof on one of his stately homes or a worn carpet he could ill afford to replace. Pockets to let for an English lord was still living quite handsomely for most folk.

No, she didn't like him at all. She opened her mouth to say precisely that.

"Don't answer me now," Bo intervened in a low tone, her eyes darting past Clara's shoulder and widening with meaning. "He's coming this way. Oh my, he is wonderfully fine-looking, Clara. I'd forgotten just how much since I saw him last at Cleo and Thornton's dinner. I'm not sure I'd be in such a rush to leave for Virginia, were I you."

Clara pursed her lips. "The appearance hides a most hideous soul, I'm sure. Devoid of all morals."

But still, she turned to drink in the sight of him striding toward her through the ballroom's heavy crush of revelers with a purpose she didn't mistake. Their eyes met, and a heavy, languid feeling sluiced over her. He was a beautiful creature, tall of form, lean of hip, his shoulders broad beneath his black evening clothes. His dark hair had been pomaded with a more judicious hand tonight, rendering it less gleaming and more lush. For some reason, she imagined tunneling her fingers through it, raking her nails over his scalp, holding his head to hers for the kind of devouring kiss he'd bestowed upon her that night in his study. The kind of kiss some forbidden part of her clamored for again.

Perhaps her brain was rotten, as her stepmother had suggested. It had to be for her to entertain the notion of ever again allowing Ravenscroft to kiss her. He reached them and bowed with formal elegance, taking their extended hands one at a time to buss the air over them. Bo's hand came first, and when it was Clara's turn, the delicious slide of his firm mouth upon her skin teased her, ever so slight but nonetheless sending her traitorous heart into a flurry.

"Forgive me if I've intruded upon you, Lady Boadicea, Miss Whitney." His tone was butter smooth and rich. Practiced.

He wasn't requesting forgiveness, not truly. Rather, he was marking his claim, Clara realized. She had aligned herself with the wickedly handsome man before her, this man who smelled of French cologne and had taken untold numbers of ladies to his bed. In a short time, she'd be his wife.

The thought gave her a shiver that she banished with the stern reminder that theirs would be a marriage in name only. "You don't strike me as the sort of man who often asks forgiveness," Clara said, harnessing the streak of boldness that wanted to come to life within her.

"Ah, Miss Whitney, how insightful you are," he remarked, an odd light in his eyes that she couldn't decipher. "Penitence isn't one of my virtues, I'm afraid. Of course, many would tell you that I haven't any virtues at all."

"Of that I have no doubt," Bo told him matter-of-factly.

Part of Clara couldn't believe her friend's insouciance but then she thought about all the nights they'd crept about their finishing school in the name of pranks and revenge. For his part, the earl flicked a casually assessing glance over Bo before turning his brilliant eyes back to Clara.

"This is the one, then," he said, and she knew he had discerned which friend had led her to his door in a mere sentence.

He was blessed with an alarming penchant for reading people with a blend of clarity and ease. She'd witnessed it before, but she was just beginning to fully appreciate its consequences. The Earl of Ravenscroft was smarter, wilier, and more aware than she'd even supposed. "Lady Bo is my dear friend," she said carefully, aware that she neither confirmed nor denied his suspicions. She didn't wish to cause any trouble for Bo, after all.

"Of course." He flashed a grin that showed off his white, even teeth. "Lady Boadicea, I have an old and treasured friendship with your sister, Lady Thornton."

His confirmation of the Duchess of Devonshire's similar suggestion days earlier stirred up an odd emotion that she refused to recognize as jealousy, for of course it wasn't. Curiosity was all it was. Bo's elder sister, the Marchioness of Thornton, shared a love match with her husband. They were a rarity in the *ton*, Clara understood. So how was it that Lady Thornton was a friend of Ravenscroft's?

She looked at Bo, who shrugged, as if to suggest it a moot point, and then back to the earl, who revealed nothing. His expression was impenetrable. Surely he would've realized the implications of his admission. But if he did, he didn't appear to care.

"I believe you owe me this dance, Miss Whitney," was all he said.

She raised a brow. "I'm sure I don't *owe* you a dance, Lord Ravenscroft," she returned. "However, I will give one to you, just the same."

Julian had to admit he found her cheek oddly endearing. As he led Clara into the glittering crush of dancers and they took up their places opposite each other, he once again experienced an irritating surge of appreciation for the plucky girl. Irritating because he wasn't meant to like her.

Lottie had cured him of any misguided notions about the finer emotions that supposedly distinguished men from beasts. The sad truth of it was that men and beasts were all the bloody same. The eyes of their fellow revelers were upon them, sudden and curious, as if to underscore his presumption.

"After this dance," he felt compelled to warn into her ear, "my interest in you will become common knowledge."

"What shall happen then?" she asked, her Cupid's bow bearing an amused slant, as though she were privy to a joke shared by no one else in the chamber—certainly not him.

He inhaled her intoxicating scent and wished she preferred something cloying and floral, something less earthy and inviting and bright. Something that didn't make him mad for her. "You'll be watched. Your every action will be fodder for the gossip mills. In short, you're about to experience firsthand the folly of your decision to enlist my aid in your schemes."

"But my lord, I have no schemes." She said the last with the ease of a practiced coquette.

He bowed, feeling grim and altogether too appropriate. They linked hands, palm to palm, and she turned her face up to his as he settled his other hand high on her waist, drawing her nearer than was entirely polite but he didn't give a damn. Her corset was a cuirass beneath her silk gown, keeping him from knowing the lush nip of her waist. He couldn't help but imagine her lovely form without the stiff girding. He would trace her soft curves, come to know the swell of her hips. A swift surge of lust kicked him in the gut, right there on the ballroom floor as the orchestra struck a waltz and they began the obligatory steps.

Waltzing involved too damn much whirling for his peace of mind. While his dancing proficiency had improved over the years, his appreciation for the art most certainly had not.

"I beg your forgiveness, Miss Whitney, in the event I prove a less than nimble dance partner." He smiled as though he hadn't a care in the world, keeping his tone equally light and low.

Several ladies and lords had actually begun making spectacles of themselves in their effort to stare. He longed to quit the ballroom, but fleeing wouldn't do a thing to further his cause. It would only invite more speculation, more whispers, more gossip to fly. The *ton* was a complex machine, powered by scandal and built upon unforgiving ruthlessness. He possessed too many black marks against him to count by now, his presence within polite society suffered for his association with the prince and the Marlborough House set.

But for Clara this would all be new. He didn't wish to make her a scapegoat, and the realization had a chilling effect upon his ardor. Then again, the urge to protect her, he supposed, was likely innate—some sort of remnant response from the days of ancient man. For there was nothing about the vibrant American beauty in his arms that made him feel differently for her than any other woman who had come before.

Or was there?

He stared at the pale, silken skin of her throat, the delicate hollow beneath her earlobe, the waterfall of golden curls spilling from her coiffure, the diamonds winking from her hair and ears. *Mine*, came an unsettling thought from deep within him. *She will be mine.* From the tip of her upturned nose to her wild eyebrow, to her red lips and small hands, her full bosom and responsive nipples…all of her. Every bit of her. He'd lay claim soon enough, and yes, he had to admit that their marriage would make her different from all the other women who had come before, whether he liked it or not. For that matter, whether she liked it or not.

Round and round they went, twirling by rote. Then he saw a flash of glossy, dark curls, a familiar profile—too handsome for conventional beauty, her patrician nose a bit long, her cheeks high slashes charged with color as she danced ever nearer in the arms of her partner. Lottie. Julian felt, for just a breath, the careening slide of anger, followed by a return to the bottomless pit of self-loathing where she'd cast him.

Jesus, her partner was leading her astray, making a fool of them all, and they were on a path to collide. Before he realized what Lottie was about, he'd pulled Clara closer, her skirts brushing his legs, nearly tangling in his feet. He turned her neatly so that it was his back that bore the brunt of the collision and not Clara's smaller and more delicate frame as Lottie and her partner jostled into them.

Despite his attempt to shield Clara, the damage had been done. This altercation, however apparently innocent and accidental, would be remarked upon by all. Lottie smiled at him, acknowledging him with a nod of her head. It was a knowing smile upon her lips. A satisfied one.

"Do forgive me, old chap," drawled her partner, equally insincere, enjoying their little farce. The Marquis of Ashburn hadn't changed a great deal since Julian had seen him at one of their set's wild house parties. It had been the very last wild house party he'd attended, in fact.

For a moment, he returned to that day, to Lottie's chamber. She'd been nude beneath Ashburn, mid rut. The unwanted image of the marquis's pale, hairy arse and thin, spider-like legs thrusting into her flashed briefly through his mind. A year had passed, but the bile in his throat was just as real and bitter as if it had been that very morning that he'd blithely walked in upon the woman who claimed to love him being fucked by a man he'd once counted as a friend.

"You'll need forgiveness, Ashburn, but not from me," he forced himself to quip with a lightness that was far from the true, dark ugliness festering within him.

Ashburn threw back his head and barked out a laugh. "Ever the ready tongue, Ravenscroft. One ought not to be surprised with all the practice you've had, eh?"

The orchestra ended its set, leaving the other dancers milling about them in a sea of colorful silk, perfect evening clothes, gleaming jewels, and unabashed curiosity. He bowed to Clara, who watched him now with a questioning expression upon her unguarded face. Damn it, he couldn't allow Lottie and Ashburn to rattle him. Nor would he allow them to insult his future countess.

"Some of us use our tongues wisely, my lord, and others do not." He kept his tone mild and cool, but his meaning was apparent, as was his deliberate slight in return.

"I don't believe we've been introduced," Lottie murmured, pursing her lips as she raked a rude stare over Clara. "Ravenscroft, won't you do the honors?"

There was something inherently wrong about the business of introducing one's former mistress to one's future wife, whether or not the former mistress was a peeress. Lottie was a duchess and a favorite of the Prince of Wales, which allowed her entrée into the best parties. However, all polite society knew damn well that, aside from the heir and spare, not one of her children belonged to her husband. Just as all polite society knew damn well that he and Lottie had indulged in a very lengthy and public affair. He'd foolishly imagined he cared for her and she for him. She'd tossed him away like a dress from last season.

"No," he said with deliberate calm.

Lottie faltered. She was not the sort of woman who had ever been denied. She'd been raised in a life of privilege, cosseted and spoiled, adored for her beauty, sought after for her charms. Men fought to win her. Even Bertie, as the Prince was known, had fallen for her with an unusual haste.

Her lips thinned and her nostrils flared, betraying her ire. "You'll not introduce me to your little nobody?"

"Oh, I daresay I'm not a nobody," Clara interrupted then, her tone as august as any peeress in her own right. She bestowed a slow, withering glance upon Lottie. "Nor am I particularly little. I *am* a Virginian, however, and we Virginians are a fierce lot. I can shoot an apple off a man's head from fifty paces."

Lottie stiffened. "How…accomplished you must be."

Her tone belied her words.

"Or a woman's head," Clara drawled, smiling sweetly.

Well, hell. His little dove never ceased to surprise him. Julian grinned, feeling the weight that had been heavy upon his chest suddenly disperse. "Good evening, Your Grace," he said in his most dismissive tones. "Lord Ashburn."

And then he whisked Clara away from the tawdry pair, giving them the cut. "Well done," he congratulated his betrothed in quiet tones as he escorted her out of the fray.

"An acquaintance of yours?"

"Former," he acknowledged, a trace of the old bitterness creeping into his voice. "I'm sorry, Clara, for the insult paid you. I'd have avoided it if I could have."

"She still seems smitten with you, but she is not a nice woman, my lord. I wouldn't consort with her ilk if I were you," she startled him by saying. "You can do far better than her sort."

He was bemused by her pronouncement, declared to him as he led her through the seemingly endless crush of the ballroom where anyone could overhear. This girl either didn't have an inkling of proper decorum, or she didn't give two shites. He rather suspected it was the latter rather than the former. No one had ever told him *he* could do better. No one but this petite, feisty American wearing an outlandishly tight midnight-blue gown that showed her waist and bosom to perfection. Damn, but she was lovely. And cheeky. And she'd bested Lottie. Hell, she'd even defended him, and he doubted she'd ever met a more debauched voluptuary than he.

Moreover, she was right. He could do better than Lottie, a woman who had professed to love him all while fucking at least two other men at the same time. Christ, but he'd been stupid. How he had trusted and believed in a woman like the Duchess of Argylle was a mystery to him now. Foolishness mixed with drink, no doubt.

"Of course I can do better than her sort," he told Clara, placing his hand over hers on the crook of his elbow for just a moment before removing it, lest it be remarked upon by anyone. "I've already found her. Or perhaps, to be more apt, she found me."

"Don't forget you cannot keep her," she reminded him beneath her breath, shooting him a sideways glance that just about undid him.

He was bloody well keeping her at his side and in his bed. Never had he been more certain of anything in his entire, admittedly misbegotten life. But he very wisely kept that to himself as he caught sight of Clara's protective stepmother and steered her back into safe waters.

Chapter Six

"Her Grace, the Duchess of Argylle," intoned her father's butler in what Clara could only suspect was grim portent.

She hadn't expected any callers, and that the duchess would arrive in the morning, outside of her receiving hours, when Clara was perfectly alone and not expecting a soul, was cause for surprise. But, she hoped, not the alarm that stirred within her as she stood with a dignity that belied her inner turmoil.

She could have claimed she was not at home, could have refused the duchess's call, and been left instead with her card on a salver and no strife to speak of. But avoidance wasn't Clara's way.

The duchess swept into the morning room where Clara had been reading, wearing a formidable visiting gown of aubergine damask and crushed velvet that emphasized her voluptuous form to perfection. She was lovely, graceful, elegant, and—worst of all—a former paramour of the earl's. A former paramour who had meant something to him. Clara had supposed as much by his reaction to the duchess at the ball, and Bo had confirmed her suspicions with a healthy dose of friend-to-friend gossip afterward.

They exchanged a proper, formal greeting. The duchess perched herself on a settee as though she were as delicate as Sèvres porcelain. Perhaps it was the tight-lacing of her lady's maid that was the source of the woman's achingly slow, deliberate movements, Clara thought rather unkindly.

Silence descended upon them, interrupted only by the steady ticking of a clock and the faint background sounds to which Clara had grown accustomed: the outside din of London traffic and the whispered footfalls of servants moving about the halls. The duchess's ice-blue gaze raked over Clara's person, her expression a study of the aristocratic dismissive. Her raven-haired beauty would have been a natural foil to the earl's dark good looks. Clara could picture the two of them together, a couple so beautiful that it would almost be painful to look upon them. A curious twinge cut through her at the notion of Ravenscroft with the exquisite creature before her.

"I have paid you an honor in this call, Miss Whitney," the duchess said at last.

Clara almost gave an indignant and thoroughly unladylike snort. The woman clearly possessed an interesting definition of the term. Over a week had passed since their inauspicious meeting, and she supposed that the duchess had followed Ravenscroft's obvious pursuit of her.

For a man who was rumored to be one of the worst rakes in England, the earl had done a grand job of properly courting Clara. He danced with her at the Earl of Margate's ball twice, once at the Marquis of Londonderry's, and two times at the Duke of Cheltenham's. He walked with her in the park. He took her for a ride on Rotten Row. In public, he was the epitome of charm. He scarcely touched her, and he certainly never said wicked things to her about his tongue or pinned her with smoldering stares that made her feel as if she stood before him in nothing save her chemise.

Clara should have been relieved. But she had grown tired of the endless social whirl. Tired of being trussed up in corsets and heavy skirts, changing five times a day, smiling pleasantly to Lady Dullard and listening with feigned concern to the Duchess of Snipe. She was weary of tea and visits, of dancing and eating and generally doing nothing of value with her time.

And now she was being ambushed by a beautiful, haughty duchess who dared to call said ambush an honor. No, facing the gorgeous former lover of her betrothed was not, in Clara's book, an honor in any form.

"Forgive me for being obtuse, Your Grace, but I don't see the reason for your call," Clara said at last, allowing her Virginia drawl to accentuate her words far more than she ordinarily would. After all, she'd been trained to speak the way a proper Englishwoman ought. But Clara was no Englishwoman, and she never would be. Which meant she had the advantage over the duchess facing her as though they had declared pistols at dawn.

The duchess stiffened, her chin raising a notch in an elegant display of ire. "Undoubtedly, you're unaccustomed to proper society. That much is grievously apparent, but that's neither here nor there. I shall be candid. I'm trying to aid you, Miss Whitney."

Clara almost laughed aloud. Trying to help her, indeed. "Pray enlighten me, Your Grace."

The duchess's eyes narrowed, revealing fine grooves caused by time. "Ravenscroft is courting you. It's common knowledge. He has been making a fool of himself all over town. I come to you with the concern of an older sister for her younger, infinitely more foolish sister. Walk away from him, Miss Whitney. If you hold yourself or your family in any esteem at all, you must throw him over at once, for his motives are not pure."

She couldn't quite stifle a smile. What irony. "I'm certain his motives aren't any less pure than your own in seeking me out, Your Grace."

The duchess's spine stiffened, her lips thinning into an angry line. "I sought you out to help you, but perhaps you are the sort of young lady who doesn't prefer to hear the truth."

"Forgive me if it seems to me that you've sought me out to help yourself," Clara said gently. It was clear that the woman before her saw her as a rival. She had orchestrated the ridiculous collision in the ballroom, and now she'd turned up holding a supposed olive branch that looked far more like a poisoned cup of wine to Clara's shrewd eye.

"Ah, American impertinence. I suppose I should've expected it. You Americans think you're all the rage now, don't you? I've seen your kind a dozen times before, Miss Whitney. You prance around with your father's wealth and your brazen attitudes and your complete lack of care for society. Some may find your gauche dearth of manners a quaint spectacle, but I am not among them." The duchess rose from her seat, sweeping her skirts back into order with an august dignity Clara couldn't help but admire, even if she didn't like or trust the woman. "Believe what you wish, Miss Whitney, but I know Ravenscroft better than any other woman alive. If you think he truly has a genuine interest in a girl as young and naïve as yourself, you're even more foolish than you appear."

"Perhaps I'm not at all foolish. Perhaps I'm very wise, and I'm a woman who isn't afraid to seek what she wants from life rather than meekly waiting about for someone else to dictate what I ought to do." Clara stood as well then, not willing to allow her opponent to tower over her. "Your Grace, I don't think it was wise for you to come here. I understand you were the earl's…particular *friend.* However, you're not his friend any longer. Whether he chooses to court me or wed me is up to his lordship, and regardless of the reasons for his actions, your *older sister* concerns are neither wanted nor necessary. Good day, Your Grace."

She didn't await the duchess's response, merely took her leave of the chamber, head held high, completely aware of the social rules she eschewed as she went. But no matter how many steps she put between herself and the earl's past, she couldn't shake the feeling that her plans had gone hopelessly awry.

She'd thought she could easily convince the earl to wed her and send her back to Virginia. Instead, she'd wound up with a courtship, a jealous former lover, and a betrothed who was handsome and wicked and wild and yet somehow also proper and…good Lord. She'd been about to think that he was kind.

Heavens, where had that rogue thought come from? Whatever the source, she'd do best to weed it out posthaste. She couldn't afford to like Ravenscroft. No indeed. Liking him was far too risky, too dangerously close to upsetting her plans. And she'd come too far for any of her plans to be dashed now. Far too far.

Miss Clara Whitney disliked corsets. She could make her lilting drawl disappear into minced, born-in-the-purple English at the drop of a coin. Her opinions were her own. She wasn't vapid, vain, or spoiled like so many ladies of the fashionable set. She was intelligent and witty, quick-tongued and passionate. She liked reading but disliked playing the piano and she'd never even bothered to attempt sketching with charcoals or painting watercolors. Her opinion of England could be summed up in one word: dreary. Her opinion of the Upper Ten Thousand could be summed up in a singularly succinct manner: absurd.

Over the course of the fortnight he'd been playing the role of dutiful, proper suitor, Julian had come to know a great deal about his future countess. Some of the facets of her character had been revealed unintentionally, others had been freely shared during the rare moments when they'd been able to speak with candor.

Walking in the park was one such particular boon, as he'd been able to lead her a safe distance from her stepmama. Her gloved hand rested lightly in the crook of his elbow. The scent of her washed over him, warm and glorious. He didn't even give a damn at the moment that public walks in the park beneath a hundred other watchful stares were the sort of thing he hated. Devil take it all, he was actually enjoying himself. Not a drop of liquor coursed through his veins, and he was properly clothed, and yes, somehow he was having a damn fine time of sporting Clara on his arm. Ah, irony.

"Women ought to be afforded the right to vote," Clara declared to him now, keeping her voice low as she turned to him, eyes flashing with the brilliance of her devotion to her subject. "Why should it be denied us? Your very sovereign is a woman, and yet every other woman in the land is denied the opportunity to allow her voice to be heard. How can it be that one woman can rule and the rest must relegate themselves to tittering in drawing rooms and accepting their husbands as their betters?"

Well damn it, how did he answer such a question? She was perfectly correct. He was ashamed to admit he'd never once given the matter much of his time or attention. Julian stood there in the park on an overcast, dreary day, on a gravel path he'd trod hundreds of times before. And for the first time, he realized what a conceited, selfish prick he'd been his whole life.

"That is the way of things," he offered at last, lacking for a better answer. In truth, there was no answer, at least not one that made a whit of sense. "You're young. You need more time to become suitably jaded and indifferent."

"I'm twenty, my lord. Not so very young and naïve, I think, to wonder why it must be so." She turned to him, her convictions bringing vivacity to her lovely face. "It seems to me that the only sex who benefits from keeping women from having a political voice is men. Where is the science that says a woman is not every bit as capable of careful thought as man?"

"I admit I'm not a man of science," he said wryly. "But I daresay no such science exists."

How had he ever thought her naïve? Perhaps she was, when it came to matters of the bedchamber, but that would be easily rectified. Her mind was sharp and vital, capable of being clever or cutting. He found her freedom of expression refreshing. This was not a woman who fretted over nothing more significant than choosing a ball gown. The woman before him was intelligent, and she wasn't afraid who knew it.

"Of course it doesn't exist." She shook her head with so much fervor that she almost knocked her elaborate hat off its dainty perch atop her golden curls. "We are all merely people. Regardless of where we were born, who our parents are, whether we are male or female, we're all equals because we are all the same. It is only the ancient trappings of society that force us to believe anything different."

How refreshing to hear her overturn the world in which he'd lived his entire life. It was all nonsense, from the trimmings of polite society to the laws that led the land. It was outmoded, antiquated, foolish and shortsighted. The world needed more Claras to upend it, by God.

"I agree with you." He covered her hand with his for just a moment.

"You do?" She turned to him, clearly having been expecting an argument from him.

She'd not garner one.

"Is it so surprising that I can be swayed by logic? I'll own that I've never given the injustice of it a second thought until now. But alas, ours is a world of vile hypocrites, darling. We must all behave properly in public, obey the tenets of polite society to the absolute letter, and yet behind closed doors, we're all just a hodgepodge of sinners and reprobates. One need only look around to see hypocrisy in action. There is Lady Darlington, speaking politely with Lord Ryland as though they are strangers, when her last daughter was sired by Ryland. She hasn't shared a bed with her husband in half a dozen years or more."

"Six years?" Clara's winged brow rose. "How can you

know for certain?"

He knew because he'd been one of Lady Ryland's first lovers after her husband had installed a famous opera singer in a house in St. John's Wood. He met Clara's inquiring stare, choosing not to lie to her. "How do you think I know, little dove?"

She appeared to take his admission in stride, her only betrayal of emotion a small swallow evident at the hollow of her throat. "I see. The Duchess of Argylle is not alone in the legions of your many admirers."

Lottie's name uttered in Clara's mellifluous voice somehow didn't seem right. The two women couldn't be more different from each other. "The duchess is not an admirer, of that I can assure you."

She'd made her opinion of him as clear as possible. He'd been nothing more to her than a source of entertainment and pleasure. She didn't wish to be encumbered by the demands of one man. He could still recall their parting, how she'd attempted to press some notes into his hand. Payment for services rendered. But how could he fault her? He had fashioned himself a whore, and it was a role he'd learned well. He was the one who had erred in thinking their arrangement was different, that it had meant something more. He hadn't accepted a pound from Lottie that day, and he never would. He'd bloody well starve in a beggar's prison first.

"I wouldn't be so certain, my lord." Clara studied him, and he couldn't shake the impression she saw more than he would have preferred. "She paid me a call, and she was most adamant that I run far, far away from your evil designs upon my person."

He'd known Lottie had a vicious streak, but he hadn't realized she'd stoop so low as to meddle in his personal affairs now. Damn her. She didn't have a right to make him susceptible to her games any longer. "Dare I hope you made good on your poorly disguised threat to use her in a demonstration of your marksmanship?" he quipped with a lightness he didn't feel. He hoped to keep their conversation away from the darkness that Lottie inevitably stirred within him.

"If she seeks me out again, I cannot promise that I won't," Clara returned. "I don't like her. Others may be dazzled by her beauty, but I can see plainly through it to the ugliness she hides within."

"She won't seek you out again." Suddenly, the pleasure he'd felt at being out of doors with Clara on his arm fled. Grim determination settled over him, icy and familiar. His past sins were never far from his heels, nor were their consequences. "I'll make certain of it."

"I can protect myself against her kind, my lord. I'm merely warning you so that you're well-armed when I've returned to Virginia." She smiled sweetly at him, but there was a wistful glint in her gaze that belied her apparent cheer. "I wouldn't wish you to fall prey to a woman like her again."

When I've returned to Virginia. Her innocent belief that such an event would occur needled his conscience. By God, he was startled to find it resurrected these days. But there it was, the nagging stab of guilt at misleading her. She would be furious with him, of that he had no doubt. He remained, however, his father's son, which meant he was a selfish bastard.

"Although I do take umbrage at the notion of myself as any woman's prey, I must ask why not, Miss Whitney?" he couldn't resist querying, allowing his eyes to travel over the soft, lovely planes of her face. If he'd had an artist's hand, he would have longed to paint her, to capture all that vivacity and passion in bold strokes on a canvas.

"Because I've begun to like you, Lord Ravenscroft." Her eyes widened as though she'd surprised even herself with her admission. "There, I've said it."

He couldn't stifle a smile, and he didn't give a damn that at least half a dozen notorious gossips watched him, remarking upon his every expression. There was something freeing about the truth, after all. He kept his gaze pinned to

Clara, the petite, complex firebrand who possessed a sharp mind, a bold tongue, and who'd had the innocent audacity to accost him in his own study. "Strange, that, for I find I've rather begun to like you as well, little dove."

The flush that tinged her cheekbones was the only answer he required.

Clara awoke to a nearly cloudless, fogless London sky. She stood by the window of her bedchamber, sipping her coffee as she'd done each morning since moving to London, and watched the parade of carriages on the street below. It was somehow fitting that her last day beneath this roof—one of her very last in England—was the most unsullied she'd ever witnessed. Why, one could almost find beauty in the grand homes parked along the road, the gleaming carriages and pristine horses, the poised and polished clamor of polite society thronging all around.

"Almost," she repeated to herself before drawing the window dressing closed. For if one looked carefully enough, stripping away the gilding, one could see that the rare world of London's aristocrats was not all it seemed.

She thought of Ravenscroft's revelations to her the day before on their walk. Of course she shouldn't be surprised that he'd taken married women as his lovers. She'd known as much before she'd ever confronted him with her plan. Somehow, hearing it from his lips rendered it different, however. Those lips had kissed hers. And though theirs would be a marriage in name only and for a short duration, she was to be his wife. There was a sense of intimacy involved now that she hadn't anticipated.

Perhaps that explained her extreme dislike of the Duchess of Argylle. She'd never admit it to a soul, but knowing that the earl had been taken in by that dreadful woman's charms irked her to no end. She'd dearly like to see her at the receiving end of one of Bo's notorious jokes.

The thought of a saucer of ink dropping into the duchess's hair and dripping down her lovely face held infinite appeal.

A quiet knock at her door startled her out of the wicked reverie. "You may enter," she called. She'd been dressed for ages, had simply been in a contemplative and somber mood, her mind sifting over the choices she'd made and the actions she'd need to take in the days ahead.

She was startled to find her father opening the door and crossing the threshold. He'd spoken little to her in the last fortnight of her whirlwind courtship with the earl, and he appeared as grim as she'd ever seen him now. Her heart gave a great pang of regret for her subterfuge.

Although her father was sometimes overbearing and misguided, she did love him. There'd been a time when he had been a stranger to her, and she'd been a young girl adrift, having just lost her mother. He had been kind and patient, enduring her confusion and her rebellion with a grace she had not expected or deserved.

"Father." She placed her coffee on the escritoire and met him halfway across the chamber, embracing him and eschewing convention in the same way he had with his unannounced visit. She buried her face against his broad chest and inhaled deeply of his familiar scent.

He was slower to embrace her, but at last his arms came around her tightly, and he pressed his face to the arrangement her lady's maid had taken care to artfully style earlier. "Clara, darlin'." There was an unmistakable thickness to his deep voice. "Are you certain? You don't have to marry him, by God. I don't want you to marry him."

The only thing she was certain of was that the more time she spent in the earl's presence, the more she doubted everything. For she was coming to believe more and more that he wasn't entirely as he seemed. He was beautiful, yes, and unrepentant to be sure. He was a voluptuary, of course, and he had bedded more women than she cared to know about or count. He was the sum of his reputation and then some.

But then there was the earl she'd glimpsed during his courtship. That Ravenscroft was odd and witty and sometimes funny, sometimes wicked, but he was also kind. He listened to her when she spoke, and not just in the way some of her suitors had, gentlemen who'd listened with half an ear only to prattle on about their own accomplishments and beliefs. He heard her, and he didn't attempt to belittle her or talk over her for beliefs that ran counter to society's whims. His intelligence simultaneously alarmed and delighted her. She wasn't sure she could trust him or herself in his presence, for that matter.

"I'm staying the course," she told him softly, for she had no other option. "I want to marry the earl."

Lord in heaven, that wasn't entirely a prevarication, either. There would be some satisfaction in seeing the expression on the Duchess of Argylle's face when and if next they crossed paths before she left for Virginia. Surely that was the sole impetus for such an irrational feeling.

"Ah, you are your mother's daughter, willful and proud to the end."

A grudging tone of admiration marked her father's words. Clara's mother had kept her existence from Father—and likewise had kept the truth from Clara as well—until she'd been on her deathbed. It had been a shock to discover the man she'd believed to be her father had not been her father at all. In the span of a week, Clara had been introduced to Jesse Whitney and had buried her mother. She'd struggled in the years since to forgive her mother for the wrongs she had committed, just as she'd struggled to fit into a world and a society that was utterly foreign to her. England simply was not and would never be home.

"I don't like to compare myself to her. She had many sins I haven't forgotten." Clara stepped back from her father's embrace and knew a moment of clarity as she met his eyes. Yes, she was very much like her mother after all, wasn't she? Lying to preserve her own aims. When had she become so much like the woman she'd spent the past five years resenting?

"She was your mother," her father said gently, his eyes glossier than usual. "She gave me you, and for that gift I'll be forever grateful to her."

Clara swallowed. Lord in heaven, she should just confess all to him now. Tell him the truth, wait for the anger she deserved. Could she have returned to Virginia by other means? Could she have convinced him to let her go, to grant her the marriage settlement free and clear, hers to use as she wished back home to aid her cause of gaining the vote?

"I'm not a good daughter." The words escaped her in a rush. "I've not been kind to you or to Lady Bella. I don't know how to be the daughter you both deserve, but you have Virginia, and I can only hope that my little sister will be a far better woman than I could ever hope to be."

"You are a fine daughter," her father corrected her, understanding and sweet now that the dye had been cast. This softer, gentler version of her father would perhaps have agreed to her wishes to return to Virginia, she thought. "A man could not ask for better."

"Father," she began, the remnants of what she needed to say lingering on her tongue.

"Lady Bella and I have happy news," her father said at practically the same time, quashing any hope she'd entertained, however fleetingly, of unburdening herself.

"Happy news?" But of course she could already tell from the smile transforming his face just what that news was.

"Another little sister or brother for you, Clara," he confirmed, grinning with pure happiness. "Lady Bella didn't want me to tell you until after the wedding, but I couldn't wait another moment. I'm so damn happy, sweetheart, so happy that my heart is near bursting with it. I want you to experience the same happiness for yourself. That is why I want you to rethink this hasty wedding to Ravenscroft. I'd hoped that this fortnight would prove to you that your feelings for him were a fleeting fancy. I wanted to believe that you'd call this nonsense off and find a man who deserves you."

What could she say to that? She swallowed, tamping down the tears that threatened her vision. "I deserve a chance to be happy," she said honestly, "and I do think I've found that, Father."

Chapter Seven

CLARA STARED AT THE CARRIAGE AWAITING HER, the knot of dread within her growing ever more intricate and insistent. Beyond, the standard bustle of the outdoors was as familiar as ever. Carriages, horses, clattering, thumping, creaking, a cacophony of smells and sounds. The London fog had decided to reassert itself with a sudden vengeance, and it cloaked the tops of the elegant mansions lining the street and fell about everyone's shoulders like a cloying ghost that couldn't be escaped.

Her fingers tightened on the earl's arm as they stopped to say their formal goodbyes. Impossible to believe that she was now this notorious, handsome man's wife. That he was her husband. That they were well and truly…

Married.

There. She'd thought it, a small word for such a frightening state. Clara experienced none of the joy that a new bride must ordinarily feel. Instead, she felt the heavy weight of the band he had slid upon her finger as though it were a manacle. She had bound herself to a stranger. The vows they'd spoken had not seemed as impermanent as she'd expected them to, and there was no denying the fact that she was now, in the eyes of God and man, the Countess of Ravenscroft.

The wedding breakfast had been a truly somber affair. Her father had worn an expression akin to a man attending the funeral of a loved one. Her stepmother had been dreadfully ill, sitting at the table ashen-faced, pushing about her food with her fork without actually eating a morsel of it. Lord and Lady Thornton, the Duke and Duchess of Devonshire, Mr. and Mrs. Levi Storm, and Lady Bo were in attendance as well, in an assortment of London friends and family. They'd all done an admirable job of feigning ignorance and promoting a false sense of cheer.

And now here she stood, Lady Ravenscroft in name but most assuredly never deed, about to say goodbye to the life she'd known for the last five years. She hadn't accounted for this moment and its bittersweet finality, for the oddity of being trundled into a carriage with the earl as though they were setting off into a life together.

"You will treat her well," her father said to the earl now, his tone one of threatening menace.

"Of course I will," Ravenscroft assured him, his charm easy and practiced. But he sent Clara a look that she couldn't quite read. It was searching. Questioning, almost. Heated. "My wife will want for nothing."

Clara flushed, not liking the way his stare made her feel or the glint of desire she recognized there. Lady Bella, still looking wan, spared her by pulling her aside and hugging her. "Be happy, darling Clara. That is my fondest wish for you."

"Thank you." She returned her stepmother's hug with true feeling.

Lady Thornton stepped in next. "He has a good heart," she told her, *sotto voce*. "Don't be fooled into thinking otherwise."

But Clara wasn't interested in the earl's heart. She wasn't interested in him. In fact, she scarcely intended to spend a fortnight with him before booking her passage back to

America. She was sure the dissolution of their brief marriage could occur with a solicitor working on her behalf.

"Of course," she said weakly, feeling as ill as Lady Bella looked. She'd never counted herself a liar, and standing before so many people she cared for and respected, engaging in an outright falsehood, shamed her.

Bo embraced her then, throwing her arms around Clara and hugging her as though it was the last embrace they'd ever share. And perhaps it would be, Clara had to admit, if neither of them crossed the Atlantic in the coming years. She returned her friend's enthusiastic clasp.

"You must tell me everything," her friend whispered into her ear. "Everything."

Clara shook her head. There wouldn't be anything to tell. "I will see you soon, dear friend," she said simply. She'd do whatever she must to see Bo before she left. Bo was the very best friend—indeed the only friend—Clara had ever made in England.

Ravenscroft held out his arm for her again, watching her solemnly. His glorious dark hair was hidden beneath a hat, and he was every inch the dashing rake from head to toe. He was so beautiful to look upon that she nearly lost her breath for a moment. It was as if the whirlwind of fashionable London around them stopped, and all she could see was him. The notorious Earl of Ravenscroft. Seducer. Hedonist. Her husband.

"My lady," he said softly. "We should take our leave now."

Yes, she supposed they should. Her final embrace was for her father, who hugged her wordlessly. She breathed deeply of his beloved, familiar scent. Clara didn't care that it wasn't done to show emotion or to embrace those she cared for on the street. She was her own woman now, and this was just the beginning of being who she was, of following her own rules, of living her life unapologetically.

"Father, I love you." She admired him. She disagreed with him. But he was a good man. Imperfect, but *good.*

"And I love you, my girl." He leveled another glare at Ravenscroft, who watched their exchange with interest. "Never forget, Ravenscroft."

"Not bloody likely, old boy," the earl drawled before raising an imperious brow. "Lady Ravenscroft?"

Lady Ravenscroft. The title sank into her conscience like a stone. Clara half expected to turn and find another, some august, lovely lady who would do him justice. Someone who wanted to be his countess, a born-in-the-purple aristocrat who didn't intend to flee him at the first opportunity.

I am not she, Clara wanted to say.

But instead, she took his arm and allowed him to lead her to the brougham. She stepped up and inside the vehicle, settling herself on the squab and trying to quell her nerves. She noted the carriage's fine, Morocco leather. Ivory damask lined the interior. This was not the same, tired conveyance he'd traveled in before, a clear sign that his fortunes had changed.

The two hundred thousand pounds he's asked for.

Her father's angry words echoed in her mind, a sharp reprimand. The earl was not a man who ought to be trusted. They had much to discuss. Ravenscroft entered the carriage and settled himself at her side, crowding her with his large body. The door slammed closed.

Suddenly, the brougham felt very small. His cologne teased her senses. Her gaze settled on his muscled thigh, brushing against her skirts. A reckless urge to touch him struck her. He was her husband. She could press her palm to him, absorb his heat through the fabric of his trousers. Such a foreign notion, the liberty to do as she wished. But no, she would not touch him. She had no desire to touch him. It must be the newness of her status that prompted her wayward compulsions.

Clara turned to the window. The gathering of well-wishers still stood in a half-circle, watching their departure with grim expressions. She waved one last time as the brougham lurched into motion. It was done. She'd gained her freedom.

"'O mistress mine where are you roaming'?"

The soft, low words skittered over her skin, leaving a trail of goose bumps in their wake. She looked away from the family and friends growing smaller and farther away with each clop of the horses' hooves. The earl watched her, his eyes probing, his expression unreadable as he removed his gloves. She hadn't expected him to recite Shakespeare, but then he seemed to have an innate skill for surprising her.

She wouldn't speak the next line to him. *O stay and hear, your true love's coming.* Clara swallowed, collecting her jumbled emotions, tamping down the unwanted warmth that threatened to steal over her. "Soon enough, I'll be roaming to Virginia."

"Newly wed and already prepared to flee, little dove? I can't be as bad as all that, can I?" He took her hand in his, bringing it to his lips for a kiss that was hot as a brand, even through her glove.

She would have tugged her hand from his grasp but he held fast. "Your reputation precedes you, my lord."

He grinned, his touch sliding to her wrist. He caught her glove with his teeth, and removed it in one fluid motion. "Call me Julian. I'm your husband now, after all."

Julian. It suited him. A strong name, equal parts bold and leonine. Becoming more familiar with him than necessary would not be wise. She'd already allowed him far too many liberties.

"Not truly," she insisted. He must not be allowed to forget the nature of their union. "Ours is a temporary joining, my lord."

"It needn't be." His bare fingers tangled with hers. "You could remain my countess, little dove."

The contact and the solemnity with which he undermined all her intentions jolted her. "I have no wish to be your countess."

But her breathless tone belied her words. Even she had to admit to herself that she was not entirely immune to him, for here she sat, watching as he took the tip of her index finger and gave her a wicked little nip. And the thoughts swirling through her mind had nothing to do with boarding a vessel bound for her homeland and everything to do with the debauched things he would do to her body if she but allowed him.

He sucked her finger, his hold on her wrist light enough now that she could escape him. "Pity." His tongue trailed a slow path to her knuckle. He bit again, catching the smallest bit of her skin in his even, white teeth.

Those teeth were as beautiful as the rest of him. It was unfair for a man so jaded with sin to be as handsome as he. She inhaled, a current of desire pooling between her legs like molten honey.

Clara snatched her hand away before he could weaken her defenses with any more of his lurid games. "The true pity would be to mire ourselves in an unwanted marriage the same as so many other men and women before us."

His direct gaze sparked with sensual promise. "Never think you're unwanted, little dove. Not for a minute."

How easily he could tempt her. She must never underestimate him, must harden her heart and her intentions. "We wouldn't suit, my lord. I don't like cynical reprobates who cozen my father out of two hundred thousand pounds."

"Ah." He smiled, but it didn't reach his eyes. "Were we not meant to split your dowry evenly? One hundred thousand apiece, no?"

She frowned. "You also requested stocks."

"Curious little dove." Idly, he stroked the satin brocade of her skirts, his finger tracing the rose pattern set against a backdrop of vivid blue. "If a man must sell himself, his price ought to be high enough to make it worthwhile."

She couldn't argue with his logic or stop tracking the mesmerizing progression of that lone finger. With a fluid grace, he trailed it to the center of her skirts, not stopping until he was directly above the juncture of her thighs. Layers of fabric were the only barriers between them. Inexplicably, she recalled how it had felt before when he'd slid his hand beneath her skirts. When he'd stroked her, told her that next time he'd use his tongue instead.

She had to keep her mind on practical matters. Drat it all, what had he said? She tore her attention from his wicked, wandering finger and looked back to his handsome face. He watched her intently, in that piercing way he had.

"I didn't buy you, Lord Ravenscroft," she forced herself to say with a cool hauteur she didn't feel. "I bought my freedom."

"What if they could be one and the same, Lady Ravenscroft?" His eyes dipped to her mouth and she felt it with the force of a caress.

It was as if he sought to seduce her by slow torture. Small touches, nips, and licks, the heat of a stare, the suggestion of his sensual mouth. The air in the brougham seemed stifling. How could he render her so helpless with such little effort? There must be some flaw in her character, some absent moral girding that he exploited. Her heartbeat quickened. Surely it was not merely *him*.

"You mustn't call me that." Her tone was prim as any governess but inside, she raged with fever. He was making her hot. Weak. Dizzy.

He opened his hand, fingers splaying over her skirts in a possessive gesture, and pressed down. She felt him through her many layers, as if he claimed her and taunted her all at once. Just barely, she suppressed the need to tip her hips as if she were seeking him.

"What mustn't I call you, little dove?" Dark amusement colored his voice.

He knew the effect he had on her. Of course he did. She thought of the first night she'd come to him in his study, how he'd been entertained by her, how he'd toyed with her. The rattler was back, coiled and ready to strike.

"Lady Ravenscroft," she snapped, irritated with herself for her damnable weakness. Why had she not prepared herself better? Why had she ever imagined she could manage a man like the Earl of Ravenscroft? "It's a mantle that ought to be reserved for your true wife. I'll not wear it for long."

He leaned into her, so near she felt his hot breath on her lower lip. "Do you know the only thing I'd prefer you not wear for long, darling?"

She tried to escape him, put some distance between them by tilting her head back against the carriage walls. But the brougham was designed to be an intimate vehicle for two passengers, and there was only so far that she could go. "This is most improper, my lord."

With his free hand, he touched the chiffon ruffle that edged her décolletage and fell in a cascade between her breasts. "This dress, little dove. I want to peel it off your luscious body, strip off all your undergarments. I want you naked and beneath me. Does that shock you?"

Of course his frank words shocked her. But they also intrigued her. They also sent tiny tongues of fire licking through her just beneath her skin. Naked and beneath him. Her limbs felt heavy, her entire being sparking with need. "This is a marriage of convenience," she reminded him. "In name but not in deed."

The pad of his thumb brushed the base of her throat. "Fucking you would be most convenient."

There it was again, that filthy word. Ridiculous that it affected her. He was depraved. She should be properly appalled. Disgusted. Instead, a fresh onslaught of molten heat blossomed through her, beginning between her thighs and radiating everywhere. Even the tips of her ears felt hot. She imagined every part of her, from her head to her toes, flushed pink.

"You agreed to my bargain." If only her mouth weren't so dry as she reminded him. If only he didn't make her so weak.

Slowly, he rubbed a circle of fire on her bare skin with his thumb. "I agreed to marry you, love. Nothing more."

"But of course you agreed to my terms."

Ravenscroft considered her, still far too near for comfort. "I professed your ruination. I orchestrated our nuptials. But I never, not even for a moment, promised never to bed you, little dove."

She thought back to their conversation on the night they'd met. To her great shock, she couldn't recall him ever promising to obey her terms. He'd been adamant, in fact, that he wouldn't wed her at all. Until her father had arrived, and Ravenscroft suddenly declared that he'd ruined her.

She stilled, an icy sensation streaking through her. How had she failed to realize he'd never actually agreed to her terms? She had no vow, no oath, no written arrangement. Not a single reassurance. And yet, like the lamb bound for the proverbial slaughtering, here she sat, Lady Ravenscroft. How thoroughly he had routed her. Now she was exposed, vulnerable to enemy forces.

Clara felt even more scattered than before. She mistrusted him. Part of her was angry that she had allowed such a clever manipulation. Part of her still longed for his lips upon hers. "Are you saying you intend to force…relations upon me?"

He grinned, flashing his teeth again. "Never."

Relief washed over her. She exhaled.

His next words set her back on edge. "Fair warning, love. I'm skilled in the art of persuasion."

There was no doubting his meaning or his intentions. But she was a Virginia girl, and she wouldn't be cowed by any English rake, no matter how pretty his face or tantalizing his touch. She tipped up her chin in defiance. "Fair warning, Lord Ravenscroft. I'm equally skilled in the art of shooting."

He laughed, the sound as pleasing to the ears as he was to the eyes. Mellifluous and low and alluring. "So you've warned before, Lady Ravenscroft. I can see you're in your papa's bloodthirsty mold. Where is your pistol, darling? Perhaps I ought to disarm you now before it's too late."

Tucked into her trunks, but she wasn't about to tell him where. Let him wonder, the scoundrel. How dare he wed her with every intention of seducing her? What else did he plan? To refuse an annulment? Keep her from returning to Virginia? Claim all her dowry for his own?

"You'll never know," she told him, catching his hands in an attempt to keep him at bay. "What else do you intend to do now that we're wed, my lord? Has this been nothing more than a game to you?"

His expression sobered. "You're not a game to me, little dove."

"Call me by my name then." When she would have disengaged from him, he tangled his fingers in hers, refusing to release her.

"Clara," he said softly in his proper English vowels as though it were a precious word to him. Or maybe a vow. And then, again. "Clara." He raised both of her hands to his mouth for a kiss to each. A third time. "Clara Elizabeth Ravenscroft."

"Clara Whitney," she countered. The mere utterance of her name in conjunction with his felt somehow just as intimate as his hand up her skirts.

"Not any longer." He turned her hands over, kissing each palm, and she realized for the first time that one of her hands remained gloved and the other bare. He'd swept her away so easily she'd failed to notice. "You're mine now."

If only his possessive proclamation didn't stir some weakness within her. "I'm my own."

"No." He leaned into her at last, kissing the side of her neck. "You're most definitely mine," he said against her skin. "I'll take great pleasure convincing you of it." Another kiss, a dart of his tongue over the sensitive place just beneath her ear before he nipped her lobe. "But for now, we've arrived."

She became aware of her surroundings all at once. The brougham no longer swayed and rocked. How long had they been parked? Mortification sunk into her, heating her cheeks all over again.

"Come," he said. "See your new home, Lady Ravenscroft."

She didn't bother to correct him.

Chapter Eight

THE BUTLER'S MIEN WAS AS GRIM AS CLARA FELT ON THE INSIDE.

By the glaring light of day, the Earl of Ravenscroft's home on Curzon Street showed itself to be even shabbier than she'd first realized. The carpet was thin and outmoded. The wallpapers were faded. Even the window dressings looked like embarrassed spinsters trying to hide themselves in the corner of a ballroom so no one would notice how gauche they were. From the dour butler to the furniture from last century—which desperately wanted a polish—the whole place was in need of a woman's touch.

Some other woman's touch, she reminded herself. She could provide the coin but she had no intention of lingering and toiling over the threadbare Aubusson. He couldn't force her to remain. She was now a woman of her own means, and as soon as she could extricate herself from the earl's hedonistic clutches, she would.

Introductions were performed to the frightfully skeletal staff. Notably absent from the ragtag grouping of servants was the housekeeper. At long last, Clara and Ravenscroft settled in for tea in the drawing room with his sisters, who had not joined them for the wedding ceremony or breakfast.

Lady Alexandra and Lady Josephine were dressed in tepid gowns that looked as if they'd been chosen by a grandmother or elderly aunt. Hopelessly out of date, they would have been all the rage a generation ago with their enormous crinolines. Someone ought to take them shopping, find them proper gowns.

Not me, she reminded herself sternly. She had other, far more important plans. *Home. Virginia. Gaining the vote.* Ravenscroft seated himself at her side, an unwanted distraction.

"We've had the greatest excitement here this morning whilst awaiting your arrival," Lady Josephine informed them breezily as they settled in for tea.

It wasn't precisely the words of welcome or congratulations—however misplaced—that Clara had anticipated. The earl's sisters appeared just as unpredictable and unconventional as he.

"The chamber maid was caught with a footman in the library," Lady Alexandra announced. "Their embrace was not chaste."

Clara almost spat her tea all over her gown. She didn't put stock in English airs, but she knew what was done and what was not done in polite company. Finishing school and Lady Bella had made certain of that. She stared at the earl's sister, who met her gaze without flinching, almost as if she were taking Clara's measure. Inspecting her mettle.

"Lady Alexandra," Ravenscroft rebuked. A muscle twitched in his jaw.

Clara couldn't quite restrain the laugh that bubbled up within her at his displeasure. At last the dissolute man had a weakness. "I'm sure that his lordship will handle the matter with aplomb."

"There are almost no servants to speak of here, so I doubt he will sack the maid for who will empty the chamber pots? Julian hasn't even the coin for a housekeeper," Lady

Alexandra continued lightly. "But I suppose you've changed that, haven't you?"

"Lady Alexandra," the earl repeated, his tone degrading into a growl of displeasure. "Have a care for your tongue."

Clara studied Lady Alexandra. They were nearly of an age unless she missed her guess. She recognized something of herself in the red-haired girl before her. Rebellious. Trapped in a place she didn't belong.

"I do hope we can be friends during my time here, Lady Alexandra," she suggested. "Lady Josephine."

"Oh, I'm sure you shall be like another sister." Lady Alexandra's tone was steeped in sarcasm.

Clara had heard whispers that the sisters more than likely had different fathers, which made sense now that she saw how different they were in appearance. Lady Alexandra was flaming, tall, bold. Josephine was tiny, dark, lovely. It would be a difficult thing, navigating this snobbish society with the hallmarks of their mother's sins obvious for all to see. Clara felt a kindred sense of pity for them both. She too had lost her mother, and her mother had not been as good a woman as she could've been either. Clara herself was a product of her mother's sins.

"One can only hope," Clara returned with as much warmth as she could manage when Lady Alexandra pinned her with the sort of glare one might reserve for one's greatest enemies. She understood now his sisters' absence at the nuptials.

"Oh yes, we shall be the greatest of friends," added Lady Josephine.

Ravenscroft muttered something beneath his breath that sounded like an epithet. Clara hid her smile behind her teacup. At least he was finally off his guard. These sisters of his were true trouble. He'd have his hands full managing their respective comeouts.

"Julian tells us we're to have dowries now since he's married such a great heiress," Lady Alexandra said next. "Thank you so much, Miss Whitney. Your marriage portion will do wonders to strip away the stink of Julian's reputation."

There it was again, reemerging like an apparition: the earl's black reputation. For a silly moment, Clara almost defended him to his sister. Then she recalled that perhaps no one knew better than she just how well-deserved his reputation was. She focused instead on the intentional slight Lady Alexandra paid her. Clara tamped down the urge to correct her, for she'd just had an argument with the girl's brother in which Clara had claimed not to be Lady Ravenscroft at all.

In truth, she was. She had married the earl. He was not as honest as she would've foolishly liked to believe. But she was Lady Ravenscroft, at least until she could legally shed the title and her marriage both. And she intended to do just that posthaste.

Ravenscroft wasn't as inclined toward good will, however. He slammed down his teacup with such force that its contents splashed everywhere. "By God, Lady Alexandra, you will treat my countess with the respect she is due."

Lady Alexandra blinked, schooling her features into an innocent expression. "Pray accept my forgiveness, Lady Ravenscroft. I meant you no insult."

Clara knew insincerity when she saw it. Little wonder the earl had scarcely mentioned his sisters to her. She smiled sweetly at the fiery viper. "Of course you have my forgiveness, dear. You needn't fear I'll cause too much of a disruption for you all. I won't be here long."

"Indeed?" Lady Josephine's interest was piqued. Her eyes narrowed upon Clara. "Where shall you be going, my lady?"

He hadn't told them. The revelation caused another stab of suspicion to niggle its way into her mind. She turned to the earl, who met her gaze, unflinching. No, he had not told them at all, which was the reason for their defensiveness. They didn't like a stranger entering their fold, disrupting their lives. But if he hadn't been truthful with his own sisters regarding the vagaries of their arrangement, it could only imply one awful thing.

Her world crumbled about her with aching clarity. He meant to keep her. The scoundrel had never intended to allow her to return to Virginia. She'd planned her escape and all the while he'd been planning her entrapment.

I agreed to marry you, love. Nothing more.

The devil. Her stomach churned as the implications hit her with the force of a hurricane. Ravenscroft held her stare, making no move to defend himself or dissuade her from her assumption. He raised a brow, as if to challenge her.

"My lady?" Lady Josephine prodded into the awkward silence that had fallen over the drawing room.

Clara settled her teacup into its saucer with an unladylike clatter and stood. "Perhaps you ought to ask Lord Ravenscroft, Lady Josephine, for it would seem he knows far better than I. If you will excuse me, I really am quite tired after all the excitement of this morning and I must retire."

Ignoring the startled expressions of the earl's sisters and the watchful gaze of the earl himself, she fled the chamber. It was only when she reached the main hall that she realized she hadn't a clue where she was retreating to. She was in a stranger's home. A stranger who had deceived her. Hugging her arms about her middle, she stopped and pressed her back against the wall, closing her eyes.

Julian watched his new wife scurrying from the drawing room in a flurry of navy and rose-patterned skirts. Damn it, he'd bungled things badly. She didn't even know her way around their home and yet she was so desperate to flee him that she dashed away as if the devil himself nipped at her heels. And perhaps he did, for Lord knew the thoughts running through his mind ever since Clara had first appeared in his study had been anything but angelic.

He'd hoped to give her time to adjust, to seduce her into seeing the merits of being his countess. But when she'd realized he'd left his sisters uninformed about the nature of their union, he'd known the moment the pieces of the puzzle had come together in her mind. He wouldn't lie to her. He respected her far too much for further pretense.

"Your new bride hardly exudes the air of a lady who is thrilled to be married," Alexandra observed, interrupting his troubled thoughts.

"She rather seemed in a hurry to remove herself from your presence," Josephine added.

He gritted his teeth and glowered at his irksome sisters. "You will mind your manners about her. Treat her with respect, and if you've bloody well got any of it in you, kindness. Lord knows she deserves all that and more."

His sisters stared at him as if he were an insect pinned for their study. Damn them, he didn't appreciate their cheek. Or their vulgarity. Or their appalling lack of tact. And he damn well didn't appreciate being observed, for he couldn't shake the impression that he'd revealed more of himself than he'd intended. Perhaps more of himself than he even knew existed.

"I didn't dare believe the scandal sheets when they proclaimed this a love match," Alexandra said.

"But it is a love match, isn't it?" Josephine asked.

"One sided, or so it seems." Alexandra's tone was wry.

Jesus. It most assuredly was not a love match, as love was a finer emotion he never cared to experience again. Lust, however, was another beast entirely. Naturally, he couldn't share that bit with the meddlesome duo before him.

"Where the hell are you getting scandal sheets?" he demanded instead. "I forbid you to read such tripe."

His sisters beamed at him. Alexandra clapped her hands. "This shall be great fun, shan't it Jo?"

Julian growled. "If you continue to refuse to behave, I'll send the both of you to a convent to live out the rest of your years."

His threat issued, he stood and took his leave of them, determined to find his wife. He'd already tarried too long in an effort to correct their infernal behavior. It didn't take him long to locate Clara. She leaned against the faded damask in the main hall, looking as if she held up the entire weight of the wall with her small shoulders. How young she appeared suddenly. How defeated. Her eyes had been closed, but they flew open when she heard him approach.

"Clara." An odd sensation settled heavily upon his chest. Surely not remorse?

"What do you want, Lord Ravenscroft?" Resignation underscored her words.

She was asking about more than just this moment in the hall. She didn't merely wonder why he'd followed her. She wondered why he'd married her. Why he'd allowed her to believe he'd load her aboard the first Virginia-bound vessel she could find after they wed. Why he'd never once corrected her when she reminded him their marriage would be in name only. Why he had her dowry in his coffers but no intention of letting her go.

It was simple.

He wanted her.

From the moment she'd appeared in his study wearing that monstrosity of a hat, blustering and offering herself to him like a feast for a starved man, he'd been drawn to her. She was a beauty, but it was more than that. She was innocent, sharp-witted, brave to a fault. She smelled of summer and her body was meant for sin. Meant for him. But Clara Whitney was not the sort of lady he could have. At least, not if he'd been entirely truthful with her.

And so, he hadn't bothered to disillusion her. He'd made clear to her that he desired her. His intention to seduce her had never been a secret. The rest, however, had been facilitated by his silence. He wouldn't regret his actions now, but neither did he like the defeated wariness in her expression.

He closed the last of the distance between them. "Need you ask, little dove? I want *you*."

When he would have stroked her cheek, she flinched away from his touch. "You cannot have me."

Stubborn woman. Julian braced a hand on the wall above her head, trapping her. "I already have you."

"Not truly." Defiance flashed in her blue eyes. "I could return to my father's home now."

"How will you get there, love? I'll not be the architect of your retreat." He couldn't resist tracing her jaw. Her skin was softer than silk, purer than cream. "Will you walk? Hire a hack? Perhaps you'll send for dearest Papa and he can barge in here bearing a six-shooter. Then you'll cry to him about your innocent intentions to dupe him into settling a marriage portion on you so that you could defy him and flee to Virginia."

A flush tinged her cheekbones. His barb had found its mark. No, they were neither of them innocent in their little drama. If she hadn't been bold enough to thwart her father's good intentions for her, she'd never have landed herself in her current predicament. But that was Julian's good fortune.

"You dare to take me to task when you tricked me into marrying you?" Her voice was cold, cutting.

He took exception to her accusation, but it didn't stop him from sliding his hand around her nape. "I didn't trick you. You *assumed* I'd accepted your offer. In truth, I never agreed to anything except marrying you, and even that matter was settled with your father."

She captured his wrist, staying his hand when he would have sunk his fingers into her lush tresses. Her anger was a pulsing, heated thing between them, as palpable as the desire. "You deliberately misled me."

"In this instance, Lady Ravenscroft, I daresay you misled yourself." He leaned closer, drank in the scent of oranges. Thoughts of everything else—his skeletal staff of servants, his interfering sisters—fled him.

"I'm going to Virginia whether you like it or not, my

lord. You cannot keep me prisoner here," she insisted, but her voice suggested she was not as unaffected by his proximity as she pretended.

She bloody well wasn't going to Virginia. He grew tired of arguing the point. His lips took hers in a long, slow kiss. She opened for him, her body yielding as her mind would not. She tasted of sweetness and tea. He wondered if she would taste as sweet everywhere and somehow knew that yes, she would.

When he withdrew from her soft mouth, he stared down at her, lust thundering through him. Every part of him longed to claim her now. To carry her upstairs to his chamber, lay her on the bed, and sink home inside her. But he wanted her more than willing. He wanted her to come to him.

"You're not my prisoner, Clara." He kissed her again. "You're my wife."

She shook her head, denying it. "I don't belong here, my lord. With my dowry—"

"Your dowry is mine," he interrupted, lest she think to reclaim her fortune and leave him. "All two hundred thousand of it, to be judiciously spent upon the refurbishing and upkeep of our homes and estates, in addition to our living expenses. Your settlement is yours by law to dispense with as you wish. Ten thousand per annum and North Atlantic Electric stock, I believe."

Clara glared at him. Her settlement was a handsome sum, but it wasn't two hundred thousand pounds. "Let me go, you brute. I'm sure my father hasn't settled the funds with so much haste. I'll tell him everything. He'll understand, help me to annul the marriage."

"No." He wasn't about to let her go. Not ever. He'd seen to it that there was no worm hole through which she could slip. "The transaction has already occurred, legally and binding, so too our marriage contract. It's all done. Don't look so distressed, little dove. We are two of a kind, you and me, selling ourselves for perceived gain. I've been at this business far longer than you, however, and I know the cost better than anyone. No one truly wins."

She pursed her lips and flattened her palms on his chest, attempting to dislodge him. "Forgive me for thinking it would rather appear that you've won, my lord. You secured yourself an heiress. Great sums of money are at your disposal, all your problems solved. It must have been so effortless. Good Lord, I came to you. And then you plied me with charm, worked your rakish ways on me, and I fell into your snare as surely as any hare."

Of course he'd won. Miss Clara Elizabeth Whitney, American heiress and unworldly innocent, was his along with a tidy sum. He wouldn't lose his homes. He wouldn't have to worry over the futures of his sisters. He would no longer have to endure snickers in polite society, rumblings over his penury and his means of staving off ruin. He could hire a bloody housekeeper and maids who didn't fornicate with footmen in the library. But she was staring at him now not with the low-lidded desire he'd come to expect from her but the full-fledged loathing of someone who had been duped.

He'd been duped before. He knew the feeling, like a blow straight to the gut. Lottie had seen to his education. Still, there was something about Clara that made a protective instinct roar to life in his breast. Something that made him want to gather her up in his arms, breathe deeply of her essence—musk and sunshine—and tell her that all would be well. That he was not a perfect man by any means, but he would never hurt her, treat her with disrespect, or ill use her.

He wanted to whisper reassurances to her now, to kiss her wayward brow, to promise he would be the best husband in his power. But instead he looked down at her upturned face, guileless and wounded, and lost all the pretty words he longed to say.

"You'll not leave me," he said instead.

But she was rebellious to the last, as proud as any queen as she stared right back at him. "Yes I will. I'll not be your wife, Lord Ravenscroft. Nor will I share your bed."

Chapter Nine

CLARA HAD NOT YET FALLEN ASLEEP. She had not joined the earl's sisters for dinner that night. Nor had she left her chamber since he had escorted her to it in the wake of their virulent row. For what must have been the thousandth time since stepping over the threshold and slamming the door in Ravenscroft's too-handsome face, she paced the room. According to the mantel clock, it was well after two in the morning.

He had not come to her. Instead, he'd left before dinner. She'd watched him step out from her window, dark and debonair. Perhaps off in search of his club or some other form of amusement. Not a mistress, she hoped, though she had no right or reason to keep him from indulging his hedonism. His departure rather stung, much as she didn't want to acknowledge it.

She detested the weakness within her that missed his presence. He was vital, a man who simultaneously sucked all the air from a room and yet breathed all the life into it. She wanted to rail against him, berate him, dress him down. She wanted to make him suffer and make him pay for deceiving her. But she also wanted him to kiss her. To knock at her door and appear, leonine and seductive, ready to strip away all her protest.

Somewhere during the course of her hours of reflection, she'd realized that part of her thrilled to the notion of being the earl's countess. And not just in name only. He had awakened her body. He had charmed her. He'd listened to her, appeared to value her thoughts and opinions. She couldn't believe his every action had been a ruse. Some men were too facile of tongue, creatures who never listened to a word a lady said. Others listened too much, pretending to care in an effort to use their feigned interest to their advantage. Ravenscroft was neither of those sorts of men. He was, she hated to admit, a law unto his own.

But what of his motivation? If it was only her dowry he'd been after, he should have been all too happy to see her off to Virginia, depositing her on the nearest docks. He didn't require her—as he'd pointed out, the marriage settlement was already in his possession. Why then, did he want her as his wife? Did he merely want to bed her? She hardly thought so, for much as she hated to concede it, he likely could have bedded her at any point during their fortnight of courtship if he'd merely pressed her enough. Her resistance was that weak.

Still he hadn't done so.

Even in the carriage that day, he'd put his hand up her skirts, touched her most improperly. But the moment she'd pushed him away, he'd respected her wishes. He could have arrived at her door, could have barged straight through it, at any point between the moment she'd slammed it in his face and now. He had not.

The Earl of Ravenscroft was a dichotomy. He had spent much of his life in sin. He was a wicked voluptuary. But he had also personally seen to the preparation of her chamber. During her many rounds of pacing, she'd begun to notice small details.

This chamber, unlike the rest of the house, was not threadbare or outmoded. Its wallpaper was crisp and new, its carpet well-padded and sculpted in a grand design. A corner bookcase possessed an assortment of volumes that were all of interest to her, from a treatise on the female vote to the poetry of Elizabeth Barrett Browning. A hand-colored lithograph of a whip-poor-will, a picture of Richmond, and some engravings of the verdant Virginia countryside ornamented the walls.

He had recalled their conversations, had tried hard to make a space for her that would appeal. It hardly made sense. But then, the man himself scarcely did. Was he gilding her cage? Attempting to win her over? Why had he not come to her? Why had he not made her his wife in deed as well as name?

Clara stilled as she heard a sudden commotion in the hall. Voices, loud and tight with worry, carried to her. Footsteps sounded, then the crashing open of the door to the earl's chamber just next door. Something was amiss.

Heartbeat kicking into a rapid pace, she donned her dressing gown, knotting the belt at her waist. In two steps, she was at the door adjoining her chamber to his, throwing it open to reveal a grim scene. Her mouth went dry as she spotted Ravenscroft's limp form being carried by the butler and two footmen. His head lolled, his midnight hair and beautiful face drenched in blood.

Dear God.

She raced across the chamber, not having a care for her state of undress, and supported his head as the men gently laid him upon his bed. Blood coated her fingers, warm and sticky. A violent wave of nausea hit her. He looked like a corpse. She pressed a bloodied hand to his chest, absorbing the gentle rise and fall of his breathing.

Not dead, thank the Lord.

But all that blood.

Her mind spun. "Call for his physician at once."

"It is already done, my lady," said Osgood, the butler.

"What happened to him?"

"His lordship was attacked outside after he returned

from his club." If she'd thought him grim before, Osgood was positively funereal now. "Fortunately, the vagabond was scared off before he could do further damage."

Attacked.

Misgiving assailed her. Someone had viciously beaten Ravenscroft outside his very own home. He was a large man, capable and muscled. His assailant must have approached him from behind. He wouldn't have had a chance of defending himself. Who would do such a thing?

But her questions would have to be answered later, for now, Ravenscroft needed all her focus and energy to be on tending him. She had never dealt with such an injury. Panic snaked through her. She gripped the earl's lifeless hand, squeezing. "I'll need clean cloths," she ordered the butler. "Hot water as well. Bring the doctor to me as soon as he arrives."

"Yes, my lady."

And then he was gone, leaving her alone with her unconscious husband and the ever-growing knot of fear within her.

Clara kept vigil at Ravenscroft's bedside after the physician had gone. By the time Dr. Redcay arrived, the earl had begun regaining consciousness, making it necessary for the doctor to administer chloroform. She had held Ravenscroft's hand as Dr. Redcay examined, cleaned, and stitched his wound. Had held her breath as she awaited the serious man's final diagnosis.

"Fortunately, there doesn't appear to be a fracture of the skull, my lady," the doctor had said. "His lordship's brain is severely concussed, but I see no reason to attempt trepanning at this juncture. Should he suffer seizures or sudden fever, call for me immediately. I've left you some bromide of potash should you require it, but his lordship is generally a strong and healthy man. Change the wound dressing daily as I've shown you, using antiseptic. He must rest for several days but he should be back to himself in no time."

Clara had nearly swooned with relief at the proclamation, for she'd gotten a good look at the instruments inside Dr. Redcay's medical case. Thank the Lord he hadn't used the insidious looking trephine upon Ravenscroft's skull.

She would not be made a widow on the second day of her marriage. No, he was not dead. He would survive. Now if only he would wake, she thought, watching him through eyes that burned from lack of sleep. The effects of the chloroform should soon wear off, she hoped.

Ravenscroft remained in his evening clothes, his form troublingly still. His skin had acquired an unusual pallor, undoubtedly from the blood loss he'd suffered. His hair was damp from her ministrations, his perfection sullied only by the bandage wrapped about his head. Her heart hurt for the pain he must have suffered. How could someone have visited such violence upon him?

Perhaps more importantly, who?

The unkind thought occurred to her that perhaps his assailant was a cuckolded husband from his past. Swiftly, she swatted it from her mind. Her first instinct had led her to believe it could have been a cutpurse, but he appeared not to have been robbed of his valuables—he still wore his gold signet ring, wedding band, a pocket watch tucked into his waistcoat. No, a cutpurse likely would not have aimed for such a grave wounding. Whoever had done this to the earl had meant to kill him. She grew more certain of it by the moment.

Her stomach clenched, bile in her throat. She feared she would vomit, worn down by the aftereffects of shock, lack of sleep, and the realization that someone intended to murder her husband. She stared at his still form, willing her nausea to abate.

One breath, two breaths, three. She would not lose her nerve now. She focused on him. *A fourth breath. A fifth.* No, she would not cast up her accounts. Ravenscroft needed her to remain calm. His evening finery disturbed her. For the sake of his comfort, she really ought to remove it. His manservant had fled the chamber long ago, squeamish at the sight of all the earl's blood.

And who else should do it, after all? Clara was Ravenscroft's wife. No, not Ravenscroft, she thought for the first time, but *Julian*. She squeezed his long fingers again, as if with her mere touch she could force him to wake unscathed. Her anger with him for his clever manipulations could wait. The sight of him, bloodied and unconscious, being carried by servants, had undone her.

She meant what she'd said to him that day during their walk in the park. She liked him. Far more than she should. In fact, as she watched him, helpless and laid low, a stern protectiveness filled her breast. How dare anyone hurt him? For all that he had a black reputation as an unrepentant sinner, a strong vein of good ran through him.

Clara released his hand and stood, moving to the foot of the bed. She had no experience in divesting a man of his clothing, and the notion of touching him so intimately made her cheeks go hot and a strange sensation unfurl low in her belly. It was a necessity, she reminded herself. And it was perfectly acceptable now, given their married state. She could tend him at his sickbed without turning into a featherhead.

She removed his fine leather shoes first, then his silk stockings. Even his large feet possessed an elegant refinement in keeping with the rest of him. They were perfectly formed, not at all ugly as one might expect of a man's feet. Next, she moved back to the head of the bed, working on his loose-fitting black jacket. His arms were heavier than she'd expected, corded with muscle that her fingers found cause to linger over a moment longer than necessary. His waistcoat proved more difficult to remove, so she settled for undoing the buttons. His crisp white shirt was bespattered with blood. She pressed her hand over his heart, feeling the steady thump and the warmth he radiated.

Suddenly, he moaned, shifting beneath her hand as he came to.

Julian became aware of his body in stages. His brain felt as though it had swelled three times its normal size and now sought to escape his skull. Pain reverberated through his head. His scalp was pulled tight. Dizziness washed over him, his mind a confused hodgepodge of questions. He was wrapped in a fog, experiencing all sensation with an odd detachment.

What the hell had happened? He struggled to open his eyes, an act that sent a fresh onslaught of pain hammering into him. The interior of his bedchamber swam before him, the sharp delineations of familiar objects blurring like melted wax from a candle. He was at home then. Thank Christ.

A small, feminine hand lay atop his chest. When he would have turned his head to identify the hand's owner, nausea churned through his gut with unexpected violence. He slammed his eyes closed again. The darkness was a comfort, a delicious void into which he could lose himself. His head pounded. Who was in his chamber?

Lottie? He groped blindly for the presence at his side. His fingers tangled in soft, billowing fabric. No stiff boning kept him from feeling the lush flesh just beneath the garment.

Not Lottie. Recognition sifted through him like awareness, small grains of sand collecting into a greater conscious. The scent of oranges and musk traveled to him then, mingling with the copper of blood. Clara. His wife. Sweet little dove. He wished he hadn't plucked the wrong name from the recesses of his aching brain, for he'd never confuse Clara with Lottie. The two couldn't have been more opposite.

His hand curved around her waist where it belonged.

Yes, he recalled now. He was a married man, and his countess had not been pleased to discover his duplicity. They'd rowed. He'd gone to his club, hadn't he? He'd intended to give her time and space to see reason. He remembered dining at his club. He'd given in to temptation and downed a whisky. The ride home had been ordinary, nothing of note to remark upon. After that, his memory was as blank as a night without stars.

"Julian?"

He forced his eyes open again, pleased to at long last hear his name in her buttery drawl. No defiant "Ravenscroft" or "my lord" this time. A worried bite made her tone almost harsh. She was a blur of colors for a moment as she came into focus. Her blonde hair fell unbound in a mass of burnished curls. Half moons darkened the creamy skin beneath her blue eyes. Her lovely face was a study in worry. Blood stained her dressing gown. His blood.

"Little dove." He tried to smile in reassurance, but even flexing his facial muscles into a semblance of cheer gave him pain. "You look as if you've been to battle." Even his words emerged slowly at first, as though his mind were a pump that needed priming after the blow he'd taken.

She looked down at herself, snatching her hand away from his chest and pressing it over the smears on her dressing gown. "I feel as if I've been to battle." Her voice gentled as her gaze snapped back to his, drinking him in or so it seemed. "You gave us all a fright. How do you feel now?"

He gingerly lifted a hand to touch his head, finding a bandage there. The devil. "I feel like hell. What happened to me?"

Clara frowned. "I was hoping you would remember. Someone attacked you, my lord. You'd just returned from your club. Your driver saw only a fleeting shadow of a figure running away. No other servants were about."

Jesus. He forced himself to think again about the drive home. He recalled debating whether or not he would knock on the door joining his chamber to hers. Weighing the merits of drawing out his seduction of her until she was mad for him or simply barging over the threshold and seducing her in one night. Then, the carriage had come to a halt and he'd alighted. He had a vague recollection of taking a few steps, but he couldn't be sure what, if anything, had occurred beyond the moment the sole of his shoe had touched the ground.

"I was attacked," he repeated, feeling fuzzy as he tried to comprehend the knowledge that someone had intentionally wounded him. And from the grinding pain in his cranium, it would seem that his assailant had meant to cause him serious injury. Perhaps even to kill him. A chill of foreboding passed over him. "I recall nothing."

"I feared as much." She caught her luscious lower lip in her teeth, pausing for a beat. She seemed to struggle for words.

As for him, he most assuredly wasn't dead yet, for watching her work her lip made his cock stir to life. "Something troubles you. What is it, little dove?"

"Who would wish you ill, my lord?"

He made another attempt at a grin. "Damned if I know. I've fashioned any number of enemies over the years. None that I'd imagine would stoop to braining me from behind just outside my residence."

The temerity of the bastard filled him with an unholy rage. It was his wedding night, by God. He was not meant to be lying abed, half clothed, with his virginal wife tending to him like a bloody nurse. He should have been in her bed, his head between her thighs, making her spend. He would find whoever was responsible for this travesty and feed him his teeth.

"I fear that whoever did this to you intended to do far worse, Lord Ravenscroft." Her face was ashen, and yet she remained the loveliest thing he'd ever seen.

His head thumped. "Never say you're worried for me, wife?"

"You mustn't call me that." Her fingers fretted with the sleeve of her dressing gown.

"Why? Are you not, in fact, the woman I married today?" It didn't matter that he'd taken a severe bludgeoning. She was still his, damn it all, and he wasn't foggy on that fact. Not one bit.

"You know quite well what I mean to say. Despite your protestations to the contrary, we will not have a true marriage. I'm returning to Virginia and you cannot stop me." She looked into her lap. "But of course I worry. How can I not? Someone almost killed you tonight, and I very much fear your assassination was the villain's primary goal."

Ah, there it was, the truth unfettered between them. They were done dancing at pretense. She was too clever for a woman of her tender age. He wondered what had made her become cynical enough to reach the same conclusion as he. Other ladies he'd known would have swooned at the sight of an injured man. They would have retired to their chamber until he regained consciousness, and then they would've made the easier and safer assumption that he'd been the victim of a random crime.

For some mad reason, her worry warmed him. Perhaps she didn't hate him for his subterfuge, then. Perhaps she even cared, just a modicum. "The bastard didn't succeed, however." He strove for a bland tone. No need to upset her more than necessary. His mind yet grappled with the implications of what had befallen him.

"Someone tried to kill you." This time, she was blunt, looking up from her nervous fingers to meet his gaze. "Are you not concerned?"

Hell, yes he was concerned. But his mind was still jumbled and muddled. His head hurt like the devil. He very much wished he had not gone to his club, spurred by his pride, and had instead gone to her.

"Surely your father wouldn't hire an assassin?" he asked, opting for flippancy, which had always served him well.

Her eyes went wide. "He would never! You cannot think my father to blame for this?"

He didn't answer her immediately, partly because although he'd posed the question in jest, he had to admit it did have some merit. Her dearest papa, after all, thought him a black-hearted despoiler of innocents, a vile fortune hunter who had preyed upon his beloved daughter. The timing seemed rather suspect. The very night of his wedding. By the contract they'd agreed upon, his demise would have left Clara with any estates that weren't part of the entail and all her marriage portion. Tidy method of solving a problem, that.

"My father is a good man," she protested, apparently reading his silence all too well. "Do not waste time misdirecting your suspicion upon him, for then the true criminal will remain free to make another such attempt on your life. You ought to carry my pistol with you whenever you're about, at least until the son-of-a-bitch is caught."

He blinked. Had his murky mind heard correctly? Somehow, an epithet coming off the lips of his sweet little dove seemed wrong. But it also aroused him. He was an absurd fellow, half his scalp cracked open and nearly bleeding to death, and his cock hard as coal. Something was wrong with him. Perhaps the blow to the head had rendered him completely mad.

And then, the rest of her words filtered through to him. She wanted to give him her pistol. His fierce little Virginian miss thought he needed her firearm. Bless her. Of course, who could blame her for thinking him an inept duffer after he'd allowed someone to all but slay him ten paces from his own door? And on their bloody wedding night, of all times.

"Allow me to reassure you that I can protect myself without your weapon, Lady Ravenscroft." He took great pleasure in reminding her of who she now was. A gash to the head had not altered that.

"Miss Whitney shall do nicely," she informed him, her tone cool and impersonal. "You must accustom yourself to the fact that I will leave you, my lord."

"Leave me to be murdered?" Some vicious part of himself, long buried, unearthed itself in that moment. "My blood already stains you, little dove, so you may as well. Tell me, why do you linger here? A servant can do as well as you."

She blanched. His words had found their mark, but he felt no pleasure in it. The aching in his head was making him peevish. He longed to call back what he'd said. Damn it, he wanted to seduce her, not to push her away. But she was ever stubborn. Ever smug in her unwavering belief that she would sail away to Virginia. He longed to shake her from her position. A woman couldn't marry her homeland. Couldn't she see how much he needed her here?

Jesus, where had that thought come from? He was the Earl of Ravenscroft, by God. He'd lived thirty-one years without ever needing a woman. A man required only funds, after all. Not a warm cunny and a luscious pair of tits. What was wrong with him, chasing after this slip of a girl as though no other woman would have him? He ought to let her go. Load her on a Virginia-bound ship. Wave goodbye.

But he couldn't.

"You need not be cruel," she said then, her voice accusatory. "I do care about you, my lord. Surely that must be apparent. A woman without feeling would not help carry a wounded man to his bed, clean away his blood, or hold his hand while the doctor stitches his wounds. A woman without feeling would not have prayed for you to wake."

Her anger coiled in his chest like a serpent ready to strike. His head ached. His mouth was dry. His stomach jerked, threatening to cast up its accounts. Devil take it. He was in no shape for this reckoning.

She had been by his side, tending to him. She'd held his hand. The jagged pieces inside him shifted, fitting together in perfect harmony. He reached for her, clasping the nearest bit of her, those agile fingers.

"Thank you," he said simply, for he meant it. Never had he been more thankful. "You didn't owe me that, Clara, and I thank you for it all the same."

Her expression softened, and she turned her hand palm up, tangling her fingers with his. "You're welcome, Julian."

Not precisely an extension of the proverbial olive branch, but he would take it. Yes, damn it, he would take it.

"TELL ME, LADY RAVENSCROFT, IS IT TRUE THAT SOMEONE TRIED TO MURDER OUR BROTHER LAST EVENING?" Lady Alexandra hadn't even waited to begin filling her plate from the sideboard at breakfast the next morning. She'd pounced the moment she stepped over the threshold.

Someone would have to teach the earl's sisters some manners. Clara had just been about to take a sip of her ritualistic morning coffee when the wayward duo bustled into the breakfast room, brimming with ill-contained curiosity. She replaced her cup in its saucer. "Lady Alexandra, Lady Josephine, good morning."

In truth, it was anything but. She'd slept in a chair at Ravenscroft's side and had only left him to the care of his manservant so that she could break her fast and inform his sisters of what had happened. Worry for him still soured her stomach, and her neck and shoulders ached from the manner in which she'd finally fallen headlong into slumber. It would seem that his sisters had already heard the news from another source. Of course they would have done.

His sisters spilled across the floor in outmoded pastel

gowns, crowding her at the table. "How is Julian?" Lady Josephine demanded. "His wits aren't addled now, are they?"

The girls before her certainly required a great deal of patience.

Lady Alexandra jostled into her sister. "Have they caught the fiend?"

"Lord Ravenscroft is as well as can be expected." As recalcitrant as the girls were, Clara knew a moment of gratification at their genuine concern. "Your brother was indeed attacked last evening and gravely injured. At last word, the criminal responsible has not yet been apprehended. Fortunately, the doctor assures me that with some rest, the earl shall recover."

"He has already recovered," came the familiar drawl of Ravenscroft himself, traveling from behind the wall of concerned femininity obscuring him from Clara's vision.

His sisters spun, Lady Josephine's flounced bell-shaped crinolines nearly knocking Clara's coffee to the floor. She rescued it just in time, righting it in its saucer, before her husband swept into her line of vision. He moved with the same easy grace as always. He wore gray trousers and a black jacket, a silver waistcoat atop his crisp white shirt. His bandage interrupted the inky beauty of his hair, but aside from it, he bore no other sign of the grave injury he'd sustained. He was handsome and debonair as ever.

What in heaven's name was he about?

Her lips compressed into a disapproving frown. "My lord, you ought to remain abed as the doctor ordered."

"My lady." His gaze met hers, warm and intimate. He bowed. "Thank you for your tender care and concern. However, I am, as you can see, mended."

No man could be mended that quickly after the loss of a great deal of blood. Clara had seen firsthand just how much of his life source had been spilled. Upon further inspection, he did appear a bit pale. "Dr. Redcay prescribed rest, my lord. In matters of an injury to the head he said it was of utmost import. I insist you return to your chamber. I'll see that your breakfast is brought to you."

"You insist?" He smiled, as if she amused him.

Perhaps she did. She supposed it wasn't every day that someone dared to gainsay a peer of the realm. But she didn't give a fig for ancient English custom, propriety, social rules, or even eloquence. What she did care about was his wellbeing, and if he was too foolish to realize that he ought to take better care of himself, she had no problem telling him.

"Yes." She stood, pinning him with a meaningful glare. "I insist, my lord."

She felt Lady Josephine and Lady Alexandra's wide eyes upon her and turned to find them staring at her as if she'd done something scandalous. Well, wasn't that rich, coming from those two? She stared them down as well. "If the earl won't have a care for his person, then who will?" she demanded.

Lady Alexandra's mouth worked, as if struggling to form words. None were forthcoming. Lady Josephine watched her from beneath raised brows. *Inspect my mettle all you will*, she told them with her silence. A Virginia girl did not back down from a challenge. Nor did she bat an eyelash at ordering about an earl.

Out of the corner of her eye, she spied Ravenscroft swaying on his feet. She rushed past his sisters and to his side, throwing her arm about his waist. His arm draped over her shoulder, as if he could steal some of her strength. She felt a tremor pass through him and knew he was not nearly as well as he pretended. Who, then, was this show of bravado for? The foolish man.

"Help me escort his lordship back to his chamber," she ordered a footman. When he hesitated, looking from her to Ravenscroft, her patience snapped. "Be quick about it, man. We haven't all day."

The servant rushed forward. *Excellent.*

"No." Ravenscroft halted him in his tracks. "I only

require the assistance of my wife."

He leaned against her, pressing his large, warm body into hers. She flushed at the contact and tried to rein in her thoughts. He'd been gravely wounded, after all. What was wrong with her?

Moreover, how did he think she alone could aid him back to his chamber? "But my lord, perhaps some more support would be beneficial."

His gaze roamed over her face, hungry, or so it seemed to her. "I'm not an invalid, my lady. I require you alone."

Stubborn man. He *was* an invalid, but why argue the matter? Very well. She would allow him to win this small battle, for there remained others to fight and win.

She looked back to the footman. "See to it that a proper breakfast is sent up for his lordship." She paused, rallying to her cause. "And get me Osgood. I require an interview with him in an hour."

It was far past time that the household possessed the proper number of servants. Well-trained servants. Servants who didn't do unmentionable things in the library.

"Perhaps she'll do after all," Lady Alexandra said *sotto voce* to Lady Josephine.

Clara's eyes narrowed on the two of them once more. For that matter, perhaps she'd found just the person to do something about his sisters' sadly lacking manners. Herself. "I'll expect tea this afternoon with you, Lady Alexandra and Lady Josephine. Do be prompt."

With that, she began guiding Ravenscroft from the room. He followed her lead, surprisingly compliant. Perhaps too compliant. Suspicion stirred in her. Had his show of inhuman strength been for her benefit? Had he forced himself from bed in the hope that she would help him to return to it? He was a calculating man, the stranger she'd wed. She'd put nothing past him.

"Lady Ravenscroft, you're as formidable as a general this morning." His low voice rumbled into her ear, his hot breath fanning over her throat.

She suppressed a shiver. "I've discovered I need to be in this household." Truly, the man needed a voice of reason. They'd been married for the span of a day, and already he'd been bludgeoned outside his home. His sisters were mayhem in frills and pink. His servants were insufficient and scandalous. His home was threadbare, in desperate need of a judicious eye and a deep purse. A woman's touch. Not her touch, however. Someone else's.

Yes, most assuredly, someone else's.

They were all—from Ravenscroft down to the chamber maid who needed sacking—someone else's problem. And yet here she was, somehow making them hers. Making *him* hers. The thought caused a pang somewhere in the vicinity of her heart. She tamped it forcefully down.

"I'm afraid we haven't precisely provided you with the welcoming I would have preferred." His tone was wry and strained.

That was an understatement if ever she'd heard one. Lord have mercy, none of this was what she'd envisioned. None of it was what she'd prepared for, what she'd waited for. And yet, somehow tending to him and seeing him at his weakest last night had changed something inside her forever.

Her heart had softened toward him. She could not deny it. Not enough to stray from her course forever, but perhaps enough to stray from her course for now. And there was the stark, unabridged truth. She wasn't prepared to leave him. Not with the shadow of an assassin hanging over him. Not when he was weak and injured. Not when he needed her.

"Whatever did you do without me, my lord?" She couldn't help but ask. They went up the grand staircase now, taking their time. The banister was in sad need of a sound polish, but Ravenscroft seemed steady enough on his feet.

"I'm sure I don't care to recall, little dove. You're here now, aren't you? That's all that matters. You cannot imagine I'll let you go after this."

A frisson of something indefinable skittered through her

entire being, warming her before she reminded herself that their union was not meant to be. They reached the top of the stairs and made their way down the hall to his chamber.

"I'm sure I cannot imagine you having the power to keep me here against my will," she challenged.

It wouldn't do for him to forget that she still intended to return to Virginia, after all. Nor would it do for her to forget. One day as his countess, and already she'd faltered. He made her want to lose herself in him.

He stopped their progress, hauling her against the wall with surprising strength, given his condition. His palms flattened to the damask on either side of her face, neatly trapping her. "I'm not planning for it to be against your will, love."

She stared up at him, wishing she could read his expression. After the blow he'd taken to the head and the blood he'd lost, he shouldn't look so inviting, so handsome. But he appeared as beautiful as she'd ever seen him, pallor to his skin and all. Not even the bandage on his head could detract from the effect he had upon her. He was magnificent. Hers.

For now.

She swallowed. Her common sense reminded her to think of his condition, of the importance of his rest. "My lord, you should be abed."

"Yes, my lady, I should." He lowered his head, bringing his wicked mouth to within an inch of hers. "With you."

A strange sensation sank through her at his words and his nearness both, starting in her belly before sinking into the very center of her. Her breasts tingled. The part of her he'd stroked when he'd put his hand up her skirt ached. This was why good women ruined themselves, she realized. This was why so many ladies had sought him. Temptation was delicious. *He* was delicious.

She shook her head, attempting to banish the dissolute thoughts he provoked within her. "No. You need to recover. Dr. Redcay stressed how imperative it is for you to rest and regain your strength."

"Redcay can go to the devil." He leaned against her, their bodies making contact from breast to chest all the way to their thighs. His legs wedged between hers, her complicit skirts billowing about him. She felt him for the first time, the hardness of him pressed straight to her center with a tip of his hips. Her dress and crinoline weren't a sufficient barrier. "You're all I need to recover, little dove. Just you beneath me. I can assure you I have enough strength for what we both want." His head dipped, his mouth opening on her throat.

The rigid shape of him against her, so suggestive and foreign and wicked, heightened her every sense. To her great shame, an echo of want pulsed within her. She didn't know how they would fit together. The vague mechanics of it had been whispered to her in finishing school. None of the girls had truly known for certain what happened between a man and a woman. She ached now with her half knowledge, needing something from him. He kissed a path to the hollow behind her ear. She tilted her head to grant him better access. His mouth played over her like velvet fire.

But she could not indulge in her newfound depravity, for she was bound and determined that their marriage would never be consummated. And he was not well. He was a man who didn't appear to take care in his own wellbeing. Were all his days just an endless string of one debauchery after the next? Did he not realize how close he'd come to being murdered the night before?

The thought chilled her. She caught his face between her palms, stilling his mouth's exploration. The stubble of his whiskers pricked her. His valet had not shaved him, and the rough abrasion felt good against her skin. The contact jolted her but she did her best to pretend as though she was unaffected.

"Lord Ravenscroft, someone almost killed you last night. Do you not have a care for yourself? You must rest and regain your strength so that you can discover what truly happened and prevent it from happening again. If someone wants you dead, he or she will surely try again once their lack of success becomes apparent."

He closed his eyes, seeming to gather his strength, leaning into her even more. "It was likely a case of mistaken identity."

It was not, and they both knew it. His attacker had meant to kill him. He'd been right outside his residence.

"I fear for you, Julian." At last, the truth was torn from her.

His eyes opened, vivid and brilliant. "You fear for me, but in every other sentence you remind me that you will leave me, and that you want no part of this marriage, no part of me. You cannot have it both ways, little dove. You must choose."

She stared at him, stricken by the one word she'd nearly blurted. *You.* But no, she wouldn't say it. Wouldn't give up on her dreams. Who was he to her? A stranger who'd taken advantage of her foolishness? The man who'd cozened two hundred thousand pounds out of her father?

She'd spent each day since her father had brought her to England longing for her eventual return home. So many years had passed that Virginia had become hazy and indistinct, a soft and warm memory, beating within her heart but not within her mind's eye. Why, she could scarcely even recall most of it with proper detail. And she would not abandon her cause of helping her fellow women to gain the vote that was rightfully theirs.

"Choose, damn you," he said again, his face so close to hers, their lips almost brushing. But he did not kiss her. "I won't force you. I won't have you knowing that you'd prefer to be somewhere else, in someone else's arms. Do you understand me?"

She still held his face in her hands. She couldn't choose. It should have been easy, a quick sentence leaving her tongue. *I choose Virginia. I want to go home.* But the words wouldn't come.

"I can't," she forced herself to say. He wanted too much from her, and too soon. They'd been wed for one day. She was not even accustomed to the layout of his household, and already all her plans had been dismantled. He'd been attacked. The unwanted feelings she'd developed for him during their impromptu courtship added to her confusion. Her body betrayed her, even now longing for him, for the weight of his frame pressing into hers, for his body against her, claiming her.

His expression was harsh, demanding as his tone, as the man himself. "I'm telling you now, Clara. You must choose. If it's a cold piece of ground you long for, I'll have my man take you straight to a hotel. You can bide your time until the next passenger ship departs for Virginia."

He shuddered against her then, swaying. She reached for his shoulders, anchoring him to her until the spell subsided. Hours before, she'd been stained in his blood. She'd watched over him, praying for him to wake. Back in her chamber that morning, she'd scrubbed her hands and face, tossed her ruined dressing gown into the dust bin. The blood was gone, but what had happened to him remained. Someone meant to do him harm. How could she sail away from him forever? What if the person who'd attempted to kill him would return, this time succeeding? How would she feel from an ocean away?

"I reckon it's Virginia then." A grim acceptance tempered his voice. He attempted to push away from her.

No.

She overpowered him in his weakened state, holding him to her when he would have retreated. "You," she breathed before she could think better of it.

Because a strangeness had overtaken her from the moment she'd first stepped into his study, a feeling that he alone could unlock the secrets within her. He was a mystery to her, a man who claimed to be a jaded cynic. A man who had misled her, who had courted her, who had listened to her opinions. He wasn't as hardened as he pretended to be.

He wasn't as careless. He had decorated her chamber, had taken in his sisters. He wanted her to be his wife when allowing her to go would be the easiest path.

"It's you," she said again, as much for her own benefit as for his. She closed the scant distance between them to press her lips to his in a quick and nervous gesture. There. That ought to be…wifely.

Wife. Suddenly the word held knew meaning. What had she done? She'd never intended to be his wife in truth or in deed. But the promises she'd made the day before resonated, as real as his hot flesh beneath her fingertips. Yes, he was hers now.

He kissed her again, fitting their lips together, setting his lower lip between hers. His teeth nipped her upper lip, tasting her, testing her resolve. "Thank you, little dove," he said against her mouth, a benediction. "Thank you."

A man could grow accustomed to such treatment.

Julian watched his wife as she directed the placement of the breakfast tray she'd ordered for him. Much as he would've loved to fuck her senseless, slide home inside her before she changed her mind and raced off to Virginia, for the first time in his life, he didn't possess the stamina. Odd bouts of dizziness struck him with an unpredictability that had rendered his intrepid venture to the breakfast room ill-advised. He must have lost a great deal of blood as well, the aftereffects of which left him uncomfortably feeble.

His pride in tatters, he'd allowed her to assist him back to his chamber and into his bed. With his haphazard valet missing once more, she acted the part without bothering to ring for him. She removed his shoes, helped him with his jacket and waistcoat, and plumped pillows behind his back. She was a capable woman, his wife.

It was all rather endearing, for he hadn't fancied her the tender sort. Fierce, foolish, and brave, yes. Determined and stubborn, also. But tender…now that was an unfamiliar side to her. A side he found he rather enjoyed. A side of her that made the strangest sensation lodge in his chest.

Indeed, the sole benefit of his unexpected brush with death was the sea change it worked upon his lovely American bride. She'd been furious with him yesterday after discovering his intentions. But her ire seemed to have faded in the face of his near-demise. She'd been hovering at his side, seeing to his comfort, checking his brow for sign of fever. Christ, she'd even taken charge of his rapscallion sisters and his sadly disreputable household.

Perhaps she didn't dislike him quite as much as she wished she did. Perhaps she wasn't as impervious as she pretended.

Suddenly, he wanted everyone who wasn't Clara gone from the chamber.

"That will be all," he informed the maid and footman dancing attendance on them. He sincerely hoped that wasn't the maid who'd been frolicking in his library, but he kept his silence as the two took their leave, despite a strong urge to warn against their impending fornication anywhere else in his home. Ah, he would freely admit that his household badly needed a woman's touch.

The door closed, leaving Julian and his wife decidedly alone. If only his bloody head would stop thumping and the room would cease spinning at the most inopportune moments. Clara stood a few paces from the bed, hands clasped at her waist. She couldn't have slept much during the night. Thrice, he'd shuddered awake to find her sleeping in the chair at his side.

But looking at her now was akin to gazing upon the verdant beauty of a summer day. She was like sunshine. Necessary. Life giving. Glorious.

Jesus, where was this maudlin tripe originating from? One blow to the head was all it took, apparently, but he couldn't look away from her. How lowering to be thus affected by such a small, fine-boned creature. He'd never imagined the like.

"Will you take your breakfast now, my lord? You do need your strength." Courtesy steeped her tone.

Damn it, back to the impersonal and circumspect form of address. Too impersonal for his taste. With Clara, he wanted anything but. He wanted familiar. Intimate. He wanted to know every inch of her, from her golden head to her dainty toes, and everywhere in between. *Especially* everywhere in between.

But not now. Not yet. For the moment, all he had in his arsenal was words. "I'm your husband. You may call me by my given name."

"Very well." She bustled to the table where the breakfast tray lay abandoned and gripped its silver handles, notably avoiding the use of his name. "Where would you have me put this?"

He wasn't hungry. The smell of food made his stomach queasy. "Leave it. I find I've lost my appetite."

"But you must eat, for how else will you get well again? Have a care for yourself, if you please." The drawl she took great pains to hide was more pronounced than usual.

"Darling, I haven't had a mother in many years, and I certainly don't require one now."

She flushed, her lush lips flattening into a line of displeasure. "Do you ever take anything seriously, sir?"

He'd spent the last decade or so of his life taking nothing seriously. A man who'd lived as he had couldn't afford to turn the sober eye of scrutiny to himself. And so, his years had been a swirl of decadence, drink, pleasure, and ruin.

Not any longer, however. Once, he'd thought that nothing changed. That life was an endless cycle of misery that only hedonism could diminish. Once, he'd thought *he* could never change. And then, a beautiful Virginia girl had walked into his study wearing the ugliest hat he'd ever seen.

The chamber stopped spinning about him. He took her in with perfect clarity, meeting her gaze. "I take *you* seriously, Clara."

His words seemed to take her aback. She swallowed, biting her lower lip before releasing it. "Sometimes, I'm not certain that you do. Sometimes, I feel as if I'm your entertainment. A joke you keep to yourself."

How little she must think of him to feel that way. Emotions were not his forte, not for some time. Feeling anything at all had become as foreign to him as that land she called home. But he didn't wish for her to misunderstand. Julian took everything about her as seriously as he had ever taken anything in his dissolute life.

He sat up and swung his feet to the floor, mustering his strength. "You're anything but a joke to me, little dove. If I laugh at anyone, it's myself."

For she made him weak. Weaker than blood loss or a blow to the head. She made him long for her. She'd captivated him and held him in her thrall from the moment she'd stepped into his dark world.

He braced his hands on the bed to leverage himself into a standing position. But she was quicker than he, flying to him and staying him with palms pressed to his shoulders. Her face hovered over his, undisguised worry hardening the soft planes.

"Please. You must rest." Her tone was gentle, cajoling.

He could almost believe she cared. Damn it, he needed to believe she cared.

"What am I to you that you should so concern yourself with whether or not I heal?" He shouldn't ask, shouldn't press her for more than she'd already given, but he was a greedy bastard. He wanted to hear it from her lips. If she wanted to be his wife in every way, there would be no more barriers between them.

She startled him by caressing his jaw. Just a fleeting swipe of her fingers over his skin before she placed her hand back on his shoulder. She treated him as if he were a wild creature she didn't dare trust to pet for longer than a moment.

"You're my husband."

Her dulcet admission undid him. His cock surged against his trousers at the combination of her small surrender and her touch both, his ballocks tightening. But he would not attempt to bed her now, not when he was weak and couldn't take his time and bring her the sort of prolonged pleasure she deserved. When the time was right, he would lay siege, batter down her every defense.

"Yes I bloody well am. I'll not let you forget it." His voice was gruff and low with suppressed desire.

"I'm not likely to forget." She pushed gently at his shoulders. "Now have a care for your wellbeing. You need to rest, and you need some sustenance. At least a bit."

He allowed her to guide him back into the mound of pillows she'd arranged for him. He doubted she realized that her ministrations put the temptation of her beautiful bosom practically at eye level. The urge to press his face into the seductive swell was strong, but he rallied his self-control and refrained.

"I don't want breakfast." He settled for resting his hands on her waist. "Come, sit with me, won't you?"

She eyed him warily. "I don't think a man in your condition ought to…"

Her words trailed off, a sweet pink flush staining her high cheekbones. Damn, but she truly was an innocent. An innocent that he would happily debauch at the first possible opportunity now that she was his.

"You needn't worry on that account," he assured her. "When I bed you, it will be with my full strength. I merely want your company now."

She hesitated, perhaps weighing her options. Or how much she trusted him against how black a reputation he possessed. "Won't you eat something first, my lord? And then I shall sit with you to your heart's content."

If she was attempting to rout him, she would have to try harder than that. He had the determination of an entire army when sufficiently motivated. And Clara was certainly ample motivation. But he excelled at games of chance, and he knew sometimes a risk predicated a great reward.

And so he capitulated, releasing her. "What would you have me eat, love? Not the *oeufs cocottes*, if you please. The mere notion of eggs makes the bile rise in my throat."

She straightened and stepped away from him with a swiftness that suggested she wasn't as unaffected as she pretended. Her aquamarine morning skirt swished as she strode to examine the contents of the tray. "Perhaps some Bayonne ham and some bread would be more the thing, then? Would you care for tea as well?"

Some devil within him toyed with the notion of asking her to feed it to him, but he knew he didn't dare press his luck. No one had ever waited upon him in such a manner who wasn't a servant. The ladies of his past acquaintance would never have dreamed of taking on such a role, as it would have been beneath them. Likely, Clara's equanimity was down to her American origins. Lesser women would have fled from the sight of a bleeding man. Lesser women would have fainted, called for a servant. Lesser women would never have shown the undeserved dedication she gave him now.

His appreciation for her grew by the second. "That will be sufficient," he said through a throat gone suddenly thick with an emotion he didn't care to question.

Silence descended upon the chamber as she removed the unwanted eggs, kidneys, and whatever else had been sent up, placing all on the table with care. At last, she lifted the tray and turned back to him. He studied the symmetry of her face and thought she would make a fine muse for an artist. Hers was a rare brand of beauty, the classical blended with the original. Cupid's bow lips and blue eyes set apart by a decadent fringe of lashes, cheekbones exotic slashes. Her forehead was high, that errant eyebrow of hers a mark of endearment.

She placed the tray gently upon his lap. "Here you are, my lord."

No, he was having none of that. His hands closed over

hers on the handles of the silver tray. "Julian."

Her gaze met his then, and he felt as if a spark settled deep into his gut. "Julian."

He smiled, liking the way his name sounded in her drawl, wilder and more lush than it had ever sounded upon anyone else's tongue. The dizziness was mercifully absent. Even the aching in his head had lessened. He released her again although the loss of touching her left him momentarily bereft.

But he was determined not to rush or press her. She would be worth the wait. "Sit with me, Clara?"

Her lips pressed together for a beat, and he feared she'd deny him. But then she nodded. "Of course." She grabbed fistfuls of her skirts and hiked them up before sidling on his bed rump first.

The act was not meant to be sexual in the least, but his cock hadn't softened since the bloody hall. Watching her scoot toward him made him even harder. She was very much in his territory now, on his bed at his side. Her musky orange scent enveloped him. As she slid her legs on the bed, he caught a glimpse of her trim, stocking-clad ankles and calves.

She attempted to settle herself with prim decorum at a safe distance from him but wound up being drawn closer by the sheer mechanics of his larger body sinking deeper into the bed. Soft, warm, delicious-smelling woman pressed to his side.

Ah, perfection.

"Forgive my lack of grace, if you please." She glanced at him, cheeks tinged more red now than ever. The growling of her stomach punctuated her apology with comical timing.

He recalled that when he'd come upon her earlier, she'd been inundated with questions from his irrepressible sisters. She had yet to break her fast. She must be starving. And yet she'd not had a care for herself. Only for him.

Julian's arm went around her waist, hauling her even closer. His hip brushed hers, the only barrier inhibiting him the crinoline cage that gave her skirts their fashionable shape. "You must be famished. Share breakfast with me. There's enough here to feed a family."

In anticipation of Clara's arrival at his home, he'd hired the best cook he could find. The fellow was French and damned expensive, but worth the price. Along with Julian's careful decoration of her chamber, it was the only expenditure he'd approved since signing the marriage contract that guaranteed him a tidy fortune. Using the funds hadn't felt right. Not, at least, until Clara would reap their benefits as well.

"It is you who concerns me now, my lord." She pressed a fork into his hand. "You need sustenance."

The chamber swirled about him in an eerie dance just then, giving credence to her words. He was still weak. His mind still jumbled. His fingers tightened over the hilt of the fork. Yes, perhaps she was right, this persistent American wife of his, and he ought to eat after all. He'd need his strength if he was going to discover precisely who the hell it was that wanted him dead.

"LADY RAVENSCROFT."

Clara looked up from the characters for domestics she'd been poring over, still startled to find herself the object of address. Whenever she heard *Lady Ravenscroft*, she half expected someone else to take her place. Someone who'd been born and raised to the position of countess. A true lady, of noble blood, rather than a native Virginian with a rebellious streak a country mile wide.

Five days wasn't long enough to grow accustomed to all the abruptly altered facets of her situation. Five days of being patient yet firm with Julian's sisters. Of contending with the badly needed refurbishing of his home, of fretting over his injuries, of taking her wifely duties to heart.

Osgood stood on the threshold of the drawing room, his face an expressionless mask. Though the rest of Ravenscroft's staff seemed dubious at best, his butler at least remained a bulwark of old world dignity.

She smiled at him now. His assistance over the last few days was an immeasurable source of comfort to her as she grappled with her newfound role. "Yes, Osgood?"

"His lordship requests the courtesy of your presence, my

lady."

The mere mentioning of the earl kindled a languorous slide of heat through her entire being. They'd spent a great deal of time together as he convalesced and she rather enjoyed her husband's company. He'd taught her to play *vingt-et-un* and told her bawdy jokes that made her cheeks flame. He'd listened with rapt attention to her stories of growing up in Virginia and her dream of founding a group dedicated to women gaining the vote. She'd yet to see him this morning, caught up as she'd been in household matters.

She'd missed him, and the sudden realization bemused her.

"Where may I find him, Osgood?"

The butler remained impervious to her good cheer. His expression was impassive. "His lordship may be found in his chamber, my lady."

One day, she vowed, she'd wring a smile from him. Surely he was capable of levity the same as anyone else. She suspected that his disapproval stemmed from her unsolicited evening call and the resulting mayhem of her father tearing through the earl's home brandishing a weapon. There was also the matter of the attempt on Ravenscroft's life. Yesterday, she'd sworn she spied a glimpse of suspicion lurking in Osgood's dark gaze.

But his suspicions were most assuredly being cast in the wrong direction. The attack on the earl had occupied her thoughts with the heaviness of iron weights. She'd already begun keeping a mental tally of who might have been responsible. For some reason, her mind kept returning to the Duchess of Argylle with fierce persistence.

"Thank you, Osgood." She gathered up the characters, deciding to bring them along with her so that she could continue her work while entertaining Ravenscroft in whatever madness he delighted in for the day.

As she took her leave of the drawing room and made for the hall, her mind flitted back—as it invariably seemed to do of late—to her husband. She knew so little of him and yet he had overtaken her thoughts just as he'd overtaken her world. It scarcely seemed real to her that she'd agreed to be his wife in truth. He'd caught her at a weak moment with his demand that she choose between Virginia and him. Staring at him, still shaken with the knowledge that he could have died, how could she have made any other decision?

But he was still a stranger to her, a mystery. And she couldn't shake the feeling that he held himself apart from her, that he was a man of many faces who merely donned whichever one suited his mood or his desires for the moment. What she did know was that he fast grew impatient with his recovery.

He didn't play the role of invalid with grace, but she was gratified that he'd remained at home, where he was as safe as he could be. Oh, he grumbled and demanded a change of scenery on a regular basis. And so she accompanied him to his study or to the library, all the while taking note of whether or not he faltered or lost his balance. Yesterday had been the first day that she'd not seen a single sign of weakness or dizziness. Even his wound appeared to be healing nicely and was no longer in need of a bandage. With his full head of dark hair, the injury was scarcely noticeable now.

As she stopped outside his chamber door, she knew a moment of unease as she contemplated that. Ravenscroft in his weakened state was rather like a caged tiger. He could be seen and admired, but he wasn't capable of doing injury. Ravenscroft at full strength was another matter entirely. The mere notion made her knees want to give out.

"Enter," called his familiar, rich voice at her knock.

A shiver of awareness danced through her as she opened the door and stepped back into his territory. He wasn't on the bed where she'd expected to find him. Instead, he sat on a chair by the hearth, clad in nothing but a dressing gown. She felt the force of his gaze like a caress. The door clicked closed at her back. Too late to flee now.

She clutched the characters to her breast as though their

mere paper and ink could form a protective shield. He was eying her as though he wanted to consume her. "Good morning, my lord."

Far easier, she found, to remain formal and impersonal when he was at his most tempting.

He stood and offered her a flawless bow, which should have been rendered ridiculous by his lack of dress but somehow made an unwanted warmth steal into her belly. He seemed as if he were truly on the mend, thank the Lord. But his recuperation also held untold ramifications for her. Ramifications that were simultaneously frightening, wicked, and altogether tempting.

"Julian," he reminded her.

How was it that each day she saw him he seemed to somehow be more handsome than the last? Looking upon him stole her breath and did strange things to her pulse. His bare calves and feet peeked from beneath the hem of his robe as he strode to her. Nary a hint of weakness today. Not a pause. Not a sway. No indeed. This morning, he was pure, seductive intention. How was it possible for a man to move with such elegance, such easy, carnal grace? She couldn't stop staring at him.

Clara took a breath, marshaled her thoughts into a semblance of order. "Osgood said that you sent for me."

"Yes I did." He didn't stop until he was near enough to touch her. And touch her he did. Nothing overtly seductive. Just a mere glance of his index finger over the characters she still held clutched to her bodice. "What's this, little dove?"

His vivid gaze held fast to her mouth. "Characters," she blurted.

"Ah, the search for domestics continues." He cocked his head, considering her. "Have you ever hired servants before?"

Of course she hadn't. She had gone from her mother's home straight to her father's. Someone else had always taken charge of the household. But she'd never backed down from a challenge and she didn't intend to do so now.

"Do you not think me capable of hiring proper staff?"

He considered her, his regard slow and thorough and so intense that she couldn't help but feel it as intimately as any caress. "I think you more than capable. You continue to surprise me, Clara."

She wondered if he meant that as a compliment and decided to accept it as such. "Thank you."

He gave her a rare smile, and she felt it all the way to her toes. His smile transformed his already gorgeous features, somehow rendering him even more irresistible. It stole some of the lines of worry from his face, abated the darkness in his eyes. Of course, he had cause for the worry and darkness. Someone had tried to kill him. No matter how devilishly handsome he was, no matter how tempting his presence and sensual gazes, she couldn't forget that disquieting fact.

"You're most welcome." He reached for the characters then, catching the sheaf of papers in his long fingers. His other hand circled her wrist in a firm but demanding clasp. "Let's leave off the characters for today, though, shall we?"

"But my lord, you haven't a housekeeper." She felt obliged—as a woman of reason and the new lady of the household both—to point out the failings of his staff. "I've had it from the Cook that his kitchen is woefully inadequate. You're in need of at least half a dozen maids and just as many footmen."

He shrugged with studied indifference. "I don't give a damn about the servants at the moment."

Some stubborn part of her refused to relinquish the characters to him. Her fingers clenched on them with determination. "But you ought to, Julian. Your household is in dire need of proper, well-trained servants. You must realize your sisters should not be subjected to the presence of servants who are so depraved that they engage in relations in your library."

His smile deepened. "And you must realize my sisters are not like most well-bred young ladies? You've spoken with them, yes? Their parents were sinners. Their brother is the worst sinner of them all."

Yes, Lady Josephine and Lady Alexandra were undeniably different from every other aristocratic young lady she'd ever met, with the possible exception of her best friend Bo. But the reminder of Ravenscroft's past sins didn't sit well with her. It made all the muscles in her body tighten, as if in anticipation of a blow. What was that other, foreign sensation swirling within her? Certainly not jealousy? Definitely not possessiveness.

For he was not truly hers.

Nor was she his.

They were two people bound by an odd concoction of duplicity and necessity, of needs and wants, danger and longing. There was no love between them. Nothing but desire.

But she didn't like the derision that always colored his tone when he spoke of his past. He was so much more than the sum total of the things he'd done. "You mustn't speak ill of yourself. I won't allow it."

His thumb rubbed a slow, delicious circle on her inner wrist. Sparks of heat shot up her arm and radiated throughout her body. "What *will* you allow, little dove?"

Everything, some wanton part of her wanted to say. Her breath froze for a beat, a scorching wash of heat flooding her. The sensitive flesh between her thighs where he'd once stroked her ached. And she knew instantly what he was about. He finally meant to claim her.

Belatedly, she realized she'd released the characters to him. That was how much power he could wield over her. He made her give in, and she didn't even notice until he was carefully placing his spoils upon a nearby table. "Why did you call for me, Julian?"

The flippancy leached from his expression, replaced by concentrated solemnity. "You don't think I called you here to read over the references for chamber maids, do you, love?"

No. Of course she didn't. But that didn't mean she was prepared for the consummation of their marriage. When she'd told him she would be his wife in truth, she'd been weak, her heart and mind a confused jumble. He'd been wounded. He hadn't been strong and leonine and half-dressed, gazing at her as if he could already see her naked before him.

She needed time. She needed space. She needed to leave the chamber and put the safety of a locked door between them. Her heart pounded against her breast. He hadn't even touched her beyond the maddening circling of his thumb, and already she was about to fly out of her skin.

"It's too soon," she protested.

His lips quirked. His other hand came to rest on her waist. "You needn't be nervous with me, little dove."

Was he mad? Of course she needed to be nervous. No man in her acquaintance had ever been able to wear down her defenses—to storm her battlements and overtake her castle—the way he did. And with an effortless ennui that suggested everything was a game to him.

She had to dissuade him. Surely this sort of thing was commonly done in the dark. "It's the morning."

He hauled her up against him in one quick tug, crushing her breasts to his hard chest. "So it is."

Her hands flitted to his shoulders, disarmingly broad and strong. "Your sisters."

His lips were so near that they almost brushed hers. "The bloody minxes are amply entertained for the day. I've arranged for them to go shopping with my elderly dragon of a great aunt. She disapproves of me most wholeheartedly but she approves of your fortune a great deal, as it turns out."

His dry pronouncement wrung a reluctant laugh from her. She didn't want to find humor in anything he said. Didn't want to soften toward him. Didn't want to allow him to make her any weaker than he already had. But wasn't that the way things had been between them from the start? He'd been able to undo her from the moment she'd stepped foot in his study. Nothing had changed except that she was now his wife. Not just in name only, for she'd agreed to more. She'd agreed to everything.

And she wanted everything. But she was also terrified of it.

"It's not my fortune any longer," she forced herself to say. There was comfort and familiarity in dialogue. Perhaps she could distract him. Perhaps she could distract herself. "It's yours now."

"It's ours." His tone was as gentle as his touch as he swept a stray wisp of hair from her cheek. "We'll build a life together, Clara. Starting today."

A life together.

How odd to hear those words coming from a hardened rake such as he. At times tender, at times scorching in his sensuality, he never failed to surprise her. But while his pronouncement may have otherwise met with cautious pleasure, they also served as a reminder that his life had recently nearly been taken. The thought chilled her as nothing else could.

She searched his fathomless gaze. "Have you forgotten that someone tried to kill you, my lord?"

He cupped her cheek, rubbing the pad of his thumb slowly over her lower lip's fullness. "Julian. There's no need for formality between us any longer."

His touch stirred a hunger within her, a blossoming ache between her thighs. She steeled herself against both. "Do you seek to distract me? You cannot believe your attentions will make me forget the grim realities we face."

"I find distraction is what I need the most just now." He traced the seam of her lips, his eyes dropping to her mouth as though it contained a secret he dearly longed to decipher. Once, twice, three times. He pressed the tip of his thumb inside her mouth, and she tasted him, salty and warm and inviting. "Can it be so grim if I'm still here, little dove?"

She nipped him, not enough to do injury, but enough to

demonstrate that she wouldn't be so easily swayed. He withdrew, bringing his thumb to his own mouth. She watched its progress, her gaze lingering on his sensual lips. So finely formed, so beautiful in their masculine perfection. He sucked his thumb for just an instant, as though tasting her, before releasing it. His eyes never left hers.

Good Lord. She wanted that mouth on her. Once, he'd told her to think of where she'd like his tongue. And she knew it now with alarming clarity. Desire unfurled within her, warm and slow and delicious.

Everywhere. She wanted his tongue to travel over every part of her body. Anywhere he chose.

But she wasn't about to tell him any of that. Good heavens, she was a lady, after all. Or at the least, her father had attempted to fashion her into one. Best to think of safer subjects. What had Ravenscroft said? Ah, yes. Their reality couldn't be so grim since he'd survived the attempt on his life.

"I'm grateful you're still here," she admitted. Knowing how close he'd come to death still shook her. He was such a big man, tall and strong, alive with energy and wit and wickedness. How could anyone dare to attempt to take him away? She needed him, and the realization simultaneously appalled and thrilled her. "But we must find out who orchestrated the attack on you. If you'll take nothing else seriously, I hope you'll at least consider your own life with the gravity it deserves."

He cocked his head, considering her. One of his hands remained on her waist, hot and possessive. The other settled on her shoulder, splaying over her collarbone, his touch as light as a butterfly. "I assure you that I have no intention of an imminent demise."

How exasperating. He could not think himself omnipotent and immortal both? "Am I meant to take heart in that? Because if I am, you're destined for disappointment. I don't think your intentions have any bearing on the matter. Someone wishes you ill, and from the severity of the attack,

I've no doubt he will try it again. You must be prepared."

He trailed a path of fire to the hollow at the base of her throat. His middle finger stroked her there with effortless seduction. Fire shot through her entire, traitorous body. "Ah, my fierce, sweet wife. I've no need for your pistol. We've already been down this road."

Yes, they had. And she'd had plenty of time to consider a course of action over the last few days. She was no society miss, no bland and sheltered English lady who'd never known a day of true suffering in her life. She'd been raised in the barren landscape of a homeland ravaged by civil war. She knew how to protect herself. Indeed, she knew how to protect him, and she would if need be. His pride be damned.

Clara shook her head, trying to ignore the way his roving hand made her feel—weak and jittery and longing for something she couldn't yet define. "You need your own pistol. I'm a crack shot. I could take a man down before he even knew what happened. I'll not part with my weapon. But you need to be armed at all times. You also need to travel with a trusted coterie of armed servants."

"All excellent suggestions, love." He found the first button on her bodice, the tiny shell disc hidden in the high collar of her smart aubergine morning gown, and effortlessly plucked it from its moorings. His index finger traced a path down the flowered brocade trim that artfully hid the remainder of her buttons from view. "But at the moment, I must confess, I'm far more interested in taking my wife to bed."

His pronouncement sucked all the air from the chamber. She was suddenly hyperaware of her surroundings, her every sense alert. Her mind whirled, grasping at any excuse to ward him off. She wasn't ready. Not for him. Not for this. Not yet. "Your injury, my lord."

"Healing." He made short work of the next few buttons. "I find myself with more than enough strength for the task. And it's Julian, little dove. No more formality if you please. After today, there will be no other man you know better."

The notion thrilled her. A fresh wave of heat bloomed from the very core of her, stretching out across her body like the ripples from a pebble in a still body of water. All he required was words and a molten stare to transform her. She wanted to become familiar with every inch of his hard, masculine form. The urge to see him stripped of his dressing robe seized her.

Something inside her broke. Her hands rose to frame his face, and she watched as if they belonged to another. Only the tantalizing abrasion of the whiskers shading his jaw told her the hands were hers. She touched him freely, as she'd wanted to do even before she'd ever spoken a word to him.

Her fingers traveled everywhere, all over his handsome face, from his high cheekbones to his angular jaw, lingering over his sculpted mouth and perfectly defined philtrum. Such raw magnetism, such undeniable beauty confined in one man. She touched him as though she could absorb him, understand him somehow with this tactile familiarity.

Her inner resolve bordered perilously on the razor's edge of surrender. One smoldering look from him, one more undone button, a ghost of a kiss, and she'd shatter. But the devil of it was that she wanted to. He made her want to experience the impossible, the forbidden. Yes, all of it. All of him.

Her index finger lingered over that faultless indentation on his upper lip, almost as though she sought to quiet him. "Julian."

His mouth quirked into a knowing, wicked grin that she felt first with her finger before it echoed through the rest of her. That dark, intense gaze of his was upon her, refusing to allow her to look anywhere else. Not that she would. There was no other sight in the world that she currently wanted to see.

He licked her. Slowly and deliberately. Up and down, firm and wanton, his tongue teased the pad of her finger. Strange how her entire body could center on the smallest point of contact. Just a finger. Barely a connection. And yet, she felt his tongue as though he plied it upon the most intimate of all her flesh.

That tongue told her what he could do to the rest of her. What he would do, as long as she remained precisely where she was, trapped in the web of desire and his penetrating stare.

Merciful heavens.

What had she done, agreeing to this? He wasn't a mere man. He was a force. A wicked seducer. A man who had dedicated his life to giving pleasure. A sybarite. A rake. A rattler. The man who had betrayed her trust.

And yet he was also himself. The man who made her feel what she'd never imagined existed. A man who listened when she spoke. A man who respected her and wanted her. He was not Ravenscroft in this moment. No, he was her own. Purely, completely, hers.

"Julian," she said again, and she wasn't certain if she uttered his name as a protest or as an encouragement. For she was equally torn between wanting him and fearing the power he had over her.

"Clara. I want you more than I ever imagined possible. Today, I'm your servant. Anything you wish, I'll do it." He kissed her fingertip with a reverence that hit her square in the chest. The last of her defenses against him crumbled. Nothing remained but her deep, abiding need for him.

Of course, she should have told him all she wanted was to leave his chamber. To flee him and the unwanted complications wrought by the things he did to her. But the truth of it was that she didn't want to leave him. Didn't want to leave his chamber. If he was well enough—and he certainly seemed so as she eyed him now—then she wanted him to take her. Though the prospect simultaneously thrilled and terrified her, it was what she longed for most.

Perhaps the time had come to be brutally honest with herself. She'd found her weakness at long last, and it was a beautiful, dark-haired, blue-eyed, silver-tongued English rake who viewed the world as his private amusement and could make her body weak with a mere look.

He caught her right hand and lowered it to his hard chest, slipping it beneath his dressing gown so that her bare flesh connected with his. He didn't stop until her palm flattened over his thumping heart.

Beat. Beat. Beat.

So steady, so reassuring. The skin beneath hers, however, was anything but reassuring. His crisp chest hairs teased her senses. His scent, masculine and spiced with his fine French cologne—a blend that was innately his—enveloped her. The slab of muscle beneath her touch flexed. His heat seared her. She never wanted to let go.

"Tell me," he said, his tone maddening, another delicious assault on her senses. "Tell me what you want."

She didn't even know. Didn't know how to give voice to the pulsing, aching need he'd brought to life within her. He was the experienced one. Shouldn't he know what she wanted? "I…" she faltered, not knowing what to say. All the suggestions that clamored to mind seemed far too improper. Far too unwise. "My lord, please."

But he was determined to be wicked, it seemed. He found her waist, caressing her there when she would have preferred his attention elsewhere. Of course he must know it, rake that he was.

His face hovered close, so beautiful and arresting, his mouth perilously near to hers. "Where do you ache, darling?"

She went crimson, her cheeks as hot as if they'd been touched with live coals. "You know."

"I want to hear it from you, little dove." He leaned into her, pressing the length of his body to hers. The protrusion of his arousal, obvious beneath the thin layer of his dressing gown, sank into her skirts. She could almost feel him prodding her center, and it took her breath. "Tell me where."

Did she dare? He was her husband. It was all very proper. She'd agreed to be his wife, fool that she was, even after he'd misled her. She'd agreed to all this, to everything. And worse, she longed for it. Yes, of course she dared, for she was just as wild and dark, as brazen and roguish on the inside as he was on the outside. It was only that she realized the wickedness of her own nature now for the first time. Perhaps he had well and truly debauched her. Perhaps she'd always been so flawed. She couldn't be sure.

Clara took the palm that wasn't flattened to the sinful lure of his broad chest and snagged his hand. Without sparing a thought for consequence, she slid that large, warm hand straight past the buttons on her bodice that he'd undone. Farther, even, beneath her corset cover, corset, and finally her shift. Until his hand curved around the fullness of her breast. Her nipple hardened into his palm.

She arched into him, never breaking his gaze. "There."

He caught the sensitized nub between his thumb and finger, not wasting a breath of time. Leisurely, he rolled and pinched. "An excellent place to begin, love."

And then his mouth lowered over hers. He fitted his lower lip between hers perfectly, the kiss slow and delicious, as though he had forever to savor her, as though he drank her like a rare wine. She kissed him back then, as if prodded into action for the first time. She didn't want slow and languorous. She wanted fast and steady, a determined claiming, a fierce joining. She wanted him to make her his in every way possible.

Clara caught his lip between her teeth. She felt suddenly ravenous, as untamed and unpredictable as the man whose heart thudded beneath her inquisitive palm. She reached behind her to capture his other hand, tugging it from her hair. Dragging it between their straining bodies, she pressed it to the part of her that begged for him the most. They were separated by her crinoline and layers of fabric, but it was a mimicry of the way he'd touched her in the brougham the morning of their wedding. Perhaps he would appreciate the significance.

"And here," she said into his mouth.

Good God.

He was nearly out of his skin. Her scent wrapped around him, orange and musk and everything delicious. Everything that was wonderfully, innately her. Clara. Wife. His. She was all those things encompassed in the finest, loveliest form he'd ever seen.

Julian had fucked more women in his life than he could count or remember. No one had ever made him feel the way he did now with her lush, beautiful innocence within his reach. Every part of her was perfection, from the sweet curve of her breast in his palm, to the fullness of her lips opening beneath his, to the sharp nip of her teeth. Her palm remained flattened to his chest, absorbing the frantic beats of his heart. She undid him, and he was helpless to stop the power she wielded.

Hell, he didn't want to. She unleashed a savage side of him, a side he hadn't realized until this moment that he possessed. He'd always been in control. He'd been the detached seducer, his skills honed from years of plying his trade. He knew how to make a woman come. He knew how to make her whimper and writhe beneath him, to prolong her pleasure and build her inevitable release into a shattering, beautiful thing.

But Clara was different. She stripped away every artifice, everything he'd believed about himself. All the games he would have played with her fled him. The blood rushed to his cock, lust roaring through him. This would not be the unhurried, controlled lovemaking he'd imagined the many times he'd envisioned in his debauched mind.

No.

This would be unrestrained fucking.

He would lose himself inside her, and he would relish the claiming.

But he would not hurt her, nor would he make her first

time anything but as pleasurable as he knew how. He reminded himself that she was an untried virgin as he ground the heel of his palm into her skirts at her urging, seeking the very heart of her that he so longed to possess. Her dress was an unwanted impediment. He longed for nothing more than her naked and spread out before him, no fabric, boning, caging, or padding between them.

He kissed her again, full and deep and plundering, a mimicry of the way he would take her. And then he broke away, gazing down on the sheer loveliness of her rounded face. Her golden hair may as well have been a halo surrounding her goodness, her blue eyes heavy-lidded with desire, her rosebud lips swelled and darkened berry-red with his kiss. She flushed a pretty pink to rival the most glorious summer rose. Even the freckles dotting her nose entranced him.

"Here?" he asked, pressing deeper into the billowing contours of her gown, wanting hot, wet flesh rather than silk. He would run his tongue over every last bit of her delectable body once he had her out of these blasted trappings.

"Yes." The single-word response hissed from her lips, telling him just how much he affected her.

Good, for she made him feel like a callow youth about to spend on the petticoats of the first woman he'd ever kissed. Those freckles of hers would drive him mad. His head had begun to pound, and he couldn't be sure if it was from pent-up desire or the remnants of his injury, but he didn't give a damn. He wasn't about to allow anything to come between him and the fiery woman who'd haunted him since she'd first appeared in his study, asking him to marry her.

Her boldness, her fearlessness, had drawn him to her then. And it was those twin attributes that drew him to her now. She didn't retreat from him. Though her flaming cheeks gave her away for the innocent she was, she didn't hesitate. She wanted this joining every bit as much as he.

Julian kissed her again, plucking at her responsive nipple and pressing ever deeper into her skirts before he withdrew entirely, standing back to survey her. She was as beautiful as he'd ever seen her in a lush creation of silk, her expression glazed with passion, bodice deliciously askew. It occurred to him that he was scarcely clothed while she was as properly dressed as though she awaited a bevy of callers during her receiving hours. Most unfair, that.

A dark urge rose up within him. He'd never wanted another woman with the all-consuming hunger that spurred him now. As undeniably lovely as she was in her French gown, he wanted it off her. "Disrobe for me, little dove."

Her eyes widened, a hand fluttering to her throat, the only evidence of her unease. "My lord?"

"Julian." He wanted to hear his name on her lips, in the mellifluous drawl she didn't bother to mask in his presence. It soothed his soul and made his cock ache at the same time. The devil of a thing. "You heard me, love. Remove your dress."

She hesitated, looking adorably uncertain. "Julian then. I'm…unaccustomed to disrobing myself, and this dress is rather complicated in construction. Perhaps we ought to wait until later. The evening? Another day? I do believe I saw you wince as though your head—"

"Come now," he interrupted, equal parts charmed and amused by her nervous attempt to procrastinate. "A Virginia lady such as yourself, one who can shoot and bluster, one who can infiltrate the study of an earl at midnight, one who tramps about London on her own wielding a pistol in her reticule, surely a lady such as this can manage to remove a mere gown on her own. Yes?"

He was testing her and the spark in her eyes said she knew it. Her gaze clung to his, her chin tipping up in her trademark show of defiance. "Of course I can. But your injury. It's too soon. You did seem to be in some pain."

"My injury is almost fully healed, fully recovered." A lie, but he didn't particularly give a damn about such a minor falsehood at the moment. “Perhaps I mistook your daring, then.”

If he’d learned anything about his new wife, it was that she never wanted to be seen as weak. Long ago, he’d mastered the art of using a woman’s weaknesses against her. It was how he’d managed to carry on for so long as he had. One of the many roles he’d been forced to play.

Only, he wasn’t playing a role now. He was hers. She was his.

“Take it off me.”

Her demand, as sudden and unexpected as it was arousing, took him aback. He stared at her, just narrowly refraining from catching her up in his arms and tearing her dress away like a ravaging beast. Gentle, he reminded himself. He would be gentle. He would take the greatest care with her. For she deserved that and so much more.

But the moment he touched the remainder of the buttons fastening her bodice, his good intentions shattered. He caught the gaping vee of her dismantled décolletage in both his hands and yanked. A shower of buttons rained to the carpet, mingling with her startled gasp.

“As you wish, little dove.” Her beautiful dress hung limply apart, revealing her embroidered corset cover. The sleeves were damned tight, clinging to her shoulders in an impediment he grew impatient to banish. He pulled again, and this time the sound of rending fabric filled the air. The sleeves went down at last, revealing soft porcelain flesh. Jesus, even her arms were beautiful, curved and feminine. He fought back the absurd desire to kiss the hinge of her elbow, to lick a path all the way to her shoulder. Her scent, bright and musky, filled his senses, even more potent now that so much of her gorgeous skin was revealed to him.

He wondered if she tasted as sweet as she smelled everywhere. Behind her knee? Her belly? The roundness of her thighs? Fuck, he had to know. Blood roared through his head, a river of lust pouring over his body, threatening to engulf him.

Dimly, he registered her protest.

"Lord Ravenscroft, you've ruined my new gown."

What an intriguing moment for her to once again revert to polite formality. She was nervous, his little dove, her eyes wide. Perhaps she feared he'd take her as roughly as he'd stripped away half of her dress. He ought to reassure her, but any civility he pretended to possess had utterly fled him.

"You required me to take it off you." The damn thing was still fastened tightly at her waist. He ripped a few more buttons and hooks, locating the ties of her crinoline and undoing them with scarcely more finesse. Down went her skirts, bodice, and dress shaper, landing in a muted swoosh around her feet. But it wasn't enough. More fabric fell to the floor until she stood before him in only her corset, chemise, drawers, and stockings. He pulled her to him, cupping her face as gently as he could manage. "And so I obliged."

She sputtered. "I didn't tell you to ruin it, my lord."

Even her dudgeon sent another arrow of heat directly to his cock. "No more 'my lord,' love."

He kissed her then because he couldn't go another second without feeling her sweet, yielding mouth beneath his. She opened. He raked his teeth over the fullness of her bottom lip before sinking his tongue inside. So sweet. Sweeter than he deserved.

Every part of him hungered to take her. To tear off her drawers, drag her chemise to her waist, take her to the carpet, and sink inside her. But he wrangled his wayward impulses. His reputation and indeed his living had been built upon bed sport. His prowess was unparalleled. He took his time, made his lover's body sing with pleasure, relished in giving her what she'd paid for—the release no man before him had known or dared to give.

What was it about Clara that dragged him to the edge? What was it that made him want to rend and tear, to rut like a beast? To fill her with his cock and after that, with his seed? In an elemental sense she was no different than any other before her. She too had bought and paid for his services, after all, with her dowry and soon her virginity.

The thought cooled some of his ardor. He dragged his mouth from hers, kissed her jaw, her ear, ran his tongue over the defined whorl that nestled against her hair. An anomalous crudeness surged to life within him then, a need to shock her and perhaps shock even himself.

"Clara, sweet, innocent Clara," he whispered into her ear. "I'm going to fuck you. I'm going to strip every last bit of covering away from you. And then I'm going to taste you everywhere. I'm going to make you spend all over my tongue first. Then all over my cock."

His words should have sent her spinning away from him in retreat. Should have made her run, flee the chamber through the adjoining door to the safety of her own space. She was a maid, after all. Untried and pure aside from his own attempts to sway her to the darker side.

But instead she did something he least expected, his little dove. Her busy fingers, the fingers he'd watched on countless occasions fretting on the folds of her gown, discovered the knot keeping his dressing gown in place. And undid it. Then those fingers skated beneath the plackets of his robe, gliding over his bare chest with pure, unadulterated fire. Her nails grazed one of his nipples.

"Do it then, Julian." Her voice was deep and throaty, at once a taunt and a dare.

So bold, his Virginian. Such audacity. As his surprise dispersed, he could sense her bravado for what it was, but that didn't mean her actions and words didn't have their intended effect upon him. His cock was rigid, and he was desperate to bury himself inside her so deep and hard that they both lost every last splinter of control.

The thin thread of his restraint snapped. She was small and fine-boned, and when he hauled her into his arms he scarcely felt the weight of her. But perhaps too that could be attributed to the rush of desire coursing through him, rendering him all but mindless. Every part of her was curved and luscious. He buried his face in the fragrant curls piled atop her head as he stalked to his bed with her. He'd never again be capable of smelling the scent of orange without going hard.

But it didn't matter. Nothing mattered but her, the blazing passion scorching the air, and the steps between where he stood and his bed. Six, as it turned out. Barely any distance at all but he rued each step for it stole seconds from him. Seconds where he could be upon her, stripping the rest of her undergarments away, parting her thighs.

Patience fled him.

He laid her upon the bed and allowed his dressing gown to fall away from his body, leaving him naked for her brilliant gaze. He'd never seen a lovelier sight than Clara half-dressed, stockings hugging her shapely calves, her ripe breasts about to spill from the top of her corset, mouth swollen from his kiss, and her gaze traveling all over him like a touch.

The ability to speak deserted him. Every practiced, pretty word vanished from his brain. Here he was, a man who'd fashioned fucking into an art, laid low by an inexperienced scrap of a woman. But then, words weren't needed now anyway and his pride could bloody well go to the devil.

He joined her on the bed, and she reached for him, bringing him against her, holding him to her with a tenderness that undid him. He found her mouth, slanted his lips over hers, sank inside to drink in the dazzling wet heat of her. Sweet and delicious. He tore her corset cover away, his fingers tangling in the knot of her corset laces until it too was opened and gone. She helped him catch the hem of her chemise and shimmy it up over her body.

Finally. For the first time, he could see her glorious breasts unobstructed. No cloth hindrance now. Full and high, tipped with hard nipples as pink and inviting as her mouth. He lowered his head and took her into his mouth, sucking the peak, nipping it. A throaty moan wrung from her as her fingers tunneled into his hair, her nails raking his scalp.

Ah, Christ. She was a quick learner, his delectable tyro. He cupped her other breast, its yielding heaviness filling his palm as he rubbed the nipple with his thumb. His cock strained against the welcoming cradle of her cunny, reminding him he sought an even greater prize. He kissed his way down her creamy skin, his mouth learning the protrusion of her ribs, the curve of her waist, the hollow of her belly button. He pulled her drawers down over her hips, leaving her stockings in place, and pulled back to survey the bounty before him.

Pale thighs beckoned from above the wicked contrast of her black silk stockings. He swallowed as a fresh onslaught of lust careened through him.

At last, he could manage discourse. "Beautiful."

A lone word and a vast understatement, torn from him. He skimmed her smooth hips, her warmth seeping into his palms. She was so soft, so perfect, and he needed to have her. To taste her. Gently, he began guiding her legs apart.

"Julian." His Christian name again, a breathy drawl that sounded half rebuke, half plea. "You mustn't."

"I must." He kissed her hip bone, thinking there was not a single part of her body he didn't adore. "Relax, little dove." His hand curved over her knee, still covered in silk, and urged it down to the mattress. She allowed him this liberty, giving in to his coax as her legs fell apart.

His hungry gaze sought the pink, glistening flesh of her cunny before traveling over her entire form. She was spread before him in erotic abandon, not a hair out of place in her coiffure, clad in nothing but her black stockings. He could gaze upon her like this a thousand times and it still wouldn't be enough.

A strange heaviness shifted in his chest but he ignored it and bowed his head, worshipping her as she deserved. His tongue found the pearl of her pleasure. She tasted sweeter than he'd recalled from the brief hint in his carriage. Her hips jerked beneath him as he used his teeth. He soothed the nip with his tongue, gripped the swells of her arse in his palms, and angled her to him. His tongue played over her, seeking her wetness as though he could somehow take her in, consume her.

His balls tightened, warning him that it had indeed been too long since he'd had a woman. Though he wanted to prolong this torture for both of them, he wasn't going to come on her thigh like some callow lad. There would be more time for exploring her. A lifetime, unless the person who'd had him beaten senseless had his druthers.

A chill skittered over him as he kissed his way back up her body. He wouldn't allow ugliness to intrude on them now. This moment, this joining, was theirs alone. Battling demons could bloody well wait for another day. He kissed the place where her shoulder and throat met, dragged his mouth back to her ear. His fingers dipped into her slick, hot folds, building the pleasure he'd begun with his mouth into a crescendo.

"Spend for me, little dove," he said into her ear.

She clutched at his shoulders, her body writhing and twisting beneath his. He knew that she was close. He tongued the sensitive place behind her ear and she shattered, crying out, shaking with the power of her release. With his free hand, he delved into her immaculate hairstyle, plucking all the pins he could feel until her long curls fell to her shoulders, unimpeded and glorious.

"Yes, love," he whispered in encouragement when she began a tentative exploration of him. "Touch me. I'm yours."

Her touch feathered over his chest, down his back to his buttocks. She kissed his cheek, his clenched jaw, his hair. "Wicked man," she said against his throat. But there was no reproach in her tone. Only wonder mingled with desire.

He knew because he felt an echoing blend of the two himself, along with a fierce and unrepentant need to possess her. He couldn't wait any longer. He positioned himself between her thighs, pressing his rigid cock to her slick entrance. "It will hurt, little dove. Only the first time."

She shifted against him, bringing them closer together. "I'm yours," she said then, repeating his words to her.

And he broke. He thrust into her in one swift stroke, tearing past her barrier. Clara stiffened in his arms and cried out. It took every shred of self-control he possessed to hold still and allow her to adjust to this new invasion. The primal impulses inside him screamed to conquer. She was so damn tight and wet.

He kissed her then, plundering her mouth as he longed to the rest of her, before breaking away. "I'm sorry, love." Of course he never wanted to hurt her. He'd never taken a virgin before, hadn't been one himself in more years than he could recall. His body and his mind were at war.

"Don't be." She moved, drawing him deeper inside her. Her breath hitched, the only sign of her discomfort. "I want this."

Her reassurance was all he needed to hear. His hand caught in the heavy skeins of her hair, his fingers tightening instinctively, holding her still so that he could gaze down into her arresting beauty. He was no novice to fucking. Pretty nothings clamored in his mind, so many silver words he could string together and seduce her with. But as he sank deeper inside her tight sheath, his entire being splintered.

Suddenly, he was jagged fragments of himself. The old Julian, the experienced rake, the man who'd earned his keep by fucking his way through the *ton*, dissipated. All he was left with was what she'd fashioned him, a man desperate to claim the only woman he'd ever want.

So many wicked, seductive poetries he could have unleashed. And instead, only one word filled his mind as he thrust into her, giving in to a primitive urge. *Mine.* He tightened his grip on her hair, making certain she met his gaze, making certain she understood the finality of their union. There would not be a Virginia for her now, not unless they went together. Not from this moment forward. "Mine," he said.

She arched into him, her fingernails raking scorching lines up his back, then to his neck, before finally settling on his skull. Her fingers tightened in his hair, holding him in a mimicry of the way he held her. "Mine," she repeated back to him before leaning up on her elbows to close the distance between them. They kissed, open mouthed and mutually ravenous. She dropped her head back to the pillow, falling away from him, breathing heavy. "Mine."

Yes.

He was hers. Nothing had ever seemed so right or true. A growl in his throat, he took her mouth with his, just as he sank inside her soft, wet heat once more. Hard and fast and deep, he went, and then he did the one thing he'd never done with another woman before. He spent inside her.

Chapter Twelve

HE STRODE DOWN THE HALL, AWAY FROM HER, and a hollowness filled her breast. The grim disquiet of mourning infected her. She felt for a moment as if she watched his funeral procession, as though this was the last time she'd ever see him. And she couldn't see his beautiful face, that wicked smile, the knowing light in his eyes. She didn't even have so much as a lock of his hair to remember him by.

He couldn't leave. Not now. Not ever. Her hands groped toward him but her body felt strangely heavy, as though her arms were held down by half a dozen unseen hands. Her legs too were stymied by something. She looked down for a moment to find her skirts sinking into brackish water. The hallway had turned into a sea.

Julian floated away from her, effortlessly gliding into the far shadows while she remained trapped, unable to follow. She tried to call out to him, but no sound emerged from her mouth.

Julian, she wanted to say. Julian, wait!

But all that left her lips was an animalistic noise of fear. Desperation coursed through her. He was leaving her, headed straight into the dark web of the dangers that had already attempted to claim him.

To kill him.

But she would not allow him to die. By sheer force of will, she escaped from the rushing sea waters, and they receded abruptly, giving way once more to the hall and its familiar, threadbare carpet. She gathered her soaked skirts in her arms and ran to him, attempting to stay his progress, to keep him safe. Finally, he was within reach. Her hands clawed through the air but she couldn't touch him. She watched in horror as he pitched forward.

He tumbled down the curved staircase, end over end. Horror stole her breath. She tried to scream as she chased down the steps after him. His descent was too quick, and she too slow. By the time she reached him, he lay in a crumpled heap at the bottom of the stairs.

No! She clutched at him. There was so much blood. Everywhere. Red and copper-scented just as she remembered, hot and sticky on her hands. My God. It couldn't be. She couldn't bear it…

Clara woke with a start, disoriented, a terrified scream strangling her throat.

"Clara?" Julian's low voice, gentle with concern, pierced the haze of half-wakefulness muddling her mind.

Sweet relief washed over her. It had all been a horrible nightmare. Awareness pierced the panic that immobilized her. He was safe, thank God. Alive and warm and here with her, his big body radiating heat into hers beneath the bedcoverings. Her hands fluttered to his broad shoulders, clutching him. Vital and real and more handsome than ever.

It occurred to her then that neither of them wore a stitch of clothing, their naked skins pressing together. The realization dashed some of her shock away, replacing it with remembrance of the wicked things he'd done to her. She drank in the sight of him, feeling simultaneously hot and cold. Cold from the awful dream. Hot from the man hovering over her.

He cupped her face and swept an errant curl from her brow. "Was it a nightmare, little dove?"

"Yes." She still reeled from the aftereffects, the rational part of her knowing none of it had been true —a mere affectation of her mind, which had been so troubled ever since the attempt on his life. "A horrible one. You were..." she trailed off. She couldn't bring herself to say the words aloud.

"I'm here." He gathered her to him, folding her against the hard sinews of his chest as if she were a small child who needed solace. "I'm here now."

His unprecedented tenderness made her want to weep. It was a side of him she'd never seen. Hadn't known existed. But the ugliness of her dream still tore through her, leaving her stomach knotted, her mouth dry.

"You don't understand." She pressed her face into his bare skin, breathing deeply of his divine scent, cologne and man and something that was undefinably *him*. "There was so much blood, just like when you were attacked." She swallowed against a sob as emotions she'd kept firmly at bay threatened to emerge. She would not cry, would not be weak. Not now, not after what they'd shared.

He'd made love to her. Taken her maidenhead. She'd fallen asleep afterward, lulled into a peaceful, sated slumber by the intense pleasure he'd shown her. How disparate that she should wake again plagued by the violence that had befallen him.

Because fear was an angry beast, hammering inside her chest. Reminding her that whoever had tried to take his life would try again. He wasn't safe. And perhaps neither was she. Those chilling realizations curled inside her heart like vines fashioned of ice. And after today, she was inextricably bound to him in the most permanent sense. No longer did she intend to leave him or annul their marriage. Something shifted inside her as she clung to him, foreign emotions sliding into place like the pieces of a puzzle. She feared for him.

And what of Virginia? A voice inside her asked. What of her dreams of returning to her homeland? Of her desire to live her life on her own terms? Would she sacrifice everything for a man she still scarcely knew? How could she bear to remain in a society she deplored for its inflexibility and unwillingness to accept change?

The questions clamoring to life within her mingled with the fear, chilling her even more. In her emotion-charged response to his attack, she'd forgotten to consider how she—with her rebellious nature and defiant spirit—could possibly be a true countess. If he expected her to develop a sudden affinity for proper manners, needlework, and vapid conversation, he'd be doomed to disappointment. She had every intention of pursuing her cause in England the same as she would have in Virginia. Women everywhere deserved the right to vote.

He seemed to sense her inner turmoil, for he withdrew to look down at her, an equally uncharacteristic sadness darkening his eyes and expression. "I'm truly sorry to be the cause of your nightmares, little dove."

But he wasn't the cause of the panic flashing through her now. What had happened to him was. She couldn't explain it, not even to herself, but the sight of him bloodied and laid low would haunt her forever. It had changed her irrevocably, and she was ill equipped to manage the aftereffects.

She held the bedclothes to her chest, seeking to put a mind-clearing barrier between them, and struggled to give voice to her misgivings. "It isn't you that's the cause. It's what happened to you."

His jaw hardened, but he grazed a finger over her cheekbone, belying the tenseness of his posture with such gentleness. "I've had enemies before, and yet here I am."

"Enemies who attempted to smash your skull in?" she demanded, the rawness of her emotions colliding with the reverberations of her dream. He had yet to acknowledge the seriousness of what had occurred. He had nearly been murdered, for God's sake. Before his own home. Beaten senseless, his broken body left to bleed out on the streets.

He flashed a wicked grin, ever his enigmatic self, and caught her hand in his, guiding it to the healing wound on the back of his head. "Not smashed, love. See? Perfectly intact, if ever it indeed was."

She was grateful his wound had not been as grievous as it could have been and that he had not suffered infection or worse. But he seemed determined to tone down both the severity of his attack and the danger facing him. She meant to point as much out to him, to dress him down with precise words of condescension.

Instead, she allowed her emotions to once more get the best of her. "Do you not think whoever tried to kill you will realize he failed and try again? What if he succeeds the next time? What then?"

His grin turned wry and he released her hand. "Then you'll be free to return to your beloved Virginia, won't you? Perhaps you ought to relinquish your wifely concern. It seems my demise would do you a good turn."

No it most certainly would not. The thought of him gone from her life forever—of the world without his engaging wit, magnetism, without *him*—seemed the most egregious thing imaginable. "How can you be so flippant about your own life?"

"Come now, little dove." He trailed a finger over her collarbone, studying her in that penetrating way of his. "Am I meant to sit about crying in a corner? Don't mistake just who it is that you married. I'm a man who has devoted his life to not giving a damn about anything, especially not my own worthless hide."

Her heart gave a pang in her chest at hearing him speak about himself in such terms. What could have happened to him in his life to make him feel so contemptible? Perhaps it was the newness of the intimacy they'd shared. Perhaps it was the result of finally acknowledging she couldn't turn away from the path she'd chosen. She'd sealed her fate when she'd lain with him. He'd seen, touched, and kissed her everywhere. He'd been inside her, had spent his seed within her. Even now she could be carrying his child.

The thought sent an odd, tingling warmth pervading her entire body. She stayed him when he would have trailed his touch lower, over the aching curve of her breast. She searched his shuttered gaze, wishing she could see within their blue depths an inkling of his innermost thoughts. "You are not worthless."

His expression hardened, a grim cast calling the angles of his features into relief. "I was a whore. There's no need to mince words or pretend. That is who I am, a man who sold his body and his soul. That is who you see before you now, the man who used his pretty face to assuage the ruin his bastard of a father left him in. You cannot do the things I did, Clara, and give a damn about yourself. And I cannot undo them now. They're forever a part of me."

She recognized the emotion coloring his voice for the first time. Not just scorn directed at himself, but shame. He was embarrassed by the things he had done to keep penury at bay. Clara wanted to weep for him, but she knew that would only shame him further.

Instead, she held his face in her hands as he had so recently done to her, relinquishing her hold on his hand and the bedclothes she'd primly attempted to pull between their naked bodies. "You did what you needed to do. You kept your sisters well taken care of. You kept your home. Stop punishing yourself for the past."

Freed of her staying grasp, his hand was once again at liberty to continue its wicked travel. He cupped her breast, making her nipple pebble into his palm. His gaze lowered to her mouth. "Watch yourself, little dove. You make it sound as if you care."

His words hit her with the force of a blow, for they pierced the confusion and emotion muddling her brain and made her recognize the truth for what it was. She did care. Of course she cared for him. If she wasn't careful, in fact, she could love him.

How stunning. How terrifying. She'd never contemplated falling in love with the Earl of Ravenscroft. He was wicked and sleek and beautiful and altogether dark and dangerous. But he was also good. He cared for his sisters. He had been gentle with her, had taken pains to inflict as little pain on her as possible. Perhaps he could learn to care for her in time as well.

Her heart hammered in her breast and she wondered if he could feel it. "I do care," she told him, tamping down her pride. For he needed to hear it from her now. "I care for you, Julian."

"Ah, a common neophyte mistake, confusing lust for something else." He rolled her nipple between his thumb and forefinger with expert attention. "Soon you'll learn the way of things."

She ignored the bloom of heat his ministrations sent directly to her core. He could not deflect her so easily. "Why do you think I'm here now?"

He tugged on the hardened bud. "Because I excel at fucking. Let me show you more, love. I'll make you come with my tongue alone. I'll sink it deep inside you and find a secret place you never dreamed existed. It'll make you go wild."

Traitorous heat slid through her, wetness and hunger pooling deep within the flesh he'd so recently claimed. It would be so easy to give in to him, to allow him to pleasure her and close her mind to the dangers surrounding them. To only feel, to bask in his seduction and forget all else. But that would be weak and wrong, for he meant so much more to her than his undeniable prowess. There was a physical pull between them but there was also something else. Something deeper and stronger.

"No." She would not allow him to dismiss her feelings for him. To suggest she'd change the course of her entire life merely because he was a skilled lover was an insult to the both of them. "I'm here because I care. For the past few years, I've devoted my life to returning home. Everything I've done—every scandal and worry I've caused my family, every madcap plan I've devised—has been with one goal in mind. To return to Virginia and the land I love. I never strayed from my course. I never intended to have anything more than a marriage in name only with you. But then I saw you bloodied and broken, and I realized that I couldn't bear to lose you. I *care*, Julian. Do not dare to insult me by suggesting I'm too naïve to understand the difference."

There. The words left her in a great rush, before she could rethink them or attempt to lessen her admission of the extent to which he had made her fall beneath his spell. Her chest heaved. He hadn't stopped toying with her nipple, but the rest of him remained oddly still. She was reminded again of her early impression of him. A rattler. Sleek and powerful and ready to strike. His gaze, formerly pinned to her mouth, met hers at last. She couldn't read the emotion simmering in the fathomless blue depths.

His silence made her flush. She felt as though all of her was displayed before him along with her body, her weaknesses and faults, her every desire and longing, before him to judge. She'd never felt such a depth of feeling, such a confused, wonderful and awful mixture of hope and dread pent up within her. He could cut her down with a word. He could render her mindless with a touch.

So much hung between them.

"Say something," she demanded at last. "Have you no response?"

"You're so very young," he said at last as he released her nipple and his hand skated lower, over the curve of her belly to the bud of her sex. His fingers worked over the sensitized nub, playing her as he would an instrument. "So innocent."

Damn him. How dare he condescend to her now, after she'd just bared the bewildering contents of her heart to him? But even as she resented him, her body responded. Her legs fell open, her body arching into his knowing touch. A breath hissed from her lungs.

"Not so innocent," she reminded him.

He slicked wetness over her seam, parting her folds to stroke her gently. "Still innocent." He kissed her then, with slow tenderness before withdrawing, his breath a hot curtain over her lips. "And sweet. So damn sweet. I want you all over again, little dove."

The stubble of his whiskers pricked her palms. She still held his face trapped between her hands, almost as if she could not let him go. The fear fueled by her dream licked at her. The chasm she'd felt at losing him was a ghost inside her that refused to leave. Why couldn't she release him? He was safe, flesh and blood before her, his skin branding hers. She wished she knew the answer.

"You toy with me," she accused him without the heat she'd intended.

"Others perhaps. Not you." He kissed the tip of her nose. "Don't be so serious, Clara mine, or I'll have to take your frown away the only way I know how."

He took her breath. His finger slid inside her slowly, and despite the sore tenderness of her flesh, a flare of desire sparked to life. She wanted him too, but his potent skills of seduction wouldn't dissuade her from her cause. He seemed as determined to dismiss her admission as he was to lure her back into another round of lovemaking. Why? Surely there was a reason for his calculated avoidance.

A thought occurred to her then. "Has no woman ever cared for you before?"

He paused, an indecipherable expression flashing across his face. Beneath her palms, his jaw hardened and clenched before releasing. "Clara." His tone was a warning. Stern. Fierce.

Could it be that no one—none of his purported legion of lovers—had ever shown him tenderness? Had they all treated him as a commodity they'd bought to amuse their selfish whims? She had to know. "Julian, tell me. I'm your wife. I deserve an answer."

He withdrew from her and returned to the nub hidden within her folds, the one that seemed to jolt live electricity through her body whenever he touched her there. Now was no different. She jerked against him, unable to help herself.

"Here is your answer." He increased his pressure and his pace. Pleasure rippled through her entire being along with need. She grew closer to the precipice of her control, her body a tightly coiled spring ready for release. "This is what I'm worth. You bought me with your dowry. Use me however you like. Fuck me, if you like. Let me fuck you."

His vulgar words touched some wicked part of her she hadn't known existed, sending a new rush of moisture between her thighs. Faster and faster his fingers moved over her, knowing somehow precisely where and how she longed to be touched, even before she did. He took her mouth and this time, the kiss was hard and uncompromising. This kiss plundered. It was as if the gentleness he'd shown her had been stripped from him. She had pushed him too far, and now he returned the favor, edging her ever nearer to the shattering bliss she knew he could bring her.

"Anything you want, little dove. Anything you want. Take it." He nipped her lip. His mouth moved hungrily over her jaw next, then to her throat. He nibbled there, all the while circling the center of her pleasure, giving her just what she wanted. What she needed. He bit her earlobe, licked the hollow beneath it. Her quim ached. Her body trembled. All the while, she refused to release him, holding him as if she could forever anchor him to her this way.

She meant to utter a protest. A staying sentence. Something intelligible. But all she managed was a moan. The hazy fog of desire suffused her mind. She could scarcely think. Damn it, he was besting her at her game of wills, and she was helpless to stop him.

"Take it," he urged hotly into her ear. "Spend for me, love."

She climaxed almost violently, arching into his hand, crying out her pleasure. Her hands fell from his face at last, moving to his bare shoulders, so strong and sleek beneath her touch, clutching him to her. She wished she could absorb him into her, take him so completely inside that he could never leave. A choked groan left her against her will. Clara gave in to the delicious ricochet of gratification, of abandon, and for a moment she forgot what she'd meant to do. What she'd meant to make him admit.

He rose above her, his glorious body naked and aroused, and held his cock in his closed fist, stroking up and down the hard shaft. She watched, sure her cheeks flushed scarlet with embarrassment, unable to look away. Surely he didn't intend to…mercy, he jerked his hand over himself, meeting her gaze without an inkling of shame.

"You're sore," he bit out. "I'll not take you again this night. Tomorrow, I'll fuck you, Clara. I'll fuck you again and again." His hand moved faster, mimicking the actions of lovemaking.

Her fascinated gaze traveled over him, taking note of every detail, from the beautiful strain of his muscled body to the strong trunks of his thighs to the very part of him that called her attention the most. A bead of moisture seeped from the head of his cock, and she licked her lips, wondering what it would be like to run her tongue over the small indentation, to taste him as he had her.

"Fuck. When you look at me like that, I want to stick my cock in your pretty little mouth." The shocking admission seemed torn from him.

Shocking but also arousing, for Clara couldn't help but imagine him doing so. Would she like such a depraved act? Yes, her throbbing body told her, she would. And then, as she watched, his body stiffened and he cried out, his seed spurting from him and landing across her belly.

"Anything you want, little dove," he repeated, his voice hoarse and breathless. "But goddamn you, don't mistake this for caring. *This* is fucking, and that is all I have to offer you."

Before she could answer him, a discreet tap sounded at the door.

"Damn it to hell," he cursed, hauling himself away from her and going in search of his dressing gown. "I warned them all that anyone who dares to interrupt me on this day will be sacked."

His anger was like a pail of cold water being tossed upon

her scorching flesh. Was he angry more at her or at himself? That was the question, though she found precious little comfort in it. A shiver went through her, leaving her covered in gooseflesh. She snatched up the bedclothes as her shield, watching him wordlessly as he donned his robe. His seed remained upon her belly, slick and warm, a reminder that she was his but that he was not yet hers. If ever he would be. No woman before her had ever shown him kindness. Of that she was now certain. And the realization produced a dreadful combination of anger and sickness.

The Marchioness of Thornton's words about Ravenscroft on her wedding day returned to her mind. They'd been spoken not so very long ago, but for all that had come to pass they may have been a lifetime ago. *He has a good heart.* A good heart did indeed beat within him. But she would allow him this retreat, for their lives had been vastly different before they'd met and hers, while far from perfect, had certainly left her with fewer scars.

"Cover yourself, madam," he ordered her, his tone cool. He'd gone to the door, his back to her, his form still and stiff as the formality of his words.

Yes, he had withdrawn from her entirely now. Although perhaps some of his reserve was due to the presence of the servant on the other side of the door. She made certain her modesty was firmly intact. "I have, my lord."

He opened the door just a crack. "This had bloody well better be important, Osgood. Something along the lines of the goddamn house about to burn to the ground, or an invading army here to storm the front door."

Clara strained to hear the butler's response.

"My lord, it grieves me to interrupt you and for that I heartily do apologize. But, we've a situation. I'm afraid it's her ladyship's father. He has arrived and he refuses to leave until he's had an audience with you."

Her father was here. It had been days since she'd last seen him, and she realized for the first time just how much she'd missed him. Why, she'd even missed Lady Bella and she'd certainly missed her sweet little sister, Virginia. How had she ever thought she could leave any of them? They'd become as much a part of the fabric of her life as anyone she'd ever known. Just as Julian had. The unwanted thought gave her pause.

"Damn it to hell. Thank you, Osgood. I'll see him in my study. That will be all." And with that, her husband slammed the door in his butler's face.

He turned back to her, his countenance even stormier than it had been before.

"Father is here?" she asked, though she hardly needed him to confirm what she'd just heard for herself. "I'll come with you, Julian."

"Not now." His tone, much like his gaze, had gone frigid. "It appears Mr. Whitney has asked for me. I'll indulge him by meeting him. Ring for your maid and tend to your toilette. You may see him afterward."

And then, without a further word, he disappeared into his dressing room, leaving her to stare after him, wondering if she'd won the battle between them or lost the entire war.

For precisely the third time in their abbreviated familial acquaintance, Julian found himself squaring off against Jesse Whitney in his study. He felt rather reminiscent of a pugilist at the moment, simultaneously attempting to defend himself and identify his opponent's weaknesses. The man was a menace who didn't give a damn for proper etiquette. Not only was it bad form to call on newlyweds until it became known they were receiving, it was bloody well terrible to demand an audience with a man upon being informed his lordship was not at home.

Particularly when the reason for his lordship not being at home was a naked and beautiful wife in his bed, sweet and warm and wet and willing. Damn everyone and everything but her to perdition. But he could not think about her now—about all they'd done and had yet to do—as he faced her father, for Christ's sake. For they had just begun, he and his little dove.

Now, however, there was another matter he needed to face. And that matter was an irate, unreasonable father who should have had the courtesy and the grace to recognize his daughter was now married. They did not require further interference. *Julian* damn well didn't require further interference. He vastly disliked being made to feel as though he were a stable boy who'd made off with the daughter of the house. Even if—his noble lineage aside—that was all too close to the mark.

Julian raised a brow, pinning Whitney with a withering look. "I don't see a pistol this time, old boy. Could it be you've one secreted in your waistcoat?"

Clara's father favored him with a scowl that would have scared the devil. "Go to hell, Ravenscroft."

The man hated him. Julian couldn't entirely blame him. If a blackguard with a reputation as bleak as his would have absconded with his own daughter, he'd feel the same. But he didn't yet have a daughter, and Clara was his in every way now. The mere thought was enough to send a sharp bolt of lust straight through him.

He tamped it down, forced his ardor to cool. Jesus, could he not regain control over himself? Was he nothing more than a ravening beast? If Whitney could see the wicked thoughts plaguing him, the poor chap would expire of apoplexy. Either that or leap across Julian's desk with every intention of throttling him.

The notion wrung a grim smile of amusement from him. For all that Clara distracted him, he still enjoyed goading her father. "One must admit that hell does indeed seem my inevitable destination."

Whitney's hands clenched into fists, the only show of his rage beyond his thunderous expression. "I'd love to send you there. Don't doubt that for a moment. But it would seem I'm not the only one. Common fame has it that you were attacked several days ago, and that the villain intended to murder you."

Blast. He'd been hoping to keep that particular ignominy from wagging tongues. "I was," he acknowledged. "Tell me, Whitney, did you hire someone to kill me?"

His wife's father threw back his head and laughed as though Julian had just delivered the finest sally. It was his turn to clench his fists as he waited for the man's loud humor to subside. Truly, how had a small and blindingly lovely creature like Clara ever been borne from the big, rough-hewn brute before him? It boggled the mind.

"I've warned you enough that you ought to know, Ravenscroft," Whitney said at last, having quelled his vociferous glee. "I served four years in the Army of Northern Virginia. If I wanted you dead, I'd do the deed myself and you damn well wouldn't be here smirking at me, gloating over my failure to bash in your skull, because you'd long be a corpse."

A bloodthirsty bastard was Clara's sire. Julian could have admired him for it, but since the bulk of his murderous intentions seemed to hinge upon Julian himself, he deemed it wise to refrain.

He kept his tone steeped in sarcasm. "Forgive me if I remain suspicious, Mr. Whitney, particularly in light of such an entertainingly murderous soliloquy. What shall I tell Clara, do you think, when she enquires about our audience? That her papa isn't responsible for my bludgeoning because he assures me I'd already be floating in the Thames if he but wanted it?"

Whitney's face reddened and Julian knew a moment of satisfaction at provoking him. Clara had accused him of fashioning everything into a game for his own personal entertainment, and perhaps she wasn't so far off the mark.

"You do amuse yourself don't you, you son-of-a-bitch? You'll say nothing of the sort to Clara. As long as my daughter assures me she is happy, I don't wish you ill. Make no mistake that I do expect an audience with her before I leave today." His glare gained intensity. "The moment she isn't happy, you'll have cause to fear me. But what concerns me now is her safety. If you've lunatics attacking you in the street, how can Clara be safe?"

The question abruptly dashed his diversion. It was, after all, a question that he had refused to allow himself to ponder. For he was selfish. He was greedy. He wanted Clara by his side. In his bed. In his bloody arms. He damn well never wanted her out of reach.

"Clara is not in danger." At least, he had no reason to believe she was. For it certainly seemed that the miscreant who'd laid him low had only been interested in his demise and not anyone else's. Of course, it did stand to reason that if a madman was targeting him, the bastard could lash out at those closest to him as well. The notion sent a chill through him.

"But *you* are, Lord Ravenscroft," Whitney noted, all but saying Julian's thoughts aloud. "And if you are in danger of further assassination attempts, how can you imagine that she might not be in danger as well? What would happen if the villain who assaulted you returns to finish the deed here in your home? What if Clara is in the way? What if she's attacked? I know you're a heartless blackguard but even you must care for her wellbeing, at least in whatever capacity you can manage. She's your wife now."

Whitney said the last as though it still made him faintly ill. Yes, Clara was his wife now. She was *his*, damn it, in every sense of the word. And he would protect her however he must. "No harm will come to her while she's in my care," he promised, relenting and taking pity on Whitney. After all, at heart, the wily bastard was only a father who loved his daughter.

And Julian could relate in a basic sense.

For somehow, Clara had made him experience something he'd thought he was no longer capable of feeling: emotion. *Jesus.* The realization hit him with the force of a blow to the gut, knocking the wind from his lungs, leaving him reeling and confused. He cared, goddamn it.

He cared for her.

That was the sensation expanding in his chest, the knot in his gut each time he looked upon her, the need to keep her from fleeing to Virginia, to touch her, to take her. All of it. Perhaps she'd hooked him, stupid fish that he was, from the day she'd stepped into this same study, bringing her warmth and her orange-scented loveliness with her.

No one would hurt her, he vowed inwardly. No one.

"Naturally, I care for her wellbeing. I'd do anything to protect her," he elaborated curtly.

"Forgive me if I cannot merely accept your assurance, Ravenscroft," Whitney drawled. "How can you keep her safe? You've nothing here but an old butler and a handful of servants for fortification. Have you even a weapon?"

Of course he didn't have a bloody weapon. He wasn't an American vagabond who invaded the home of a peer of the realm, waving a pistol and threatening to do him bodily harm.

"This isn't war, Whitney," he said gently. "We live in a civilized world. What would you have me do, hire a phalanx of soldiers to guard the damn door?"

"You need to be prepared." Whitney scrutinized him, appearing to take his measure and making him want to squirm in the process. "I've lived through war, my lord. Man can be a savage when life requires it. I'll never forget that. Whoever wants you dead will try again. Don't make it easy for him. Don't put Clara in danger."

"I would never put Lady Ravenscroft in danger," he said coldly, for Whitney's words had affected him more than he cared to admit. Christ, how could he be so selfish? So stupid? He'd hire every brawny, willing man in London to protect Clara if need be. But he couldn't bear to part with her. Couldn't countenance the thought of sending her away as Whitney seemed to imply he ought. "Believe of me what you like, Mr. Whitney, but know that I hold your daughter in the highest regard."

Clara's father stared him down, seeming to attempt to judge the veracity of his words. Before he could form a response, the study door opened unannounced. The subject of their conversation sailed over the threshold in an elaborate afternoon gown of deep, riveting navy silk trimmed with gold cording.

From her elaborately styled braid to her hem, she was faultlessly elegant, more beautiful than any lady he'd ever before seen. To look upon her, he'd never guess she had so recently been nude and sated in his bed. He shouldn't have been so coarse with her and well he knew it, but he'd been consumed, too caught up to control himself. Her cheeks were flushed, the sole sign of any discomposure on her part.

"Father," she exclaimed, her voice tinged with a vibrant affection that would have made him jealous indeed had she addressed any other man.

He was so distracted by drinking in the sight of her that he nearly forgot to stand. Damn it, what was wrong with him? He stood a full half minute after Whitney swept from his chair and met Clara halfway across the study, clasping her to him in an undignified embrace that spoke to the depths of his love.

Julian fought the urge to look away from the unabashed display. He was not familiar with such unfettered emotion and it made him deuced uncomfortable. He was quite certain that neither his mother nor his harsh bastard of a father had ever treated him with a tenth of the adoration Clara's father so freely showered upon her.

"Clara darlin'." Whitney's drawl was infinitely more pronounced as he stepped back, appearing to remember himself. He surveyed Clara as if inspecting her for a sign of ill treatment. "Are you well?"

Clara's gaze slipped to Julian's for a moment, and he felt the clash as keenly as he would her touch. The glittering depths of her blue eyes spoke of the abruptness of their last meeting in his chamber. He had been cold to her. Had spilled his seed on her as if he were no better than a rutting animal. And she—regal, elegant, and lovely—*she* had accepted his every act. She had not questioned. Had not railed against him.

Had he told her all he could offer her was fucking? Suddenly he wondered if it were true. For how could she inspire such fierce feelings within him, the likes of which he'd never known? No other woman had ever made him feel the way Clara did: possessive, bewildered, helpless but to bask in the brilliance of her presence.

He'd never know what his wife read in his expression. Jesus, he liked to think she could read nothing at all, that he wasn't a book pried open for her thorough inspection. But whatever the case, she turned back to her father with the air of a woman who had reached a decision.

"I'm very well, Father." She bestowed a beatific smile upon Whitney and embraced him yet again. "How are you and Lady Bella and Virginia? I must confess that I've missed you."

He felt like an interloper in his own home as he awkwardly watched the tableau before him. Never had he even heard his wife speak with such a soft, lilting drawl. And she'd yet to acknowledge him, a slight that was perhaps unintentional but nevertheless unmissed.

"As I've missed you, my dear daughter." Genuine emotion marked Whitney's low voice. He stepped away from her then, clearing his throat to ward away what sounded like deep sentiment.

By God, was the devil…*weeping*? Julian found himself straining closer, longing to see the pistol-wielding, threat-issuing American brought to his knees. And wasn't that the best bloody joke of them all, one man laid low by Clara hoping that his nemesis was as well?

Hellfire, he was a wreck. Perhaps the blows he'd taken to the head had rendered him prone to madness. Yes, surely that was the explanation for the confounding round of emotions churning through him now. *Emotions*. From a man who'd believed he no longer had the capacity to sustain them. What irony.

"Oh, Father." Clara said in soft tones, her smile warm and indulgent. "I'm not far from you here. You're always welcome in our home. Is that not true, Lord Ravenscroft?"

Her vivid eyes pinned him once again, bringing him back into the conversation as though he'd just stepped into the room for the first time. He gathered his faculties, took a breath. It wouldn't do to appear undone or affected before Clara. And most especially not before her violent hound of a father. He was the Earl of Ravenscroft. He'd fashioned apathy into an art form.

"Of course, my lady." He kept his tone as mild as possible given the wildness of his inner thoughts. With great effort, he smiled at Jesse Whitney, who watched him now with the careful air of a man who'd just spotted a rattler in his path and sought how best to distract him to avoid being bitten. "Mr. Whitney, we would be humbled if you and Mrs. Whitney would join us for dinner in the upcoming weeks. Lady Ravenscroft will send a formal invitation, of course."

The pleased smile Clara sent his way was worth the pride he had to swallow to invite the man to dinner. There was something about Jesse Whitney that went against the grain. The man didn't like him, didn't trust him. Part of Julian couldn't blame him. Part of him wanted to prove him wrong.

"We would be happy to accept I'm sure," Whitney said easily, sparing Julian half a glance before looking back upon Clara. "Clara, daughter. Might I have a word alone with you?"

Clara's eyes swung from him to her father. Julian felt his face settling into a familiar mask. Here was a new experience. No one had ever before forced him to vacate his own study, threadbare and dilapidated though it was. Indeed, he'd come frighteningly near to being evicted from the entire home, but that danger was now a thing of the past. Still, he supposed there was a first for everything, and being dismissed from his inner sanctum was certainly that.

"My lord?" she asked, her gaze questioning. Probing. Seeing more than he damn well wanted her to see.

The truth of it was that she didn't need to ask him permission. He was not her bloody gaoler. Unable to keep the twist of self-derision from his smile, he bowed with as much formal elegance as he could muster. "Of course, my lady. Pray excuse me. I find I've important matters to attend elsewhere."

Another bow and he stalked from his study, wondering what the hell was wrong with him. But just as soon as he asked himself the question, he'd already acquired the answer. Clara. His little dove. His *wife*, damn it. She'd changed everything. She'd even begun to change him.

But one thing remained the same. Her oaf of a father could still bloody well go straight to hell. As he stalked from the chamber, Julian comforted himself with that thought.

Clara tried not to flinch at the sound of Julian slamming the study door. She wished, not for the first time, that she was able to read his shuttered expression and grim gaze with absolute certainty. She thought she'd seen a hint of concern, a spark of caring. Along with something else. The rigid set of his jaw bespoke…what? Irritation? Dissatisfaction?

So much of Ravenscroft remained an enigma to her. At the moment, he was doing his best to keep her at arm's length. But persistence had always been one of her best qualities. She could meet his determination with some of her own.

Her father's beloved face drew her attention from her husband's abrupt departure. Lines of apprehension carved grooves in his forehead and bracketed his mouth. She wondered if he remained this grim as a result of her marriage.

He dispelled her curiosity by breaking his silence. "Clara,

tell me the truth. Are you happy? Ravenscroft does not treat you with disrespect, does he?"

Once again the specter of Julian's reputation had returned. She wanted to rail against the unfairness of it, that others' judgments of him should always be colored by his past. Somehow, she'd acquired an inexplicable sense of defensiveness on her husband's behalf. She longed to banish the sadness she sensed in him forever.

Clara met her father's gaze now unflinchingly. "I'm happy, Father. Truly. Lord Ravenscroft has been a model husband."

Well, perhaps not entirely a model, she inwardly amended. To be sure, they had much yet between them that would need ironing. Perhaps even mending. Her reaction to Julian confused her as much as the man himself did. She had never known a man as dangerous to her inner balance. He'd had her hopelessly off kilter from the moment she'd entered his study and he'd approached her, as cagey as any predator. She didn't know where she stood. Didn't know what the future held in store for them.

But despite all that, telling her father she was happy was not prevarication. For with Julian, she felt as happy and at home as she'd ever been in England. Being his wife would not always be easy, but it was the path she'd chosen. The path that was right for her. She didn't regret her decision, and she knew that in time they could find happiness together.

Her father's lips compressed into a tight line of disapproval, as though he weighed his next words. Perhaps he'd anticipated an outpouring from her of how miserable she was in her new role. His undisguised distaste for Julian had not gone unnoticed. She'd been hoping he may have softened. But he had not. He wasn't brandishing a pistol on this occasion, but his mien was forbidding enough without it.

"Our doors are always open to you," he said at last. "Should you desire to leave him, Clara, you have a home with myself and Lady Bella."

His obvious displeasure and distrust of Julian nettled her on her husband's behalf. "Thank you, Father, but why do you insist on believing that I made such a great error of judgment that I shall need to one day retreat back to you?"

Her father made a sound of exasperation deep in his throat. "Forgive me if I believe you acted impetuously in your decision to marry a known blackguard who compromised you so that he could eliminate his debts with your dowry. He knew I'd consent to nearly any of his terms to save you from ruin and see you settled, the blighter."

Guilt settled over her, heavy as a boulder. How had it not occurred to her that part of her father's poor opinion of Julian was due to her subterfuge? She had to tell him the truth, to unburden herself.

Clara placed a hand on her father's coat sleeve in an imploring gesture. "Father, there's something I must confess to you. Marrying Lord Ravenscroft was my idea."

Her father's brows snapped together. "The hell you say it was. Don't try to protect him, darlin'."

Ah, if only she were half the angel her father imagined her to be. But she was not. She was wicked and willful and rebellious. Impetuous too. Lord have mercy, it seemed she had not many virtues in her possession at all if she were to truly consider the matter.

"I'm not trying to protect him," she told her father gently, almost in the tone she'd use to inform someone that a death had occurred. For she feared his reaction to her full revelation. He would be angry and hurt. Disappointed in her. But regardless, she must tell him everything. "Coming here to his home that night, attempting to be compromised, it was all my idea. I'd never met the earl before that day but I knew of his reputation, and I thought he'd make an excellent foil for my plan to return to Virginia. I offered to pay him to marry me and then annul our union and let me go home."

Her father's face went ashen. "Damn it, Clara, tell me

you're lying. Why the hell would you do something so foolish?"

Yes, she had to admit, her actions had been foolish indeed. How naïve of her to ever imagine she could've made a man like the Earl of Ravenscroft do her bidding. "You told me you wouldn't allow me to return to Virginia, that even after I'd reached my majority you wouldn't settle a penny on me. I didn't want to remain here. It seemed the best means of circumventing you."

"If all this is true, why not tell me? You could have spared yourself so much." He waved his hand in a broad, encompassing gesture. "You could have spared yourself *this*. If I'd realized you wanted to go back to Virginia so much you'd shackle yourself to a devil like Ravenscroft, I'd have sent you there myself."

His angry words gave her pause, but she didn't believe for a moment that he would have mildly acquiesced to sending her to Virginia on her own. He was too protective of those he loved. "Julian is not the devil you think he is, Father."

"Yes he damn well is." His face contorted. "Did he or did he not compromise you that night? I saw the two of you with my own eyes, Clara. His conduct was not that of a gentleman."

Perhaps not. She winced. "He didn't…that is to say, I allowed you to believe he had lured me to his home and compromised me because it facilitated my objective. If I had told you the truth, you wouldn't have allowed me to marry him."

Her father shook his head, clearly trying to force his mind to accept everything she'd just told him. There it was, her secret laid bare. She was not a good daughter. She wasn't sure she knew how to be. But she did love her father, and she did care for her husband, and she knew a rush of relief at confessing the truth.

"That lying whoreson." His tone had grown positively murderous now. "He looked me in the eye and told me there was a possibility you carried his child. Fed me some tripe about you two falling in love and then demanded two hundred thousand pounds and a hundred thousand in North Atlantic Electric stocks. By God, don't tell me you're too blind to see that man for the fortune hunting vulture he is."

Clara had no excuse to offer. It seemed that she and her husband were not so very different. When they wanted something, they were dogged in their perseverance. "He's not a vulture."

"I'm taking you home with me. This is insupportable. The blackguard dares to put you in danger, keeping you here while someone is out to kill him." He clenched and unclenched his fists. "I'll spare the villain the trouble and kill him first. I'm of half a mind to gut him like a hog for his manipulations."

Lord. This was fast unraveling. "I don't want to go home with you, Father."

"I don't give a goddamn. I'm your father and it's my duty to protect you, especially if you refuse to protect yourself." His blue gaze snapped with fury.

"I won't go with you," she denied again, for she was where she belonged. Nothing in her life had ever felt so simply, preciously *right*. Yes, there was no other word for it except one. One she'd refused to think up until this moment as she faced her father's paternal wrath and protectiveness.

One simple and terrifying word. An emotion as powerful as it was bewildering.

"I've fallen in love with Lord Ravenscroft," she blurted. "I won't leave him."

Chapter Thirteen

JULIAN STARED INTO THE DARKNESS and willed his fierce arousal to abate. His head ached with a low, steady throb, a needling reminder that he wasn't entirely healed of his injury. That alone should've been enough to keep his mind from Clara, who was likely sleeping the slumber of the innocent just next door while he tortured himself with images of her lovely curves. Now he knew the precise color of her nipples. A lush, warm pink, sweeter than any rose he'd ever seen abloom. Now he knew her taste as intimately as he knew her musky citrus scent. And he bloody well knew how it felt to sink inside her tight, wet heat and lose himself.

It felt like pure heaven on earth, that's what.

And if the sentiment rendered him nothing more than a mooning imbecile, well, it couldn't be helped. For she had infected him, had ravaged his body and his mind as completely as any disease. He could only think of her. Of wanting her. No, damn it, more than that. Of *needing* her.

Ah, it was true. He needed Clara more than he'd ever needed anyone or anything in his life. He needed her more than money, more than liquor, more than sin. *I'm here because*

I care, she'd said to him, earnest and without artifice. She cared for him. The idea had been so laughable—that a lovely innocent as pure and true as Clara could somehow care for a reprobate like him—that he'd been ill equipped to deal with his reaction.

So he'd made an ass of himself, settling into his familiar mantle of aloof apathy. He'd pushed her away. He regretted his actions now as he waited for sleep to claim him. He wished he could be a man worthy of her love, one who had not given away so many pieces of himself that almost nothing remained.

But sleep didn't seem to be forthcoming. He'd damn well tried everything to lose himself into the abyss of slumber. He'd tossed back a not insubstantial quantity of whisky before settling into bed. He'd taken a tepid bath in an effort to cool his ardor. He'd turned up a lamp and settled on a volume of particularly dry poetry. He'd turned the lamp back down and tossed the volume aside.

He'd used his own hand to reach his release twice already.

Nothing he'd tried thus far had been effective. He was still hard as marble, his thoughts consumed by her, wishing he hadn't decided to let her rest for the night without taking her again. Surely she was sore. She'd been a virgin. He'd done his best to blunt the pain but he'd still torn into her like a savage, and there'd been blood enough to show that their lovemaking hadn't been entirely pleasant for her.

Tomorrow he would make it up to her. Tomorrow, he'd woo her and charm her, strip her bare and touch and kiss and lick every beautiful bit of her. Tonight, however, was another matter. Tonight, he was tortured and frustrated, feeling like an amnesiac who'd woken within a strange body, uncertain of who he was and how he ought to act.

To hell with trying to sleep. He threw back the bedclothes and turned the lamp up, searching for the trousers he'd discarded in one of his fitful attempts to distract himself. As he pulled them up over his hips, an odd sound cut into his heavy musings.

Very odd indeed. It was muffled and high, almost like a cry. A series of muted thumps followed the sound. His mouth went dry as a surge of unadulterated fear surged up his spine and exploded into a thousand jagged splinters. For a moment, he remained still, listening, praying he was wrong, that he was overreacting. Another high, shrill sound split the night.

A muffled scream.

Jesus, it was *Clara's* muffled scream.

Heart hammering in his chest, he ran to the door adjoining their chambers. The knob refused to turn. Locked, goddamn it. Who had the key? Did he? Damn it, the chamber had been empty for so long, and his servants were so sparse, that only God knew where the key could possibly be. There wasn't time to ring for a servant. There wasn't time to try the hall door. Clara was within, and she needed him.

No one would hurt her. Not his Clara. No.

Without a moment's hesitation, he threw himself into the door, shoulder first. Wood cracked. The door didn't budge. Bracing himself, he summoned all the strength and unholy anger, the fierce urge to protect his wife, and slammed himself back into the portal. He'd break down the bloody door, and when he crossed the threshold, Lord have mercy on the bastard on the other side.

Because Julian was going to fucking kill him.

She woke to a heavy body pressing her to the mattress. As sleep left her and awareness returned, part of her knew something was wrong. The body atop hers was too heavy and bulky. The scent of him was all wrong too. He was breathing heavy, and the smell of spirits and smoke clung to him.

No, it was not Julian who had laid himself upon her

above the bedclothes. It was a stranger. A large man. A man who intended to do her harm.

She let loose a scream but a hand clamped over her mouth and nose. She could scarcely breathe. She struggled to free her arms, but they were trapped beneath the bedclothes and her attacker's weight. Dear God, he meant to kill her. Whoever had attacked Julian had come for her this time. And he was going to murder her in her bed.

Still fighting to breathe, she forced her mouth open and sank her teeth into the fleshy pads of her assailant's fingers. She bit him as hard as she could. Until she tasted the copper tang of blood and heard him curse her.

"Damn it, you bitch." His other hand snagged in her hair, gripping it so hard that tears ran down her cheek at the awful, wrenching pain.

But she was in a fight for her life, and if she had any say in the matter, her husband would not wake up in the morning to find her body, limp and broken lying in her bed. She would live for him, for herself, for the life they'd build together. She bit down harder, summoning up all the fury within her.

He released her hair. "Goddamn it."

His fist connected with her cheek, gnashing her teeth together. White stars flew before her eyes in the inky darkness. In her shock, she released her grip on his finger, and he didn't waste a moment in striking. His hands clamped on her neck, tightening.

"You're going to die tonight, you little American bitch," he growled.

Dear God. Perhaps she was. She choked, struggling to breathe in, but no air would find her lungs. His grip was so tight. And the blow to her head had made her weak. The lack of air made her weaker still. But she had to continue fighting. She thrashed her legs on the bed, thumping as hard as she could. Perhaps someone would hear. Her fingers clawed at her attacker's manacle-like hands, scratching and scraping and trying to draw more blood, then to his face when she failed. He kneed her in the stomach, sending a fresh wall of pain crashing over her.

She couldn't free herself. Her vision seemed hazy and indistinct now, even in the darkness. The stars returned, along with a buzzing in her ears. So this was it. She was going to die after all, she thought in grim horror. And she hadn't even gotten the chance to tell Julian she loved him. To bear him children. To take away his sadness.

Life seemed to slip from her. She could feel it leaving. The darkness was there, beckoning, waiting to claim her. Another minute and it would all be over. She'd be gone. She wanted to fight, but her body, attacked and starved of air, wouldn't cooperate.

Suddenly, her assailant released her throat and rolled away from her, his weight leaving her body. She gasped, the breath returning to her aching lungs a violent shock. Her hands went to her neck where just seconds before, her unseen attacker's fingers hand been. She rubbed, trying to bring the life back, trying to erase the pain and the violence both.

A part of her processed the sound of her attacker cursing and then the quick, hefty thuds of his footfalls racing across her chamber. A second set of footfalls sounded. She braced herself, uncertain if they belonged to one of his confederates. Just as quickly, the footsteps hastened back to her side. Someone else was upon her then, and this time it was a welcome embrace, for she smelled his cologne, felt his arms around her in their familiar, beloved strength. His bristled cheek pressed to hers.

Julian, thank God.

"Clara!" His voice was hoarse, and he clasped her to his bare chest as though he could pull her inside himself and keep her there forever. "Jesus, Clara, are you hurt? Speak to me, love. Say something."

"I'm alive," she croaked in awe, her brain still stupid with lack of air and shock, still trying to process what had just occurred.

"Thank Christ. My God, what did he do to you? I'll hunt him down and draw and quarter him myself." There was a vicious, raw edge to his tone she'd never heard before.

When he would've left her and chased after her attacker, she clutched at his shoulders. "No, Julian, please. Don't leave me."

Terror, wide and deep and all-consuming, filled her chest at the thought of being alone in the dark again. What if whoever had tried to kill her would return? What if Julian wouldn't be there to frighten him away and keep her safe? Her pistol had done her no good tonight, tucked into her reticule as it was and too far out of reach. She shook so badly that she knew she'd never have managed a good shot anyhow.

If she'd ever fancied herself invincible, that illusion had been thoroughly dashed. She'd never felt more desperate or helpless than she had with a stranger's hands clamped around her throat and the life seeping from her body. A sob rose in her chest, and to her shame she couldn't contain it.

"Hush, darling." He caressed her hair, rained kisses all over her face. "I'll not leave you. He won't hurt you again. You have my word."

His reassurance somehow helped to banish some of the horror that threatened to take hold of her. She continued to gulp air, and breathing—never before a luxury—felt better than it ever had. "Julian, he wanted to kill me. He told me I was going to die tonight."

"Any man who dares try to hurt you will need to go through me. I'll damn well kill him first," Julian growled. "Listen to me, love. Whoever he is, he cannot come after you and expect to get away with it. I'll hunt down the son-of-a-bitch myself and make him pay."

If only his words could assuage her fears entirely. For tonight had made it painfully clear that whoever was determined to do him harm wouldn't stop until he'd accomplished his evil task. Either that or meet his own end first. And now he'd come after Clara as well. A shiver tore through her. Her thoughts raced to Julian's sisters next. "Do you think he's still within the house? We need to find Lady Josephine and Lady Alexandra."

He kissed her again before standing. "Stay here, love. I'm going to ring for the servants and turn up the lamps."

Clara hugged herself, her body shaking with a combination of cold and shock. Her nightdress was only a thin impediment to the night air. Light flared to life, illuminating the chamber in a dull glow. Ordinarily, the sight of Julian clad in only trousers slung over his lean hips, his chest broad and bare, would have made her warm and wanton. But panic was beginning to set in now. She rubbed her neck where the stranger's fingers had pressed. How much longer would it have been until he'd taken her life?

Never mind her own brush with death. There could still be a lunatic on the loose. Others could be in the selfsame danger while they lingered in her chamber. Clara summoned her wits, took a calming breath, and slid from her bed. "We must find your sisters, Julian," she said again.

He was looking at her strangely, an inscrutable expression on his face, his gaze going from her neck to her throbbing cheek. "Jesus, Clara. Why didn't you tell me he'd hit you?"

She shook her head. "It's nothing. Lady Alexandra and Lady Josephine could be at peril even now."

"The bastard ran for the stairs, not toward their chamber." He held out a dressing gown for her, his jaw a hard, grim line. "Put this on, love. You can't go running about the house like that."

She allowed him to help her into the robe, and when she would have tightened the cord at her waist, he gently brushed her away, doing it himself. "I could have managed it," she told him.

"I know." The words seemed torn from him. "But I wanted to. I—goddamn it Clara, I need to touch you. To know you're still here."

His tone held a note of incredulity, as though he could

not believe he felt that way, much less confessed it aloud. Then he hauled her to him again, the gesture devoid of his usual seductive charm. The motion was jerky, nearly bringing their faces colliding together. His eyes roamed over her as his fingertips traced, gliding across her smarting cheek, past her lips, across the bruises she was sure had begun to mottle her throat. It was the closest he'd ever come to admitting he cared for her.

A sudden burst of love blossomed inside her chest, warm and altogether foreign, doing its part to chase away some of the lingering shadows. "I'm here," she told him, kissing his cheek, his chin, every patch of his skin available to her. Finally, she settled on his mouth.

The kiss they shared was long and fierce and deep. It said more than either of them could as they rejoiced in their relief to be in each other's arms, life still a vibrant creature of fragile possibility. For now, they had each other. They were safe. And it was enough.

With great reluctance, she drew away from him. "We must see to the rest of the household, Julian."

"Of course. Forgive me. I've never…" He allowed the thought to trail off, as though thinking better of it, before catching her hand in his, their fingers tangling. "I'll not let you out of my sight for the rest of the night."

She tightened her grip on him. With Julian, she felt safe. She felt as though they could battle whatever menace sought to claim them and come out the victors. "I wouldn't let you," she assured him. "Not tonight or ever again."

But as they ventured off together to find his sisters who, as it turned out, remained peacefully sleeping in their beds, having been unaware of any commotion at all, it occurred to Clara that he had remained troublingly silent.

Chapter Fourteen

HOURS LATER, JULIAN FOUND HIMSELF in much the same position he'd been in before all hell had cut loose within the walls of his home. Nude in his bed, his cock rigid as ever. But this time, a beautiful woman, smelling of orange and musk, just as nude as he, curled her sweet body to his. Her cheek rested on his bare chest. His hand stroked over her glossy, fragrant curls. It wasn't right to want her as much as he did now, not after all she'd been through. But his body wouldn't heed his bloody mind, so he kept his lower half angled away from her, hoping like hell she hadn't noticed what a depraved bastard he was.

Ah yes, much the same position indeed. Hungry for his wife. Unable to sleep. But beyond the physicality of it all, everything was different. Strange how in such a short amount of time, so much could change.

Everything could change.

He could have lost Clara tonight.

It had been a litany hammering through him the entire time he'd roused the servants, checked upon the safety of his sisters, and scoured the house for any signs of the intruder. In the end, they hadn't found a damn thing. The police had been summoned, and they'd taken statements but had accomplished precious little. They certainly hadn't discovered any clues as to who had attempted to murder Clara.

The mere juxtaposition of his wife's name and *murder* in the same thought left him feeling as though all the air had been sucked from his lungs. As though the weight of a cartload of bricks sat upon him, as though his gut was tied in knots, his skin a bizarre blend of hot and cold, simultaneously numb and on fire. A world without Clara. He couldn't fathom such a travesty. By God, there ought not to be a world at all without her in it.

He had not lost her, and he could thank the Lord for that a hundred thousand times and his gratitude would still never be adequately expressed. If indeed the Lord cared to listen to a sinner like him, that was. But not losing her wasn't the point any longer, not now.

For he *could* have lost her. Had he been any slower to break down the door, had he been sleeping instead of awake and brooding, had she not been as strong and fierce a fighter as she was, he wouldn't have her warm, lovely curves draped over him. She'd have been murdered in her bed, just next door, because of him. Because he had unwittingly brought danger into her life.

Whitney's words echoed through his mind. *How can you keep her safe? What would happen if the villain who assaulted you returns to finish the deed here in your home? What if Clara is in the way?* And what had Julian done but mocked him? *This isn't war*, he'd scoffed. But tonight had proved him wrong. Dead wrong. It *was* war. He'd tear out the throat of the man who'd dared to create such bruises on Clara's tender skin, who'd dared to attempt to choke the life from her while she slept in her bed.

A hunger for retribution burned through him. A bloodlust. A desperation to right the wrongs of the night. Tonight, he'd done what he did best his entire life: he'd failed. He'd failed Clara, much as he'd failed at everything he'd ever tried. Being a good son, rescuing himself from debt without selling his soul, keeping his bloody wife safe.

Christ, it was his fault. Every bit of it. He could have left her alone. He could have taken the hundred thousand pounds and marched her off to the nearest ship for Virginia. Even today, he could have sent her to her father's home, at least until he could be assured of her safety.

But he was a selfish fucking bastard. And he had wanted her from the moment he'd first seen her. He had seen her innocence, her brightness, her intelligence and beauty and daring, and he'd wanted to possess it all for himself.

He'd wanted to possess her.

Hell, yes. Everything could change. For now he knew that he needed to let her go. To rid her of him. To send her back to safety. Let her go to Virginia. By God, let her go anywhere else in the goddamn world, so long as she was away from him and *safe*. He couldn't bear to be the cause of her death. To be the reason she was in grave danger. Until tonight, he'd thought he couldn't bear to set her free.

Tonight, he'd realized his capacity to love hadn't withered away entirely from his black soul. He loved Clara. Loved her more than he'd ever experienced. It terrified him. Terrified him as much as the notion of being responsible for her death did.

Because of his love for her, he knew he could no longer keep her tied to him. The danger surrounding them aside, she was too good for him. He'd been too caught up in his own needs to acknowledge it before, but he could damn well see the truth for what it was now. He didn't deserve a woman like her.

And she didn't deserve a man like him, a jaded bastard who'd manipulated her, seduced her, deceived her, and all because he had wanted her for himself. Because the good and the innocence in him had died the day he'd accepted Lady Esterly's proposition. He'd become what he hated most, and if Clara remained his wife, he would only ruin her as surely as he had been ruined. The binds between them needed to be severed for her safety as much as for her own good.

And so, he would send her back to her papa by any means necessary. Anything to secure her safety, to give her the sort of future he could never provide. She was a stubborn woman, his little dove, and he knew she would not go easily. But go she would, for he loved her enough to make certain there would never be another day she suffered because of him.

For the moment, however, he couldn't bear to push her away. He needed this precious time, needed the feeling of her wrapped around him, the luxurious strands of her hair beneath his palm, her even breathing, her lush breast pressed against him. He needed to drink in this one last night they would have together before he said goodbye to her forever.

"Thank you for chasing him away," she said quietly into the stillness that had descended between them, disrupting the bleak turn of his thoughts at last.

He'd supposed she'd fallen asleep, worn out as she must be from the horrors of the attack she'd endured. He swallowed against a sudden thickness in his throat. "I'm sorry I wasn't there for you sooner. I wish to God I'd been there before..."

He couldn't bring himself to give voice to what had happened to her. That bastard's hands on her throat. The purple fingerprints on her otherwise flawless skin. The angry bruise on her cheek. His fists clenched.

Her hand traveled over his chest in a tentative caress, almost soothing. "You came for me just when I needed you, Julian."

Jesus, could it be that *she* was reassuring *him*? How utterly ridiculous. How thoroughly Clara. He trapped her wandering hand in his, stilling it. "Don't fancy me a hero, little dove. I'm a man, weak-willed, selfish, and more flawed than you can imagine."

His biggest flaw of all was being incapable of protecting the woman he loved. How helpless he'd felt, attempting to slam his way through the door, hearing the muffled sounds of the breath being choked from her. To think someone in the world felt such malice toward him that he'd intended to kill not only Julian but his wife as well was jarring indeed.

Even more jarring when one considered the pathetic fact that he hadn't an inkling as to who would wish him such ill or why. He'd been of half a mind to suspect Whitney of hiring someone to remove him, blight that he was, from the earth. But Jesse Whitney loved his daughter, and he would never have consented to her being injured, which left Julian hopelessly adrift.

She pressed a kiss to his chest, sending a fresh arrow of heat to his groin and effectively cutting through the morose bent of his mind. "You are a good man, Julian, for all that you choose to believe you're not. Besides, I wouldn't be here now if it weren't for you."

Her drawl remained more pronounced than usual, and her voice felt like honey sliding slowly over him. He didn't want to think about how near she'd come to death. Didn't want to entertain for one more moment the knowledge that if anything had happened differently earlier, she would be forever gone. Gone from him he could bear because he loved her too much, but gone from the earth he could not.

She pressed another kiss to his skin, her tongue flicking out to taste him, and he wasn't sure which urge was stronger, the one to catch her in his arms and flip her on her back or the one to fling her from him for her own good. His fingers tightened over hers, twining with them.

"Damn it, don't you see? You wouldn't have been in danger at all, wouldn't be in this very house like a lamb ripe for slaughter, if it weren't for me." His voice was rougher than he'd intended, but there was the truth of it.

"Nothing that happened was your fault." She seemed to read his mind in that canny way she had. She kissed higher, her hot mouth roaming to his neck. "You mustn't blame yourself."

"Ah, but I must, for that is where the blame lies." And to do penance, he would see her safe and far, far away from him. An ocean away if he had anything to say about it. "I'm so very sorry for all the pain I've caused you. How is your cheek, love?"

He'd wanted to summon her a doctor but she'd been adamant in her refusal. With the fight drained from his body, he'd made her promise to agree to an examination in the morning. She had acquiesced with extreme reluctance.

"Sore, but it will heal," she assured him, and by now her enterprising lips had kissed their way up the cord of his throat, lingering over his Adam's apple, before finding the solid angle of his jaw. She disentangled her fingers from his grasp, her hand flitting to his shoulder. "What of you? It must have hurt when you broke down the door."

In truth, he hadn't felt a damn thing. Fear and determination had pumped through him, washing out any other sensation. He'd never been so frenzied, so terrified. All that had mattered was getting to Clara. Now she fretted over him, as though ramming his shoulder into a piece of wood was the equivalent to even a bloody twentieth of the pain she'd endured. His brave, sweet little dove. How he would miss her when he set her free from her gilded cage on the morrow. But it needed to be done. He was no bloody good for her. No good for anyone.

"Do not concern yourself over my worthless hide." He couldn't resist slipping his hand beneath the soft curtain of her hair and stroking up her spine.

She framed his face in both her palms then, her face so near to his that he could distinguish each fleck of navy in her vividly blue eyes. After what had happened earlier, neither of them had been willing to extinguish the lights entirely, and he was glad for it now.

The warm glow of the lowered lamps bathed her ethereal beauty. He studied her, attempting to memorize her features: the rosebud mouth, wayward eyebrow, the freckles, tipped chin, retroussé nose. Perfection. Every inch of her was lovely. Jesus, he would more than miss her. Losing her would be akin to losing a part of himself. The best part of himself. How had she gotten beneath his skin, into his very blood, in such a short span of time?

"I never want to hear you call yourself worthless again," she told him then, her tone passionate. Dictatorial, almost. "You are anything but. You've proven yourself kind and true and brave more times than I care to count. I won't stand for you to speak ill of yourself ever again. Am I understood, Lord Ravenscroft?"

A wry smile tugged at his lips. "You are understood, Lady Ravenscroft." If only he—or anyone else in England, for that matter—esteemed him as highly as the plucky, nude American woman draped over his chest and issuing him orders did. But that was part of why he loved her, wasn't it? She saw beneath him, saw past the ugliness of his past, saw him better than anyone ever had. And she had chosen *him*. Against all odds, against logic and reason and goddamn it, even common sense, she had chosen him.

For tonight, at least, she was still his. Before he could say anything else, she kissed him. It wasn't a skilled kiss. It wasn't even a sensual kiss. Rather, it was a sudden setting of her mouth upon his, hard and fast. But it was borne from the emotions arcing between them in the night with the force of electricity.

Tonight only, they were man and woman, two people who had nearly lost each other in the darkness. For the time being at least, there was light. There was warmth and there was pleasure, and there was something else that was far more defining and powerful.

There was his love for her, impossible yet true, and *that* was all that mattered.

Her attempt at seduction was rather clumsy, even she had to admit. She'd meant to give him a soft, languorous kiss, a kiss that enticed and hinted at greater pleasures in store. Instead, she'd been so overwhelmed by love for him, a fierce surge of protectiveness rippling through her, that she'd mashed their lips together as though she could confess the depth of her emotions with aggression. She doubted he'd ever suffered such awkward inexperience.

Her cheeks heated with mortification and she made to pull away from him, but he caught her shoulders and held her still when she would have retreated. His lips firmed over hers, taking control of the kiss, teasing her mouth open for his exploration. His tongue delved inside, claiming and coaxing. He tasted of whisky and desire, and her fingers sank into his hair as she gave in to him, telling him without words what she most longed to say.

She slid her leg over his thigh so that she straddled him, bringing their lower bodies into full, torturous contact. *Take me.* He was hard and hot, the tip of him brushing her slick folds in a maddening precursor of what was to come. *I'm yours.* A low growl of pleasure rumbled from him. She arched into him, wanting his possession so badly she ached with it.

I love you.

Clara kissed him back with all the fiery sensations burning though her: relief, fear, hope, desire. If only she could tell him how she felt. But it was too soon, her emotions too new. And her body clamored for revelations of a different sort entirely. She rubbed the sensitive bud of her sex on his cock. He pumped against her, nipping her lip. His hands came between them to cup her breasts, his thumbs drawing quick, delicious circles over her nipples.

Yes. This was what she needed so desperately after what had happened. She needed to become one with him, for the joining to be frenzied and intense. To lose herself, lose every memory of evil and terror and replace it with the wonder of Julian's body against hers, on hers, inside hers. She inhaled deeply, savoring the scent of him, cologne and hot-blooded man.

He broke the kiss at last and worked his way down her throat, lingering with sweet tenderness where her skin was sore and bruised. He rained kisses on her, erasing the violence and pain inflicted upon her with each brush of his lips.

"I'm so sorry for this," he crooned. "I'm so very sorry, my love."

"It will heal," she promised, continuing to torment herself by gliding her slick folds over him again and again. "Take away the pain for me, Julian. Replace it with pleasure."

His tongue flicked over her neck, tasting and licking and banishing every trace of the brigand who'd dared to assault her in her own bed. "I'd take it for you, darling. I'd bear it all for you if I could. That's how much I—goddamn it, Clara, I will hunt the bastard responsible for this down. I'll hunt him down and I'll choke the life from him, and I'll watch him die."

His words sent pinpricks of ice through the sensual haze enveloping her. Her husband was not a violent man. But he meant what he'd just said. She had no doubt of that. His deep voice vibrated with a complex blend of rage and passion. This beautiful, enigmatic man she'd married would kill to avenge what had happened to her. The realization left her shaken. Humbled.

"The police will find him," she said with far more confidence than she felt. The inspector who'd been sent to conduct interviews with the household had seemed rather green and overwhelmed. "The law will see him punished."

"*I'll* see him punished," Julian vowed before bestowing another series of quick, devoted kisses to her neck. "That's my promise to you. You'll never know another moment of fear if I bloody well have a say in it."

Here was the rattler in him re-emerging. She hadn't been wrong about that part of him. With everything in her, she believed that if there was indeed a way for him to hunt down the villain who'd attempted to kill them both, he would. And he would extract his own vengeance. But she didn't want to think any more about vengeance or murders or evil men who attacked in the darkness of the night.

No, she most certainly did not. What she wanted now was her husband. The man she loved. The notorious Earl of Ravenscroft, a man who seemed to regard the entire world around him—even his own life—as some sort of private joke, the man who had married her without ever intending to uphold his half of the bargain, the man who cared for his trying sisters and had committed all manner of sins in the name of providing for them, the man who tried so hard to never allow anyone to see the real him. That was the man she loved. Complicated, baffling, more handsome than any man had a right to be, protective and wild and strong.

And most importantly of all, hers.

She guided his head back to her for another kiss, and this time she took great care not to bungle it as she had before. She angled her mouth over his, kissing him slowly, running her tongue over the seam of his lips until he parted for her, letting her inside. She plundered him, taking and tasting, nipping at him, teasing him, leaving them both breathless. And then she undulated her hips against him, not stopping until the head of him rested at her slick entrance.

"Make love to me, Julian," she ordered against his mouth.

In one swift motion, he rolled them both so that she was pinned beneath him on his bed. Her thighs opened, welcoming him. His fingers dipped into her folds, working the nub that was so greedy for his touch. She jerked against him, crying out. He kissed her again, deep and voracious, before taking the tip of her breast in his mouth and sucking.

A mewling noise split the air, and she realized dimly that it had come from her. He caught her nipple between his teeth and tugged. Her hands went to his broad back, her nails sinking into his warm, muscled flesh. He played with her, working her fast and hard and bringing her perilously close to release. Then his fingers brushed lower, parting her, sinking inside her body. She twisted and moaned, still unaccustomed to the invasion but knowing now what it meant. Wanting more. She arched into his hand, bringing him deeper inside her, crying out with need.

Her nipple popped from his mouth with a wet sound and he stilled, his gaze meeting hers. "Are you sore, my love? I don't wish to give you any more pain tonight."

The discomfort from earlier had gone, and in its place was only a wild, ravaging hunger. A need to have him inside her again. "I'm fine. Please, Julian. I want you."

Her reassurance was all he needed, for in the next moment, he withdrew his finger and his cock was once more at her entrance, poised. "Are you certain, little dove?" His voice was strained, his expression tense.

She moved against him, bringing the tip of him inside her. "Yes," the lone word left her lips as a hiss. "Oh yes. I need you inside me."

"Fuck, Clara. Tell me again."

His guttural demand was as wicked as it was enticing. He liked when she said sinful things to him, she realized, things she would never have before dared to say aloud or even known existed.

She met his gaze, unwavering. "I need you inside me. Now."

The breath left his lungs in a hot rush, billowing over her bare breasts like a kiss. In one long thrust, he was fully sheathed inside her, deep and rigid and wonderful. Every part of her—her skin, her breasts and limbs and mercy, her entire body—hummed with pleasure. His mouth took hers again as his touch traveled everywhere, stroking her nipples, her back, dipping between where their bodies joined to tease her hungry flesh.

She was wet, so very wet, and he slid in and out of her more easily this time than the last, her body stretching to welcome him, tightening to bring him deeper. It was a beautiful rhythm, and it didn't take long for her to shatter, clenching around him as waves of bliss licked over her. He continued to thrust inside her, absorbing the ripples of her pleasure.

With another growled curse, he withdrew suddenly from her body and she felt the warm wetness of his seed on her belly. He kissed her again, a possessive claiming as powerful as their coupling had been, and then rolled to his side, his chest heaving, head upon the pillow.

"My God, little dove," he said, his voice hoarse. "My God."

The next morning dawned grim and bleak. Julian woke with Clara pressed trustingly to his side, the scent of sunshine and citrus and some indefinable note that was simply her—lush and effervescent and gorgeous—enveloping him. He ached with everything inside him, every instinct and nerve and raw, pulsating emotion, to keep her forever there. To never let her go.

For the first time, he understood what had been missing from his life. She had been. A complex and determined woman with a keen mind and a sound dose of daring, who'd been bold enough to make him want her and steadfast enough to make him love her. It was the sight of the purple bruises circling her neck like some sort of sick necklace that broke the spell she cast upon him, a reminder that he dared not linger or stray from his course.

He had brought the darkness of his world into her light, and he alone could remove the blight.

He knew what he must do, and so he pressed a kiss to the silken cascade of golden hair at her crown and gently extricated himself, taking care not to wake her. He dressed in haste, without the aid of his valet, and made certain two of his most reliable footmen guarded the chamber door.

Though he doubted the miscreant who'd attacked Clara would have the bollocks to make another attempt by the light of day, he wasn't about to take any further chances with her safety.

He took a brief moment to confer with Osgood, leaving the household preparation in his capable hands before settling into his carriage for what felt like the longest drive of his life. With each sway of the conveyance, he felt sicker, the knot inside his gut tightening until he feared he'd cast up his accounts like a sailor on his first day to sea.

Yes indeed, this was the fates' way of meting out punishment for the reckless sin that had marked his life. Finally, he must do penance. He'd bloody well take it, though, if it meant protecting the woman he loved. The plum-colored flesh of her elegant throat and cheek mocked him as the carriage came to a halt outside the townhome of Jesse Whitney. His visit was unannounced, unexpected.

He'd come to bow and scrape to Clara's father, to see to it that she remained far from the path of the malevolence he'd unwittingly brought into her life. Far from him and anything and anyone who would hurt her. Swallowing his pride today was the least of his worries. Jesus, someone had almost killed her. On his watch. Because of him.

Another surge of nausea nearly made him wretch but he tamped it ruthlessly down as the carriage door swung open and he descended, gulping the cool morning air despite its familiar stench of horse dung and soot. He entered the stately home in a dreamlike state, only half aware of his surroundings.

As the butler led him to Whitney, Julian rehearsed half a dozen different things he might say. But how the hell did one tell a man that his daughter had almost been murdered in her bed and it was all his fault? Given Jesse Whitney's searing dislike of him and his propensity for defending his daughter with the business end of a pistol, he wouldn't be surprised if he left this interview with a gunshot wound.

Whitney stood upon his entrance, looking tense and ill

at ease, his mouth drawn into the ferocious frown he'd come to expect. "Ravenscroft."

"Whitney." Julian sank into a chair, his legs betraying him. He'd never felt more weak, more pathetic and useless than he had in the hours since Clara's attack. It left him limp and drained, floating in a sea of self-disgust.

Clara's father sat, steepled his fingers, and raised an expectant brow. "To what do I owe this visit, my lord? Have you squandered my daughter's dowry already? If it's more money you're after, I'm afraid you're bound for disappointment. I'll not give you another godforsaken penny."

On any other day, he would've taken umbrage that the man held him in such low regard that he imagined him capable of losing a fortune in the span of a few days. But today was a different goddamn sort of day.

"I don't want your bloody money, Whitney," he bit out. "I want you to assure me that you'll abide by Clara's wishes and send her back to Virginia as soon as possible."

"Well I'll be damned." Whitney sat back in his chair, regarding him as he would a thief who'd just approached him on the street with every intent to fleece him. "Is this what you planned all along, you cold-hearted son-of-a-bitch? To get her dowry and then rid yourself of her?"

"No," he denied, his voice hoarse with the tenseness of the emotions roiling through him. "Her leaving me is the last thing I want in this world. But it's what needs to happen. Someone attacked her last night. If I hadn't been able to break down the door when I did…"

His words trailed away, cut off by the sudden thickness in his throat. By God, he would not weep before Jesse Fucking Whitney. He would not. His hands tightened into impotent fists on the chair's carved mahogany arms. He took a steadying breath.

"My God." The color drained from Whitney's face, leaving him as ashen as Julian was sure he appeared. "Where is she now? What happened to her?"

"She's safe," he reassured. "She is sleeping under guard as we speak. But the bastard strangled her. She's badly bruised. His intent was clear. I can only surmise that the person responsible for attacking me is behind this as well and he'll stop at nothing until he reaches his objective. I'll not have Clara in danger. Not for all your American gold. Not for all the gold in the bloody world. I want her safe and far away from me and any enemies I've made over the years. The farther away the goddamn better."

"Sweet Jesus, she was strangled? My daughter was *strangled*? In your home? What kind of a monster are you?" Whitney flew from his seat, his face going from white to red in an instant. "How dare you put Clara in danger? If ever there was a man deserving of a beating, it is you, Lord Ravenscroft. I'd punch you in your smug, lordly face now if I didn't fear that I couldn't stop, and I've no wish for my children and wife to see me cast to gaol for your murder."

Julian rose as well, grimly accepting every last drop of the anger Clara's father spewed at him. He deserved it all and more. "I can assure you, Whitney, that no one loathes me more than I loathe myself. I never, not in my wildest imaginings, not for one second, believed my wife was in danger. I don't have an inkling who is behind all this or why, but after last night, I'm determined to remove everyone I love from harm. That's why I'm here now, to beg you to take in Clara and my sisters both as expeditiously as possible."

"Everyone you love?" Whitney sneered. "Don't expect me to believe you're capable of such an emotion, my lord. Do me the favor of ceasing to maintain your pretense of caring for my daughter. She is and always has been worthy of far more than a man who's whored himself for half the *ton*. She confessed the truth of your union to me, and I know it for the hogwash it is."

So Clara had revealed the truth to her father. It startled him to realize she had done so and had never said a word to him about it. What else could she have said to her father?

he wondered. And what was her motivation for telling him?

He couldn't think about any of that now, though, could he? For the moment, he needed to focus on what was the most important task: securing safety for Clara and his sisters by their distance from him. "In that we are very much in accord. Clara is worthy of a far better man than I, and that's why I'm setting her free. Look, I don't expect you to believe a word I say, Whitney. But it may surprise you to discover that your opinion isn't the arbiter of my finer emotions."

Whitney scowled, striking his desk with his fist with enough violence to make pen and papers dance about. "Nothing surprises me, Ravenscroft. Particularly when it comes to fortune hunting vultures who prey on innocent, good-hearted girls like my Clara. She may be foolish enough to fancy herself in love with you, but I see you for the blackguard you are. You don't fool me, goddamn your hide."

Clara fancied herself in love with him? Something inside him, some stupid hope he couldn't seem to quell, rose to the surface. "Clara said she loves me?"

Whitney's eyes narrowed. "Of course she did. The girl lives with her head in the clouds. She's too much like her mother, easily swayed by a handsome face. I all but begged her to come with me and she wouldn't leave your sorry arse. Much good it did her. Nearly murdered in her own bed. Jesus, I'm of half a mind to kill you myself, earl or no, and beat whoever's after you to the punch."

His heart ached in his chest, ached to think that she felt what he did, this bone-deep connection, this all-consuming desire to be one with her and protect her. He wanted to be the only man who ever touched her, to make her his forever. But perhaps she was just a dream sent to taunt him, to prove to him how contemptible he was, how what he needed the most would forever remain beyond his reach.

Something inside him, raw and true, broke free in that moment. He met Whitney's glare without flinching. "Believe whatever you like of me, Mr. Whitney, but know this: I love Clara. I don't deserve her. I never have and I never will. She's good and smart and caring and brave. She swept into my life with the force of a bloody summer thunderstorm, and I've relished every second I've been in her presence."

He paused, warming to his cause before continuing. "I love her and I want her safe and happy. I want her on a ship bound for Virginia as soon as possible—that's what she's wanted all along, and she ought to be far enough away from me and whatever faces me there. I want her to have the life she's dreamed of. As for my sisters, I hope that they can stay in your home until I can be certain that whoever wants me dead would not come after them as well. I ask you all this as one man who loves Clara to another."

Whitney stared at him wordlessly, appearing to take his measure. "My God," he said at last. "I must be losing my mind, for I'm almost persuaded to believe you."

"Believe me," he said fiercely. "I've never met as fine a woman as Clara. I'll do anything to protect her, even if it means giving her up forever. I want her safe more than anything. I'm no good for her, and I never will be."

The fight seemed to seep from Whitney's body. "I don't like you, Lord Ravenscroft."

The feeling was fairly mutual. "You don't need to like me. We have the same goal: keeping Clara safe. She isn't safe with me. I was too damn stupid to realize it, but I won't make the same mistake again."

Clara's father sighed, and it was the sigh of a man who felt every one of his years in his very joints. "She won't leave you easily, you know. When Clara is determined, Lord help anyone who stands in her way."

Julian nodded. "She's too stubborn for her own good. That's why I'm enlisting your help, sir. I know she won't listen to me alone."

Whitney inclined his head in acknowledgment. "You seem to know my daughter well, Lord Ravenscroft. I begin to think I may have misjudged you."

Ah, how ironic. On any other day, he would have appreciated the change of tides. It seemed that Jesse Whitney was realizing that he wasn't the only man in the world capable of loving his daughter. Indeed, the usual rancor that had underscored their every conversation had dissipated.

Even so, never let it be said that he couldn't own his faults. "You didn't. I'm not worthy of your daughter, sir. My reputation is as black as you think and then some. But I love her with everything in me. And the thought of anything happening to her…I can't bear it. Help me, please."

"You needn't beg, man." Whitney skirted the desk and delivered an awkward clap on his back, the first show of anything other than enmity between them. "I'll be happy to welcome her and your sisters into my home. And if I've any say in the matter, she'll be Virginia bound by this time tomorrow."

Thank God. The assurance left him feeling hollow and shattered. In less than a day, Clara would be sailing away from him. But by God, at least she would still be alive.

"Thank you, Mr. Whitney." Relief coursed over him, blunting the soul-sick dread that threatened to overwhelm. "Now if you'll excuse me, I have some other matters that require my attention."

The biggest matter of them all was uncovering who was behind the attempts on his and Clara's lives and getting retribution. More and more, he couldn't seem to keep one name from swirling through the murk of his thoughts.

Lottie.

And if she was somehow behind all this, there'd be hell to pay.

Chapter Fifteen

THE FAINT STRAINS OF LIGHT EMERGED THROUGH THE WINDOW DRESSING, piercing the depths of Clara's slumber and forcing her to wake. She rolled over, stretching, her body singing still with pleasure. She fully expected to find her husband at her side. The bed was empty and cool to the touch, counterpane carefully drawn tight to the pillow as if to suggest he'd never even been there at all.

But he had been there, and a niggling sense of foreboding settled in her gut that he was not there any longer. Aware of an unprecedented amount of footsteps sounding in the hall outside and doors opening and closing, she rose with grim intent, determined to find out what was happening.

Her dressing gown awaited her, neatly laid out on a chair by the bed. Had he done that? It was difficult indeed to imagine the Earl of Ravenscroft collecting her dressing gown and laying it out for her like a lady's maid. She threw it over herself, belting it with care, and made her way to the door joining their chambers.

The door had splintered from his effort to break it down

the night before, and it no longer closed properly. She would need to see to its repair, of course. The abundance of footfalls in the halls and the broken door were the least of her concerns, however, and that much became apparent when she stepped over the threshold to find a most unexpected tableau unfolding before her.

No, nothing about the day was as troubling as what she saw now. What *was* troubling indeed was that a number of servants were currently engaged in packing up her personal effects. She stopped, mouth opening in shock.

The contents of her wardrobe were scattered over the chamber, her gowns and undergarments separately arranged, trunks laid out, some already closed. The maids working diligently to pack her belongings all stilled at her unexpected entrance. Where had they come from? She'd yet to select domestics from the characters she'd been reviewing the day before.

She found her lady's maid in the crowd. "Anderson, what is the meaning of this?" she demanded.

"My lady." Anderson curtsied and hastened to her side, her expression lined by worry. "His lordship instructed Osgood that we are to pack up all your things as you'll be moving back to live with Mr. Whitney."

Betrayal settled deep into her bones, cold as winter and just as merciless. He was sending her away. Sending her back to live with her father. And he hadn't even had the nerve to inform her of his decision to her face. No, instead, he'd abandoned her in his bed as if she were no better than a harlot he'd paid for the night so that she could learn the truth from her lady's maid and her own two eyes.

"Where is his lordship, Anderson?" she asked, trying to keep the violence of her emotions from coloring her voice. She would be calm. She would confront him, learn the meaning of this. She would not, by God, be sent away. Not like this.

Anderson blanched. "He's not at home, my lady."

Not at home. Her teeth ground together. "Where has he

gone, if you please?"

"I'm sure I'm not privy to his lordship's schedule for the day," Anderson said faintly. "I'm so sorry, my lady, for what happened to you last night. It's given the household quite a fright. Are you well today?"

"No," she admitted, her gaze traveling back over the chamber once more. The other maids had continued their work, diligently sorting and folding. "I'm not well at all."

"Let's get you dressed, my lady. The doctor will be arriving soon at Lord Ravenscroft's request." The lady's maid's gaze dropped to Clara's throat, her brow furrowing. "Begging your pardon my lady, but are you in much pain?"

Yes. She hurt everywhere. Most especially in the vicinity of her heart. "I'm not seeing a doctor," she decided.

Julian could make as many high-handed decrees as he chose, but their issuance didn't necessitate her submission. For never let it be said that Clara Elizabeth Ravenscroft had ever obeyed the edict of any man. If he thought he could simply pack her up and excise her from his life without putting up a fight, he was wrong.

"But my lady, surely you ought to see the doctor as his lordship wishes?" Anderson persisted gently. "You've a great deal of bruising, I'm afraid."

Clara's hand stole to her neck, absentmindedly stroking the reminder of the previous night's horrors. "I'll see no one other than the earl himself."

A reckoning was in order.

The time to confront his past had arrived, though the act gave him no satisfaction. Indeed, he knew only a deep-seated tug of anger mingled with self-loathing in his gut as his carriage stopped on a familiar street.

He was no stranger to the Duke of Argylle's Mayfair home. Indeed, he suspected he'd spent more time there than Argylle himself, who preferred rusticating in the country or staying in St. John's Wood with his mistress when in the city. After Lottie had produced two healthy sons, she'd been free to pursue as many lovers as her heart desired. And as it turned out, her inconstant heart had desired a great many.

Julian had been only one of an endless procession, though he'd been witless enough to believe their affair was different than the others who'd gone before him. Fucking came easy to Lottie—she had a beautiful face and body, a husband who didn't give a damn, and a voracious sexual appetite. As a favorite of Bertie's, she enjoyed free reign of the Marlborough House set.

But she also had a reputation beyond her eagerness in the bedchamber, one that he'd ignored in his lust and her declarations of love. A reputation for vindictiveness. She had a history of cutting and ostracizing the wives of her lovers. There had been whispers that she'd had a helping hand in Lady Morehaven's madness and subsequent incarceration in an asylum in Chiswick after Viscount Morehaven had very publicly flaunted their affair. That had been before Lottie and Julian became lovers and he hadn't paid the gossip much mind at the time. Naturally, Lottie had dismissed such notions with the wave of an elegant, well-manicured hand.

Julian had simply accepted her word, for the Morehaven scandal wasn't any of his affair and he had enough whispers darkening his own reputation not to give a damn for idle gossip. Now, however, he had every cause to wonder. There had been the troubling altercation at the Devonshire ball, after all. Not to mention the call Lottie had later paid upon Clara. It had left Clara with enough misgiving that she'd seen fit to share it with him.

He descended from his carriage and strode up the front walk in a fog of troubled thoughts. As Julian gave the butler his card and cooled his heels, his mind sifted feverishly through the facts. He didn't want to believe Lottie capable of hiring a thug to commit murder on her behalf. She was frivolous, callous, and faithless, but he'd never for an instant before today believed her dangerous.

Sill, someone was responsible for the two acts of violence perpetrated upon his home, that much was certain. It seemed Lottie had the best motive of anyone he could countenance. And if she was behind the attacks, Lord have mercy on her soul, for he couldn't be certain what he'd do to her.

The butler returned. "Her Grace is not at home."

Of course he shouldn't be surprised that she'd refuse his call. Anger boiled within him. "Kindly inform Her Grace that I'll not leave until I receive an audience. It's a matter of grave import."

The servant's brows snapped together but he did as he was asked, his distaste of Julian's gauche refusal to accept polite pretense quite clear. Julian didn't give a goddamn what the butler, the Duchess of Argylle, or anyone else thought of him. All he cared about was finding out who had dared to cause Clara harm.

The butler returned just when Julian had begun to contemplate storming into the home and finding her himself. "Her Grace will see you, my lord."

Biting back a retort, he stalked to the big, cheerful drawing room where Lottie had always preferred to receive callers. As usual, it was bursting with flowers. He'd never known if she had such a surfeit of admirers or if she sent the bouquets to herself. Whatever the case, they were an omnipresent installation.

He found her sprawled elegantly on a settee, looking sated and relaxed. "Julian," she greeted him throatily, extending a hand. "I hope you don't mind if I don't rise? I'm not accepting callers this morning, you see."

He bowed but refused to take her hand, not wanting to so much as touch her. This near to her, he could see that her pupils were large and onyx in her eyes. Perhaps she'd once more taken to playing with opium. For Lottie there would never be a thrill great enough to cure her appetite.

"Thank you for accepting my call, Your Grace," he said

stiffly, careful to remain formal. "Do you know why I'm here?"

She raised an indolent brow before raking her gaze down the length of his body and lingering on his cock. "You're not satisfied with that little American jezebel you married? What's the matter, darling? Doesn't she like to be tied up?"

His skin went hot at her allusion to the depraved romps they'd once shared. "Do not speak of my wife, madam."

"She likes being tied up, then?" Lottie's full lips curved into a feline smile. "Perhaps I do her discredit. You've come here to suggest an assignation between the three of us? Would you like me to taste her cunny while you watch, Julian?"

He struggled to maintain his composure. An unholy rage rattled through him, straight to his bones. How dare she speak of his wife as though she were no better than some tart he'd hired for the night? How dare she imagine for even a moment that he would consider subjecting Clara to such debauchery? That he would want it?

Jesus, he was disgusted. Disgusted with her, with himself. Disgusted he'd ever imagined he could care for such a vapid woman, whose only care in life was her own pleasure.

Just barely, he suppressed the urge to yank her from the settee. "Enough, Lottie. I'll not hear another world of filth from you. I didn't come here for that."

Her lips formed a moue of disappointment. "Why are you here then? I'll admit, when I first saw you I was reminded of how well we got on in bed. It made me miss you, darling."

He ignored that. "Someone attacked my wife in her bed last night." He studied her reaction for any sign that she knew more than she pretended.

Her face remained a delicate mask of lethargy, as though she hadn't a care. Perhaps she didn't. "Attacked her? Whatever do you mean?"

"Someone attempted to murder her," he bit out. "He

strangled her in her sleep."

At long last, the words seemed to percolate the opium cloud she currently inhabited. "Good God, Julian, I don't like the chit but that's truly awful. How is she?"

Not the words he would expect from the person who had orchestrated such a violent crime. He swallowed. "As well as can be expected."

"Why are you here telling me this when we haven't spoken intimately in months?" Her gaze narrowed. "You think I had something to do with it?"

"Someone tried to kill me as well," he said instead of answering her question. "Two such incidents in such a small span of time are very suspicious. Wouldn't you agree?"

"Of course they're suspicious, you dolt. Someone is trying to kill the both of you by the sounds of it. But if you fancy that I care enough about you and that American bit of skirts you married to hire someone to do you both harm, you're sorely mistaken, Ravenscroft." Her smile faded. "When I heard you were marrying some green chit, I was jealous. I'll own that. I tried to scare her away from you. That much is true. But you cannot believe I'm capable of murder. Not even *I* am that depraved."

Julian stared at her, wishing he could see straight through her to the contents of her conscience. Of course, that was supposing she had one, and he was inclined to believe she didn't. Even so, everything she said, her manner and affectation, the calmness of her tone, suggested that she spoke the truth.

"What of Ashburn?" he asked. "Has he anything to do with this?"

"Percy?" She wrinkled her nose. "The only thing Percy cares about is cunny, drink, and horses. He's not the sort."

He wondered where the duchess had gotten the mouth of a sailor. Perhaps it was the opium talking. Whatever the case, he couldn't shake the feeling that he'd caught her with her guard down, in a state that would render it far more difficult for her to prevaricate. And everything she'd said held a glimmer of veracity.

"You swear that you know nothing of this, Lottie?" he demanded.

Not that he would take her at her word, damn it, but he was beginning to feel the fool for even having supposed that a woman more concerned with the next hard cock and vial of laudanum she could find than anything else would be capable of such a vicious plot. Looking at her now, pale and unaccountably relaxed by the potency of the opium she'd no doubt ingested, he couldn't imagine her capable of much of anything, really.

She stretched her arms above her head and yawned like a sleepy cat. "I swear, Julian. If you want to find out who's after you, perhaps you should look closer to home. Your brother doesn't have many kind words to spare for you these days."

"Edward?" His blood went cold at the unexpected mentioning of his brother. "He's on the Continent. I haven't had word from him in years."

Hadn't missed him either. Recalling the last time they'd spoken still filled him with acrimony. They had been young and stupid, Edward railing against him for the hedonistic lifestyle he'd adopted to save the estates from ruin. *You're a whore*, Edward had sneered, *just like our mother.* Their mutual rancor had never been more poisonous, and it had led to an angry round of fisticuffs that day that ultimately resulted in his brother's departure from the country.

"On the Continent? How strange." Lottie attempted to flash him one of her rare smiles, but her ever growing stupor seemed to impede her. "I ran into him at the Duke of Rutherford's soiree just the other day. Or was it the other week? Dear me, the days do seem to blend."

Jesus. Edward was back in London? He hadn't sent word. Not a single bloody word. A sharp surge of foreboding hit him then, starting at his spine and shooting straight through his body. He felt as if he were about to explode. "What did he say to you?"

But Lottie was fading. Her eyelids appeared to get heavier by the moment. "I don't recall, darling. Only that it wasn't pleasant. Have a care, won't you? I shouldn't like to see a man with such a beautiful face go to his rewards before his time. I always did love your face." She yawned again. "Dear me. I do believe I'm due for my nap. See yourself out, won't you?"

Before he could say another word, her eyes slid closed and she sighed, apparently succumbing to however much laudanum she'd consumed. For the first time since his entrance, he noted an empty vial and a drained teacup. Jesus, she must have drank it right before he'd entered. To hide a guilty conscience? He couldn't be certain of anything or anyone, it seemed. Least of all his instincts.

Either way, further conversation with Lottie was a moot point. She had passed out on her settee. With a muttered curse, he fetched her butler, instructing the man to see to his mistress. He wouldn't have her death on his shoulders, and he couldn't be sure how much of the poison she'd taken.

He stalked back to his carriage, weighed down by more questions.

What the bloody hell was Edward doing back in London?

It seemed he would need to locate his brother and find out. But first, he needed to return to Clara. Before he did anything else, he needed to make certain that she was removed from all harm, by whatever means necessary.

Clara was waiting for Julian in his study when he returned. He strode in, his expression troubled, looking so unfairly virile and handsome that he made her ache despite the anger trapped inside her. She'd been pacing the threadbare carpet but halted at his entrance, every part of her body attuned to him with razor precision. The mere sight of him made heat sluice through her, pooling in a steady ache between her thighs.

But no. She mustn't allow the way he made her feel to inhibit this audience. She wouldn't allow him to send her away from his life. They could damn well face the danger together. She wanted to be by his side or nowhere else.

"My lady." He came to her, taking her cold hands in his, that glacial blue gaze skating over her, lingering on the bruises that Anderson had taken pains to hide with a high-necked gown and some pearl powder. "How are you this morning?"

She knew he asked after her physical wellbeing, but bruises would heal far easier than hearts ever could. "Not well."

His jaw tensed. "Are you in pain? What did Dr. Redcay say?"

"I didn't see the doctor. My only interest was in seeing you." Clara searched his gaze. "I'm not going back to my father's house, Julian."

"Yes, damn it, you are," he growled. "You're not safe here. That much was amply demonstrated last night."

Her lips tightened. If he wanted to be stubborn, she could outmatch him any day. "I won't leave you. Do whatever you must to ensure my safety here. I'll keep my pistol beneath my pillow. Station a footman by my door. I don't care. Only don't send me away."

"Listen to me." His voice was low and intense, his face a mask of cold determination. "There is no way in hell I will allow you to be in further danger because of me. Someone is trying to kill me, and he's so desperate to get to me that he targeted you as well. I've made arrangements with your father. You and my sisters will be going to him this afternoon. He'll arrange passage for you to Virginia as soon as possible. And you'll go, goddamn it. You'll go and forget all about me."

"Forget about you?" The anger swirling through her froze. Her stomach felt as if it bottomed out. "What are you saying, Julian?"

He released her hands and stalked away from her, going to a decanter and pouring himself an ample amount of whisky before tossing it back and pinning her with a dispassionate look. "It's over, Clara. We'll have the marriage annulled. You'll be free to return to the land that you love unencumbered. I'll transfer your dowry to you. You'll want for nothing."

His words tumbled through her, clawed at her insides along with the icy fingers of shock. *It's over. Annulled. Unencumbered. You'll want for nothing.* He didn't just intend to send her to her father's home for her safety. He meant to leave her. To force her to leave him.

She swallowed, her mouth suddenly going dry. "All that I want is you, Julian. I don't want an annulment. I don't even want to return to Virginia unless it's with you by my side."

He tossed back another swallow of liquor, staring at her. "I'm doing you a favor, little dove." His tone gentled. "One day, you'll thank me for it. You don't belong here, and you don't belong with someone like me. This is for the best."

How utterly highhanded and wrong of him. She closed the distance between them, not liking the gulf it seemed to create, and didn't stop until her skirts brushed his trousers and she could see the shadows beneath his eyes and the whiskers shading his cheeks. He wasn't as unaffected as he pretended.

"You're wrong," she told him. "With you is precisely where I belong. I'm not going. Whatever danger there is lurking out there, we'll face it together. We'll find out who is responsible."

He took another draught of whisky, draining the glass before depositing it on the side table with a loud clunk. "Ah, little dove. I warned you against mistaking lust for something more, did I not?"

It was as if the caring, passionate husband of last night had been replaced by a bloodless stranger. Her heart gave a pang in her chest. "Don't do this, Julian." She was not above begging, not when it came to this man, the man she loved. "Don't try to push me away in some misplaced sense of keeping me safe."

"Don't you see?" He skimmed his fingers over her jaw, down her throat. "We will never suit. I can't give you my heart because I don't bloody well have one, and a woman like you deserves nothing less. I brought all this on myself, and I'll face it as I must. I won't allow my darkness to sully you or put you in danger for one moment more."

"No." She shook her head, refusing to listen, refusing to give a modicum of credence to his words. "It is you who doesn't see, Julian. I love you."

If her revelation affected him, he didn't show it. His gaze became shuttered. "I was fourteen years old when Lady Esterly propositioned me. My mother had passed on earlier in the year after giving birth to Josephine and my father had just died. I was only sorry for the death in that it saddled me with all his debts. He loved gambling, whoring, and drinking almost as much as he loved beating me, you see. Not much to be missed. Lady Esterly approached me at the old bastard's funeral. Her husband, Lord Esterly, was one of my father's friends. She wanted me to fuck her. Offered me money. Do you know what I did, Clara?"

Her heart ached for the young man he must have been. So terribly young. To have had a father who beat him instead of loving him and left him swimming in debt, to have felt he had no recourse other than sacrificing himself. "You don't need to tell me this, Julian. You were just a boy, and that awful woman preyed on you, abusing your innocence and vulnerability. Regardless, your past doesn't change the way I feel about you."

"But I do need to tell you." His face came closer to hers as he took her chin in his thumb and forefinger and held her there, trapped as any butterfly pressed to a pin board. "You need to hear this, to understand what I am. Who I am. I fucked her, Clara. I accepted the money. I became a whore that day. And that's how I've lived my life ever since, servicing widows and unhappy wives for money. I've fucked so many women I lost count. I haven't a bloody clue how many enemies I've made over the years. It could be any cuckolded man in London trying to kill me. Do you understand?"

He felt responsible for the attack. That was what she understood. And fear was making him build walls between them that should never exist. Her hand closed over his. "I understand more than you know."

He tore his hand from hers. Anger emanated from him in almost tangible waves. "Then for Christ's sake, don't throw your love away on a man like me. I'm not worth it, goddamn you. Go to Virginia. You'll be safe there. Find a good man, one who'll make you a decent husband, one who's deserving of you."

"I don't want another man. I want you." She placed a hand on his arm, feeling the tenseness of his muscled flesh even through his coat. "I love you, Julian."

He shrugged away from her touch and clamped his hands on her waist, setting her away from him as if she were a flame that had burned too near. "But I don't want you. I don't love you. I'm not capable."

She didn't believe him. "Everyone is capable of love."

"Not me." With a muffled curse, he reached for his empty glass and hurled it against the wall. It shattered on impact, shards raining to the carpet. "Leave, Clara. Get the hell out of here while you still can."

Stricken, Clara looked from the broken glass to her husband's grim countenance. "Please, Julian. Don't do this."

"Go. *I don't want you here.*" He spun her around so that she faced the door, his touch unusually rough. "Leave me now. And don't come back."

Tears threatening her vision, she found herself numbly obeying him, walking from his study. Leaving him. What could she say in the face of his anger? She'd laid her heart bare before him, and he'd turned it down before smashing it beneath his boot heel. Something inside her splintered, leaving her fragmented and hopelessly adrift.

Perhaps he didn't love her after all, at least not enough to fight for her. To fight for them and what they'd only begun to build. *I don't love you. I'm not capable. Don't come back.* The awful words echoed through her mind, a mocking litany. Pressing a hand over her mouth to muffle the sobs she couldn't suppress, she rushed over the threshold.

More breaking glass sounded behind her just before she closed the door.

Chapter Sixteen

SHE HAD GONE.

Thank the bloody Lord. Odd how life had a way of working in circles. Demented circles. For here he sat, alone in his study, going about the business of getting thoroughly soused. He tossed back the rest of his brandy, wishing it could obliterate everything with its heady burn. How long ago had it been that he'd sat in this very chair on a similar night, and Clara had upended his world?

A lifetime, it seemed.

But the lifetime had come and gone now, taking with it every trace of brightness, every bit of joy she'd brought him. He would never find another like her. The Lord wouldn't dare make a copy, nor would Julian settle for one. He loved her so much he ached with it, need of her an agony so searing he didn't think he'd ever recover. Forcing her away from him had nearly been his undoing.

As had revealing all the ugly truths about himself. For try as he might to forget about the sins of his past, he couldn't erase the indelible marks they'd left upon him. The evidence of it was everywhere, in the whisky and glass-soaked floor he'd refused to allow the servants to clean, in the incessant thumping of his head, in the pain tearing through him, and most damning of all, in the plum finger marks bruising Clara's delicate throat.

His self-hatred was raging like a hurricane, threatening to blow him apart. Perhaps he ought to make it easy for the bastard who wanted him dead and drink himself to death. The idea had merits.

Nothing mattered now that Clara was back at her father's house and safe. Whitney had sent word that they'd stationed guards everywhere in an effort to protect Clara and his sisters. That and the fact that they were removed from Julian's ambit ought to prove enough to keep them safe. The best news of all: Whitney had managed to secure passage for Clara back to her homeland as well.

Knowing he would never see her again felt akin to a knife stuck in his chest. Whenever he thought about it—which was every other breath—raw, unadulterated anguish paralyzed him. Understanding it was for the best didn't mitigate the pain. But he loved her too much to try to keep her. Even if the bastard who wanted him dead was caught, Clara deserved far better than a jaded rake who'd diddled half the ladies of the *ton* to keep the roof over his head. She deserved the best, and nothing but happiness, a man worthy of basking in her brilliance.

Julian was not that man. Nor would he ever be.

He took another gulp of brandy. Damn it, if only he hadn't thrown his entire decanter of whisky against the wall. He was nearly out of brandy and he had yet to find the stupor he sought.

A discreet knock sounded at the door, disrupting his black thoughts. Couldn't his butler ever do as he was bloody well told and leave a man the hell alone? He'd been explicit that he didn't want to be disturbed. No matter how much crashing or breaking glass might be heard from within. By God, if he wanted to tear the entire study from floors to rafters and leave it nothing but a pile of rubble, he would.

He would, if that's what it took to expunge Clara from

his blood.

"Damn it, Osgood," he roared, "I told you not to interrupt me. Not even for the devil himself."

"Forgive me, sir, but a very urgent note has arrived from the Whitney residence," Osgood intoned from the other side of the door. "I thought perhaps you may excuse the interruption in such an event."

His blood went cold. An urgent note from the Whitney residence. What the bloody hell could it mean? He shot to his feet and stalked across the chamber, trouncing through broken glass, books, and papers without a care. He wrenched open the door himself to find his butler wearing a strained expression, a silver salver bearing a single missive in his hands.

Julian snatched it up and tore it open, desperate for news, praying for the first time in his life. *Please God. Don't let anything have happened to her. Take me instead.* But why would the heavens want to listen to a man whose sins far outnumbered his years?

He scanned the contents of the note, dread sinking into his gut with the heaviness of a boulder. "Bloody, bloody hell."

The message was penned in Jesse Whitney's bold scrawl. And the words were the very last in the world that he wanted to see.

Clara had disappeared. So too had a footman instructed to guard an exterior door. But there was more. A single gunshot had been heard just outside the home. A frantic search of her chamber had turned up nothing.

Jesus. Everything in him withered.

No. He refused to believe something had happened to her. Anything but that. His sweet, lovely, bold Virginian lass could not be gone. Taken from the world when he'd done everything in his power to see her safe.

No, goddamn it.

He must have said the words aloud without realizing it, for they echoed now in the eerie silence of the hall like a war cry. It was the same hall where he'd pinned her to the wall and kissed her senseless on the day of their wedding. He thought of her soft, full lips beneath his, how innocent and sweet she'd tasted. How badly he'd wanted her. She could not be gone. Not his Clara. Not his little dove.

"My lord?" Osgood was a steadfast presence at his side, predicting action would be required.

"Have a horse brought round at once, Osgood." He hadn't time for the encumbrance of a carriage. But he would find her. By God, he'd ride all over London, tear the city apart with his bare hands if he must. Whatever he needed to do, he'd do it. And gladly, if only it meant that he could make her safe. If only it meant she hadn't been shot or worse. He stared at his butler, feeling as if the entire world had gone horribly off-kilter. "Lady Ravenscroft has…gone missing."

Saying it aloud hit him as surely as a blow to the chest. The air rushed from his lungs. For a moment, he couldn't breathe. Saying the words aloud made them real, and brought with them all their crushing depths of primeval fear.

"Yes, my lord. May God be with her." Osgood hastened away from him.

"Amen," Julian whispered to his butler's departing back. By Christ, she'd even won old Osgood's wizened heart.

Stealing away from her father's house now that it was under rigid guard was simultaneously easier and riskier than Clara had supposed. Easier than she'd supposed for she'd managed to succeed when she'd feared she had not a hope of escaping unnoticed. Riskier because taking a hostage had been, as it turned out, necessary.

It hadn't taken long for her to realize what she needed to do after her arrival back at her father's home. Lady Josephine and Lady Alexandra had run off to settle in to their temporary lodgings with a grim acceptance as she faced an unwanted interview with her family. She'd endured her father's smothering comfort and Lady Bella's equally smothering attempts to console her—all out of a place of love, she knew, but nevertheless difficult for her to accept.

Clara's eyes had been swollen from crying, her head ached, her throat throbbed, and her heart hurt. There was nothing in the world she wanted to do less at that moment than speak with anyone. Her husband had just rejected her. Sent her away from him. Told her he was incapable of love.

"Lord Ravenscroft was right to bring you and his sisters here," her father had said on a frown as he patted her arm. "You're safe with us, my darling girl. Lord only knows what manner of fiend he's brought down upon himself after so many years of debauchery. You cannot think to put yourself in harm's way because of his past sins."

Her father's words had done nothing to stem the flow of misery careening through her like a flooded river. "He is my husband," she'd argued. "It's my duty to stand at his side."

"Just as it's his duty to protect you, dear heart," Bella had intervened then, unable to refrain from gazing upon Clara as she might a motherless kitten she'd found on the street. Perhaps it was her delicate condition that caused her every emotion to be written across her beautiful face. Whatever the case, Clara found herself feeling most unappreciative of her stepmother's sweet kindness. She didn't want to be told that Julian was right to send her away. She wanted to rail against his decision, his self-loathing, his fears. She wanted someone to tell her to run straight back to his arms and put up a damn fight like a true Virginian.

But no one had, and all at once, understanding had dawned on her.

She loved her father. She loved Lady Bella. But everything in her told her that this was not where she belonged. She belonged with Julian. And if he was in danger, then she would face the danger with him. She would not, by all that was holy, cut stick and run, abandoning him to his fate.

No she would not. Virginia girls were made of sterner stuff.

The sternest stuff.

Naturally, her father had other ideas. He'd proved his usual obdurate self and had refused to allow her to leave, citing the recent attack on her as ample proof that being beneath Julian's roof was dangerous. He'd even booked her passage to Virginia. But the victory she'd once fought for—the return to her homeland—was hollow now.

She knew where she was meant to be. She had one home, and it wasn't a place.

As the hired hack she'd caught swayed through Belgravia, she kept her pistol trained on the brawny young footman she'd taken hostage. She rather pitied him, but her back had been pressed to the proverbial corner.

"You shot at me, my lady," he said dumbly for what had to have been at least the third time since she'd made good her escape.

"I shot into the ground," she corrected him gently. "And I'm sorry for it, but it was necessary. You weren't listening to reason."

She'd managed to convince the footman guarding her chamber door to allow her a visit to the library for a book. Once inside the library, she'd turned off the electric lights and made a run for it, knowing the layout of the house quite well. But upon reaching the side door she'd chosen for her exit, the footman guarding it had attempted to waylay her. When he'd begun shouting as she hailed a hack, she'd feared he would bring the entire household down upon them.

Clara had no wish to be discovered and forced back inside where she could spend the next several sleepless hours ruminating over why her husband had sent her away. And why she'd let him. No, sir. She had every intention of accomplishing what she'd set out to do. And so she'd raised the pistol hidden in the pocket of her skirts and shot.

Unfortunately, her action had not produced the desired

effect, for the alarms had been raised in her father's house. She'd decided at the last moment that perhaps bringing the lad along for her protection wouldn't be a bad idea. And so, just as the front door had been thrown open, she'd disappeared into the hack with the footman, guiding him with the best incentive mankind had ever produced: the barrel of a firearm.

"Begging your pardon, but I think you're mad, my lady."

She frowned at him. "You aren't precisely in a position to be tossing about insults, young man."

But the footman was either too shocked or too simple to know when he ought to hold his tongue. "I'm sorry, my lady, I am. But why would you want to leave a house where you're being kept safe to run out into the night? Only a madwoman would do such a foolish thing. Why, you're merely asking for mischief, as my ma would say."

Clara sighed. "Silence, if you please."

The lad was likely not far from the truth. Fleeing her father's home was, in hindsight, not the cleverest notion she'd ever entertained. But never let it be said that Clara Ravenscroft was afraid of taking a chance. And never let it be said that she wouldn't do anything for the man she loved.

Even if it meant humbling herself before him. Even if it meant abducting a poor footman at gunpoint and galloping through town back to her husband. Even if it meant taking a stand against whoever or whatever evil threatened them.

For in the hours since she'd allowed herself to be evicted from her home and Julian's life both, she'd discovered that she was stronger than she'd ever imagined. She was strong enough to face anything, to beat anything, to take a risk and feel the wind in her face. She was strong enough, which meant she would fight. She'd fight for Julian, fight for herself, fight for the life they were meant to live together.

The hack slowed as they reached the familiar neighborhood of Ravenscroft's townhome. In the darkness with only the glow of the street lamps, it looked more imposing than it truthfully was. Her heart hammered in her breast. Home, she thought.

"We're here," she informed the hapless footman, waving her pistol at him. "You alight first. I've no desire to cause you harm, but if you attempt to stop me, consider this fair warning. I can shoot an apple off a man's head from fifty paces."

It wasn't the first time she'd used that threat. Very likely, it wouldn't be the last. The footman blanched and did her bidding, preceding her out of the conveyance. She paid the hack driver, a grinning fellow with more black space in his mouth than teeth. If the sight of a lady brandishing a weapon and forcing a servant inside his conveyance had alarmed him, he still didn't show it. The coin she'd given him prior to their departure had certainly helped to ease any concerns he may have had.

She hurried to the front door. It was answered in two swift knocks. Osgood appeared, his ordinarily imperturbable countenance brightening into an expression of genuine relief. "My lady! You're home."

"Of course I am. Please see to it that this young man has a nice meal and a warm bath." She gestured to the footman with her pistol, which she perhaps ought to have hidden, given the startled look that raced across the butler's face. Belatedly recalling the trappings of civility, she tucked the small weapon back into the pocket in her skirts. "I'm afraid I've given him quite a fright this evening. Where is his lordship?"

The redoubtable butler frowned. "He isn't with you, my lady? He left a short time ago. He'd had word from the Whitney residence that you'd disappeared. His lordship was extremely concerned, as you might imagine."

"Oh dear." Perhaps her escape plan hadn't gone as well as she'd imagined after all. Firing the pistol had, in retrospect, been a grievous error. "Have you any idea where he was headed?"

"I'm afraid not, my lady," Osgood said gently, apparently recovered from the sight of her waving a pistol about like a common street criminal. Much to his credit. "He didn't advise as to his plans as he was in quite a rush."

Well, this was certainly an unexpected predicament of her own foolish making. She could either go back into the night in search of Julian or await his return. She hadn't intended to cause such a frenzy with her departure. It seemed she'd never cease landing herself in scrapes.

Rather than continue to chase her husband all over town, the best course of action would be to stay in one place, she reasoned. If he'd rushed out at word of her disappearance, then his destination was likely her father's home. "Osgood, would you please have a note sent to the Whitney residence to let them know I've arrived here safely and that I'll await Lord Ravenscroft's return?"

"Of course, my lady," reassured the competent butler. "And may I say that I'm heartily relieved your ladyship has returned to us?"

She smiled, touched by the thawing in his ordinarily frigid hauteur. "Thank you, Osgood. I'm equally relieved to be back."

Now if only her husband's welcome would be as warm. She made her way to his study, intending to wait for him in its comfortable confines. But she wasn't prepared for the disaster that greeted her upon her entrance. Books had been flung, their spines cracked. Glass shards littered the worn carpet. The entire room smelled heavily of spirits. Several dark stains marred the faded wallpaper. Chairs were overturned.

Good Lord, it looked as though a regiment of marauding soldiers had ransacked the chamber.

"Oh Julian," she whispered as she took in the evidence of how much it had devastated him to send her away. The door closed softly at her back and for the briefest flash, the sensation that she wasn't alone overcame her.

Before she could react, a voice sounded behind her.

"Lady Ravenscroft, we meet again."

Clara's entire body froze, her skin going instantly

clammy, her breath hitched and shallow, her mouth dry as sand. Fear curled around her chest in a crushing grip. The last time she'd heard that voice, there had been a pair of large hands wrapped around her neck.

By the time Julian returned to his home and was instructed by a relieved Osgood that Clara awaited him in his study, he felt as if he'd been to the bloody gates of hell. First, a paralyzing dread had snared him in its unforgiving maws as he'd raced to Whitney's house, desperate for news, any clue as to what had happened or how he could possibly find Clara. He'd been conferring with an extremely tense Jesse Whitney when word had arrived that the wayward minx was alive, thank God, and safe, waiting for him at home. Relief had come next, swift and searing. Following closely in its wake had been an almost unholy rage as the remainder of the succinct message had been read aloud.

Lady Ravenscroft escaped of her own volition.

No one had abducted her. She hadn't been shot. Hadn't been killed. However, she *had* put her life in jeopardy. He'd done everything in his power to send her from him, had stripped his soul bare to secure her safety, and instead of seeing reason, she'd defied him and her father both. Not to mention that it appeared she'd somehow taken a servant along with her, after firing a shot at the poor fellow.

Julian had found himself torn equally between anger and reluctant admiration for the entirety of his ride back. One moment, his blood thundered through his veins, his temples throbbing with suppressed anger, that she would be so bloody foolish. That she would not stay where no one could harm her and seize her reprieve from marriage to him with both hands.

The next moment, he couldn't help but appreciate her audacity and determination. Some lack-witted part of him, the part that loved his maddening wife to distraction, felt buoyed by hope that her actions carried a far greater significance than her mere willfulness. That she loved him, enough to foolishly risk all to stay with him.

Buffeted by his turbulent emotions as a ship in a storm-tossed sea, he crossed the threshold of his study, expecting to find his wife awaiting him, tucked into a wing chair. Or perhaps even standing, color staining her high cheekbones in her dudgeon. What he did not expect, as the door closed almost soundlessly at his back, was to see Clara, beautiful and stricken, her face wet with tears, trapped in his brother's arms. The barrel of a gun was pressed to her golden curls.

"Jesus, Edward." His eyes were only for Clara at first, drinking in the sight of her. She didn't appear to be harmed, thank God. His gaze went to his brother, a sickening sense of realization hitting him straight in the gut. He'd thought with such certainty that an enemy from his past—some cuckolded husband or jilted lover—had attacked him and Clara both.

But it had been a different sort of enemy from the past altogether. His very own flesh and blood. Betrayal tore through him like a gunshot, swift and ravaging in its aim. Edward had tried to kill him. *Edward* had attempted to strangle Clara. How the hell could it be?

His shocked brain attempted to make sense of the scene before him. He wanted to believe that the man holding Clara against her will was a stranger. But his eyes didn't lie. Edward had inherited their father's short, bullish build and plain features. Ten years had worked some change upon him—his body was stockier, his dark hairline receding as the former earl's had, grooves marking his forehead—but the man facing him now with murderous intent etched into the hard lines of his face was none other than his brother.

"Edward," he said again, his thoughts whirling with how the hell he could get Clara to safety. Perhaps he could overpower him, disarm him, at least tear her from Edward's grip. He stalked forward. "Is it you?"

"Don't take another step or she dies." Edward's tone

was flat and emotionless. Menacing.

Some instinct deep within Julian cried out, forced him to continue. Another step. Two. *Mine*, he thought grimly. *I protect what's mine.* And no one else in the world belonged to him the way Clara did. The way he belonged to her. She was his wife. His love. He'd do anything to save her and protect her. Even if it meant offering his own life. Especially if it meant that, for a life without Clara in it was one he didn't want to live.

But Edward didn't react well to his challenge. The arm he had locked around Clara's neck tightened and she cried out in pain. "Stay where you are, goddamn it."

Julian stopped, willing his mind to remain calm, to find some way out of this. "Let her go, brother. Your quarrel is with me."

"Damn right my quarrel is with you." Edward's face curled into a sneer that was so reminiscent of their father that for a moment Julian's body recoiled at the remembrance of the earl's fists connecting with his flesh. It was almost like staring at their father's ghost. An even more vicious, deranged ghost.

Julian raised his hands in a slow, placating gesture. "Tell me what you want from me. I'll do anything you ask as long as you release my wife. She is an innocent in all this."

"Your wife, innocent?" Edward laughed. "Best bloody joke I've heard in some time, *brother*. From what I hear, you've spent the last fifteen-odd years fucking your way through the *ton*. Any bride of yours would be tainted the instant you touched her. She's likely already carrying your heir. And that makes her dispensable indeed, for I have no wish for competition."

The air seemed to leave the chamber. Or Julian's lungs. He couldn't be sure. All he could be sure of was that his brother meant to kill him and claim the earldom for himself. More than likely, he intended to kill Clara as well.

Julian wasn't about to allow Edward to carry out whatever evil plan he'd hatched. No one would harm so much as a hair on Clara's head ever again. Not even over his dead fucking body.

"She's not carrying my heir," he denied, hoping to deflect some of his brother's attention away from Clara, perhaps even to release her. "I haven't touched the chit."

Edward's gaze narrowed to reptilian slits. "You expect me to believe you didn't bed her? A young, innocent beauty like this?" He relaxed his hold on Clara's throat to cup one of her full breasts in his hand. "Don't tell me you could resist such pretty tits."

A guttural sound tore from him and he lunged forward, blinded by rage and the need to defend Clara from being manhandled. Edward sprang backward, dragging Clara with him as though she were nothing more than a helpless heap of skirts.

"Not another step closer, damn you," Edward warned, once again tightening his hold on Clara's neck. "Or I'll choke the life from her. I almost managed last night. This time I won't fail. The choice is yours."

"Julian," Clara spoke for the first time. Her tone was hesitant, starved for breath. A plea. "He's mad. He means to kill you."

"Shut up," snarled Edward, tightening his hold until Clara made a choking sound.

Julian just barely restrained himself from launching himself at his brother. The only thing that kept him planted to the spot was the gun Edward kept trained to Clara's head. "Let her go. She has nothing to do with what's between us. She's leaving for Virginia in two days. Her passage is already secured. Release her and you'll never hear from her again. Your quarrel is with me."

"*Quarrel.*" Edward spat the word as though it left a bad taste in his mouth. "This is not a quarrel, goddamn you. This is about righting a grievous wrong. Now you've landed yourself a fat dowry and I mean to collect what's owed me. I'm the rightful Earl of Ravenscroft, and I've wasted too many years waiting for you to drink yourself to death."

He flinched. Perhaps a bit too close to the truth, that last statement. But Edward had been so mired in his bitterness that he'd failed to notice Julian advancing another half step nearer. If he could distract his brother with idle talk, inch close enough, there was a chance he could knock the gun from Edward's hand.

His gaze met Clara's for just a moment, long enough to spy the fear in the glittering depths of her eyes. Jesus, how he wished he could promise her he'd spring her from this hell safely. He wanted to allay her every fear, to kiss the beloved rosebud of her lips, the soft curve of her cheek, that wayward eyebrow. But he had to focus on the task at hand. A deadly one.

He wrenched his gaze back to Edward. "You're the rightful heir?" he demanded, his tone mocking. "Pray tell me, brother, how can that be when I am indisputably the first born?"

Edward's jaw tensed. "Our mother was a bloody whore. Little wonder you turned out in her mold. She came into the marriage to Father unchaste, a bastard in her belly. She never would tell him whose by-blow he'd accepted as his heir."

"You lie," Julian growled, creeping closer.

"I speak truth. Father confessed everything to me on his deathbed." Edward smiled, resembling the previous earl more than ever. "Our mother pretended to be an innocent, tricked Father into marriage. Then you were born far too early, a weak and pathetic babe by all accounts. Father knew at once you could not have been of his blood. He wanted to smother you but our mother begged to keep you safe and he was merciful. When I was born a year later, he never forgave himself for giving in. He wished to his dying day that he could have ended you, removed your false claim upon the Ravenscroft line. At long last, I've decided to be the one who does."

The story sounded like the sort of rot the old earl would spew. Then again, it could explain a great deal. He and

Edward had never shared a resemblance. The earl had relished in beating and scorning him while he'd only ever heaped praise and adulation upon Edward. Their mother had undeniably taken lovers—Josephine and Alexandra were proof of that.

In truth, none of it mattered any longer, for their parents were long gone, and he couldn't afford to be distracted. His entire being needed to be focused on freeing Clara, even if it meant getting himself killed in the process. He didn't give a damn what happened to him, as long as she lived.

He'd inched closer yet again during Edward's ramblings but stood still now as his deranged sibling's eyes scoured him, looking for even a hint of forward motion. "If your aim is sending me across the River Styx, let Clara go. She's done you no harm."

Edward cocked his head, considering him in a shrewd manner that belied his lunacy. "I'll strike a bargain with you, brother. As long as you swear she's not carrying your get, I'll let her go free."

Julian swallowed. He would say anything to save her. Lie or truth, it didn't matter. "She's not. I swear it."

"This won't end well for you," Edward warned grimly, almost as if he had a conscience. "I'm afraid you must die so that I can become earl as I ought to have been from the first. It's the only way. I waited on the Continent for so long, you know. Waited and did the honorable thing, hoping you'd drink or whore yourself to death. But then word reached me that you were courting an heiress, and I couldn't allow an heir to supplant me and take the earldom that's been mine all along, now could I? Her fortune is, of course, a boon."

Julian's blood went cold to hear his brother's casual confession. Jesus, he made it sound as if his greedy bloodletting was a natural step in the process of regaining what he felt was rightfully his.

"Of course you couldn't," he said easily, not daring to step closer with Edward's attention pinned on him. "But neither could you realize that she and I reached a bargain. We have a marriage in name only, in return for my portion of her dowry, while she goes home to Virginia. She's not a threat to the earldom, Edward. She's not carrying my child."

Edward appeared to be relenting. "I'll strike a bargain with you. There's a vial of poison in my pocket. Drink it, and I'll let her go."

"No," Clara cried out. "Don't do it, Julian. He'll only kill us both."

"Silence," Edward ordered, tightening his arm on her throat.

Clara's hands scrambled to Edward's coat, clutching at it as he choked her.

Nausea hit Julian straight in the gut. Damn it, Edward was going to kill Clara unless he acted. Unless he agreed to drink the poison. From there, with Clara freed from the pistol pressed to her head, perhaps he could finally make a move.

"I'll do it," he said definitively. "Let her go, Edward, and I'll drink the bloody poison."

Clara cried out, tears dashing down her cheeks. "No, Julian."

"Hush," he told her with a calm he little felt. "All will be well. This is what must be done." With his eyes, he tried his best to tell her how much he worshipped her, to communicate to her the endless depths of his love. He looked to Edward then. "Let her free."

Edward released her, shoving her away from him and in the opposite direction of Julian. Clara stumbled, gasping for her breath before catching her skirts in her hands and righting herself.

"Go sit in the chair," Edward ordered Clara, waiting as she haltingly made her way to the chair behind Julian's desk before turning his attention to Julian, the pistol trained upon him now. He reached inside his jacket and extracted a small vial. "You'll drink this now or I'll kill her and then I'll kill you."

Julian stared at the vial of poison, his mind spinning. He could knock it from Edward's hand, jump on him, grapple for the gun. But would that put Clara at risk? *Think,* he told himself frantically. *Think, goddamn it.* He could stall him, delay him, distract him. Those were his best options. And when he saw his opportunity, he would act.

"How do you imagine this will play out, Edward? I die and then what? You don't think the authorities will find this suspect?"

"You don't think I've thought this out?" Edward taunted. "Of course I have. It's a shame you suffered an apoplectic fit like our father. I'll be grieving, of course. Not many questions will be asked. And if they are, isn't it commonly known that poison is a woman's weapon? Perhaps one of your lovers finally sent you to hell. Perhaps even your own wife."

Julian's fists clenched at his side as he struggled to remain calm. The plan didn't sound nearly as deranged as it ought. But what chilled him the most was not his brother's betrayal or even his greed. It was that he intended to frame Clara for Julian's murder.

"You're a sick bastard," he said, staring at the stranger who shared his blood. Half his blood if he were to be believed, but blood nonetheless.

"Drink the poison or I'll make you watch her die," Edward snarled, holding the vial out to him.

Julian prepared himself to strike, knowing he would need to act fast, to take Edward by surprise and overpower him or all would be lost for he and Clara both. He reached out as if to accept the vial.

And just that quickly, a gunshot exploded into the silence. Almost simultaneously, a bullet found its home in Edward's skull. Blood spattered across Julian's waistcoat, the wall, the carpet. Edward fell, a wound on his forehead blossoming scarlet. His eyes stared sightlessly into the ceiling. The gun and poison fell from his limp fingers.

It was over. Edward was dead.

"Julian, are you injured?" Clara's shaky voice cut through the haze of shock clouding his mind.

He turned to find her standing, her face a pale mask, a pistol in her hand. Jesus, she'd shot Edward and saved them both. He'd never have imagined she'd have it in her. Everything he should have said to her before clamored to his tongue. But instead of any of them, all he could manage was a numb reply.

"Clara, you shot him."

Her beautiful mouth tugged up into a half-smile. "I told you I could shoot an apple off a man's head at fifty paces."

"My little Virginian warrior princess." His throat was thick, his mind and body and heart bombarded with all that had unfolded this night. But one thing he knew for certain. He loved her with everything in him. She was fierce and brave and better than he deserved. "My love. Come here."

He didn't need to say it twice.

She flew into his arms, and he held her to him as if he could forever keep her there. If he clasped her with more force than necessary, it couldn't be helped. Never in his life had he been more relieved. The full, blinding force of emotion exploding inside him was overwhelming. Thank Christ she was safe. Trembling in his embrace, but *safe*.

He buried his face in her fragrant hair, breathing deeply of her scent, and blurted the words he should have said long ago, the words that it seemed had begun simmering within him the very first night he'd laid eyes on her in his study. "I love you, Clara. I love you so damn much I ache with it. More than I ever imagined possible. When I almost lost you, it was more than I could bear. I would do anything for you. For you, I would have gladly swallowed the goddamn poison." His hoarse voice broke on the last confession but he didn't feel a bit of shame.

Her face was pressed to his neck, her arms around him in a grip that rivaled his own in its vehemence. She tipped back her head to look up at him, tears and unrestrained love shining in her eyes. He'd never seen a more beautiful sight.

"And I love you, Julian. I love you so much that I couldn't stay away, regardless of the danger. I never want to be anywhere but with you ever again. You're my home."

Perhaps he shouldn't have revealed his feelings. He still had no right to keep her from pursuing what she truly wanted, from returning to Virginia. He still wanted only the best for her. He was still an imperfect man with a past marred by too many sins to count. But something about the way she gazed at him now made him believe he could be a better man. That he had changed, and that she alone was responsible for it.

He swept a stray tendril of hair from her soft cheek, caressing her with his thumb. "I thought Virginia was your home."

She shook her head. "Not any longer. Anywhere in the world is home to me as long as I'm by your side."

He took her lips with his, the kiss fierce and deep as he dared for a moment to imagine a future for them. It was a kiss that would have gone on much longer if the servants, alarmed after hearing the fatal gunshot, hadn't chosen that moment to storm into his study. With reluctance, he tore his mouth away, for there was much to be dealt with yet this night and many grim hours looming ahead.

Chapter Seventeen

THE SUN WAS RISING OVER LONDON, painting the sky with fingers of brilliant yellow and bold orange, by the time Clara tied the robe on her dressing gown and slipped into Julian's chamber. A flurry of activity had descended upon the household in the moments after the gunshot rang out. The authorities had been called, statements taken. Word had been sent to the Whitney residence that all was well and that Lord and Lady Ravenscroft were safe at last, merely in need of some rest.

It was finally over. Relief and shock still pulsated through her, leaving her mind as thick as London fog. But there was one thing she knew: she and Julian had been given a second chance, and she meant to take it.

He stood with his back to her, his tall, lean form clad in only a dressing gown as well, his feet bare. He had the curtains pulled back, and he was still as a marble statue, surveying the street below.

Her hands shook as she crossed the room to him so she folded them together at her waist. She had killed a man tonight, and though she would make the same choice again in a heartbeat, she regretted the necessity. If only there had been another way.

She hadn't wanted to do it. Though she was a crack shot and always had been, she'd never had need of that particular skill until tonight. But greed and jealousy had turned Julian's brother into a madman, and he wouldn't have stopped until he'd killed them both.

She stopped a few feet from her husband, feeling hesitant despite his earlier words of love. He seemed to be unaware of her approach. Had he been in shock when he'd told her he loved her? Did he regret it now? Dear God, she hoped not.

"Julian," she said quietly.

He turned away from the grim vigil he'd been keeping, his beautiful face hard and tense. As his gaze settled on hers, he softened, holding his arms open to her. "My love."

She didn't hesitate. In another breath, she launched herself into his chest. He caught her to him, holding her tight. Her breasts crushed against him, and without the barrier of her everyday layers, each inch of his hard maleness was a delicious, reassuring thing. She held him with a matching fervor, desperate to be as close to him as she possibly could after coming so close to losing him for the second time. He pressed a kiss into her unbound curls.

"Thank God you weren't hurt." His voice was a low, deep rumble. Beloved. "I could hold you forever and it wouldn't be long enough."

She listened for a moment to the steady, reassuring thud of his heart beneath her ear before speaking. "I'm so sorry, Julian."

"It is I who should be apologizing to you, for bringing you into this mess. What can you be sorry for, darling?" He withdrew a bit to look down at her, his vibrant eyes probing.

Clara hesitated, her mind grappling with what she had done. "Your brother. I'm so sorry…I didn't want to do what I did."

"Jesus, Clara." He cupped her face. "You saved my bloody life. You saved *our* lives. Edward was unhinged. He tried to kill each of us on two separate occasions, and tonight he would have succeeded if it weren't for your bravery. Never be sorry for that. Christ knows I won't."

She searched his expression, feeling the guilt that had been festering inside her in the hours since she'd shot Edward begin to dissipate. "But he was your brother. And I…I killed a man, Julian."

"You were fearless," he said gently, rubbing his thumb over the fullness of her bottom lip. "My own plucky Virginia girl. You mustn't let this weigh on your heart. If I'd had a pistol, I would have shot him myself. He was mad, and was bent on murder. You did the only thing you could have done."

She believed him, and the last of the guilt lifted from her. "I couldn't bear for anything to happen to you. I would do it again."

"Ah, my love." He crushed her mouth beneath his on a groan, his lips taking hers in a fierce, claiming kiss. "I don't deserve your goodness or your daring. I don't deserve a single, goddamn thing about you. I don't deserve *you*, little dove."

"Don't say that." Reverently, she traced the contours of his face. The slash of his jaw, the hollows of his cheeks, the high, proud bones above it. She absorbed the prickle of his whiskers, the comforting heat of him, the sensual curve of his lips. "Don't ever say such nonsense again. I'll not hear of it."

"It must be said." His voice was harsh, steeped in self-deprecation. "Everything I told you about myself was true, Clara. Everything you've heard about me, I've no doubt, is true and then some. I'm not a good man. I've done things in my life that I deeply regret. As my wife, scandal will always follow you. Some doors will never be opened to you because of me. My past will always dog me."

"Hush," she cried out, her heart hurting for him, for the complete vulnerability he revealed to her. "I don't care about your past."

"But you should, Clara." He tone was passionless, relentless. "I'm giving you this chance now to leave me. I damn well should have given it to you before, but I wanted you too much. From the moment you stepped into my study in that godforsaken hat, I knew I'd do anything to have you. You were beautiful and innocent, so much the opposite of every woman I'd ever known, and I couldn't bear the thought of any other man having you. I told your father I'd ruined you. I bargained for your dowry. I never intended for you to leave for Virginia."

"Julian," she tried to interrupt, wanting to tell him that none of it mattered. That she loved him. That she too would do anything to have him.

But he wasn't finished. "No, you need to hear this. You need to listen and make your own choice. I tried to take your choice from you once, and I won't do it again. I love and respect you far too much for that. If I'd been the kind of man who is worthy of you, I'd have sent you on your way that day in my study without touching you. I wouldn't have dragged you into my sordid world, wouldn't have put you in danger. But I did, and now we're both paying for it. So for Christ's sake, Clara, listen to me when I tell you again that *I am no good for you*. You should leave me. I won't keep you from Virginia. I won't keep your dowry. Say the words now, and I'll let you walk out that door and on to the life you long for."

She swallowed against the emotion brimming within her, framing his beloved face in her hands. "This is the life I long for, with you. I love you. I love you more than I ever imagined possible. You are the only man for me."

"Clara, think this through. I'll not stand in your way. I'm offering you what you've always wanted, the very objective that led you to my study that first night." He paused, his countenance equal parts harsh and forbidding. "You can return to Virginia, free and unencumbered, with all your dowry at your disposal. I'll not keep a ha'penny."

"I've already thought it through, Julian." She beamed up

at him, happiness swelling within her like a hot air balloon, displacing all the tumult of the night. He loved her so much that he would set her free. Her strong, sensual, beautiful man. So many people had wronged him. She would not be yet another. "As I already told you, my home is with you. My place is at your side. Do you love me?"

"Hell yes I love you," he all but growled. "Never doubt that. I love you so much that I can barely think straight."

"Then that is all the answer you need." She kissed him then, taking his mouth with hers for a change, sliding her tongue inside to invade and claim the same way he'd done to her. "I'm not going anywhere."

"Jesus." He kissed her again, his eyes traveling over her face, her body, her lips. Almost as if he didn't quite trust himself. As if he didn't believe she was real. "I love you so bloody much. Do you mean it, little dove? Will you stay with me?"

She didn't need to think. "Forever if you'll have me."

A low sound tore from him. "Of course I'll have you. You're the only woman I want. My only love. Now and forever. Last chance to run, darling."

Not a chance, the silly man. How she loved him. She shook her head. "I'm not going anywhere. Now kiss me, if you please."

"With pleasure." His mouth descended, claiming and hungry. An almost frantic need took over them both. His tongue slid inside to duel with hers.

She wanted his bare, heated flesh, his body atop hers. A hollow ache pulsed between her thighs, wetness flooding there as he plundered. She raked her seeking fingers over his broad back, his strong shoulders. Her nails sank into his tight buttocks, and then she traveled over his lean waist to the knot on his robe, her fingers making short work of it.

He gripped her dressing down in both hands and tore it apart, heedless of the belt as he ravished her mouth. The silken robe fell to the floor, leaving her bare for him. His hands were everywhere. Kneading her breasts, thumbs working over her hard nipples, branding her curves.

"Mine," he whispered reverently, dragging his mouth down her throat, nipping and licking and kissing as he went.

"Yes." Her complete surrender was torn from her, so easy, so right. There was nothing else she wanted in the world than to be in her husband's arms now in this moment, reveling in their love. "Take me, Julian. Make me yours forever."

Julian's fingers dipped into the folds of her sex, finding the pearl that made her mindless with want. "You're so wet for me." He sucked a nipple into his mouth, raked his teeth over the sensitive nub, gave her a gentle bite that had her crying out and her knees going weak. He caught her to him when she would have turned into an aspic, puddling to the floor. "Tell me what you want, my love." He kissed the curve of her breast.

Desire surged through her, coiling in the center of her being, the very core of her where she longed for him most. "You, my love. Take me. Please." She tore his robe off him at last, mindless in her need for him.

He took her in his arms, carrying her to his bed before depositing her gently in the center. In the next moment, he was atop her, his powerful body between her thighs, spreading them wide. He rained kisses over her skin, from breasts to thigh to the inside of her knee. Lower, to her calf. Higher to the jut of her hip bone. And then, when she thought she'd melt with desire, his dark head settled between her thighs.

"Mine," he said again, the word a delicious brand against her most sensitive flesh. "Come for me, little dove." And then he licked her, plumping the bud of her sex before tracing wetly over her seam. His tongue sank inside her in long, hot thrusts before he replaced it with his fingers. When he nipped at her pearl and worked it in slow slashes, he sank inside her so deep that she couldn't contain herself. She cried out, finding her release, her body twisting and jerking into his.

"Yes, my love, just like that." Lovingly, he ran his tongue over her, lapping up the wetness of her spend, savoring her in a way that made a fresh onslaught of desire make her weak.

And then he was over her, above her, his thighs between hers, spreading her wide. "Tell me what you want," he commanded, his voice strained.

The hard tip of him nudged her folds. She reached between their bodies, grasping his velvety length and stroking. "You," she said. "I want you, my darling husband."

"Put me inside you."

Clara guided him to the hungriest part of her, tipping her hips to welcome him at the same moment he pushed inside. The breath hissed from his lungs as he thrust into her, hard and sure. They rode the wave of pleasure as one, bodies slamming together, eager, desperate, longing. She reached her climax at the same moment he found his. He pulsed inside her, his seed a warm, delicious flood inside her sated body.

Slowly, they both descended back to earth together. He kissed her throat, took her lips, grazed her jaw. "I love you, Clara. I love you so bloody much it hurts."

She held him to her, kissed him back with all the love in her heart. "And I love you," she whispered. "I love you so."

He stared into her eyes, beautiful and fierce and beloved. "Do you promise, little dove? You'll not change your mind and long to go back to Virginia without me one day? I made you choose between the place you loved and me once, and I'll not do it again."

She kissed him lingeringly. "I promise. And if I ever do go back to Virginia, it will only be with you by my side."

Julian pressed his forehead to hers and closed his eyes. "Thank you, my love. I'll do my damnedest to see that you never regret choosing me."

Clara smiled, heart bursting with love. "I have no fears on that account, my darling man. You're quite stuck with this Virginia hoyden."

He grinned. "I wouldn't have it any other way."

And then he kissed her again.

Epilogue

CLARA RESTED HER HANDS on the scrolled wooden railing of the balcony off her bedchamber, tilted her head back to feel sun warming her skin, and leaned into the solid presence of the man she loved at her back. Birds chirped, the air was redolent with freshly mown grass and the pink roses blooming in the gardens below.

She inhaled deeply, eyes closed. "Is there anything sweeter than a Virginia summer?" she asked Julian on a pleased sigh.

He pressed his wicked mouth to her throat just below her ear and gently nibbled at her skin. "You are sweeter than a Virginia summer, my love. Far sweeter." He nipped her ear lobe and then traced his tongue over the shell.

An answering heat slid straight to the pulsing ache at her core. They'd just made love not an hour ago, and even though she'd restored her gown and hair to a semblance of order, she was already contemplating luring him back to bed. It was their honeymoon, after all.

A sigh of approval hummed from her as she inclined her head to grant him better access. "Perhaps you ought to keep tasting me to see where I'm sweetest," she suggested with cheeky intent.

"With pleasure, Clara mine." He kissed her jaw, her cheek, nuzzled into her throat, his tongue playing over her with delicious, insistent little strokes. "Tell me where I shall taste you. Here?" He found the sensitive dip where her neck and shoulder met, tasting it as well. "Or perhaps here?"

Anticipation sparked through her, making her nipples tighten into hard points against her corset. How she loved their easy familiarity with each other. Julian had proven himself a tender and attentive husband as well as lover. He listened to her, was patient and kind even to her bear of a father, he made her laugh with his wit, and simply put, he made her melt. Everywhere.

She found the small buttons hidden on the front of her bodice and slipped the first few from their moorings. "I had somewhere else in mind. Somewhere…lower."

"Ah, I know just the spot." His low drawl sounded simultaneously proper and debauched.

A thrill went down her spine. The moment he came into a room, looked at her, touched her, *existed*, she wanted him. She couldn't touch him, smell his divine masculine scent, or look upon him without feeling an ache deep inside her. A need to be filled and claimed. And it seemed that the feelings only grew stronger with each passing day. Each day she loved and wanted him more than the last. She'd never imagined it possible, but it was true.

"What spot is that?" she asked, feeling like a wanton and not knowing even a trace of shame for it.

She expected to feel her skirts rising. Instead, he took her hand in his and brought it to his lips. Her head swiveled to the side to drink in the sight of him, bronzed and dark and beautiful. Virginia agreed with him. She was so very happy that she'd allowed him to persuade her to spend a month here for a belated honeymoon. He'd rented a grand old home in the countryside that was only half a day's drive from Richmond. His sisters were thriving in London under the clever tutelage of Lady Bella in preparation for

Alexandra's comeout. It was nothing but the two of them and a handful of staff, and Clara reveled in the chance to be unfettered and free and simply enjoy married life.

After their honeymoon was at an end, they would travel by train to New York, where they'd meet with Levi Storm and his wife Lady Helen Storm. Julian had been keen on creating his own source of wealth so that his estates would never again fall into ruin. He was partnering with Levi in a company that would manufacture steam turbines, set up with the help of Clara's father. It seemed that everything—all the pieces of their puzzle—had fallen together.

Staring at her now in that rakish way he had that never failed to undo her, Julian ran his tongue over one of her knuckles. "Here." He licked again.

Moisture pooled between her thighs. Her husband could make even the most innocent part of her body into a seduction. And she loved him all the more for it. "That wasn't the spot either."

He sucked the tip of her finger into his mouth before releasing it. His gaze was like electricity sparking straight through her. "Here?"

"Anywhere," she confessed. "Surely you know by now. I'm helpless to resist you."

He pressed a passionate kiss to the top of her hand. "That's what I like to hear, little dove."

With her free hand, she tunneled her fingers through his thick, dark hair. How she loved this man. "You already knew that, my lord."

He kissed her inner wrist, his grasp curling lightly over her. His touch sent a fresh wave of longing through her. "You could tell me every hour of every bloody day and I'd never grow tired of it."

She smiled, realizing in that moment that she was the happiest she'd ever been, at ease on a summer day with her husband in her arms and the sun shining down upon them. All was right in the world. "What if I told you every minute? Perhaps you'd grow weary of it then," she teased.

With a growl, he spun her to face him, trapping her between the balcony's railing and his body. He cupped her cheek and fitted his mouth over hers, taking her lips in a possessive kiss. He tasted of tea and sin and of their earlier lovemaking.

When he tore his mouth from hers, they were both breathless. "You could tell me every minute, love. I still wouldn't mind as long as you're mine and as long as you love me."

Her gaze traveled over his handsome, beloved face. "You know the answer to both."

"Tell me," he commanded.

Her smile softened. "I love you, and I'm helpless to resist you."

He gave her a roguish grin. "You didn't seem helpless to resist me earlier when I found you at your correspondence. Tell me, what letter had you frowning so ferociously until I eventually convinced you to join me in bed? You never did say."

"Nor did you ask." She swatted his chest playfully. "You were far too busy tempting me away from my letters. But if you must know, the letter was from my dear friend Bo."

Julian groaned. "Not the troublesome one."

"She's not troublesome," Clara defended her best friend. "She has a good heart. We'll always be bonded by terrorizing our enemies at finishing school. She's an original. True, sometimes she gets herself into scrapes, but it isn't as if I couldn't say the same for myself. Bo is bold and unique and…"

"Troublesome," her husband finished for her. "I'll be forever in her debt for sending you to me, but my gratitude aside, I can see her for the hoyden that she is."

"She isn't a hoyden." Clara frowned at him. "She wrote me with news of the inroads she's been making on behalf of our Lady's Suffrage Society."

Clara and Bo had decided to create a group of ladies who could advocate for women receiving their rightful vote. It went against the grain of the *ton* elite, but Clara didn't give a damn and neither did Bo. They both believed firmly that women should be treated as man's equal, in law and deed, and they meant to do something about it.

Thus far, they hadn't accomplished much. Their membership was thin at best. But when Clara returned to London, they would begin recruiting. If enough women banded together, they could accomplish something. She just knew it.

"Inroads?" Julian arched a brow, his interest piqued. He had encouraged her to take action about her beliefs. Creating a group with influence that could potentially sway parliament had been his idea.

"Yes," she said on a satisfied sigh as he kissed her neck again and his fingers found the buttons she'd already undone on her bodice. "An MP is sweet on her, and she hopes to influence him. He's the younger brother of the Duke of Bainbridge."

"Bainbridge is an arrogant, pompous, unyielding stone wall of a man," Julian said against her skin, his tone suggesting he found the notion humorous. "I doubt very much he'd allow someone as free-spirited as Lady Bo to bend his brother's ear."

Clara thought of what her friend had said about the duke. *Frigid as Wenham Lake ice. Disapproving of everyone save his superior self.* "She's been invited to the family home, so it couldn't be as bad as all that. It's some sort of country house event, or so I gather."

"Good luck to her. Or perhaps I ought to say good luck to Bainbridge." Julian made short work of the remainder of the buttons on her bodice, peeling it open. In another breath, he'd loosened her corset and tugged it and her chemise down, allowing her breasts to spill free into the humid summer air. "Either way, I've more pressing concerns at the moment."

She moaned and arched into him as he sucked a nipple. "More pressing concerns? What could they possibly be?" As she asked him the question, she slid her hand down his taut belly to the rigid protrusion of his cock beneath his trousers. She cupped him, feeling an answering ache between her thighs.

He caught her nipple in his teeth before releasing it with a lusty sound. "I have a feeling you already know, Lady Ravenscroft."

"Do I, Lord Ravenscroft?" She attempted a look of innocence. "Perhaps you ought to show me, just to be certain."

In one swift motion, he scooped her up in his arms. "With pleasure."

She threw her arms around his neck and kissed him soundly, her heart bursting with happiness. "I love you, Julian," she said again, for she couldn't speak the words enough, it seemed. She never wanted him to forget. He was a man so very much in need of love and so very worthy of it too.

"I love you too, little dove," he said against her lips. "More than you know. Now, if I could only find the spot where you taste the sweetest."

"It may require some research, my love," she told him with mock seriousness.

He grinned down at her as he carried her back inside. "Never let it be said I'm not an excellent student."

And he proceeded to show her just how excellent he was.

Read on for an excerpt of Book 6 in the Heart's Temptation Series, *Darling Duke*.

Darling Duke
Heart's Temptation Book 6

An untamable hellion…

Lady Boadicea Harrington is a scandal waiting to happen. She's too outspoken, too opinionated, and far too much of a flirt to ever land a good match.

But that doesn't concern her. The last of her sisters on the marriage mart, she isn't about to settle down. In fact, she doesn't plan to marry at all. If only she could tone down her wild streak and force herself to behave…

A rigidly proper man…

The Duke of Bainbridge is one of the most powerful men in England, so frigid that it's rumored his own wife committed suicide to escape him.

When Spencer learns his madcap younger brother is pursuing the unsuitable Lady Boadicea, he's determined to put an end to their ill-advised flirtation. But his best intentions go awry when he discovers his own baffling inability to resist her.

Ice meets fire…

Spencer never meant to so thoroughly compromise Lady Bo that he's duty-bound to wed her. Bo certainly never intended to enjoy being in his arms or to find him so wickedly tempting.

Can her passionate fire prove enough to melt his icy heart, or are they forever doomed to a cold marriage of convenience?

Chapter One

1884

OF ALL THE CHITS IN ENGLAND HIS NONSENSICAL BROTHER COULD HAVE GONE LOVESICK OVER, Lady Boadicea Harrington was, indisputably, the most unsuitable. Spencer had never been more certain of it than the moment he caught her in his library with a bawdy book in her hand.

Oh, she'd disguised the tripe in a pretty, embroidered cover. The ordinary observer would never guess the contents of the small book she'd held nestled in her elegant, fine-boned hands. But she'd dropped it when he startled her from her rapt reading.

Naturally, he'd played the gentleman despite his acute dislike of her. He'd known without a doubt that she was trouble. Everything about her—from her bold auburn hair to her vivid blue eyes and her beauty so singular that the first time he'd seen her at close proximity, a jolt had gone straight through him—yes, *everything* about her was in bad taste.

She flirted with each able man in her vicinity. She smiled

too much. She laughed too loudly. She was gauche and opinionated. Even her dress, a dark scarlet satin trimmed with velvet rosettes, was far too attention-seizing and daring for an unmarried lady. Fresh from Paris unless he missed his guess, the gown hugged her body as though fashioned to bedevil any poor sod who gazed upon her in it.

But he wouldn't think of the gown now. Nor her perfectly shaped mouth with the tiny beauty mark offset to the right like a planet in orbit around a blazing sun. And he most certainly would not contemplate the sudden snug fit of his trousers as the scent of her, jasmine and lily of the valley, hit him with the force of a blow to the gut.

Dear God. He could not possibly be aroused by such a creature. No. He was not.

Spencer forced himself to read another sentence in the small volume he held in his hands, just to be certain he hadn't misjudged.

I was well-pleased at the tumescence of the shaft I held in my hand.

Jesus Christ. He snapped the book closed and pinned Lady Boadicea with the most cutting glare he could manage. "Lady Boadicea, you are trespassing in my personal library."

A charming flush traced her cheeks. Her eyes were wide upon him, attempting, it seemed to him, to judge precisely how much of the obscene drivel he'd read. "Your Grace, please forgive me. I do have a tendency to wander, and I'm afraid the beckoning sight of a fire and these lovely windows proved too much of a temptation to resist. I hadn't realized, of course, that it was your private library."

Damn it, that flush on her skin went down her throat and disappeared beneath her décolletage, making him wonder if even her lush breasts were tinged pink. Bloody hell, this wouldn't do.

His brows snapped together in a frown. "See that you do not come here alone again, my lady. Not only is it most improper, but I treasure my solitude."

"I have heard, Your Grace." She held out her hand impolitely. "Once again, I do offer my sincerest apologies.

If you'll just return my book to me, I'll be on my way."

She had *heard*. He stiffened, wondering what else she'd heard. The whispers about him seemed to always abound, regardless of how much he tried to remain above reproach.

"You heard?" he repeated, unable to keep the displeasure from his voice. He despised being the target of others' conjecture above all else.

Lady Boadicea blinked at him, a tentative smile curving that beautiful mouth of hers. "Why yes, from Lord Harry of course. Don't worry. I shan't tell a soul."

Bloody hell. He didn't need her promises. And he damn well didn't need her smile. "Forgive me if your assertion is far from reassuring, my lady." His tone was deliberately frigid and forbidding.

He'd feared her unacceptability from the moment Harry had requested he extend an invitation to their annual Boswell Manor house party for Lady Boadicea and her sister and brother-in-law, the Marchioness and Marquis of Thornton. But Thornton was a potential political ally for Harry, and Spencer had relented on that account alone.

Look what good his equanimity had done him.

"Make of it what you will," the chit dared to snap at him in dismissive tones now, her hand still stretched out in anticipation of the lecherous volume he had no intention of returning to her. "My book, if you please, Your Grace?"

He tucked the slim volume inside his jacket. "No. I don't think I'll be relinquishing it."

Her smile was gone, and some ridiculous part of him—a part he'd thought long buried—felt the loss like a physical ache in his chest. She considered him, lips pursed, her expression shifting to one of irritation. Her hand remained open, waiting. Rude, damn it all. Even if some far more ludicrous part of him contemplated running a finger over her palm just to see if the circle was as soft as it looked. To trace the lines bisecting it with his lips and tongue.

"I'm afraid I don't see why you're so unwilling to return my property to me, Your Grace." She cast a sweeping glance around her. "Surely you have a more than ample supply of reading material at your fingertips?"

The baggage had more temerity than he'd imagined. "Indeed, though perhaps nothing quite so…edifying. I wonder what Lord and Lady Thornton would make of your reading proclivities, my lady."

Her eyes flared. "Are you threatening me, Your Grace?"

"Perhaps." It occurred to him that he could use this discovery to his advantage. "Here is what I propose, Lady Boadicea. I'll hold on to your little book and keep it our secret. In return, you stay the hell away from Harry."

At last, she withdrew her waiting hand, bringing it to her waist as she struck a defensive pose. "You mean to bribe me?"

Had he thought she possessed temerity? That wasn't the proper word for the impudence emanating from the lush beauty before him. First, she'd dared to trespass upon his private library. Not to mention he'd caught the hoyden reading the sort of filth that should make any proper, unmarried female faint from horror. Instead of being duly chastised, she dared to challenge him. She stood, as fierce and defiant as the warrior queen who was her namesake.

No question of it.

The wench was as troublesome as she was comely.

He gritted his teeth. "Bribery is rather an ugly word, is it not? I prefer to think of it as bargaining to achieve our mutual ends. Keep away from my brother, and I'll give your lecherous book back to you at the conclusion of the house party. No one ever need be made aware of your depraved nature, and Harry won't find himself shackled to a wanton tart masquerading as a lady."

The alluring pink that had clung to her skin vanished as she paled at his viciousness. He ought to be ashamed, he knew, to speak with such savage indifference to a lady, albeit one with unseemly tendencies and a vulgar reading habit. Had Millicent destroyed all the good in him so that there was nothing left save cruelty and ice? Or, a more troubling question prodded him, was there merely something about Lady Boadicea that unleashed the beast within him?

Lady Boadicea didn't remain silent or pale for long. In a heartbeat, twin flags of angry red rose on her patrician cheekbones. "Did it ever occur to you that it's Lord Harry's prerogative who he decides to marry?" She paused. "Or, for that matter, that perhaps a wanton tart wouldn't want to marry into a family with the reputation of yours?"

The arrow of her insult found its intended target with deadly accuracy. He stalked toward her, closing the distance between them before he could think better of it, and stared down into her upturned face. But she didn't stare at him, as some in polite society did, with fear or suspicion. Every bit of her, from the irritatingly lustrous auburn locks that had been woven into an intricate series of braids, to the firm set of her sensual mouth, oozed defiance.

"The Marlow family is one of the wealthiest and most well-known families in England, madam," he growled as another note of her airy scent swept over him. Tuberose, and damn if he didn't actually go hard in his trousers right then and there.

She raised a brow, challenging him still, seemingly unmoved by his proximity. "Is it? I confess, I hadn't realized."

Without warning the words he'd read returned to him. *I was well-pleased at the tumescence of the shaft I held in my hand.* Bloody, bloody hell. The vulgar words and her scent entwined, inciting a fire in his veins that pulsed through him and shot straight to his groin. For a moment, he imagined that fine-boned, slender hand of hers—the one that had awaited her book's return—on his cock. Stroking.

What the hell was the matter with him? His brother was wearing his heart on his sleeve for the vixen. Yet here he stood, the Duke of Bainbridge, a man who had not wanted any woman in three goddamn years, fantasizing about *her*. A minx who was altogether unacceptable in every way, who read obscene books in his bloody library and dared to defy him, whose very name was as ridiculous and fierce and lovely as the rest of her. Hadn't the last few years taught him anything?

The familiar coil of resentment and bitterness tightened within him as memories of Millicent returned to him again, chasing lust back into the dark recesses of his soul like Cerberus. He could control himself. His time of penance had cured him of the need to fulfill his desire.

He sneered down at her. "Hundreds of ladies would do anything to marry Lord Harry, and any one of them would be far more deserving of being his bride than you."

But she refused to stand down like any rational, well-bred miss in her place would. Instead, her eyes flashed up at him. Her chin upturned with stubborn firmness. "Then perhaps he ought to ask for one of their hands, for the very last thing I should like to do is marry a man with such an insufferable nodcock for a brother. Kindly return my book to me and go browbeat someone else with the misfortune of being beneath your roof."

He didn't bloody believe her. She still wanted the book. Still believed she could best him. Still tried him at every turn, as though she were in the right and he was the interloper here on his own turf.

"No," he snapped. "Now get the hell out of my library and consider yourself lucky I don't take this book and your behavior both to Lord and Lady Thornton."

"Very well," she said grimly.

But if he'd thought she had at long last chosen to show him deference and humbly go on her way, he was wrong. For in the next instant, she closed the final step between them. Her face was so near he detected a smattering of bewitching freckles over the bridge of her nose. Her full skirts swished against his trousers, and his cock went hard all over again.

"My lady," he warned tightly.

"Oh do shut up," she told him, and then she locked her arms around his neck and pulled his mouth down to hers.

Before you go...

If you enjoy steamy Regency and Victorian romance and second chance love stories, don't miss the Wicked Husbands series.

Fiercely independent, dazzlingly beautiful, and married to handsome scoundrels, these American heiresses are ready to turn the tables on the insufferable English lords they've wed. What happens when their wicked husbands start falling for the wives they never thought they wanted?

Corsets come off, bed chambers ignite, the passion sizzles, and more than one stubborn English rake gets reformed by love.

Read on for an excerpt of the latest book in the series, *Her Reformed Rake.*

Her Reformed Rake
Wicked Husbands Book Three

She refuses to behave...

American heiress Daisy Vanreid prides herself on bucking convention at every turn. Equally well-known for her beauty and her rebellious nature, she has no choice but to entrap the notorious Duke of Trent to avoid marriage to the aging aristocrat her father chose for her. Or so she thinks.

But once she becomes Trent's duchess, he disappears. Now, she's on a mission to stir up enough scandal to force his return.

He refuses to be chained...

An elite spy, Sebastian, the Duke of Trent, is on a mission of a different variety, and his wild, trousers-wearing wife is creating the sort of distraction he can't afford. He returns to London to take the minx in hand, but the woman he married as a pawn proves a wilier opponent than any enemy of the crown.

His inconvenient attraction to her complicates an already tangled web of danger and deceit.

Love is the most perilous risk of all...

When Daisy uncovers Sebastian's secret life, she's swept into his world of intrigue and straight into his arms. Together, they become locked in a battle of passion and wits that they can only survive by trusting each other.

Chapter One

London, 1881

THE BRASH AMERICAN CHIT HAD NOTHING TO DO WITH DYNAMITE. Sebastian would wager his life upon it. He watched her from across the crush of the Beresford ball as she flirted with the Earl of Bolton. He was trained to take note of every detail, each subtle nuance of his quarry's body language.

Studying her wasn't an unpleasant task. She was beautiful. A blue silk ball gown clung to her petite frame, emphasizing the curve of her waist as it fell in soft waves around lush hips down to a box-pleat-trimmed train. Pink roses bedecked her low décolletage, drawing the eye to the voluptuous swells of her breasts. Her golden hair was braided and pinned at her crown, more roses peaking from its coils. Diamonds at her throat and ears caught the light, twinkling like a beacon for fortune hunters. She wore her father's obscene wealth as if it were an advertisement for Pears soap.

Everything about her, from the way she carried herself, to the way she dressed, to her reputation, bespoke a woman who was fast. Trouble, yes. But not the variety of trouble that required his intervention.

She tapped Bolton's arm with her fan and threw back her head in an unabashed show of amusement. Her chaperone—a New York aunt named Caroline—was absent from the elegant panorama of gleaming lords and ladies. Dear Aunt Caroline had a weakness for champagne and randy men, and provided with sufficient temptation, she disappeared with ease.

Sebastian wasn't the only one who was aware of the aunt's shortcomings, however. He'd been watching Miss Daisy Vanreid for weeks. Long enough to know that she didn't have a care for her reputation, that she'd kissed Lords Wilford and Prestley but not yet Bolton, that she only smiled when she had an audience, and that she waited for her aunt to get thoroughly soused before playing the devoted coquette.

As he watched, Miss Vanreid excused herself from Bolton, hips swaying with undeniable suggestion as she sauntered in the direction of the lady's withdrawing room. Sebastian cut through the revelers, following her. Not because he needed to—tonight would be the last that he squandered on chasing a spoiled American jade—but because he knew the Earl of Bolton.

His damnable sense of honor wouldn't allow him to stand idly by as the foolish chit was ravished by such a boor. Wilford and Prestley were young bucks, scarcely any town bronze. Manageable. Bolton was another matter entirely. Miss Vanreid was either as empty-headed as she pretended or her need for the thrill of danger had dramatically increased. Either way, he would do his duty and by the cold light of morning, she'd no longer be his responsibility.

He exited the ballroom just in time to see a blue train disappearing around a corner down the hall. Damn it, where the hell was the minx going? The lady's withdrawing room was in the opposite direction. His instincts told him to follow, so he did, straight into a small, private drawing room. He stepped over the threshold and closed the door at his back, startled to find her alone rather than in Bolton's embrace. She stood in the center of the chamber, tapping her closed fan on the palm of her hand, her full lips compressed into a tight line of disapproval. Her chin tipped up in defiance. He detected not a hint of surprise in expression.

"Your Grace." She curtseyed lower than necessary, giving him a perfect view of her ample bosom. When she rose with equal grace, she pinned him with a forthright stare. "Perhaps you'd care to explain why you've been following me for the last month."

Not empty-headed, then. A keen wit sparkled in her lively green gaze. He regarded her with a new sense of appreciation. She'd noticed him. No matter. He relied upon his visibility as a cover. He flaunted his wealth, his lovers. He played the role of seasoned rake. Meanwhile, he observed.

And everything he'd observed thus far suggested that the vixen before him needed to be put in her place. She was too bold. Too lovely. Too blatantly sexual. Everything about her was designed to make men lust. Lust they did. She'd set the *ton* on its ear. Rumor had it that her cunning Papa was about to marry her off to the elderly Lord Breckly. She appeared to be doing her best to thwart him.

He fixed her with a haughty look. "I don't believe we've been introduced."

She gave a soft, throaty laugh that sent a streak of unwanted heat to his groin. "You mean to rely on your fine English manners now when you've been watching me all this time? How droll, but I already know who you are just as you must surely know who I am."

His gaze traveled over her thoroughly, inspecting her in a way that was meant to discomfit. Perhaps he'd underestimated her, for in the privacy of the chamber, she seemed wilier than he'd credited. "I watch everyone."

Tap went her fan against her palm again, the only

outward sign of her vexation aside from her frown. "As do I, Your Grace. You aren't nearly as subtle as you must suppose yourself. I must admit I found it rather odd that you'd want to spy upon my tête-à-tête with Viscount Wilford."

Miss Vanreid was thoroughly brazen, daring to refer to her ruinous behavior as though nothing untoward had occurred. It struck him that she'd known he watched her and had deliberately exchanged kisses with Prestley and Wilford, perhaps even for his benefit.

He crossed the chamber, his footfalls muted by thick carpeting. Lady Beresford's tastes had always run to the extravagant. He didn't stop until he nearly touched Miss Vanreid's skirts. Still she held firm, refusing to retreat. Some inner demon made him skim his forefinger across the fine protrusion of her collarbone. Just a ghost of a touch. Awareness sparked between them. Her eyes widened almost imperceptibly.

"Wilford and Prestley are green lads." He took care to keep his tone bland. "Bolton is a fox in the henhouse. You'd do best to stay away from him."

She swallowed and he became fascinated by her throat, the way her ostentatious diamonds moved faintly, gleaming even in the dim light. "I'm disappointed you think me as frumpy and witless as a hen. Thank you for your unnecessary concern, Your Grace, but foxes don't frighten me. They never have."

Her bravado irritated him. Even her scent was bold, an exotic blend of bergamot, ambergris, and vanilla carrying to him and invading his senses. He should never have touched her, for now he couldn't seem to stop, following her collarbone to the trim on her bodice, the pink roses so strategically placed. He didn't touch the roses. No. His finger skimmed along the fullness of her creamy breast. Her skin was soft, as lush as a petal.

"You do seem to possess an absurd predilection for your ruination, Miss Vanreid."

She startled him by stepping nearer to him, her skirts billowing against his legs. "One could say the same for you. Why do you watch, Your Grace? Does it intrigue you? Perhaps you would like a turn."

Jesus. Lust slammed through him, hot and hard and demanding. He'd never, in all his years of covert operations, gotten a stiff cock during an investigation. Thanks to the golden vixen before him, he had one now. While he'd already decided she was not involved in the plot, he was still on duty until he reported back to Carlisle in the morning. He wasn't meant to be attracted to Daisy Vanreid, who was not at all as she seemed.

Still, he found himself flattening his palm over her heart, absorbing its quick thump that told him she wasn't as calm as she pretended. The contact of her bare skin to his, more than the mere tip of a finger, was jarring.

"Are you offering me one?" he asked at last.

Her lashes lowered, her full, pink lips parting. "Yes."

And he knew right then that he'd been wrong about Daisy Vanreid. She bloody well *was* the dynamite.

Get your copy of *Her Reformed Rake* today! And don't miss books one and two in the series, *Her Errant Earl* and *Her Lovestruck Lord.*

About the Author

Award-winning author Scarlett Scott writes contemporary and historical romance with heat, heart, and happily ever afters. Since publishing her first book in 2010, she has become a wife, mother to adorable identical twins and one TV-loving dog, and a killer karaoke singer. Well, maybe not the last part, but that's what she'd like to think.

A self-professed literary junkie and nerd, she loves reading anything but especially romance novels, poetry, and Middle English verse. When she's not reading, writing, wrangling toddlers, or camping, you can catch up with her on her website www.scarsco.com. Hearing from readers never fails to make her day.

Scarlett's complete book list and information about upcoming releases can be found on her website.

Follow Scarlett on social media:

www.twitter.com/scarscoromance
www.pinterest.com/scarlettscott
www.facebook.com/AuthorScarlettScott

Other Books by Scarlett Scott

HISTORICAL ROMANCE

Heart's Temptation
A Mad Passion (Book One)
Rebel Love (Book Two)
Reckless Need (Book Three)
Sweet Scandal (Book Four)
Restless Rake (Book Five)
Darling Duke (Book Six) (Coming Soon)

Wicked Husbands
Her Errant Earl (Book One)
Her Lovestruck Lord (Book Two)
Her Reformed Rake (Book Three)

CONTEMPORARY ROMANCE

Love's Second Chance
Reprieve (Book One)
Perfect Persuasion (Book Two)
Win My Love (Book Three)

Coastal Heat
Loved Up (Book One)

24690538R00176

Printed in Poland
by Amazon Fulfillment
Poland Sp. z o.o., Wrocław